The critics on Stephen Coonts

Fortunes of War

'A stirring examination of courage, compassion, and profound nobility of military professionals under fire. Coonts' best yet' *Kirkus Reviews*

Flight of the Intruder

'[Coonts'] gripping, first-person narration of aerial combat is the best I've ever read. Once begun, this book cannot be laid aside' *Wall Street Journal*

The Red Horseman

'One of the most thrilling post-glasnost thrillers to date' *Publishers Weekly*

Under Siege

'Mr Coonts knows how to write and build suspense. His dialogue is realistic, the story line mesmeric. That is the mark of a natural storyteller'
New York Times Book Review

The Minotaur

'A fast-paced, graphic thriller with harrowing insights into the thankless, razor's-edge world of the navy test pilot and the labyrinth of superpower espionage'
Washington Post

Stephen Coonts is a former naval aviator who flew combat missions during the Vietnam War. He is the author of thirteen published novels. A former attorney, he resides with his wife and son in Las Vegas. He maintains a website at *www.coonts.com*.

THE RED HORSEMAN

STEPHEN COONTS

ORION

An Orion paperback

First published in USA in 1993
by Pocket Books
a division of Simon & Schuster Inc.
This paperback edition published in 2003
by Orion Books Ltd,
Orion House, 5 Upper St Martin's Lane,
London WC2H 9EA

5 7 9 10 8 6 4

A CIP catalogue record for this book is
available from the British Library.

ISBN 0 75284 907 7

Typeset at The Spartan Press Ltd,
Lymington, Hants

Printed and bound in Great Britain by
Clays Ltd, St Ives plc

www.orionbooks.co.uk

The author gratefully acknowledges the assistance of the following people on various aspects of this novel: William C. Cohen, Oleg Kalugin, Fred Kleinberg, and George C. Wilson. A special tip of the hat goes to Barnaby Williams, who conceived the idea of personal binary poisons and graciously allowed the author to twist it to his own perverted ends.

And there went out another horse that was red: and power was given to him that sat thereon to take peace from the earth, and that they should kill one another: and there was given to him a great sword.

Revelation 6:4

The Cold War is over; the Soviet Union is no more . . . In the past, we dealt with the nuclear threat from the Soviet Union through a combination of deterrence and arms control, but the new possessors of nuclear weapons may not be deterrable.

—Les Aspin,
US Secretary of Defense

CHAPTER ONE

Toad Tarkington first noticed her during the intermission after the first act. His wife, Rita Moravia, had gone to the ladies' and he was stretching his legs, casually inspecting the audience, when he saw her. Three rows back, four seats in from the other aisle.

She was seated, talking to her male companion, gesturing lightly, now listening to what her friend had to say. Now she glanced at the program, then raised her gaze and spoke casually.

Toad Tarkington stared. In a few seconds he caught himself and turned his back.

How long had it been? Four years? No, five. But it couldn't be her, not here. Not in Washington, DC. Could it?

He half-turned and casually glanced at her again.

The hairstyle was different, but it's *her*. He would swear to it. Great figure, eyes set wide apart above prominent cheekbones, with a voice and a touch that would excite a mummy – no man ever forgets a woman like that.

He sat and stared at the program in his hand without seeing it. He had last seen her five years ago, in Tel Aviv. And now she's here.

Judith Farrell. No, that was only an alias. Her real name is Hannah something. Mermelstein. Hannah Mermelstein. Here!

Good God!

Suddenly he felt hot. He tugged at the knot in his tie and unfastened his collar button.

'What's the matter? Are you catching a cold?' Rita

slipped into her seat and gave him one of those looks that wives reserve for husbands whose social skills are showing signs of slackness. Before Toad could answer the house lights dimmed and the curtain opened for act two.

He couldn't help himself. When the spotlight hit the actors, he looked left, trying to see her in the dim glow. Too many people in the way. Hannah Mermelstein, but he had promised to never tell anyone her real name. And he hadn't.

'Is something wrong?' Rita whispered.

'Uh-uh.'

'Then why are you rubbing your leg?'

'Ah, it's aching a little.'

That leg had two steel pins in it, and just now it seemed to Toad that he could feel both of them. The Israeli doctors inserted the pins just a day or two before he saw Judith/ Hannah for the last time. She came to see him in the hospital.

Toad Tarkington didn't want to remember. He folded his hands on his lap and tried to concentrate on the actors on the stage. Yet it came back as if it had just happened yesterday, raw and powerful — the night he made love to her, that Naples hotel lobby as the man with her gunned down a man in the elevator, the assault on the *United States*, the stench of the ship burning in the darkness . . . that F-14 flight with Jake Grafton. He found himself gripping the arms of the seat as all the emotions came flooding back.

What is she doing here?

Who has she come to kill?

'Come on,' he whispered to Rita. 'I want to go home.'

'Now?' She was incredulous.

'Yes. Now.' He stood.

Rita collected her purse and rose, then preceded him toward the aisle, muttering excuses as she clambered past knees and feet. In the aisle he took her elbow as she walked toward the lobby. He glanced toward where Judith Farrell was sitting, but couldn't spot her.

2

'Are you feeling okay?' Rita asked.

'I'll explain later.'

The lobby was empty. He led Rita to the cloakroom and fished in his shirt pocket for the claim check. The girl went to fetch the umbrella. He extracted two dollars from his wallet and dropped them into the tip jar, then wiped the perspiration from his forehead with his hand. The girl returned with the umbrella and handed it across the Dutch door counter.

'Thanks.'

When he turned, Judith Farrell was standing there facing him.

'Hello, Robert.'

He tried to think of something to say. She stood looking at him, her head cocked slightly to one side. Her male companion was against the far wall, facing them.

'Rita,' she said, 'I'm Elizabeth Thorn. May I speak to your husband for a few minutes?'

Rita looked at Toad with her eyebrows up. So Judith Farrell knew about his wife. It figured.

'Where?' Toad asked. His voice was hoarse.

'Your car.'

Toad cleared his throat, 'I don't think—'

'Robert, I came tonight to talk to you. I think you should hear what I have to say.'

'The CIA is open eight to five,' Toad Tarkington said, 'Monday through Friday. They're in the phone book.'

'This is important,' Judith Farrell said.

Toad cleared his throat again and considered. Rita's face was deadpan.

'Okay.' Toad took his wife's arm and turned toward the door. The man against the wall watched the three of them go and made no move to follow.

They walked in silence across the parking lot. The rain had stopped but there were still puddles. Toad unlocked the car doors and told Farrell, 'You sit up front. Rita, hop in the backseat, please.'

Once in the car he started the engine and turned on the

defroster as the women seated themselves. Then he reached over and grabbed Judith Farrell's purse. Farrell didn't react, but Rita started. Still, she remained silent.

No gun in the purse. That was his main concern. There was a wallet, so he opened it. Maryland driver's license for Elizabeth Thorn, born April 17, 1960. The address was in Silver Spring. Several credit cards, some cash, and nothing else. He put the wallet back into the purse and stirred through the contents. The usual female beauty paraphernalia, a box of tissues, a tube of lipstick. He examined the lipstick tube, took the cap off, ran the colored stick in and out, then replaced the cap and dropped the tube back into the purse. He put the purse back on Farrell's lap.

'Okay, Ms Thorn. You have your audience.'

'I want you to give Jake Grafton a message.'

'Call the Defense Intelligence Agency and make an appointment.'

'Obviously I don't want anyone to know that I talked to him, Robert. So I came to you. I want you to pass the message along, to him and no one else.'

Toad Tarkington looked that over and accepted it, reluctantly. Rear Admiral Grafton was the deputy director at the DIA and Toad was his aide. Both facts were widely known, public knowledge. At the office every call was logged, every visitor positively identified. Admiral Grafton lived in general officers' quarters at the Washington Navy Yard and was guarded by the federal protective service. While it would be easy enough for a professional to slip through the protective cordon, doing so would require the admiral either to report the conversation to his superiors or violate the security regulations. Presumably this way it would be up to the admiral to decide if this conversation had to be reported, a faint distinction that didn't seem all that clear to Toad.

'Rita and I will know.'

'You won't tell anyone. You're both naval officers.' That was also true. Rita was an instructor at the navy's Test Pilot

School at NAS Patuxent River. Both of them held the rank of lieutenant commander, both had top secret clearances, both had seen reams of classified material that they couldn't even talk about to each other.

Toad turned and looked at Rita, who was staring at the back of Elizabeth Thorn's head and frowning.

Toad Tarkington gazed out the window at the empty parked cars as he considered it. 'Why tonight? When I'm out with Rita?'

'If I had walked up to you when you were alone, you would have brushed me off.'

That comment irritated him. 'Pretty damn sure of yourself, aren't you?'

Farrell didn't reply.

Toad again glanced over his shoulder at his wife, who met his eyes. She was going to be full of questions as soon as they were alone. Now she opened her door and stepped out of the car. She walked around to the front of the vehicle where she could watch the other woman's face.

'This better be good,' Toad said. 'Let's hear it.'

It took less than sixty seconds. Toad made her repeat it and asked several questions, none of which Elizabeth Thorn answered. From her coat pocket she took a plain white unsealed envelope, which she passed to Toad. He opened it. It contained a photo and a negative. The photo was a three-by-five snap of a middle-aged white man seated at a table, apparently at an outdoor restaurant, reading a newspaper. There was a plate on the table. His face registered just a trace of a frown.

'Want to tell me who this is?'

'You find out.'

'Any hints?'

'CIA. You'll talk to Grafton?'

'Maybe, if you'll help me with the caption.' He wiggled the photograph. 'Like when and where.'

'Jake Grafton can figure it out. I have a great deal of faith in him.'

'But not much in me.' Toad sighed. 'How about this: just before he took his first — and last — bite of eggs Benedict injected full of arsenic trioxide by beautiful spy Hannah Mermelstein, Special Agent Sixty-Nine realized that the *Sauce Hollandaise* had a pinch too much salt?'

Her face showed no reaction whatever.

Toad Tarkington shrugged. He put the photo back in the envelope and placed the envelope in an inside jacket pocket. 'So how did you know Rita and I were coming to this play tonight?'

Judith Farrell opened the car door and stepped out. 'Thank you for your time, Robert.' She closed the door and walked away. Toad watched her go as Rita came around the car and climbed into the front passenger seat.

'Who is she?'

'Mossad.' The Israeli intelligence service.

'You were in love with her once, weren't you?'

Trust a woman to glom onto that angle. Toad sighed and pulled the transmission lever into reverse.

When the car was out on the street, Rita asked, 'When did you know her?'

'Five years ago. In the Med.'

'Her real name isn't Elizabeth Thorn, is it?'

'No. She got out that name right up front, so I wouldn't call her anything else.'

Rita waited for him to tell her more, but when it became obvious he wasn't going to, she remarked, 'She's very pretty.'

Toad merely grunted.

'Are you going to tell me what she said?'

'No.'

Rita seemed to accept that with good grace. And she had gotten out of the car without being asked. She was a player, Toad told himself, a class act, every inch the professional Judith Farrell was. Perhaps he should have been nicer to Farrell.

This thought was still tripping across the synapses when

Rita remarked, 'I think you're still in love with her. Not like you love me, but you care for her a lot. That was obvious to her, too. If you didn't care you would have been nic—'

'Shut up!' Toad snarled.

'Listen, husband of mine. In three years of marriage neither one of us has told the other to shut up. I don't think—'

'I'm sorry. I retract that.'

'I feel like I'm trapped in a soap opera,' Rita said. After a pause she added, 'And I don't like it.'

No fool, Toad Tarkington decided to let her have the last word.

Later, as they waited for a traffic light, Rita asked in a normal tone of voice, 'So what does Elizabeth Thorn do for the Mossad?'

Toad considered before answering. He decided maybe the truth was best. 'Five years ago she was running a hit squad. Maybe she still is. She's a professional killer. An assassin.'

Toad awoke at dawn on Saturday and took his clothes into the kitchen to dress so he wouldn't wake Rita. After enough coffee had dripped through to make a cup, he poured himself some and went out into the backyard of the little tract home he and Rita had purchased last year near Andrews Air Force Base. The morning was expectant, still, with the diffused sunlight hinting of the heat to come in a few hours. Not even the sound of jet engines of planes from the base. Too early yet. Someone somewhere was burning last fall's leaves, even though it was against the law, and the faint smell seemed to make the coffee more pungent.

Judith Farrell. Here.

Although he would never admit it to Rita, seeing Judith had been a jolt. And Rita knew anyway. Blast women! All that crap about body language and nonverbal speech that

7

they expected men to sweat bullets acquiring was just the latest nasty turn in the eternal war between the sexes. And if by some miracle you got it they would think of something else you needed to know to meet tomorrow's sensitivity standards. If you suffered from the curse of the Y chromosome. Aagh!

He sat sipping coffee and pondering the male dilemma.

After a bit his mind turned to Judith Farrell's message for Jake Grafton. Probably Farrell hadn't tried to contact him when he was home alone because even he and Rita never knew when that would be. This was his first free Saturday this month. That crap about brushing her off . . . Well, it was true, he would have.

Someone told Farrell – told the Mossad – that he and Rita had tickets to that play last night. Who?

He tried to recall just when and to whom at the office he might have mentioned that he and Rita were going last night. It was hazy, but he seemed to recall that the play had been discussed several times by different people, and he may have said he had tickets.

He purchased the tickets over a month ago by calling a commercial ticket outlet and ordering them. And there was no telling to whom Rita might have mentioned the planned evening out. It was certainly no secret.

So that was a dead end. Frustrated, he went inside and poured himself another cup of coffee.

He got out the envelope and looked again at the photo. A very ordinary photo of a very ordinary man. He held the negative up to the light. It was the negative of the photo, apparently. Given to prove the genuineness of the photo. Okay, so what was there about the photograph that made it significant? Toad studied it at a distance of twelve inches. The guy's sitting in front of a restaurant. Where? No way to tell. When? Nothing there either.

Well, Jake Grafton would know what to do with it. Grafton always knew how to handle hot potatoes, a quality that Toad had long ago concluded was instinctive. The guy could be tossed blindfolded into a snake pit and still avoid the poisonous ones.

The water began running in the bathroom. Rita must be taking a shower. He replaced the photo and negative in the envelope and put it into his shirt pocket.

Toad was outside trimming weeds along the fence when Rita appeared in the door wearing a flight suit, her hair braided into a bun that was pinned to the back of her head. 'I'm leaving, Toad.'

He paused and leaned on the fence. 'Back for supper?'

'Yes. Are you going to call Admiral Grafton?'

'I dunno. Haven't decided.'

'You are, then.'

Toad resumed the chore of cutting weeds, trying not to let his temper show.

Rita laughed. He tossed the hedge shears down and turned his back on her.

In a few seconds she appeared in front of him. 'I love you, Toad-man.'

He snorted. 'I'm gonna ditch you and run off with ol' Lizzie Thorn. Won't be nothing here tonight when you get home except my dirty underwear and busted tennis racket.'

She stretched on tiptoe and kissed his cheek. 'See you this evening, lover.'

The numbers . . . the numbers appalled him, shocked him, mesmerized him. He wrote them on the back of an old envelope that he used as a bookmark. The stupendous, incomprehensible quantity of human misery represented by the numbers numbed him, made it impossible to pick up the book again and continue reading.

Jake Grafton stared out the window at the swaying trees in the yard without seeing them, played with his mechanical pencil, ran his fingers yet again through his thinning hair.

And he looked again at the envelope. Fifteen million Russians died fighting the Germans during World War I.

Fifteen million! Dead! No wonder the nation came apart at the seams. No wonder they dragged the czar from his palace and put him and his family against the wall. *Fifteen million!*

The new republic was doomed. The Bolsheviks plunged the land into a five-year civil war, a hell of violence, famine and disease that cost another fifteen million lives. Another *fifteen million!*

Then came Josef Stalin and the forced collectivization of Soviet agriculture. Here the number was nebulous, an educated guess. One historian estimated six million families were murdered or starved to death – another believed at least ten million men, women, and children perished; young and old, vigorous and infirm, those struggling to live and those waiting to die. The Red Army had gone through thousands of square miles robbing the peasants of every crumb, every animal, every potato and cabbage and edible kernel, then sealed the districts and waited for every last human to starve.

Ten million! A conservative estimate, Jake thought.

Then came the purges. Under Josef Stalin – and they had called the fourth Ivan 'the Terrible!' – Soviet citizens were worked as slave labor until they died or were shot in wholesale lots because they might not be loyal to their Communist masters. The secret police murder squads had quotas. And they filled them. Through the use of show trials and extorted confessions, the soul-numbing terror was injected into every nook and cranny of Soviet life. Citizens in all walks of life denounced one another in a paranoid hysteria that fed on human sacrifice. Those who survived the horror had a word for it: *liquidation.*

Over *twenty million* human beings were liquidated, possibly as many as forty million. Only God knew the real number and He had kept the secret.

World War II – the raging furnace of war, famine and disease consumed another twenty-five million Soviet citizens. *Twenty-five million!*

10

The numbers totaled eighty-five million minimum. Jake Grafton added the numbers three times. It was too much. The human mind could not grasp the significance of the numerals on the back of the tattered envelope.

Eighty-five million human lives.

It was like trying to comprehend how many stars were in a galaxy, how many galaxies were in the universe.

'Jake?' His wife stood in the doorway. 'Amy and I are going to the Crystal City mall. Won't you come with us?'

He stared at her. She was of medium height, with traces of gray in her dark hair. She had her purse in her hand.

'The mall . . .'

'Amy wants to drive.' The youngster had just received her learner's permit and was now driving the family car, but only when Jake was in the front seat with her. Callie had announced that her nerves were not up to that challenge and refused the honor.

Jake Grafton rose to his feet and glanced out the window. Outside the sun shone weakly from a high, hazy sky. On this June Saturday all over America baseball games were in progress, people were riding bicycles, shopping, buying groceries, mowing yards, enjoying the balmy temperatures of June and contemplating the prospect of the whole summer ahead.

The envelope and its numbers seemed as far away from this reality as casualty figures from the Spanish Inquisition.

'Okay,' Jake Grafton told his wife.

He eyed the envelope one last time, then slid it between the pages of the book. With the book closed the numbers were hidden; only the top half inch of the envelope was visible.

Eighty-five million people.

But they were all long dead, as dead as the pharaohs. The earth soaked up their tears and blood and recycled their corpses. Only the numbers survived.

He turned off the light as he left the room.

*

Toad Tarkington called after the Graftons returned from the mall. Callie invited him to dinner. Five minutes later she answered the phone again.

'Jack Yocke, Mrs Grafton. I'm leaving for an overseas assignment on Monday and I wondered if I could stop by and chat with your husband this evening.'

'Why don't you come to dinner, Jack? Around six-thirty.'

'I don't want to put you to any trouble.'

Callie was amused. She enjoyed entertaining, and Jack Yocke, a reporter for the *Washington Post*, was a frequent guest. Jake habitually avoided reporters, but Yocke had become a family friend through an unusual set of circumstances. And he had never yet turned down a dinner invitation. Friends or not, he had the most important commodity in Washington – access – and he knew precisely what that was worth. Callie undoubtedly knew too, Yocke thought: she was perfectly capable of slamming the door in his face if she ever thought he had taken advantage of her hospitality.

'No trouble, Jack,' she told him now. 'Where are you going?'

'Moscow! It's my first overseas assignment.' The enthusiasm in his voice was tangible.

Callie stifled a laugh. Yocke had been maneuvering desperately for two years to get an overseas assignment. Other than a short jaunt to Cuba, he had spent most of his five years at the *Post* on the metro beat covering police and local politics. 'Good things come to those who wait,' she told him.

'Actually,' Yocke said, lowering his voice conspiratorially, 'I got the nod because our number two man over there had a family emergency and had to come home. My biggest asset is that I'm single.'

'And you've been asking for an overseas assignment.'

'Begging might be a better word.'

'Moscow? He's going to Moscow?' Jake Grafton repeated when his wife went into the study to give him the news.

12

Callie nodded. 'Moscow. It's dangerous over there, I know, but this is a big break for him professionally.' She left the room to see about dinner.

'He'll certainly have plenty to write about,' Jake Grafton remarked to himself as he surveyed the piles of books, newspapers and magazines strewn over the desk and credenza.

He was reading everything he could lay hands on these days about the Soviet Union, the superpower that had collapsed less than two years ago and was now racked by turmoil. Like a ramshackle old house that had withstood the winds and storms long past its time, the Communist empire fell suddenly, imploded, shattered like old crystal, all in a heap. Now ethnic feuds, runaway inflation, famine and a gradual disintegration of the social order were fueling the expanding flames.

'Plenty,' Grafton muttered listlessly.

Yocke's enthusiasm for his new adventure set the tone at dinner. Almost thirty, tall and lean, he regarded his new assignment as a great challenge. 'I can't stand to go into that District Building one more time. This is my chance to get out of metro once and for all.'

His chance to get famous, Jake Grafton thought, but he didn't say it. The young reporter oozed ambition, and the admiral didn't hold that against him. Ambition seemed to be one of the essential ingredients to a life of great accomplishments. Lincoln had it, and Churchill, Roosevelt . . . Hitler, Josef Stalin.

Grafton played with his food as Jack Yocke talked about Russia. Toad Tarkington seemed preoccupied and quieter than usual. Tonight he listened to Yocke without comment.

'It's hard to imagine the Russian empire without a powerful bureaucracy. The bureaucracy was firmly entrenched by 1650 and became indispensable under Peter the Great. It was the tool the czars used to administer the empire, to run the state. The Bolsheviks just adopted it pen

13

and paper clips when they took over. The problem at the end was that the bureaucracy lost the capability of providing. The infernal machine just ground to a halt and nothing on this earth could get it started again without the direct application of force.'

'Not force,' Jake Grafton said. 'Terror.'

'Terror,' Yocke agreed, 'which the leadership was no longer in a position to supply.'

'Where did they go wrong?' Callie asked. 'After the collapse of communism and the dissolution of the Soviet state, everyone was so hopeful. Where did they go wrong?'

Everyone at the table had an opinion about that, even Amy. 'No one over there likes anyone else,' she stated. 'All the ethnic groups hate each other. That isn't right. People shouldn't hate.'

Toad Tarkington winked at her. Amy was growing up, and he liked her very much. 'How's the driving going?' he asked when there was a break in the conversation.

'Great,' Amy said, and grinned. 'Except for Mom, who sits there gritting her teeth, waiting for the crash.'

'Now, Amy . . .' Callie began.

'She knows it's going to be bad – teeth, hair and eyeballs all over the dashboard.' Amy sighed plaintively. 'I've decided to become a race car driver. I'm going to start in stock cars. I figure in a couple of years I'll be ready for formula one.'

'Amy Carol,' her mother said with mock severity. 'You are not—'

'Talent,' Amy told Toad. 'Some people have it and some don't. You should see my throttle work and the way I handle the wheel.'

After dinner Jack Yocke asked to speak with the admiral alone, so Jake took him into the study and closed the door. 'Looks like you've been doing some reading,' the reporter remarked as both men settled into chairs.

'Ummm.'

'This is my big break,' Yocke said.

14

'That's what you said when the *Post* let you write a column during the '92 presidential primary campaign.'

'Well, that didn't work out. And it wasn't a column – it was just a signed opinion article once a week.'

Jake reached for a scrapbook on a bookshelf and flipped through it. 'Callie saved most of them. I thought some of your stuff was pretty good.'

Yocke shrugged modestly, a gesture that Grafton missed. The admiral adjusted his glasses on his nose and said, 'Let's see – this was written in January, before the New Hampshire primary. You said, "Now Bush admits that he didn't know the country was in a recession. He's the only man in America who hadn't heard the news. The man's a groundhog who only comes out of his hole every four years to campaign."'

'Acceptable hyperbole,' Yocke said and squirmed in his seat. 'A columnist is supposed to be interesting.'

' "If George Bush had been president during World War II, allied troops would have stopped at the Rhine and the Nazis would still be running Germany."'

'Well . . .'

Grafton flipped pages. He cleared his throat. ' "The American people don't want George Bush and Clarence 'Coke can' Thomas deciding whether their daughters can have abortions."' Grafton glanced over his glasses at Yocke. 'Coke can?'

'There was a mix-up on that. That comment should not have gotten into the paper. I wrote that as a joke to give the editor something to shout at me about and somehow he missed it. He and I almost got canned.'

Grafton sighed and flipped more pages. 'Ahh, here's my favorite: "Even if Arkansas Governor Bill Clinton is absolutely innocent, as he claims, of having an adulterous affair with bimbo Gennifer Flowers, that by itself would not disqualify him to be president. America has had two presidents this century, perhaps even three, who were faithful to their wives. A fourth would not rend the social

15

fabric beyond repair. It's an indisputable fact that such dull clods rarely seek public office in our fair land and almost never achieve it, so if one does squeak in occasionally, once a generation, how much harm could he do?"'

'A parody of David Broder,' Yocke muttered with a touch of defiance. 'A satire.'

'Everything written in our age is satire,' the admiral said as he closed the scrapbook and slid it back into the bookshelf. When he looked at Yocke he grinned. 'You should be writing for *Rolling Stone.*'

'The *Post* pays better,' Jack Yocke said. 'Y'know, I've written a lot of stuff through the years, yet I still have to spell my name for the guy at the laundry whenever I drop off my shirts. And he's seen me twice a week for five years, speaks English, can even read a little.'

Still wearing a grin, Grafton took off his glasses and rubbed the bridge of his nose. 'Your stuff's too subtle. You should try to give it more punch.'

'Words to live by. I'll remember that advice. But we have a hot tip that I'm going to try to chase down when I get to Russia. The story is that some tactical nukes are on the open market. For sale to the highest bidder.'

'You don't say?' Jake Grafton said. He pushed his eyebrows aloft. 'Where'd you hear that?'

Yocke crossed his legs and settled in. 'I know you won't confirm or deny anything, and you won't breathe a word of classified information, but I thought I'd run this rumor by you. Just for the heck of it.'

Jake Grafton ran his fingers through his hair, pinched his nose, and regarded his guest without enthusiasm. 'Thanks. We'll look into it. Be a help if we knew the source of this hot tip, though.'

'I can't give you that. It's more of a rumor than a tip. Still, if it's true it's a hell of a story.'

'A story to make you famous,' Jake agreed. 'And to think we knew you when. All you have to do is live long enough to file it.'

'There's that, of course.'

Jake stood and held out his hand. 'If worse comes to worst, it's been nice knowing you.'

Jack Yocke looked at the outstretched hand a moment, then shook it. He got out of his chair and smiled. 'One of your most charming characteristics, Admiral, is that deep streak of maudlin sentiment under the professional exterior. You're just an old softie.'

'Drop us a postcard from time to time and tell us how you're doing.'

'Yeah. Sure.'

Jack Yocke opened the door and went out, and Amy Carol came in. She carefully closed the door behind her. 'Dad, I have a question.' She dropped into the chair just vacated by the reporter.

'Okay.'

'It's about sex.'

Jake opened his mouth, then closed it again. Amy was growing up, no question about that. She had filled out nicely in all the womanly places and presumably had consulted with Callie about plumbing, morals and all that. Under his scrutiny she squirmed slightly in her seat.

'Why don't you ask your mom?'

Amy shot out of the chair and bolted for the door. On her way down the hall he heard her call, 'Toad, you owe me five bucks. I *told* you he'd duck it.'

After Yocke said his good-byes, Jake and Toad Tarkington took coffee into the study and carefully closed the door.

'You're not going to believe this, Admiral, but last night at the Kennedy Center Judith Farrell walked up and said hi.'

Jake Grafton took a while to process it. It had been years since he'd heard that name. 'Judith Farrell, the Mossad agent?'

'That's right, sir. Judith Farrell. Now she calls herself Elizabeth Thorn. She had a Maryland driver's license.'

'Better tell me about it.'

17

Toad did so. In due course he got to the message. 'You remember Nigel Keren, the British billionaire publisher who fell off his yacht a year or two ago while it was cruising in the Canaries?'

Jake nodded. 'Found floating naked in the ocean.'

'Stone cold dead. That's the guy, Nigel Keren. Then his publishing empire went tits up amid claims of financial shenanigans. But nobody could ever figure out how Keren got from his stateroom aboard the yacht over a chest-high rail into the water while wearing nothing but his birthday suit.'

Jake sipped coffee. 'He was a Lebanese Jew, wasn't he? Naturalized in Britain?'

'Yessir. Anyway, ol' Judith Farrell says the CIA killed him.'

'*What?*'

'That's the message she wanted you to have, Admiral. The CIA killed Nigel Keren. Oh, and this photo.' Toad took the envelope from his pocket and passed it to the admiral, who went to his desk and turned on the desk lamp to examine it.

'I know who this is,' he told Toad.

'Yessir. I recognized him too. Herb Tenney, the CIA officer who is going to Russia with us. If we go.'

Jake got a magnifying glass from his desk drawer and examined the photo carefully as he tried to recall what he had read of Keren's death. The financier had been alone on the yacht with its crew until he turned up missing one morning. Several days later his nude body was fished from the ocean. All twelve crewmen claimed ignorance. The Spanish pathologist had been unable to establish the cause of death but ruled out drowning, due to an absence of water in the lungs. So Keren had been dead when his body went overboard. How he died was an unsolved mystery.

Finally Jake laid the glass and the photo on the desk and regarded it with a frown. 'Herb Tenney reading a newspaper.' He sighed. 'Okay, what's the rest of the message?'

18

'You got it all, Admiral. "Tell Admiral Grafton that the CIA killed Nigel Keren and here's a photo and negative. 'Bye." That's all she said.'

Jake used the magnifying glass to examine the negative. It appeared to be the one from which the print was made. Finally he put both print and negative back in the envelope and passed the envelope back to Toad. 'Take these to the computer center on Monday morning and have them examined. I want to know where and when the photo was taken and I want to know if the negative has been altered or enhanced by computer processing.' He doubted if the negative had been altered, but Farrell had offered it as evidence, so it wouldn't hurt to check.

'Yessir. But what if word of this gets back to Tenney?'

'What if it does? Maybe he can tell us about the photograph.'

'If the CIA killed Keren and Tenney was in on it, maybe they won't want anyone to see this picture.'

'Toad, you've been reading too many spy stories. We'll probably have to ask Tenney about that picture. Farrell knew that. She probably wants us to question Tenney.'

'Then we shouldn't.' Toad said. 'At least not until we know what this is all about.'

Jake Grafton snorted. He had been on the fringes of the intelligence business long enough to distrust everyone associated with it. The truth, he believed, wasn't in them. They didn't know it. Worse, they never expected to learn it, nor did they care. 'Take the print and negative to the computer guys,' he repeated. 'Stick a classification on it. Top secret. That should keep the technician quiet.'

'What about Farrell?' Toad demanded.

'What about her?'

'We could get her address from the Maryland department of motor vehicles and try to find her.'

'She was told what to say and she said it. She doesn't know anything.'

Toad Tarkington flicked the envelope with his forefinger,

then placed it in an inside pocket. He drained the last of his coffee. 'If you don't mind my asking, what did Yocke want?'

'He's heard a rumor that some tactical nukes are for sale in Russia to the highest bidder.'

'*Shee-it!*'

'I know the feeling.' Jake Grafton said. 'The most sensitive, important, dangerous item on the griddle at the National Security Council and Jack Yocke picked it up on the street. Now he's charging off to scribble himself famous. Makes you want to blow lunch.'

CHAPTER TWO

Richard Harper was a priest of the High-Tech Goddess. He spent his off-hours reading computer magazines and technical works and browsing at gadget stores. He thought about computers most of his waking hours. There was something spiritual about a computer, he believed. It was almost as if it had a soul of its own, an existence independent of the plastic and wire and silicon of which it was constructed.

So he habitually talked to his computer as his fingers danced across the keyboard. His comments were low, lilting and almost unintelligible, but it was obvious to Toad Tarkington that Harper was in direct communication with whoever or whatever it was that made the machine go. That didn't bother Toad – he had spent years listening to naval aviators whisper to their lusty jet-fueled mistresses: he didn't even classify Richard Harper as more than average dingy.

Just now he tried to make sense of Harper's incantations. He got a word or two here and there. '. . . time for a hundred indecisions, a hundred visions and revisions . . . Do I dare, do I dare?' After a few minutes he tuned out Harper and scanned the posters, cartoons, and newspaper articles taped to the wall. All over the wall. On every square inch. Computer stuff. Yeck!

Tarkington regarded computers as just another tool, more expensive than a screwdriver or hammer but no more inherently interesting. Of necessity he periodically applied himself to making one work, and when required could even give a fairly comprehensive technical explanation of what went on down deep inside. But a computer had no pizzazz, no romance, no appeal to his inner being. This Monday morning he leaned idly on the counter and without a twinge of curiosity watched Harper and his computer do their thing.

But he had a restless mind that had to be mulling something: once again his thoughts went back to Elizabeth Thorn, alias Judith Farrell. He had loved her once. One of the male's biological defects, he decided, was his inability to stop loving a woman. Oh, you can dump her, avoid her, hate her, love someone else, but once love has struck it cannot be completely eradicated. The wound may scar over nicely, yet some shards of the arrowhead will remain permanently embedded to remind you where you were hit. If you are a man.

Women, Toad well knew, didn't suffer from this biological infirmity. Once a woman ditches you her libidinal landscape is wiped clean by Mama Nature, clean as a sand beach swept by the tide, ready for the next victim to leave his tracks like Robinson Crusoe. And like that sucker, he'll conclude that he is the very first, the one and only. Amazingly, for her he will be.

Biology, you old devil.

Ah, me.

Then Toad's thoughts moved from theoretical musings to the specific. He poked around the edges of the emotions that the sight and sound and smell of Elizabeth Thorn created in him and concluded, again, that it would be unwise to explore further. Yet he couldn't leave it. So he circled it and looked from different angles.

He felt a chill and shuddered involuntarily.

'Commander Tarkington?'

It was Harper. This was the second time he had said Toad's name.

'Yeah.'

'Just what is it you want to know about these prints?' Harper flexed his fingers like a concert pianist.

'Ah, have they been enhanced? Touched up? Whatever the phrase is.'

'Well, the two prints are identical.' Toad had given Harper two prints, the original that Elizabeth Thorn had handed him Friday night and one he had made yesterday evening from the negative at a one-hour photo shop in a suburban mall. 'I ran them through the scanner,' Harper continued, 'which looks at the light levels in little segments called pixels and assigns a numerical value, which is how the computer uses the information. The prints are essentially identical with only minor, statistically insignificant variations. Possibly caused by dust on the negative.'

Toad grunted. 'Did anybody doctor it up?'

'Not that I can see.' Harper punched buttons. Columns of numbers appeared on the screen before him. 'What we're looking for are lines, sharp variations in light values that shouldn't be there. Of course, with a sophisticated enough computer, those traces could be erased, but then the resultant print would have to be photographed to get a new negative, and that would fuzz everything. I just don't think so. Maybe one chance in a hundred. Or one in a thousand.'

'What can you tell me about the picture?'

Harper's fingers flew across the keyboard. The photo appeared on the screen. 'It's a man sitting at a table reading a newspaper. Apparently at a sidewalk café.'

'Do you know the man?'

'No, but if you like I can access the CIA's data base and maybe we can match the face.'

'That won't be necessary,' Toad Tarkington said. 'Is there anything in the photo that would indicate where it was taken?'

The computer wizard stroked the mouse and drew a box over the newspaper. He clicked again on the mouse button and the boxed area filled the screen. The headline was in English and quite legible, but the masthead was less so.

'We'll enhance it a little,' Harper muttered and clicked the mouse again.

After a few seconds he announced, '*The Times.*'

'*New York Times?*'

'*The Times*. The real one. London.'

'What day?'

'Can't tell. The date is just too small. But look at this.' The whole photograph was brought back to the screen and the cursor repositioned over a white splotch on the café window. Now the splotch appeared. Toad came around the counter and stared over Harper's shoulder. 'It's a notice of the hours the café is open. You can't read the language in this blowup – the picture is too fuzzy – but if the computer uses an enhancement program to fill in the gaps it should become legible.'

His fingers danced. After a minute or two he said, 'It's not English. It's Portuguese.'

'So the photo was taken in Portugal.'

'Or in front of a Portuguese café in London, Berlin, Zurich, Rome, Madrid, New York, Washing—'

'How about the front page of the paper? Can you give me a printout of that?'

'Sure.' Richard Harper clicked the mouse on the print menu and in a moment the laser began to hum. Toad waited until the page came out of the printer, then examined it carefully. There was a portion of a photo centered under the paper's big headline, which contained the words 'Common Market ministers.' He folded the page and put it back into his pocket.

'Well,' he said, 'I guess that's everything. Give me back the prints and erase everything from the memory of your idiot box and I'll get out of your hair.'

Harper shrugged. He put the prints in the envelope that had originally contained them and passed it to Toad, who slipped the envelope into an inside pocket. Then Harper clicked away on the mouse. After a few seconds of activity he sat back and said, 'It's gone.'

'I don't want to insult you,' Toad said, 'but I should emphasize this little matter is a tippy top secret, eyes only. Loose lips sink ships.'

'Everything I do is classified, Commander,' Harper said tartly. He reached for the folder on the top of the pile in his in basket.

'No offense,' Toad muttered. 'By the way, what were those lines you were saying about "visions and revisions"?'

Now Harper colored slightly and made a vague gesture. ' "The Love Song of J. Alfred Prufrock." '

'Umm.'

An hour later in the media reading room in the Madison Building of the Library of Congress Toad found the page of the London *Times* that had been captured in the photo. Several weeks' editions of the newspaper were on each roll of microfilm. He selected the roll that included the date Nigel Keren died, placed it on a Bell & Howell viewing console and began to scroll through the pages. The headline he wanted was on page twenty-three of the scroll, the edition of November 1, 1991.

Rear Admiral Jake Grafton spent the morning in a briefing. As usual, the subject was nuclear weapons in the Commonwealth of Independent States, which was the old Soviet Union. This matter was boiling on the front burner. The locations of the strategic nuclear missiles – ICBMs – were known and the political control apparatus was more or less public knowledge. But the Allied intelligence community had lost sight of the tactical nuclear weapons – weapons that were by definition mobile. They were hidden behind the pall of smoke rising from the rubble of the Soviet Union.

Listening to experts discuss nuclear weapons as if they were missing vases from a seedy art gallery, Grafton's attention wandered. He had first sat through classified lectures on the ins and outs of nuclear weapons technology as a very junior A-6 pilot, before he went to Vietnam for the first time. In those days attack plane crews were each assigned targets under the Single Integrated Operational Plan – SIOP. The lectures were like something from Dr Strangelove's horror cabinet – thermal pulses, blast effects, radiation and kill zones and the like. When the course was over he even got a certificate suitable for framing that proclaimed he was a qualified Nuclear Weapons Delivery Pilot.

But the whole experience was just some weird military mind-bender until he was handed his first target the day after the ship sailed from Pearl Harbor on his first cruise to Vietnam.

Shanghai.

He was assigned to drop a nuclear weapon on the military district headquarters in Shanghai. It wasn't exactly downtown, but it was on the edge of it.

Actually he was not going to drop the bomb: he was going to toss it, throw it about forty-three thousand feet, as he recalled. That was how far away from the target the pull-up point was. He would cross the initial point at five hundred knots, exactly five hundred feet above the ground, and push the pickle on the stick, which would start the timer on the nuclear ordnance panel. The timer would tick off the preset number of seconds until he reached the calculated pull-up point – that point forty-three thousand feet from the target. Then a tone would sound in his ears. He was to apply smooth, steady back-pressure on the stick so that one second after the tone began he would have four Gs on the aircraft. At about thirty-eight degrees nose-up the tone would cease and the weapon would come off the bomb rack and he would keep pulling, up and over the top, then do a half roll going down the back side and scoot out the way he had come in.

He had practiced the delivery on the navy's bombing range in Oregon. With little, blue, twenty-eight-pound practice bombs. The delivery method was inherently inaccurate and the bombs were sprinkled liberally over the countryside, sometimes a couple miles from the intended target. A good delivery was one in which the bomb impacted within a half mile of where you wanted it. With a six-hundred-kiloton nuke, a miss by a mile or two wouldn't matter much.

'Close enough for government work,' he and his bombardier assured each other.

Months later on an aircraft carrier crossing the Pacific with a magazine full of nuclear weapons, the insanity of nuclear war got very personal. Figuring the fuel consumption on each leg of the run-in, working the leg times backward from the hard target time – necessary so he and his bombardier wouldn't be incinerated by the blast of somebody else's weapon – plotting antiaircraft defenses, examining the streets and buildings of Shanghai while planning to incinerate every last Chinese man, woman and child in them, he had to pinch himself. This was like trying to figure out how to shoot your way into hell.

But orders were orders, so he drew the lines and cut and pasted the charts and tried to envision what it would feel like to hurl a thermonuclear weapon into Shanghai. The emotions he would feel as he flew through the flak and SAMs on the run-in, performed the Götterdämmerung alley-oop over a city of ten million people, and tried to keep the airplane upright and flying as the shock wave from the detonation smashed the aircraft like the fist of God as he exited tail-on to the blast – emotions were not on the navy's agenda.

Could he nuke Shanghai? Would he do it if ordered to? He didn't know, which troubled him.

Fretting about it didn't help. The problem was too big, the numbers of human lives incomprehensible, the As and Bs and Cs of the equation all unknown. He had no answers. Worse, he suspected no one did.

So he finished his planning and went back to more mundane concerns, like wondering how he was going to stay alive in the night skies over Vietnam.

That was twenty-three years ago.

Today listening to the experts discuss the possibility that nuclear weapons might be seeping southward from the Soviet republics into the Middle East, the memories of planning the annihilation of half the population of Shanghai made Jake Grafton slightly nauseated.

The voice of the three-star army general who headed the Defense Intelligence Agency jolted his unpleasant reverie. The general wanted hard intelligence and he was a bit peeved that none seemed to be available.

'Rumor, surmises, theories . . . haven't you experts got one single fact?' he demanded of the briefers. 'Just one shabby little irrefutable fact – that's not too much to ask, is it?'

The three-star's name was Albert Sidney Brown. After thirty-plus years in the maw of a vast bureaucracy where every middle name was automatically ground down to an initial, he had somehow managed to retain his.

The briefer was CIA officer Herb Tenney, who briefed Lieutenant General Brown on a regular basis. Today he tried to reason with the general. 'Sir, the place is bedlam. Nobody knows what's going on, not even Yeltsin. The transportation system's kaput, the communication system is in tatters, people in the countryside are quietly starving, armed criminal gangs are in control of—'

'I read the newspapers,' General Brown said acidly. 'Do you spooks know anything that the Associated Press doesn't?'

'Not right now,' Herb Tenney said with a hint of regret in his voice. Regret, Jake Grafton noted, not apology. Tenney was several inches short of six feet. His graying hair and square jaw with a cleft gave him a distinguished, important look. In his gray wool business suit with thin, subtle blue stripes woven into the cloth he looked more like a Wall Street buccaneer, Jake Grafton thought, than the spy he was.

'Congress is performing major surgery on the American

28

military without benefit of anesthetic,' General Brown rumbled. 'Everybody east of Omaha is tossing flowers at the Russians, and that goddamn cesspool is in meltdown. There are *thirty thousand tactical nuclear weapons* over there just lying around loose! And the CIA doesn't know diddly squat.'

Jake Grafton thought he could see a tiny sympathetic smile on Herb Tenney's face. His expression looked remarkably like the one on the puss of the guy at the garage giving you the bad news about your transmission. Or was Grafton just imagining it? Damn that Judith Farrell!

Tenney's expression seemed to irritate General Brown too. 'I am fed up with you people palming off yesterday's press clippings and unsubstantiated gossip as news. You're like a bunch of old crones at a whores' picnic. No more! I want facts and you spies better come up with some. Damn quick!'

Brown's fist descended onto the table with a crash. 'Like yesterday! I don't give a shit who you have to bribe, fuck, or rob, but you'd better come up with some hard facts about who has their grubby hands on those goddamn bombs or I'm going to lose my temper and start kicking *ass!*'

When the briefers were gone and he and Jake were alone, Albert Sidney Brown rumbled, 'They'll never come up with hard intelligence. Nobody on our side knows anything. Not a goddamn thing. Now *that's* a fact.'

'We just don't have the HUMINT resources, General,' Jake Grafton said. HUMINT was human intelligence, information from spies. The CIA had never had much luck recruiting spies in the Soviet Union. Prior to the collapse the counterintelligence apparatus had been too efficient. It was a different story now, but a spy network took years to construct.

'The world is becoming more dangerous,' General Brown said softly. 'It's like the whole planet is on a runaway locomotive going down a mountain, faster and faster, closer and closer to the edge. The big smashup is waiting around the next bend, or the next. And those cretins in Congress are in a dogfight to divide up the "peace dividend." Makes you want to cry.'

Jake had had numerous wide-ranging conversations with General Brown since he reported to this job six months ago. Brown was convinced that the proliferation of weapons of mass destruction was the most dangerous trend in an increasingly unstable international arena. And Jake Grafton agreed with him.

Recently the United States and other Western nations had agreed to spend $500 million to pay for destruction of the Soviet nuclear arsenal, but the work wasn't going quickly enough. 'They've got bombs scattered around over there like junk cars,' Brown told Jake Grafton. 'They don't know what they've got or where it is, so it's imperative that we get someone over there to keep an eye on the situation and prod them in the right direction. You're that someone.

'The ambassador is talking to Yeltsin right now, trying to sell military-to-military cooperation at the absolute top level. As soon as we get the okay, you're on your way. Keep your underwear packed.'

'Aye aye, sir.'

'Jake, we have got to get a handle on this nuclear weapons situation. I want you to get the hard facts. Ask the Russian generals to their faces — and don't take no for an answer. There isn't time to massage bruised egos. They must be as worried as we are. If their criminal gangs or ragtag ethnic warriors start using nukes on one another, Revelation is going to come true word for word. And if those fanatics in the Middle East get their hands on some . . .' Brown lifted his hands skyward.

Jake Grafton finished the thought. 'This planet will be history.'

'A radioactive clinker,' Brown agreed, and swiveled his chair toward the map of the old Soviet Union that hung on the wall.

*

'The first day of November 1991,' Toad Tarkington repeated, 'just three days before Nigel Keren went for his long swim.'

Toad fell silent. He had completed his recital of what he learned this morning. Jake Grafton was bent over the photograph on his desk, staring at it through a magnifying glass. Finally he straightened with a sigh.

'We could ask the CIA where Herb Tenney was that week,' Toad suggested.

'No.' Jake squirmed in his chair. He flexed his right hand several times, then let it rest limply on the arm of the chair. 'For the sake of argument, assume that the CIA did kill Keren. Either the president authorized it or someone in the CIA was running his own foreign policy. The Mossad must have concluded the assassination was without authorization or they would not have approached anyone in the American intelligence community, no matter how obliquely. Assuming the CIA did kill Keren. A rather large assumption, but—'

'Sir, we've got to do something about this,' Toad said with a slight edge in his voice.

'What is this evidence of?' Jake gestured toward the photo. 'What?' That was the nub of it. At best this photo might destroy one alibi. 'We've got nothing. Absolutely nothing.'

'Do you think the CIA killed Keren?' Toad asked.

'I have no idea. If the Mossad knows and wanted us to believe, they could have given us real proof. They didn't. Which raises another question – is Farrell still working for the Mossad?'

Toad spent several seconds processing it. 'I can't see her working for anyone else. She . . .'

Toad ran out of steam when Jake Grafton gave him one of those cold glances. With thinning hair and a nose a tad too large, Jake Grafton's face wasn't memorable. It was just another face among the throng. Until he fixed those gray eyes on you with one of those looks that could freeze water, that is – then you got a glimpse of the hard, determined man inside.

'Maybe they wanted to smear Herb,' Toad added lamely.

'That's one possibility. Another is that they want to discredit me.'

'You?'

'I'm not going to be around here very long if I sally forth to slay a dragon armed with nothing but a peashooter and one pea. You see that? The dragon will fry my britches. And if there's no dragon I just immolated myself.'

Jake rooted in his desk drawer for a pack of matches. He found them, then dumped the trash from his wastecan onto the floor. One by one he lit the prints and dropped them into the gray metal wastecan. The negative went last. When the celluloid was consumed, Jake picked up the trash and tossed it back into the can.

Then he picked up a file on the Russian army and opened it. Several minutes later Toad remembered the computer printout of the front page of the London *Times* that was inside his pocket. He wadded it up and tossed it into the classified burn bag.

CHAPTER THREE

June in Washington is very similar to early summer in any other large city in the northeastern part of the United States. The days of clouds and rain come regularly, interspersed with periods of sunshine and balmy breezes, perfect days when it seems the whole world is ripe, flourishing, vibrantly alive. Weekends are for shopping expeditions, yard work, an occasional party.

Workdays in the nation's capital begin here like everywhere else. Most people turn on one of the television morning shows as they dress and drink a cup of hot chocolate or coffee. While they take a quick squint at the morning newspaper and gobble a fat pill, Willard Scott tells them about the weather and a lady having her hundredth birthday. Why supposedly sane people choose to spend the worst moments of the day with Willard Scott, Bryant Gumbel and their colleagues on the other networks is a phenomenon that will probably intrigue archeologists of a future age.

With the kids shoved out the door to swimming lessons or other summer activities, working people fire up their horseless chariots and join the commuting throng. Tooling out of the subdivision they tune in another set of fools on their car radios. On each of the morning 'drive shows' one or two jaded disk jockeys and one syrupy sweet, eternally cheerful female crank out some combination of pop music, weather and crude humor interspersed with reports from a helicopter pilot about the traffic jams that form every morning around stalls, wrecks and road construction projects. This mix is occasionally enlivened with a blow-by-blow account of a spectacular police chase of a freeway speeder who suddenly remembered his thirty-two unpaid parking tickets when he saw the cop's flashing light.

And 'news,' lots of it. Usually 'news' is presented in short snippets, 'sound bites,' some of them worth the ten seconds of air time they get, most not. To prevent the working citizen creeping through traffic from getting too down from an overdose of reality, the producers of these shows leaven the mix with the inane doings of show business celebrities and the latest risqué tidbits from the court trials of current cretins. Nothing heavy, nothing in depth, just a once-over-lightly on items that would only interest a heavy metal groupie or a social scientist from planet Zork.

Jake Grafton never listened. Callie had the television going every morning while she fixed Amy's breakfast, but Jake read the newspaper. If the *Washington Post* thought an international story was worth the front page, the American intelligence community was going to be wrestling with it before lunch.

In the car Jake turned off the radio the instant it babbled to life. Amy and Callie always left the squawk box on, he always turned it off.

Today he drove in the usual blessed silence while he reviewed the crises of yesterday and the likely flaps on today's agenda. The Middle East was boiling again: another assassination, more riots protesting ongoing Israeli set-tlement in the occupied West Bank, more terrorism and murder. Chaos in the Balkans, another wave of Haitians heading for Florida, the usual anarchy in the new Com-monwealth of Independent States, or as the bureaucrats had labeled it, the CIS – all in all, this was just another day in the 1990s.

Normally there was little the Americans could do to improve any international situation. Nor, as the optimists noted, was there much they could do that would make things worse. Still everything had to go through the gristmill and be forwarded on to the policymakers for their information. And in the case of the DIA, to the appropriate units of the military to ensure they weren't luxuriating in blissful ignorance.

Besides the usual international crises, the top echelons of the military and civilian policymakers were still trying to formulate America's response to the shape of the post-Communist world. The world had changed almost overnight, yet change was the bureaucracy's worst enemy, the crisis to which it had the most difficulty responding.

This morning Jake Grafton thought about change. The knee-jerk reaction had been to reorganize, to draw more lines on the organization chart. That had been easy, though it hadn't been enough. The brave new world had to be faced whether the policymakers were comfortable or not.

They were uncomfortable. Very uncomfortable. Men and women who had spent their adult lives as warriors of the cold war now had to face the unknown without experience or perspective. Mistakes were inevitable, grievous mistakes that were going to cost people their reputations, their careers. This sense of dangerous uncertainty collided with the extraordinary dynamics of the evolving geopolitical landscape to produce a stress-filled crisis atmosphere in which tension was almost tangible.

This situation is like war, Jake Grafton decided. Every change in the international scene reveals a new opportunity to the bold few and a new pitfall to the cautious many.

He was musing along these lines when the Pentagon came into view. It was a low, sprawling building much larger than it looked.

As he parked the car he was wondering if there was any place at all for nuclear weapons in this changing world. Were they obsolete, like horse cavalry and battleships? He also wondered if he was the only person in the Pentagon asking that question.

*

'Everyone would have been better off if Russia had had another revolution and shot all the Communists.'

General Albert Sidney Brown delivered himself of this opinion and stopped the strategy conference dead. Which was perhaps what he intended. The subject was the growth of virulent anti-Semitism in the former Soviet states.

'General,' CIA deputy director Harvey Schenler said wearily, 'I don't believe fantasies of that type contribute much to our deliberations.'

Brown snorted. 'Most of the problems the new regimes in eastern Europe and the old Soviet Union are now facing were caused by the Communists' grotesque mismanagement, incompetent central planning, believing their own propaganda, lying to everybody, including themselves, cheating, bribery, favoritism – the list goes on for a couple dozen pages. Now that the Commies have become the political opposition, they're preaching hatred of the Jews, trying to blame them for the collapse of the whole rotten system. It's 1932 in Germany all over again. Now you people in the CIA seem to think that if the Communists get back in power, in some magical way this nuclear weapons control problem will just disappear. Bullshit!'

Schenler's tone sharpened. 'I think you owe me and my staff an apology. General. We have said no such thing here.'

'You've implied it. You just stated that we have to keep our lines of communication open to the Commies, treat them as legitimate contenders for power.'

'We're *not* suggesting the United States should aid their return to power.'

Brown cleared his throat explosively. 'Then I apologize. I've become so used to double-talk and new age quack-speak from you people, I'm easily confused. Perhaps today we can dispense with the bureaucratic mumbo jumbo and get down to brass tacks.'

Schenler paused for several seconds as he looked at the page before him. He had an apology and a challenge. He

36

decided to accept the apology and return to the agenda items.

Brown's outburst was the only bright spot in the meeting, Jake Grafton found to his sorrow. These weekly strategy sessions, 'strategizing' the civilian intelligence professionals called it, were usually exercises in tedium. Today was no exception. No facts were briefed that hadn't already circulated through the upper echelons. Most of what ended up on the table were policy options from CIA analysts, career researchers who were theoretically politically neutral. Jake Grafton didn't believe it – the only politically neutral people he had ever met were dead.

So the items discussed here were really policy alternatives that had made their long, tortuous way through the intestines of the Central Intelligence Agency, perhaps the most monolithic bureaucracy left on the planet. Like General Brown, Jake Grafton looked at these nuggets without enthusiasm. Larded with dubious predictions and carefully chosen facts, these policy alternatives were really the choices the upper echelons of the CIA wanted the policymakers to adopt. The researchers gave their bosses what they thought the bosses wanted to hear, or so Brown and Grafton believed.

Alas, these two uniformed officers well knew they couldn't change the system. So they listened and recorded their objections.

Schenler sometimes argued. Most of the time he just took notes. Grafton never saw the notes. About fifty, with salt-and-pepper hair and an ivy league education, Schenler was an organization man to his fingertips. 'I'll bet the bastard hasn't farted in twenty-five years,' General Brown once grumbled to Jake.

Jake also took occasional notes at these soirées, doodled and watched Schenler and his lieutenants perform the usual rituals.

Today, when he finally concluded that General Brown had given up, he went back to doodling. He used his pencil to doctor up his copy of a reproduction of a current Russian anti-Semitic poster that had been handed around before Brown fired his salvo. The crude drawing depicted two rich Jews – they had to be Jews: guys with hooked noses wearing yarmulkes – counting their money while starving women and children watched. In one corner a man with a red star on his cap observed the scene. Jake penciled a swastika on his chest.

'What is this?' Jake held up a piece of paper and waved it at Toad Tarkington.

'Ah, Admiral, if you could give me a little hint . . .'

'You put this here, didn't you?'

Jake Grafton had been going through his morning mail pile when he ran across Toad's masterpiece, a summary of everything in the computer about the demise of Nigel Keren. It was short, only one page, but pithy, full of facts. Toad knew the admiral was partial to facts.

'Oh,' Toad said when Jake held the paper out so he could see it, 'that's just a little thing I put together for your information.'

The admiral stared at him with humor. 'I know everything I want to know about Nigel Keren.'

Toad had rehearsed this, but looking at Jake Grafton, his little speech went out the window. 'I'm sorry,' he said contritely.

'I know how he was killed,' the admiral said.

Toad gawked.

The admiral put the paper on the desk in front of him and toyed with it. 'A publishing mogul alone on a large yacht, no one aboard but him and twelve crew members, all male. The ship is three days out of the Canaries when he eats dinner alone – the same food that all the crew was served – and spends the rest of the evening walking the deck, then goes to his stateroom. The next morning the crew can't find him aboard. Two days later his nude body is found floating in the sea. A Spanish pathologist found no evidence of violence, no water in the lungs, no heart disease, no burst blood vessels in the brain, no evidence of suffocation. In short, the man died a natural death and his corpse somehow went into the sea. None of the crew members knows anything. All deny that they killed him.'

When Jake fell silent Toad added, 'Then his media empire broke up. Apparently large sums of money, hundreds of millions, may have been taken. If anyone knows, they aren't saying. Keren's son says the deceased father just made too many leveraged deals and the worldwide recession caught them short.'

The admiral merely grunted.

'Perhaps there was a stowaway aboard the yacht,' Toad suggested. 'Or a small vessel rendezvoused with the yacht and an assassin team came aboard.'

'No. The British checked with every ship in the vicinity and interrogated the crew thoroughly. And if he was assassinated, how was it done?'

'You tell me,' Tarkington muttered.

'Remember that top secret CIA progress report that went through here a couple of months ago on the development of binary chemicals?'

Toad nodded once.

'When I saw it then, I thought of the Keren case,' Jake Grafton continued, 'but I forgot all about it until the other day when I was staring at that photo Judith Farrell donated to the cause. And I confess, I used the computer yesterday after you left to reread the Keren file.' He smiled at Toad. 'It would have occurred to you sooner or later.'

'Binary chemicals.'

'That's right. The poisons of the past – arsenic, strychnine, that kind of thing – all had a couple of major drawbacks. If given in sufficient quantity to do the job they killed very quickly, before the killer had a chance to leave the scene of the crime. And there was always the problem of killing too many people, anyone who ingested the poisoned food or drink. Binary chemicals remove those drawbacks. You give your victim one chemical, harmless in itself, perhaps serve it in the punch at a party. Everyone drinks it and no one is the wiser. It's absorbed by the tissues and so remains in the body for a lengthy period, at least several weeks. But it's benign, produces no ill effect. Then at a later date the assassin serves the other half of the poison, also quite benign by itself. And the second half of the brew combines with the first half in the body of the victim and becomes a deadly poison. The victim goes home and goes to bed and the chemical reaction takes place and his heart stops. No one will suspect poison. Even if they do, investigation will reveal that everything the victim ate and drank was also ingested by other people.'

Jake Grafton turned his hand over.

'So Keren could have been given the first drink of the chemical at any time in the preceding few weeks,' Toad said.

'Correct. At a party, a luncheon, a dinner, whatever. It could have been in anything he ate or drank. And that everyone else ate or drank.'

'Then aboard ship . . .'

'The second chemical could have been in the food when it came aboard, maybe in the ship's water tank. Probably the food, which would be consumed or thrown away. When Keren had ingested a sufficient dosage and chemical reaction was complete, his heart stopped. And no one aboard the ship knew anything about it. They were all innocent.'

'Wouldn't this stuff still be in his body?' Toad asked.

'Probably. If the pathologist had known what to look for. Zero chance of that.'

'But why did the body go into the water?'

'That's a side issue,' Jake Grafton said. 'Nothing in life is ever neat and tidy. Someone panicked when they found him dead. You can make your own list of reasons. Maybe the British found out who threw him overboard and kept quiet to protect the dead man's reputation. Extraordinarily wealthy man, pillar of the community, why smear him after he's dead? The British think like that.'

'But later they said Keren committed suicide. That's certainly frowned on by the upper crust.'

'If you have a corpse floating in the ocean and no proof of murder, what would you call it?'

'He was a Jew from the Levant,' Toad said carefully. 'Emigrated to Britain as a young man. Poor as a church mouse.'

'Then he made hundreds of millions and the Mossad was right there when he died to snap a photo of a CIA agent. Makes you wonder, doesn't it?' Toad said, eyeing the admiral.

'Not me,' Jake Grafton said with finality. 'I have no reason to go prying into someone else's dirty little business. And no levers to pry with even if I were foolish enough to try.' He tossed Toad's summary at him. 'Put this into the burn bag and let's get back to work.'

On Friday evening Jake took Callie and Amy to a movie. Afterward they stopped for ice cream. It was a little after eleven before Amy wheeled the car into the driveway and killed the engine. Jake got out of the passenger seat and held the rear door open for Callie.

'Well, Mom, what'd'ya think?' Amy asked.

'You drive too fast.'

'I do not! Do I, Dad?'

'Wasn't that a great movie?' said Jake Grafton.

'Dad!' Amy exclaimed in anguish. 'Don't avoid the issue. Oooh, I just hate it when you do that!'

From the porch – this rambling three-story brick built in the 1920s still had its porch – Jake waved to the federal protective service guard standing on the corner under the light, then opened the door with his key.

'You two are just so narrow bandwidth,' Amy continued, 'so totally random.' Still talking in a conversational tone of voice, she made for the stairs and started up. 'It's like I'm

41

stuck in an uncool fossil movie, some black-and-white Ronald Reagan time warp with all the girls in letter sweaters and white socks and the boys in duck's ass grease-cuts—'

'Amy Carol,' Callie called up the stairs. 'I'll have none of that kind of language in my house.'

Her voice came floating down. 'I'm the last kid in America growing up with Ozzie and Harriet . . .'

'You're very narrow bandwidth, Harriet,' Jake told his wife, who grinned.

'What does that mean?' she asked softly.

'I don't know,' her husband confessed. He kissed her on the forehead and led the way to the kitchen. After Callie made coffee and poured him a cup, he took it upstairs to the study.

He flipped on the light and started. A man was sitting behind the desk. Another sat on the couch.

Automatically Jake's eye went to the door of the safe. It was still closed.

The men were in suits and ties. The man on the couch had blond hair and spoke first. 'Come in and close the door, Admiral.'

Jake stood where he was. 'How'd you two get in here?'

'Come in and close the door. Unless you want your wife and daughter to hear this.'

Jake obeyed.

'Want to tell me who you are?' he said.

Now the man behind the desk spoke. 'You haven't hit the right question yet, Admiral. Ask us why we're here.'

Jake remembered the coffee in his hand and sipped it as he examined the visitors. Both under forty, but not by much. Short hair, clean-shaven, reasonably fit.

'Get out of my chair,' he said to the man behind the desk.

'Admiral, that confrontational tone is not going to get us anywhere. Why don't you sit down and we'll—'

Jake tossed the remainder of the coffee at the man's face.

42

The liquid hit the target, then some of it splashed on the desk. The man grunted, then wiped his face with his left hand. He stood up slowly. As he got fully erect the blond man on the couch uncoiled explosively in Jake's direction.

Jake had been expecting this. He smashed the coffee cup into the side of the blond man's face with his right hand – the cup shattered – and followed it up with a hard left that connected with the man's skull and jolted Jake clear to the elbow. But then the man had his shoulder into Jake's chest and slammed him back against the bookcase. The other man was coming around the desk.

Jake tried to use a knee on his assailant's body. No. He tried to chop with both hands at the back of the man's neck. He succeeded only in getting himself off balance, so his blows lacked power.

The man from the desk drew back a right and delivered a haymaker to Jake's chin.

The admiral saw stars and lost his balance completely.

When his vision cleared he was on the floor, the blond standing and the other man kneeling beside him. Blondie was using a handkerchief on the side of his face. When he withdrew it Jake could see blood.

'You've had your nose in a matter that doesn't concern you, Admiral. You're not Batman or Jesus H. Christ. This visit was just a friendly warning. You've got a wife and kid and it would be a hell of a shame if anything happened to them. Do you understand me?'

'Jake?' It was Callie's voice. She was outside the door. She rattled the knob. The men had locked it. 'What's going on in there, Jake?'

'What matter?' Jake asked.

'The same thing that happened to Nigel Keren could happen to you. It could happen to your wife. It could happen to your daughter.'

Outside the door Callie's voice was up an octave. 'Jake, are you all right? *Jake, speak to me!*'

'Be a hell of a shame,' Blondie said, 'if your fifteen-year-old daughter died of heart failure, wouldn't it? A hell of a shame. And you'd have only yourself to blame.'

'*Jake!*'

'Think about it,' the first man said, then stood up. He unlocked the door and pulled it open.

'Excuse us, please,' he said to Callie and walked by her for the stairs, the blond man at his heels.

Stunned, Callie stared after them, then rushed to Jake, who was getting up.

He was still dizzy. He leaned on the bookcase. 'Make sure they leave,' he told his wife and pushed her gently toward the door.

He sagged down onto the couch and lowered his head onto the arm. His jaw ached badly. He felt his teeth. One seemed loose.

When Callie came back he was sitting at his desk. 'Jake, who were those men?'

'I dunno.'

She started to speak and he held up his hand. She cocked her head quizzically. He held a finger to his lips. Then he reached for paper and wrote:

The place may be bugged. I'll search it later. Please go downstairs and throw away all the food in the house. Everything except the stuff in sealed cans. All milk, soda pop, beer, frozen food, coffee, everything.

She read it and looked puzzled.

'I'll explain later,' he said. 'Please, go do it.'

She went.

Jake Grafton sat looking out his window for about fifteen seconds, then he knelt by the safe and opened it. His gun was still there, an old Smith & Wesson .357 Magnum that he had carried when he flew in Vietnam. All the classified documents seemed to be as he had left them. After he closed and locked the safe, he rooted through his bottom desk drawer for the box of shells. He loaded the pistol and stuck it in the small of his back, under the belt.

Downstairs in the kitchen he kissed his wife. 'Where are the car keys?'

'In my purse.'

Jake helped himself, then snagged his coat from the hall rack. 'I'll be back in a little while,' he said.

'Where are you going?'

'Tarkington's. There's a chance those guys stopped here first. They're delivering messages tonight.'

'Why don't you call Toad?'

'I want to see these guys again.'

'Jake, be careful.'

'You know me, Callie. I'm always careful.' He kissed her again and let her close the door behind him.

The uniformed guard was walking the beat on the sidewalk. Jake stopped beside him and rolled down his window. 'Did you see two men come out of my house?'

'Yessir. They got into a car parked across the street.'

'What kind of car?'

'I don't know, sir. It was a sedan with government plates. Is there a problem, Admiral?'

'No. No problem. They forgot something, that's all. Thanks.' He took his foot off the brake and got the car in motion before the man could ask any more questions.

The pistol was a hard lump where his back pressed against the seat.

A white Ford sedan with government plates sat in Tarkington's driveway behind Rita's car, which was in the carport. Toad's Honda Accord was parked at the curb. A light in the living room window made the drapes glow. Jake drove past and parked on the next block.

As he walked back he kept looking in parked cars. He saw no one.

These guys were sloppy. No lookouts, no driver waiting behind the wheel, a *government sedan*, for Christ's sake! They were just out putting the fear of God in a few people tonight and not bothering to do it right.

Jake tried the door of the sedan. It was unlocked. He popped the hood latch and eased the door shut. Feeling in the darkness he jerked the leads off the spark plugs, then let the hood down gently. Then he got behind the front of Rita's car, got the pistol out, and waited.

Jake was under no illusions. This was going to be dicey. He was going to have to get control of this situation quickly before these two clowns had a chance to think about it. If he pulled the trigger the cops would be here in short order, someone was going to be arrested, and someone was going to have a lot of explaining to do. And someone – Jake suspected that he might wind up as this someone – would probably find himself in more trouble than he could get himself out of.

He had waited no more than three minutes when he heard the Tarkingtons' front door open.

He got down on his hands and knees in front of Rita's car and looked under it. He saw their feet. They got into the sedan. A muttered oath.

The passenger door opened and a set of feet came around to the front of the car. Grafton straightened and peered through the window of Rita's car.

The sedan's hood was up. The blond man was looking into the engine compartment.

Jake went to his left, around Rita's Mazda. The hood obscured the driver's view and the blond had his back to Jake. He heard Jake coming at the last instant and started to turn just as the pistol butt thunked into his head. He went down like a sack of potatoes.

Jake grasped the butt of the revolver with his right hand and stepped around to the driver's door. He jerked it open.

'Get out.'

The dark-haired man looked slightly stunned.

Jake reached with his left hand and got a handful of shirt and tie. He jerked hard. The man half fell out of the seat. Jake jabbed the gun barrel into his ear and kept pulling.

'Jesus, you can't—'

'Get up and walk or I'll blow your brains out.' He jabbed savagely with the gun barrel.

The man came along.

'Tarkington,' Jake called. 'Get out here.'

The door opened and the stoop light came on.

'Toad, turn off that light and get out here.'

Tarkington came out. He was in his pajamas and they were torn half off his chest. 'That one on the ground,' Jake said, nodding. 'Clean out his pockets. Everything. Put him into the sedan and bring all the stuff inside.'

Rita held the door.

In the living room Jake hooked the dark-haired man's leg and sent him sprawling.

'Search him, Rita, and tell me what happened.'

Rita Moravia was wearing a robe over a nightie. Her hair was down. She began pulling things from the man's pockets as she talked. 'They rang the doorbell and told Toad they were from the DIA and you sent them over here. He let them in. I heard a scuffle out here in the living room and came out and they had knocked him down. They made some threats.'

'How long were they here?'

'Seven or eight minutes. No more.' Rita had finished with the man's rear trouser pockets and side coat pockets. She rolled him over without ceremony and emptied his inside jacket pockets. She turned his front trouser pockets inside out.

'Feel him all over for weapons.'

Rita did so. 'Nope. Just the one wallet, and this.' She held up a card encased in plastic attached to a chain. Jake had seen ones like this before. It was a pass to the CIA's Langley facility.

Jake picked up the wallet and examined it. He extracted the driver's license and held it out so he could read it. 'Okay, Paul Tanana of 2134 North Wood Duck Drive, Burke, Virginia. Want to tell us who sent you on this little errand?'

Rita was finished. She gathered the CIA pass and the change, keys and pens and placed them on a coffee table.

'I asked you a question,' Jake said.

Tanana glowered. 'You'll be sorry for this.'

'I'm sorry I ever laid eyes on you. Who sent you?'

Silence.

'Rita, check on Toad.'

The gun felt heavy in Jake's hand. He kept it pointed at Tanana, who was rubbing his ear. Jake rubbed his fingers back and forth across the stiff plastic of the driver's license.

In a moment Rita and Toad came in. 'Guy didn't have a gun,' Toad said. 'Just a wallet and a CIA pass and a little pack of lock picks.'

'Who sent you to see me tonight?' Jake asked Tanana.

The man snorted. 'You ain't gonna shoot me.'

What's wrong here?

Jake looked again at the driver's license, at the clear plastic, the perfect edges.

He put the license into his pocket and eared back the hammer of the revolver. He approached Tanana. He bent down and placed the barrel of the weapon against the man's temple.

'You're right. I'm not going to shoot you tonight. But if anything ever happens to my wife or kid – if you ever get within a mile of my wife or kid – if I ever see you within a mile of my house – I'll blow your fucking brains out and I'll take a great deal of pleasure in doing it, Paul-baby. Are you getting the message?'

'I got it.'

Jake rose and backed off. 'I jerked the wires off the spark plugs on your car. Put them back on and get the hell out of here.'

Tanana got slowly to his feet. 'What about our stuff? Our wallets?'

'We'll keep them. Maybe I'll frame the CIA passes and display them over at the DIA. They'll be wonderful souvenirs. Now get out.'

Tanana went.

Jake watched from the doorway as Tanana worked on the car. It took a couple minutes. 'Rita, get a pencil and write this down. US government plate, XRC-five-four-five.'

He was wondering if he'd hit the blond man too hard when Tanana slammed the hood down. He got behind the wheel, started the engine and backed out onto the street.

'I think you cracked the other guy's skull,' Toad said as the sedan drove slowly away. Typical Tarkington, Jake reflected. He could almost read his boss's mind.

Jake closed the door and locked it. 'I could sure use a cup of coffee.'

Callie was sitting on the stairs waiting for him when he came through the front door. After he ensured the door was locked behind him, he hung up his coat and took a seat on the step beside her.

'Who were they?'

Jake passed her the wallets. She opened them and looked at the licenses, credit cards, and other items. When she had finished he handed her the CIA passes.

'CIA,' she whispered.

Jake extracted his own wallet from his right hip pocket and took out his driver's license. He held it out so he could see it. 'I got this about a year and a half ago. Look how it's curved from being in the wallet and how the edges have frayed. Now look at those other licenses.'

Callie did so. 'They're like new,' she said.

'They shouldn't be. They were issued a couple years ago. And the credit cards. Notice how the black ink on the raised numbers has yet to rub off. I don't think they've ever been used.'

'So?'

'These two clowns were over at Tarkington's when I got there. I slugged one and we searched the other.'

'They let you do this?'

'That's an interesting question.' Jake pulled the pistol out

49

and showed it to Callie. 'You wave a gun around and everyone does what you tell them, just like in the movies.' And he had had the opportunity to surprise them. A couple of klutzs, or were they?

'What if they had had guns?'

'Then I'd have cheerfully shot the bastards and called the cops.' He stood. 'So they didn't have guns. They were betting I wouldn't panic.' The more he thought about it, the more sure he was that the whole scene was just an act. But why?

'Let's go to bed.'

He helped her to her feet.

'I still don't understand,' she said. 'Were they CIA or not?'

'I don't know,' Jake said slowly. 'Through the years several people have accused the CIA of using agents to deliver warnings — of intimidation attempts. Yet in every case where the accusation was made public, it turned out that the CIA had no agents like the people supposedly involved. Now you tell me — were those two guys CIA agents carrying their own ID, CIA agents carrying false ID, or someone else's hired help using false CIA ID?'

'But the message is clear. Lay off.'

'Precisely. It's from someone very powerful, someone who cannot be reached. And that is part of the message.'

He had the toothpaste on his brush and the brush in his mouth when it hit him.

He took the brush out of his mouth and stared at it. Then he examined the toothpaste tube. Nothing could be easier than poisoning a tube of toothpaste. Merely unscrew the cap and stick a syringe in, then screw the cap back on.

But they had had no syringe on them. At Tarkington's house, anyway. For all he knew they could have thrown it in the gutter or put it in the garbage pail out behind the Graftons' house where it would be hauled away on Tuesday.

A knot developed in his stomach.

He started to put the toothbrush back into his mouth, but he couldn't.

Damn!

He rinsed out his mouth, then threw the toothbrush and the toothpaste into the wastebasket under the sink.

When he and Callie were in bed with the lights out, she asked, 'How do you get yourself into these messes, anyway?'

'You make it sound like I'm a juvenile delinquent.'

'I'm scared.'

'That's what they intended.'

'They succeeded. I'm frightened.'

'Me too,' he told her.

CHAPTER FOUR

On Monday morning at seven-thirty Toad Tarkington opened the door to the DIA computer facility and signed the log. 'Richard Harper, please,' he said to the receptionist when she came over to examine his pass. She had a cup of coffee in her hand and was polishing off the last of a doughnut.

'I'm sorry, but he doesn't work here anymore.'

'Say again.'

She shrugged. 'He doesn't work here now. He's gone.'

'Did he quit or what?'

'I don't know. He didn't come in last Wednesday. Or maybe Wednesday was his last day. Anyway, I heard someone say he transferred to another government agency. Can someone else help you?'

Toad Tarkington leaned his elbows on the counter and gave her a shy grin. 'He was in one of our baseball pools and won a hundred bucks.'

'Maybe he'll call you.'

'He doesn't know he won. We don't roll for the numbers on the grid until Friday.'

She smiled and shrugged. 'I'm sorry. Maybe if you call personnel . . .'

'I'll try that,' Toad said. 'In the meantime, I need a little work done. I need someone to check the CIA data base.'

'Mabel can help you. Right over there.' She pointed.

Mabel's terminal was in a corner. Toad removed a sheet of paper from a manila envelope stamped top secret and laid it in front of her. On it were two names: Paul R.

Tanana and Rodney D. Hicks. 'Please see if these two are on the CIA data base,' Toad asked.

Mabel apparently knew her way around a computer. Thirty seconds later she spoke. 'No.'

'Nothing?' Toad asked.

'*Nada.*'

'Not employees?'

'Nope.'

'How about the FBI data base? Can you access it?'

'It'll take a bit,' she murmured as she whacked keys. Toad watched the words and letters on the screen come and go, come and go. Last week when Harper played with the computer Toad had other things on his mind. Today he was interested.

All this high-tech . . . before it came along you would have just looked in the telephone directory.

The telephone book!

Toad spotted a directory under the desk and reached for it. He should have done this yesterday.

'I don't have any Roger Hicks,' Mabel told him. 'I have a Robert Hicks and a Rose Hicks and two R. Hicks.'

Toad flipped pages. 'Could you print out what you have on the R. Hicks entries?'

'Sure. And you don't have to look in the phone book. We have access to the phone company's files. If they have an account with the phone company, we'll see it. Maybe if you could tell me what you're looking for?'

'Whatever I can get,' Tarkington said. He put the phone book back on the bottom shelf of the desk. 'Check Tanana, then the Virginia Department of Motor Vehicles. And how about the Visa and MasterCard lists. I'll take anything.'

But he already knew what the answers were going to be. When Mabel gave him the printouts there it was in black-and-white. Each man had both Visa and MasterCard credit cards, but they had never made any charges on the cards. These accounts were less than a month old. The driver's licenses were real, but the addresses weren't. Burke, Virginia, had no such street as Wood Duck Drive, where Tanana's license said he lived. Hicks' address was equally bogus. The telephone company had never heard of either man.

So the identities were fake.

'Anything else?' Mabel asked. She was still on the right side of thirty and had a cute, intelligent face.

'Well,' said Toad Tarkington, and grinned conspiratorially. 'There is one little thing. Richard Harper won a hundred bucks in our baseball pool this weekend and we don't know where to get in touch with him. Could you check him on the CIA data base?'

'That isn't official business,' Mabel told him primly.

'I know. But I'll bet Richard would like the hundred.'

'Commander, we're not supposed . . .'

Toad gazed into her eyes and gave her an undiluted dose of the ol' Tarkington charm that had melted panties on three continents. 'Call me Toad. All my friends do.'

Mabel swallowed once and lowered her eyes. 'Okay,' she said and turned back to the keyboard. She punched keys.

'Here it is,' she told him. 'He transferred to the CIA computer facility at Langley. His office phone number is 775-0601.'

'Lemme write that down,' Toad said, and did so on a piece of scratch paper he snagged from beside the terminal. 'Thanks a lot, Mabel. I'll tell Richard he owes you a lunch.'

'You were right,' Toad told his boss. 'Tanana and Hicks are fake identities.'

Jake Grafton just nodded.

'How'd you know?'

Jake shrugged. 'They wanted us to see that ID.'

'And the analyst who worked on the photo of Herb Tenney, Richard Harper, now works at the CIA. As of this past Wednesday or Thursday.'

'So he was probably the leak,' Jake said.

'Yessir.' Toad found a seat. 'What are we going to do now?'

'I don't know,' Jake said.

Toad frowned.

'If you have any suggestions, let's hear them.'

Toad shrugged. 'I'm just the hired help around here, Admiral. You're the guy getting the big bucks.'

'Someone thought this out very carefully,' Jake said after a moment. 'They wanted to scare us, and they did, but there was the possibility that we could be induced to impale ourselves on our own swords. So they came equipped with fake identities and bogus Langley passes. And they drove leisurely from my house to your house to give me time to call you or catch up.'

'I didn't check the passes,' Toad said.

'Oh, they're as fake as the driver's licenses and credit cards. You can bet on it. And if I charged off to the front office with this wild tale about CIA employees threatening us and demanded that General Brown go after someone's head, I would have merely discredited myself, made myself look like a fool. And put General Brown in a difficult position.'

'Too bad we didn't take photos of those clowns.'

'Umm.'

'So what are you going to do?' Toad asked again.

'I'll have to think about it. If I go to General Brown I'm going to have to tell him about that Herb Tenney photo, and I don't know that that's a good idea. We still don't know a goddamn thing.'

'The CIA's reaction to the photo proves that they helped Keren depart for eternity.'

'If those two worked for the CIA. What if Tanana and Hicks were Mossad agents trying to make me suspicious of the CIA?'

'We're going to have to tell General Brown just to cover our fannies,' Toad said.

'Maybe. And that may make General Brown overly

suspicious of the CIA, which might have been the Mossad's goal when they gave us that photo. If it was the Mossad. The whole thing's a mare's nest. A military that stops believing its intelligence service is fumbling around in the dark. As if we had a lot of light now . . .'

Toad was thinking of Judith Farrell. Grafton had implied before that Farrell might have been intentionally trying to harm the United States, but Toad had automatically rejected it. Now he began to consider the possibility seriously.

'I'll bet someone at Langley would like to know where we got that photo,' Jake muttered.

But if that was the case, wouldn't that be the first priority? Why the simple intimidation attempt? It didn't compute. If it were the CIA. But the Mossad angle was even more unlikely.

What was wrong here? He was missing something. It was right in front of him and he couldn't see it. But what?

His eyes came to rest on Tarkington, who was staring at him. Toad looked away guiltily.

What? He went over it again, from Judith Farrell's meeting with Toad all the way through this morning's verification of the false identities of the agents.

Toad said something.

'What?'

'It's like Rubik's Cube, isn't it?' Toad repeated.

Rubik's Cube had a solution, although the solution was complex and one needed a good sense of spatial relationships to figure it out. Jake Grafton had spent a miserable week wrestling with a cube some years back when Amy gave him one for Christmas. Finally his next-door neighbor showed him how the trick was done.

The problems Jake had learned to solve had much simpler solutions: one usually became apparent when you backed off and looked at the forest instead of the individual trees.

Okay, Jake thought, by the numbers – One: if someone at

Langley knows about the photo, why isn't he trying to discover where and how I acquired it?

Maybe he is but I don't know about it.

Unlikely, Jake decided. He and Tarkington were the only people who knew the answers. And Rita and Judith Farrell. But they don't know about Rita. They might know about Judith Farrell or have an agent in the Mossad, but that would be a complex solution, only acceptable if there are no simple ones. There *must* be a simple explanation.

Two: the person who sent the goons on Friday night isn't curious.

Why not? Because he already knows.

How?

Jake Grafton's eyes focused and he looked again at Toad, who was watching him askance.

'No,' Jake said.

'No?'

'Not like Rubik's Cube.'

The admiral pulled around a sheet of paper and picked up a pencil. On it he wrote 'This office is bugged.'

Toad came over and looked at the words. 'You think?' he murmured.

Jake nodded. He got up, removed his jacket and draped it over the back of his chair, loosened his tie and began to look. Toad started on the other side of the room.

In five minutes they had ruled out the obvious, a microphone behind a painting or under a desk. 'Let's go for a walk,' Jake suggested.

'It's nothing obvious,' Jake told Toad as they walked toward the cafeteria. 'Nothing conventional. If it was, the sweeps would have discovered it.' The office was swept for listening devices twice a week at random intervals.

'Maybe it's the telephone. We'll have to take that apart. And how about the window vibrator?' Toad suggested. This device used elevator music to vibrate the glass pane and foil any parabolic listening device aimed at the window. 'What if it isn't a real vibrator?'

'Perhaps our eavesdropper has a parabolic antenna aimed at the window,' Jake said, 'and is unscrambling the tape with a powerful computer, like a Cray?'

'That's a possibility,' Toad admitted after he thought about it. 'Are you sure about the bug?'

'No,' Jake told him. 'But a listening device would explain a lot. And not some simple piece of Radio Shack junk. Something computerized, something so sophisticated we don't see it for what it is.'

'If they're using that window as a sounding board, about all we can do is put another music source near the window, like a portable radio, and complicate the signal. But I think we should search that office until we find a bug or can swear there isn't one.'

'Go down to the maintenance office and get tools. Screwdrivers, pliers, wrenches, and a voltage meter.'

'Aye aye, sir.'

'And a pipe wrench.'

They started on the telephone. They disassembled the plastic box and tested the microphone in the headset and in the desk unit to see if it really went dead when the phone was on the hook. It worked as they thought it should.

Next the light fixtures were removed from their sockets and examined, then reinstalled. The soundproof ceiling tiles were taken down and the overhead and tile framework examined. They moved the furniture and rolled back the carpet. Nothing.

The heating and cooling duct vents were dirty but innocent.

Toad pointed toward the polished walnut molding that framed the door and window and edged the walls.

Jake examined the trim. He rated it because he was the deputy director of the DIA. The nails that held the wood in place were covered with varnish.

He shook his head at Toad and pointed toward the radiator.

The old steam radiator was no longer in use, but the steam pipes were still installed. They used the pipe wrench on the ring nuts.

And there it was.

With the nuts off the steam intake and outlet pipes, they wrestled the radiator out a half inch or so, just enough to reveal the insulated wire that went through the inlet pipe.

So the whole radiator was a sounding board. Inside the cast-iron unit there must be a sensing unit, more likely two or three of them. The signals went out through the wire to God knows where, and there the readings were tape-recorded. An analysis of the tape using the known vibration characteristics of the radiator would produce an electronic signal that could be processed into speech.

There was nothing for an electronic sweep to find. Yet whoever had installed this unit had merely to run the signal through his computer to hear everything said inside the office.

Jake used the pipe wrench to pound a hole in the wall. The pipe made a left turn inside the wall.

'Come on.'

Out in the corridor Toad was ready to pound another hole in the drywall when Jake stopped him. 'Let's find the telephone switchboxes. They probably have it routed through the phone system. Go call the telephone repair people and get someone up here on the double.'

The telephone switching boxes were in the basement. The system technician opened one of the boxes and Jake drew back in amazement. Hundreds of wires. 'How do you know which is which?'

'Well, sir, just tell me the phone number and I'll show you the connection.'

'I don't know the phone number.'

'Well, everything coming into this box has a number.'

Now Jake understood. Somewhere in the building there was a tape recorder or recorders — a monitoring station — hooked up to a telephone. All the eavesdropper had to do was telephone the proper number, punch in a code and the monitoring station would obediently belch forth all its data, which could then be processed by a computer into speech.

The technician was still talking. '. . . they built this building during World War II and have been hooking up telephones ever since. The last big telephone update we did we added more lines and used the old ones where we could. But there's no blueprints or diagrams or anything like that. It's fucking spaghetti.'

They could establish what line it was, of course, by trial and error. Some of the lines were undoubtedly not supposed to be hooked up. But why bother? 'Thanks, anyway,' Jake said. 'I appreciate you showing us this.'

Back in Jake's office Toad Tarkington cut the wire going into the radiator.

'They know everything,' he said disgustedly.

'Apparently.'

'They even got the conversation about binary chemicals.'

'Yep. And one of those goons alluded to it Friday night. He said what a terrible thing it would be if Amy died of heart failure. I should have known right then. Goddamnit!'

The more he thought about the situation the angrier he became.

'*Goddamn those bastards!*'

General Albert Sidney Brown didn't get angry, he went ballistic. He listened to Jake tell him about the bug in the radiator with an air of disbelief and growing bewilderment, but when Toad used the pipe wrench to disassemble the radiator in the general's plush corner office and he saw *his* wire, he went into an apoplectic rage. He spluttered, his face turned a deep crimson. When he recovered slightly he began to curse. He gave a rich performance at a full-throated volume that would have done the crustiest drill instructor proud.

Only when Brown began to wind down did Jake signal to Toad to cut the wire. If the CIA had someone listening he

60

wanted them to know they had just pissed on and royally pissed off the very upper echelons of the American military. If they cared.

Then the general got on the phone. Sixty seconds after he hung up, the DIA's security officer, an army colonel, was standing in front of Brown's desk. The general led him to the radiator and showed him the wire.

By this point Brown's mood had coalesced into cold fury. 'I want to know how many of these goddamn listening devices are in this agency's offices. I want all the sensors and wire and telephone equipment removed. And take out these' – he whacked the radiator with Toad's pipe wrench – 'fucking antique radiators. I want to know why these bugs weren't detected by your staff. I want to know what it's gonna take to make sure something like this doesn't happen again. And when you have finished with all of that, you and your entire staff are going to stand in this office and swear me a blood oath that there are no more goddamn bugs in any of our spaces.'

The colonel left in a hurry. Brown then eyed Jake Grafton without warmth. 'You and I are going to have a little chat, Admiral. And not in this damned building. Get your hat and let's go see if we can find someplace private.'

They ended up in an exclusive restaurant in Alexandria, Virginia, after a silent ride in Brown's limo. Brown apparently knew the owner, who admitted him after he pounded on the door. After listening to Brown's request she escorted the two officers to the far back corner of the empty dining room.

'I know you don't open until five, but could we please get coffee?'

'Of course, General,' the lady said. 'Make yourself comfortable and we'll bring it out in a few minutes.'

'I appreciate your hospitality, Mrs Horowitz.'

She smiled and left for the kitchen.

'Well?'

Jake told his boss everything, from Judith Farrell's

meeting with Toad to the discovery of the bug. The recitation took thirty minutes and was broken only by the delivery of a pot of coffee and two cups. Brown listened without interruptions.

When Jake finished the general said, 'Admiral, I'll lay it on the line with you. You should have reported the contact by a foreign agent to me as soon as possible. You fucked up.'

'Yessir.'

'You fuck up again, you'll be a civilian by noon the next day.'

Brown refilled his coffee cup and stirred it with a spoon. A slow grin twisted his lips. 'Tell me again about sticking the pistol in that CIA weenie's face.'

When they had finished dissecting Jake's adventure, General Brown began to talk of the CIA and the personalities of the men who ran it. Finally he became philosophical:

'All intelligence services are bureaucracies, of course. The output is always mangled to some extent as it goes through the pipe. But when the people in the intelligence business start editing the raw data to support their policy recommendations, the output becomes fiction. It's worse than worthless − it's fantasy as fact, so it's just plain dangerous. Policymakers think they're getting the big picture and they're making the decisions, but in reality the decision-making function has been appropriated by the person editing the data. The elected policymaker is being manipulated. He becomes a mere rubber stamp.'

'Do you think that is what's happening at the CIA now?' Jake Grafton asked.

Brown grimaced. 'Historically the heads of intelligence services have usually stood right by the throne. Often in Europe the spymasters were the second most powerful men in the government. But not in the United States. The cloak-and-dagger boys have always put the fear of God in our elected politicians, and rightfully so. Are they manipulating our government, now, here?'

He leaned across the table toward Jake. 'They missed the collapse of communism. The biggest political event on this planet since World War II and they missed it. Apparently not a soul at Langley ever predicted it or suggested it as a possibility. They said the Soviet economy was three times larger than it was. They said the Soviet military was much stronger, more capable, more combat-ready than turned out to be the case. They sat there looking at a society in meltdown and never saw a wisp of smoke. The fact is that for the last five years you could have gotten a better picture of what was happening inside the Soviet Union by reading the *New York Times* than you could from reading the CIA intelligence analyses. But was that intentional?

'These damned CIA briefings and intelligence reports give me a queasy feeling,' Brown continued after a moment's pause. 'Nothing I can put my finger on – the stuff is too slickly written for that. Maybe that's the trouble. Maybe it's too slick, every mousehole carefully papered over. I don't know. I just get this feeling. I'd really like to see the raw intelligence, *all* of it.

'What I think . . . what I *think* we're looking at in Russia is merely an interlude between dictatorships, like the 1917 republic after they toppled the czar. The problems are too big, the people are bigots intolerant of dissent and diversity, they are too easily swayed by demagogues spouting bull-shit and hate, they readily swallow any hint of a conspiracy, they despise anyone with a ruble more than they've got. The average Russian can't conceive of a loyal opposition: the concept doesn't compute. That's the background for the biggest economic experiment ever tried on this planet, the conversion of a centralized socialized economy into a free market one. But the CIA downplays all that. The folks at the CIA aren't worried. And no one over at the White House seems to be in a sweat. Our politicos have bigger fish to fry, like squabbling over Clinton's tax increases and waggling their fingers at the Japanese.'

Brown rearranged the salt and pepper shakers. 'I'm not

sure what the National Security Adviser thinks. At the CIA briefings sometimes he acts like he smells a rat, other times he sits there like he was getting the gospel in Sunday school.

'What's happening in the former Soviet Union right now may turn out to be the seminal event that determines the course of human life on this planet for the next century. The old union is in the midst of total social and economic collapse. Nothing works. Nothing! No one knows how to make a decision. All look to central authority, which is corrupt, incompetent, self-absorbed. The republics constitute the most highly polluted nation on earth. It's one giant petrochemical sewer, thousands of square miles of soil so radioactive that humans can't survive on it, social systems that have completely collapsed. Doctors are poorly trained and incompetent – they routinely misdiagnose ailments, sick people go to unbelievably bad hospitals where they are butchered by quacks, there isn't enough medicine, equipment, food, clothes, anything . . .

'I could go on for hours.' He picked up a pepper shaker and tapped in on the table, hard. 'I think the pollution is what did in the Communists. Too many people are getting sick. Best guess is at least a million people in the old union are sick with radiation poisoning. Lack of basic sanitation and immunizations causes epidemics of diphtheria, dysentery, polio, influenza – fifty percent of their conscripts are rejected for military service. It's estimated only one in fourteen of the people in uniform could pass a flight physical.

'You can only run a society for the benefit of the elite at the top for so long before the whole thing implodes.' He shrugged.

Jake Grafton found himself leaning forward and lowering his voice. 'So what about those nuclear weapons?'

'CIA hasn't told us the whole story. You can bet your pension on that. Reality has a feel, a texture, that's unique.

It's seasoned with insanity and random chance. This stuff the CIA's selling hasn't got that feel.'

'You sure?' Jake pressed.

'I wish I was. But no, I ain't sure. The key is money. If nuclear weapons are leaving Russia, someone is paying big bucks for them. CIA is looking and says they can't find the trail.'

'Perhaps we should do some looking on our own,' Jake suggested.

'How?'

'Well, we need to draft a computer expert.'

'You say that like you have one in mind.'

Jake did. He just nodded.

'CIA, Treasury, and State won't like it.'

'If we find the trail their objections won't matter much.'

'If it's there to find,' Brown said without enthusiasm.

Jake decided to change the subject. 'What are you going to do about the bugs, General?'

Albert Sidney Brown pushed back his chair and stood. 'I'm going to write a report to the president and send copies to everybody on the list. The CIA will think I'm a patsy if I don't. But just the bugs. Nothing about Nigel Keren or Mossad photographs or intimidation efforts. You were right about that. If we run those shitty rags up the flagpole now, you and I'll be diving headfirst into a foxhole to keep from getting squashed.'

The whole mess was pretty bizarre, Jake Grafton reflected later. It was like climbing a mountain: the higher you got the worse the visibility became, the thicker the cloud. And if it was like this at his level, presumably the president, the man at the top, couldn't see his hand in front of his face. No wonder the government stumbled from crisis to crisis!

That night Jake and Toad searched the Grafton house from top to bottom for bugs. They didn't find any, which merely increased Jake's sense of unease. Then they went over to Tarkington's house and turned it inside out. Rita helped. And they found nothing.

'So what are we gonna do, Admiral?' Toad asked when they had finished and were drinking beer in the kitchen.

Rita flipped on the radio and cranked up the volume.

'Do?'

'Yessir. About Herb Tenney and going to Russia with him and all of this.'

'I dunno,' Jake said. 'Any suggestions?' He glanced at Rita Moravia, who stood with her back against the sink, trying to look deadpan. She wasn't supposed to know about the Russian trip, which was still highly classified. Her hair was pulled back and held with a clasp tonight. Tall for a woman, she had the sleek look of solid, healthy muscle. She colored slightly when she met the admiral's eyes. Feeling a touch of amusement, Jake's gaze returned to Toad Tarkington. 'What would you suggest?'

'I'd like to go over to Langley and sweat somebody.'

'Who?'

'I'd start with Herb.'

'He wouldn't tell you jack, even if he knew anything to tell.' Jake sighed. He drained the last of his beer, then sat the glass out of the way. 'Got a phone book?'

'Sure.'

'Let's go calling. There is a fellow who works at Langley that I'd like to talk to.'

There were fourteen Richard Harpers and eleven R. Harpers listed in the Washington metro telephone directory. Rita did the calling while Toad listened on the living room extension. She worked for a pizza company and they had lost a delivery address.

'This won't work if his wife answers,' Rita pointed out.

'I don't think he's married,' Toad told her. 'He isn't the type.'

'Oh, and what type is that?'

'Sensitive, warm, loving, wholesome, handsome, sharing, caring—'

'Shut up. It's ringing . . . Hello, Richard Harper please . . . Mr Harper, did you order a pizza about a half hour ago? No? Well, a Richard Harper on Gordon Street ordered a large pepperoni and olive and our driver can't find the house . . .'

She fell silent as the man on the phone talked. From the living room Toad signaled no. Rita made her excuses and thanked him for his time.

They got lucky. They found him on the fifth call. An address in Chevy Chase.

'Let's go,' Jake said.

Richard Harper wasn't going to invite them in. Toad shoved the door open and pushed past him. Jake Grafton followed. 'It's two in the morning,' Harper squeaked.

'I know,' Toad Tarkington said. 'But I wanted you to meet my boss, Admiral Grafton. Admiral, this is Richard Harper, late of the DIA and now with Central Intelligence.'

Jake stuck out his hand. Reluctantly Richard Harper took it. While Harper was still wondering how to handle this intrusion, Jake dropped into a chair and turned on the light on the reading stand beside him. 'Let's all sit down and visit a minute.'

Harper moved toward a chair, but he didn't sit. 'This won't take long,' Jake assured him. Harper perched on the front edge of the seat.

Jake displayed his green military ID card and his DIA office pass. Harper refused to touch them. Jake made a show of replacing the cards back in his pocket, then began. 'There's been a security violation at the DIA and we're trying to find the leak. We have to do this after office hours since people don't want to talk about their colleagues at the office. You understand?'

Harper nodded reluctantly.

From Toad's attaché case Jake removed a tape recorder – borrowed from Rita – and placed it on a low table between himself and Harper. He pushed the play button and made sure the tape was turning. 'This is Rear Admiral Jacob L. Grafton. It is now two oh seven A.M. on June eighteen. I am interviewing Richard Harper. Mr Harper, last Monday did you conduct a computer search of CIA records at the request of Lieutenant Commander Robert Tarkington at the DIA computer facilities?'

'Now wait a minute—'

'No, you wait a minute, Mr Harper. Someone revealed classified information about that computer search to persons without access. Top secret information has been compromised. This is an official investigation. If you fail to cooperate you can be dismissed from government service and prosecuted. Do you understand?'

Harper's face contorted. A tear rolled down his cheek. 'I've already been fired.'

'Say again.'

'The CIA fired me this afternoon. They found out about my record.'

The two naval officers exchanged glances. Jake reached over and turned off the tape recorder. 'Maybe you'd better tell me about it,' he murmured.

The recitation took most of an hour. Periodically there were tears. Richard Harper was twenty-seven and had been fascinated with computers since he was in high school. Just for the challenge of it, he became a hacker, a person who breaks into industry and government computer files for the sheer joy of outwitting the security devices that guard the files. He had been caught once while he was in college and received a suspended sentence. The second time, when he planted a virus program, he had gone to jail.

The computer industry refused to hire him. Computers were his life and he was blacklisted. He had managed to secure a temporary appointment at DIA by lying on his employment application. He knew the FBI would learn the truth sooner or later, so when agents of the CIA approached him about supplying them with information about DIA projects, he had agreed if they would give him a permanent computer job. A month went by, he supplied all the information they asked for, including Toad's bizarre request, and they had him start work at Langley last week. Then today they pretended to have just learned of his previous convictions and fired him. It wasn't fair. He had quit the DIA, the CIA had canned him, the FBI would eventually learn of his record. Computers were his whole life yet he couldn't work in computers.

'Do you have a computer setup here at home?' Jake asked.

It was in the guest bedroom at the back of the little house. There Jake and Toad were treated to a proud recital of hard disk capacity, extended and expanded memory, CPU speed, and all the rest of it as they stared at screens, keyboards and the innards of computers that were scattered everywhere.

'How good a hacker are you?' Jake asked.

'I'm good. Real good. If I hadn't done that virus way back when . . . And it was nothing, just tidbits of zen philosophy that popped onto the screen at holidays and all. It didn't hurt anyone and . . .'

Back in the living room, Jake told Harper, 'I have a job for you. I can't promise a permanent job at the DIA until we get a final FBI check and go over it line by line. But I can pay you by the hour on a temporary basis if you can do this job. It would be here at home, on your own equipment.'

Harper was enthusiastic. Yes. He agreed before he even knew what the job was. Jake felt as if he were throwing a rope to a drowning man. He thought he had the authority to hire Harper on a temporary basis, but if it turned out he didn't he would pay him out of his own pocket.

'I want you to find a river of money,' Jake said, intently watching Harper's face, 'a subterranean river flowing through the world banking systems. The task won't be easy. I'm not even sure that you will be able to recognize the river when you see it. The mouth of the river is in Moscow, but I don't have any idea where it begins.'

'Banks?'

'Banks.'

'I'll need computer access telephone numbers, user names and passwords. If I go after that stuff myself they'll be on to me in hours.'

'I thought—'

'Hackers get into computers by conning the phone number and codes out of somebody. I can do that. But I can't do it three dozen times and get away with it. The National Security Agency has that stuff. They monitor bank transactions on a daily basis.'

'If NSA has it, we can get it,' Jake said, glancing at Toad.

'You give me that stuff, and if the money is there, I'll find it,' Harper said confidently. Too confidently, Jake Grafton thought.

'Don't be so quick to make promises. And I don't want anyone to know you're looking.'

'Maybe you'd better tell me what I'm supposed to be looking for so I'll know it when I see it.'

Fifteen minutes later Harper knew everything Jake did, which was precious little. So Jake devoted another hour to discussing the possibilities and the probabilities. 'The problem,' he told Harper, 'is that I don't know who I can trust. I've got to trust my boss, but who else? I can't call friends in the FBI, in the CIA, people I've known for years. If there is a small cabal in the CIA, only the people involved know it is a cabal. Everyone else thinks they are doing their duty when they report conversations, fill out reports, do what they are told to do. That's the problem.'

'How do you want me to report to you?' Harper asked.

'Well, written reports would be okay. Mail them to my wife. She'll see that I get them wherever I am. I may be out of town for a few weeks.' He gave Harper his address.

When Jake and Toad left at four in the morning, Rita was asleep on the front seat of the car.

Under the streetlight Toad said, 'I have a real bad feeling

about this, Admiral. If Harper steals money or screws up some accounts, you and I will end up in prison.'

'I hope they give us separate cells,' Jake told him. 'A rear admiral ought to rate a private cell.'

CHAPTER FIVE

'Yeltsin said yes. Two hours ago.'

'Sure took him long enough,' Jake Grafton muttered. 'If I were sitting on all those weapons I'd have got a hot seat months ago.'

General Brown consulted his watch. 'Fifteen hours ago two army bases were attacked. The Russian government says the attackers stole machine guns, artillery, APCs and at least ten truckloads of ammunition.'

'Truckloads?'

'Yeah,' General Brown said. 'They killed sixty soldiers at one base, fifty at another, and blew up all but the trucks and APCs they drove out.'

'Who?'

'They aren't sure. Maybe criminal gangs, maybe Armenians again. Maybe some ex-soldiers who are starting their own private army.' General Brown stepped to the map on the wall and pointed. 'Here and here.'

When he had resumed his seat, he said, 'The CIA's man went over yesterday.'

'Tenney?'

'Yes. He'll meet you at the embassy. Ambassador Lancaster will brief you. The president wants the nukes neutralized and the Russian government strengthened. Talk to those people. Let us know what you need to do the job.'

Jake Grafton didn't laugh. It was too ridiculous for that. How in hell had he gotten into the middle of this mess?

'And,' General Brown continued, 'if you can piss on any of those outlaw or rebel gangs, that'll be all right too.'

His stomach felt like there was a rock in it. 'Yessir,' he managed.

'The air force will have a C-141 at Andrews in six hours. Be on it.'

'Aye aye, sir.'

Albert Sidney Brown came around the desk and held out his hand. 'Good luck, Admiral.'

'Don't worry, sir. I'll take my rabbit's foot along.'

'You're going to need more than a rabbit's foot,' Callie told Jake as she passed him aspirin and toilet articles to put in his bag. He had just mentioned his parting remark to General Brown. She didn't think it was very funny. As she watched him stuff underwear around his Smith & Wesson .357 Magnum and shoulder holster, she tartly added, 'You're also going to need more than that little popgun.'

She pushed her hair back out of her eyes. 'Oh, you men! Jetting off into the middle of a revolution. It's so damn pathetic.'

'It isn't really a revolution,' her husband replied as he folded underwear around a box of pistol ammunition and added it to the bag. 'Yeltsin's still in the driver's seat, still in control.'

'For how long? What does anyone think you and Toad can really accomplish?'

'Oh, we'll have some help. Too much probably. But if we can just prod the Russians into—'

'Don't change the subject,' Callie said sharply. 'You know precisely what I mean. Even with the entire United States Army over there you'd still be outnumbered ten to one. Sending you and Toad over there is some kind of insane joke.'

'Umph,' Jake grunted.

Toad Tarkington's opinion had been more colorful but

no more optimistic: 'Once again our politicians are saving the world from foreign politicians stupider than they are. And we nincompoops in uniform smartly salute and grab ankles. BOHICA!' Ah yes, that lovely old acronym, BOHICA—Bend Over. Here It Comes Again.

Callie jerked a pair of trousers away from him that he was rolling up. She folded them carefully and handed them back. 'Not that they'll send the entire army,' she said. 'You'll be lucky to get two privates and a corporal. One of the privates will be the cook and the other will peel potatoes. Presumably the corporal will have a few minutes a day to help you and Toad when he isn't busy supervising the privates.'

She sat heavily. 'Oh, Jake. Why you?'

He sat down beside her and took her in his arms.

'Everything will work out. It always does.'

'No. Everything doesn't always *work out*. I'm really tired of hearing that trite little phrase.'

'You know me, Callie,' Jake Grafton said. 'Trust me.'

'Hey, babe. It's me, Toad. We're leaving today.'

'Now?' Rita asked.

Toad gripped the telephone tightly. 'Plane leaves Andrews at six.'

'I'll see if I can get the rest of the day off,' she said. 'You're at home?'

'Yeah. Packing.'

'If I don't call in ten minutes I'm on my way home.'

'Okay.'

'I have a bad feeling about this, Toad.'

'It'll be okay.'

'I love you.'

'I know that, babe. And I love you.'

'See you in a while.'

The C-141 headed north on the great circle route to Moscow. After it climbed above the stratus clouds covering

74

the East Coast of the United States, it flew in a clear sky illuminated by the sun low on the horizon.

Jake Grafton came up to the flight deck and visited a moment with the pilots, then stood looking at the vastness of the sky. 'It doesn't ever get dark at this time of year at these latitudes,' the copilot told him.

'How many times have you guys flown this route?' Jake asked.

'Couple dozen times for me, sir,' the pilot, an air force major, replied. He nodded at the copilot, a first lieutenant. 'This is his second trip.'

Cold. The sky looked bleak and cold, even with the sun shining. The cockpit was a tiny capsule of life adrift in an indifferent universe.

Jake shivered once, then returned to the little passenger section. There were only eight seats and Toad was asleep in one of them. In the next row the liftmaster, a senior sergeant, also snoozed. The rest of the plane was filled with military rations bound for orphanages and soup kitchens for the elderly. The admiral opened the door to the cargo compartment and stood there looking. Overhead lights illuminated the cargo compartment and the sea of boxes stacked on pallets.

The incongruity of the situation appalled him, filled him with a sadness devoid of hope that seemed to drain the energy from him. Insanity, Callie had said. Yes, that was the word. A nation with enough nuclear weapons to kill half the life on earth and doom the rest couldn't feed its old people, its children.

Jake closed the door and sagged into a seat.

He tried to sleep but it wouldn't come. Finally he turned so he could look out the window at the cold, infinite sky.

At Sheremetyevo Airport near Moscow, the C-141 was parked next to a Soviet military terminal across the field from the regular passenger terminal. Jake and Toad exited the plane through the rear cargo door after it had been opened. Although the plane had been airborne for twelve hours and it was 6 A.M. in Washington, it was two o'clock in the afternoon here on a pleasant summer day. Small puffy clouds floated in a blue sky. They stood on the concrete ramp beside their bags and watched a limo driving toward them. It came to a halt and a man in a US naval officer's uniform climbed out.

'Lieutenant Dalworth, sir,' said the young officer after he had saluted. He pulled open the back door of the car. As Jake and Toad climbed in he added, 'You don't have to go through customs.'

'How come?'

'I arranged it, sir. I've become pretty good friends with several of the customs and emigration guys.'

Jake was taken slightly aback.

'Don't worry, sir. With diplomatic passports, the whole deal is just a formality. I've partied with those guys, given them some sacks of groceries and gotten drunk with them. They know I won't screw 'em.'

Three minutes later, after Jake's and Toad's baggage was loaded in the trunk, Dalworth climbed in and got the car in motion. Toad Tarkington mused, 'Dalworth. Dalworth . . . By any chance, are you Spiro Dalworth?'

A look of discomfort crossed the young officer's face.

Tarkington grinned broadly and seized the lieutenant's hand. He pumped it heartily. 'As I live and breathe.'

Jake Grafton recognized the name too. Lieutenant Dalworth had been assigned to the navy's public relations staff in New York City when he somehow wound up on a television talk show panel discussing 'women in the modern military.' After thirty minutes of weathering abuse from a prominent feminist fanatic who shared the panel with him, Dalworth lost his temper. His parting shot at her had been, 'Oh, Spiro Agnew.'

Three days later someone told the female warrior that the former vice president's name was an anagram for 'grow a penis.'

She charged into the navy's cubbyhole office in the Manhattan federal building with a television reporter and cameraman in tow and proceeded to assault Dalworth with an umbrella while she hurled invective. After she shouted herself out and departed, a stunned Dalworth told the reporter that the feminist had a brain like a prune and a body to match.

The episode was marvelous television.

Alas, Dalworth's new status as a media celebrity interfered with his work and embarrassed the navy, still reeling from the 1991 Tailhook Convention scandal, so now he was a very junior naval attaché at the American embassy in Moscow, eight time zones away from the nearest militant feminist armed with a television camera and umbrella.

'That whole thing was almost eight months ago,' Dalworth muttered. 'You'd think people would at least start to forget.' He was a rangy young man, several inches over six feet, with wide shoulders and bulging biceps. At some point in his athletic past his nose had been slightly rearranged, and the effect was a memorable face. Not handsome, but unique.

'What an honor, Spiro! I sure am pleased to meetcha,' Toad enthused. He playfully tapped Dalworth on the shoulder.

'Did you have a good flight?' Dalworth asked.

'Terrific. Filet mignon over the North Pole and all the free champagne we could drink.'

'The cold chicken box lunch, huh?'

'Yeah. You wonder what the air force does to the chicken to make it taste so bad.'

'Ever been to Moscow before?'

'Neither one of us,' Toad said.

'Sleepy?'

After a glance at Grafton, Toad told him, 'Not too.'

'Drive you around the downtown a little before we go to Fort Apache.' Fort Apache, Jake knew, was the complex behind the embassy where the residents lived, a tag that came straight from the movie *Fort Apache, The Bronx*. 'Give you the hundred-ruble tour.'

The endless rows of concrete apartment buildings were soon in view. Nine and a half million people, Jake knew, lived in Moscow, most of them stuffed into tiny apartments in these crumbling mausoleums. Yet on a sunny June day they didn't look bad. Almost as if he could read Jake's thoughts, Dalworth said, 'Place looks a lot different in the winter. Then it's the devil's own refrigerator, gray and terminally dismal.'

Soon the car was bucketing down a broad boulevard toward the center of the city, a chip afloat in a stream of little sedans and huge trucks, all emitting a noxious miasma that stung the eyes and throat. 'Bad pollution, about like Delhi, India. Sorta like Seoul without the kimchi.'

Dalworth piloted them into the center of the city. Soon they were circling the brick walls and onion-topped towers of the Kremlin. Jake's eye was caught by the cars on the side of the road with their hoods up and people bending over the engines. Someone seemed to be broken down in every block.

Dalworth pointed out the naked pedestals where once statues stood. 'See those? They even tore down the statue of Felix Dzerzhinsky in front of KGB Headquarters, presumably while the KGB types watched out the windows. Now I'll show you my favorite place in Moscow. I found this the other day when I was out walking.'

After three more stoplights, he turned and crossed the Moskva River and went down one of the side streets. In one of the river channels a cruise ship sat listing in the mud, gutted and abandoned. Ahead across the sidewalk was a park. A dirt road for park maintenance vehicles was blocked by steel crowd-control railings. Dalworth drove the car onto the sidewalk, stopped, then got out and moved the railings. He pulled the car through, then replaced them. The park was young trees and grass, but the grass was half weeds and hadn't been mowed. Here and there women with strollers sat taking the sun. After Dalworth drove about a hundred yards, he pulled the car to a stop.

Just to the left, surrounded on three sides by more haphazardly placed crowd-control railings, stood three huge bronze statues amid the dandelions and grass. A smaller marble statue lay on its side in front of the others. Behind them half-hidden by the foliage of the trees one could glimpse rows of apartments.

'This is where they dumped some of the statues,' Dalworth explained. He parked the car and the three men got out.

Jake Grafton ran his hands over the marble defaced with swatches of paint. The lower portion of the statue was broken off and lying in the grass. He moved to the head and stared down into the paint-daubed face of Josef Stalin.

'Who are these others?'

The standing bronzes were three or four times life size. 'They look to me to be three likenesses of the same guy, Admiral,' Dalworth said. 'Dzerzhinsky, I think, but I don't know for sure. Maybe Lenin with hair. For sure he was some big Commie mucky-muck that they were tired of looking at and hearing about. He looks sort of like a Slavic Thomas Jefferson, doesn't he?'

'More like Jefferson Davis,' Jake Grafton murmured, and looked around. 'What's that over there?' He pointed at a huge gray concrete structure three or four stories high a hundred yards away, beside the river. The parking lots were empty, and even from this distance he could see the building was shabby, the facade crumbling.

'Some kind of cultural thing. Just beyond it across that boulevard is the entrance to Gorky Park. See that huge gate?'

'Umm.'

Jake Grafton turned back to Stalin. He ran his hands over the marble and looked again into the stone eyes.

'"Look on my works, ye mighty, and despair,"' Toad Tarkington said.

Lieutenant Spiro Dalworth was more down-to-earth. 'Be fun to have one of these out in the backyard, wouldn't it? To piss on whenever you felt in the mood.'

US Ambassador Owen Lancaster was not a career diplomat – rather he was one of those political insiders who had been repeatedly appointed to key embassies by both Democratic and Republican administrations. His political affiliation was a subject that never seemed to get mentioned by anyone, even the press. In short, he was The Establishment from fingertips to toenails.

And he looked it, Jake Grafton concluded. Tall, lean, patrician and impeccably turned out in a tailor-made wool suit and a handmade silk tie, Owen Lancaster looked exactly like central casting's idea of an heir to a nineteenth century Yankee merchant's fortune, which he was. It seemed as if this room in Spaso House were designed around him: the lighting, color scheme, expensive furniture and carpeting – the room was an exquisite tribute to the interior designer's art. God would have a living room like this if He had the money.

In a chair to the left of the ambassador sat one of the career diplomats, a woman in her mid to late thirties – maybe early forties – it was hard to tell. She wore modest, expensive clothes and no makeup that Jake could see. Her name was Ms Agatha Hempstead, with the emphasis on the Ms. She hadn't yet opened her mouth but Jake Grafton already suspected that she was three or four notches smarter than Old Money Lancaster.

On the other side of the ambassador sat Herb Tenney. He was wearing a suit and tie this afternoon and looked as if he had merely dropped in to pass a few social moments. After he had smiled and nodded pleasantly to Jake and Toad, he devoted his attention to the ambassador's plea-santries.

'I don't pretend to know just what instructions you have been given in Washington, Admiral,' the ambassador was saying, 'or what we Americans can do to improve this situation. I don't know that we can contribute anything to the solution of this particular problem, but it certainly won't hurt to try. The Russians must learn that they can cooperate with us on matters of mutual interest and, indeed, it is in their best interests to do so. I think that's critical . . .'

Jake Grafton twisted in his ornate, polished mahogany chair. Herb Tenney looked *innocent*, Jake concluded. His whole presence radiated comfort, proclaimed to everyone who saw him that here was a man at peace with humanity and his conscience, a man who knew in his heart of hearts that he had nothing to regret, nothing to apologize for, nothing to fear.

All of which somehow irritated Jake Grafton.

'. . . We *can* help,' Ambassador Lancaster was saying, 'solve problems in a constructive way that will . . .'

Toad Tarkington caught Jake's eye with a warning glance. Apparently he could see that his boss was struggling to keep a grip on his temper.

God! Was it that obvious?

The fact that Tenney could probably also see the effect of his innocent act was gasoline on the fire. Jake felt the heat as his face flushed. Herb Tenney and his CIA bugs . . . Sunday op-ed drivel from the ambassador . . . if he had to sit here in this museum exhibit of bureaucratic good taste for another two minutes he was going to be in a mood to strangle them both.

'Mr Ambassador,' Jake interrupted as he struggled to rise from the overstuffed chair. 'I didn't get any sleep on the plane and I've just spent an hour with the naval attaché. I've got to lie down for a few hours. Is there anyplace I can crash?'

'Oh, of course, of course. You must be rested when you meet General Yakolev in the morning. I should have thought of that. Would you like something to eat before you go to bed?'

'No, thank you, sir. Perhaps a light breakfast in the morning?'

'No problem, Admiral. We'll talk again then.'

Jake Grafton shook the ambassador's hand, nodded at Ms Hempstead, then turned and tramped out without even a glance at Tenney.

He woke up at midnight after four hours' sleep and found he was wide awake. He turned on the bedside light and examined his watch. What time was it in Washington? What the hell was the time differential? Eight hours? Four o'clock in the afternoon in Washington. No wonder he couldn't sleep even though he was tired.

From the window he could see the Moscow skyline as the anemic city lights made the clouds glow. And the sky wasn't completely dark – sort of a twilight.

He dressed quickly in civilian clothes and pulled on a light jacket. He picked up the phone and was quickly connected to the enlisted marine at the duty desk. 'Could I get a car and driver? I'd like to do a little sight-seeing.'

'I'll see what I can do, sir.' The marine's voice was matter of fact, held not a trace of surprise. Perhaps these requests were common, Jake mused, from new arrivals suffering from jet lag.

'Okay.'

'It'll be just a few minutes, sir.'

The driver, a sergeant, motored slowly on a journey without a destination as Jake Grafton took it all in from the backseat. The city didn't resemble any city he had ever visited. The streets were poorly lit and had private cars parked everywhere. There seemed to be no shortage of parking spaces. At least there was one thing Russia had enough of. Only because they didn't have many cars. Occasionally he saw a few soldiers at street corners, here and there some civilians.

Now and then the driver told him the name of some public building, softly, almost whispering it.

Yes, Jake too felt like a trespasser.

The public buildings were large and grand, but once away from them the streets were lined with endless blocks of concrete buildings designed without imagination and constructed without craft. What these buildings would look like covered with snow and ice was something Grafton didn't want to think about. Some of the buildings were abandoned, mere shells with sockets where the windows had been.

He always got depressed at first in foreign cities — culture shock, he supposed. Tonight the empty streets and the dark blocks of miserable flats reflected a people devoid of hope. It was a sadness that shook Jake Grafton to the marrow.

Inevitably his mind turned to the eighty-five million. Murder on that scale must have a profound effect on those left behind — an effect beyond anything encompassed by grief or tragedy. To live with evil on such a scale was beyond Jake Grafton's comprehension. These people were all *guilty*, all of them; those who gave the orders and those who pulled the triggers and those who buried them and those who pretended it never happened.

Where does responsibility stop? Is it an exclusive property of these miserable, impoverished people crowded into these miserable, mean buildings, fighting for survival?

Jake Grafton thought not. He rode through the summer twilight streets looking at the new sights with old, tired eyes.

CHAPTER SIX

Herb Tenney arrived at the breakfast table as the orange juice and coffee were served.

'Morning, Admiral. Commander.' He nodded at each of them in turn and gave his order to the waiter.

'Your first time in Moscow?' Tenney asked as Jake Grafton turned his attention back to his coffee cup.

'Uh-huh.'

Tenney launched into a discourse on the city that sounded suspiciously like the text from a guidebook. He looked rested and fresh after a good night's sleep, which wasn't the way Jake felt. He had gotten only one more hour of sleep after the excursion last night. This morning he felt tired, listless.

Tenney poured himself a cup of coffee without missing a beat in his monologue. He added a dollop of cream to the mixture and half a spoonful of sugar, then agitated the liquid with a spoon. He paused in his discourse and took a sip.

'Ahh, nothing like coffee in the morning. Anyway, Peter the Great built . . .'

Jake stared at the black liquid in the cup in front of him. He had already had a sip and the slightly acid taste lingered still in his mouth. Would there be a taste to binary poison? What had that report said?

Tenney took another sip of his coffee, then added another smidgen of sugar and languidly stirred with his spoon while he rambled on about the city of the czars.

When the waiter slid a plate of bacon and eggs in front of him, Jake Grafton could only stare at it.

'Something wrong, Admiral?'

Tenney was looking at him solicitously.

Jake Grafton gritted his teeth. Then his face relaxed into a smile. 'Jet lag.'

'Takes a while to get over,' Tenney said. 'The main thing is to sleep when you're sleepy and not try to fool Mother Nature.'

Jake Grafton slid his chair back. 'I wouldn't dream of it,' he said, then glanced at Toad. 'Come up to my room when you're finished here.'

'Yes, sir.'

General Nicolai Yakolev, the Russian Army chief of staff, was a short, ugly man with bushy eyebrows, a huge veined nose, a lantern jaw, and ears that stuck out like jug handles. The wonder was that he could see anything at all with the eyebrows and clifflike nose obstructing his vision. Still, once you ignored nature's decorations you caught a glimpse of lively blue eyes.

Yakolev squeezed Jake's right hand with a vise grip, then shook hands with Herb Tenney as Jake flexed his right hand several times to restore the circulation and watched that impressive, ugly face.

'Bad news, she rides a fast horse,' the Russian said in easily understandable English.

'So I've heard,' Jake Grafton replied and looked curiously around the room, a vast cavern with ceilings at least eighteen feet high. Mirrors, chandeliers, a massive wooden desk atop a colorful Persian carpet, walls covered with books and several oil paintings – apparently Communists were as fond of perks as Democrats and Republicans. They were on the second floor of the Kremlin Arsenal, a two-story yellow building inside the walls.

'Nice room,' he commented.

The general smiled. 'So, Admiral, what did the American government really send you here to do?'

'Watch you take tactical nuclear warheads apart, General.'

'Sounds very boring.'

'I'm also supposed to count them.'

'Ah, one . . . two . . . three . . . four . . .' Yakolev laughed. 'And you, Mr Tenney?'

'I'm with the State Department, sir. Here to assist the admiral.'

Yakolev nodded and shifted his eyes to Jake. 'Is that true?' he asked.

Jake mulled it for about two seconds, then said, 'He's here to keep an eye on me all right, but he's CIA.'

'Ahhh, a political officer, a commissar. I've known a few of them in my time. But as you gentlemen know, our *zampolits* are at the moment unemployed. The world changes. So, please, Mr Tenney, since I am at the disadvantage, I ask you to let the admiral and me converse alone. Then no harm will be done if we inadvertently make any little political mistakes.'

Tenney glanced at Grafton, then rose and left the room.

Jake got a glimpse of twinkling eyes behind Yakolev's bushy brows, then the general turned his attention to a file that lay before him. 'Your dossier,' he said, indicating the file. 'The GRU is very thorough, one of their few virtues.'

He flipped from page to page. 'Let us see. You had combat experience in Vietnam, the usual tours aboard numerous aircraft carriers, command of two air wings . . . Ah, here is a summary of a regrettable incident in the Mediterranean that we thought would surely end your career – and that involved nuclear weapons, I believe.'

'I can neither confirm nor deny that.'

The general laughed, a hearty roar. 'Very funny. Admiral. You make a little joke, and I like that. We Russians laugh to make the pain endurable. But I tell you frankly, if you expect to work with me, you and I must learn to tell each other the unpleasant truths.' He wagged a finger at Jake. 'Regardless of what our politicians say or the lies they tell, you and I must treat each other as professionals. We must work together as colleagues. No lies. All truth. Only truth. You comprehend?'

Jake studied the Soviet general in front of him. He held out his hand. 'May I see the dossier?'

'It is in Russian.'

Jake nodded.

The general closed the file and passed it across the desk. Jake opened it on his lap. It was thick, contained maybe thirty pages of material. Most of the pages were indeed in Russian, some typewritten, others in script. There was a front page of the *New York Times* with his photo and another photo taken on a street somewhere several years ago. He had been in civilian clothes then. Also in the files were several photocopies of newspaper and magazine articles about the A-12 Avenger stealth attack plane for which he had been the project manager, before full-scale production was canceled. One of the articles was from *Aviation Week and Space Technology*, a magazine commonly referred to as *Aviation Leak* by the American military. The file also contained a photo of Toad Tarkington. Jake closed the file and passed it back.

'I don't read Russian.'

'I know. That fact is in the dossier.'

'You speak excellent English.'

'I spent several years in Washington and two in London. But that was years ago, when I was just a colonel.'

'This is my third trip to the Soviet Union – Russia.' This of course was a lie. It was Jake's first trip.

The general merely nodded and lit a cigarette. The heavy smoke wafted gently across the desk and Jake got a dose. It stank.

Jake looked around the room again. Hard to believe, after all those years of reading intelligence reports about the Soviet military, all those years of planning to fight them, here he was in the inner sanctum talking to a Soviet – now Russian – four-star. And the subject was nuclear weapons. The whole thing had an air of unreality. He felt like an actor in a bad play devoid of logic. Life without reason – that's the definition of insanity, isn't it?

Jake Grafton scanned the room yet again, rubbed his hands over the solid arms of his chair, reached out to touch the polished wood of the desk.

But are these guys on the level? Do they really intend to destroy their tactical nukes? Or is this whole thing some kind of weird chess game with nuclear pieces, something out of one of those wretched thrillers about crazed Communists out to checkmate all their opponents and take over the planet?

'Do you play chess?' Jake Grafton asked the general behind the desk, who was watching him through the drifting smoke.

'Yes,' Yakolev said, 'but not very well.' His lips twisted. This was his grin. After the lie came the grin. Very American, like a used-car salesman.

Jake Grafton grinned back. 'I looked at your dossier in the Pentagon a week or so ago. It says you like to fuck little boys.'

The lips twisted again. 'I like you, Grafton. *Da!*'

Jake cleared his throat. 'We know your politicians are' – he was going to say 'less than accurate' but thought better of it – 'lying about the degree of control they have – the army has – over these weapons. I am here to evaluate the extent of your problems and make a report to my superiors. And to offer suggestions if you are receptive.'

Jake Grafton paused as he eyed the Russian general. 'My superiors want the Yeltsin government to succeed in the revolution that Gorbachev began. They do not want the Communists to regain power, nor do they want to see the Soviet Union balkanized unless there is no other way. Baldly, they want to see a stable government in this country that has the support of the populace, a government that indeed is trying to improve the lot of its citizens.'

'They are humanitarians,' General Yakolev said lightly.

'Don't ever think that,' Jake Grafton shot back. 'They are

damn worried men. Their primary concern is nuclear weapons. They do not want to see nuclear, chemical or biological weapons technology exported. They desperately want you to establish a viable democracy here, but first and foremost – the most important factor – your government must keep absolute control of *all the nuclear weapons that exist on your soil.*'

'Yeltsin is not in control of anything right now. He is at the center but the storm revolves around him. How I say it? – he is like one of your cowboys on a crazy bronco horse. He is still on the saddle but the horse goes his own way. Understand?'

'I will give you the frank, blunt truth, General. I will not repeat the platitudes of the politicians. The Americans will deal with whoever has these weapons, be it a Communist dictator, fascist demagogue, religious fanatic, or a criminal gang leader. Whoever. And I suspect the same is true of the British, the Germans, the French – all the Western democracies. But their liaison officers can tell you that themselves.'

Yakolev came around the desk and pulled a chair closer to Grafton. He sat. 'You and I can work together. We are both military men, both patriots. I serve Mother Russia. You understand?'

Jake nodded.

'I am not blind. Russia must join the world. This planet is too small to sustain an isolated society of three hundred million people. We have tried dictatorship and it failed; now we must try democracy. But I lay out the truth for your inspection: no matter who rules the Kremlin, *I* serve Russia.'

Russia the grand abstraction, Jake thought ruefully. Well, every nation is an abstraction if you stop to think about it. He irritably dismissed the thought and asked, 'And the army? Whom does the army serve?' When the Russian was slow to answer, Jake sharpened the question: 'Will the army obey your orders?'

General Nicolai Yakolev spit out the word, 'Yes.'

That, Jake Grafton suspected, was the biggest and baldest lie so far. And mouthed like a pro. And yet . . . 'These weapons distort everything,' he said.

'I know.'

'While they exist, you serve only them,' Jake said.

'Control all the nuclear weapons that exist, you said. I noted your choice of words, Admiral.'

'They must be destroyed,' Jake Grafton said, 'before they destroy you. You asked for truth. There it is.'

The Russian leaned toward Jake. 'You are a soldier, not a politician. I like that. I think we can do business. Come.'

He led Jake to a table under a huge oil painting that should have been in a museum. There was a large map on the table. The Russian general pointed and explained where the weapons were and what might be done with the plutonium after the warheads were disassembled. Through the tall windows Jake could see the soft summer sun sifting down, gently bathing everything in a surreal light.

An hour later the men were back at the general's desk drinking strong, black tea in tall glasses with metal holders. At the general's suggestion Jake had stirred in juice from a slice of lemon and a spoonful of something that looked like blackberry jam.

'Perhaps you could tell me a little about yourself, General,' Jake Grafton said, jerking his thumb at the dossier.

The Russian laughed. 'All the time, effort, and expense that goes into compiling dossiers, and you know what yours tells me? That you are a professional officer. Nothing else. And that I knew before I opened it.

'But it is me you want to know about, even after reading my dossier in the Pentagon. Dossiers are the same the world over. I am old, seventy years. I fought in the Great War. I was young enough to enjoy killing Nazis. In Berlin I saw Hitler's bunker, helped search it. I saw the patio where they burned his body, his and Eva Braun's. I walked

90

through the rubble. All Europe was rubble then, my friend. I tell you that.'

So Yakolev had once been a shooter, a warrior. Maybe down deep under the wrinkles and gray hair he still was. Most of the top men in the world's military organizations weren't: they were bureaucrats and cocktail party politicians.

The general shook his head. 'I was very young then. And that is the only fact about me that would be of interest. The rest is obvious. I survived. I *survived!*'

Ahh, Jake mused, at what cost? How many men have you sold out, General, how many lies have you told, how much of your honor can possibly be left after you clawed and scratched and gouged your way to the top of this squirming snake pile of criminal psychopaths? The scars must be there . . . unless you have become one of them, a man without conscience, a man to whom the end justifies whatever it takes to get there. If so . . .

The general rumbled on. 'But no stories. Old men tell too many stories, stories of a dead past that are of little interest to the young, who think their own problems unique.'

'And I am too young,' Jake Grafton said.

General Yakolev's eyes searched his face. 'Perhaps. Your youth . . .' He shook his head. 'You Americans turn out your officers to fatten in the pasture so very early, just when they grow old enough to have a bit of wisdom, just when they are old enough to understand all the things that they are not, all the things that they can never be, will never be. Just when they are old enough.'

Jake sipped his tea. It wasn't like American tea, weak and insipid. He liked it.

'What do you *know* of Russia?'

Jake drank the last of the tea and set the cup in its saucer. 'The usual, which is not much . . . the bare essentials, twenty years of reading intelligence briefs, a few books.'

'Tolstoy?'

'A little. Chekov I liked. Andreyev's *The Seven Who Were Hanged* was too Russian.' Oops! He should not have said *that!* 'Solzhenitsyn . . .' What could he say about Solzhenitsyn's descriptions of hell on earth? They had horrified Jake Grafton, painted communism as one of the foulest evils ever perpetrated by man upon man. 'I have read him,' he finished lamely.

'Hmmm,' said Yakolev, his face a mask. 'Dinner tomorrow night, yes? The military observers from Britain, Germany, France and Italy will also be here. You know them, yes?'

'No, sir. I've never met them.'

'I will send my car for you at the embassy. About eight.'

'May I bring my aide, sir?'

'If you like. We will take the time to learn to know each other better. I will be interested to learn where you draw the line between Russian and too Russian.'

Jake was led back through the long cold hallways with their dim lights and dark oil paintings that could barely be seen. Herb Tenney was standing near the door, waiting. Outside the summer sun of the Kremlin grounds made Jake squint. The contrast between inside and outside hit him hard. He held his hat on his head as he climbed into the car.

Culture shock, Jack Yocke decided. He felt depressed, alone, listless. He could count on one hand the number of people he had met who spoke English. The constant fumbling with the paperback Russian-English dictionary frustrated him. The heavy, fatty mystery meat and greasy vegetables were clogging his bowels. Culture shock, he told himself, hoping that sooner or later he would adjust.

How good it would be to be back in the *Post* newsroom, talking on the phone to someone who spoke American, understanding the nuances of what wasn't said as readily as he captured the intent of what was. Oh, for a bacon and egg breakfast, with eggs from a lovely American chicken and crisp fried bacon from a handsome American pig! To go across the street to the Madison coffee shop for a hot pastrami on rye! And an American beer, a tall cold American beer in a frosty glass with foam spilling over the top.

He was gloomily contemplating the difference between American beer and the Russian horse piss product when the motorcade came around the corner into view. Three vehicles. Black. Limos.

He was stuck off to one side of the platform where the speakers were going to address the rally. Perhaps a thousand people, mostly men and babushkas, milled around the square and luxuriated in the sun, rolling up sleeves to brown their white arms, drinking juice from glass bottles. The few children were messily eating ice cream bars sold by a sidewalk vendor, who was doing a land office business today. Apparently the vendors, for the city sidewalks seemed crammed with them, were something new, fledgling capitalists trying the new way right here beside a Communist rally. The irony of it made Yocke smile.

The paper's Russian stringer translator was sucking on a foul cigarette and chatting in Russian with his counterpart from the *New York Times*. *The Times* reporter was on the other side of these two and busy scribbling notes, no doubt literate political insights that would form the heart of an incisive think piece. Damn *The Times!*

Jack Yocke took off his sports coat and hung it over one arm. He wiped the perspiration from his forehead. And damn these Commies! Why can't they hire a hall like politicians in more civilized climes?

The senior *Post* correspondent was over at the Kremlin today buttonholing Yeltsin lieutenants, so Yocke was stuck covering this rally of nationalistic Commie retrogrades, people who thought that the Stalin era was Russia's finest hour. Yes, there were still live human beings on this planet who believed that, and here were some of them, waving red flags and posters with slogans. Some of them even wore red armbands, but the red flags were the grabber: to Yocke's

American eye the blood red flags looked like an image straight from a museum exhibit. That there were still people who firmly believed in the gospel of Marx, Engels, and Lenin was a fact that he knew intellectually, yet seeing it in the flesh was a jolt.

These people were obviously committed. Just below the platform four older men were arranged in a circle, shouting at one another. No, it was three against one. Yocke couldn't understand a word of it and thought about asking the stringer what it was all about, then decided against it. He thought he already knew the answer.

Yegor Kolokoltsev was their guru, a man who could rant anti-Semitic filth that would have been too raw for Joseph Goebbels and in the next breath extol the glories of Mother Russia. As Yocke understood Kolokoltsev's message, the Communists never had a chance to purify the Soviet Union and make her great because the Jews had subverted them, stolen the fruit of the proletariat's labor, betrayed the revolution, sucked blood from the veins of honest Communists, etc., etc.

So now he stood sweating as the motorcade drew to a halt and burly guards jumped from the cars and began opening a pathway to the platform. Idly Yocke looked around for soldiers or uniformed policemen. There were none in sight. Not a one.

The bodyguards in civilian clothes had no trouble clearing a path. The crowd parted courteously, as befitted old Communists. And these were mostly old Communists, workers and retired grandmothers. Here and there the mix was leavened by better-dressed younger men, probably bureaucrats or apparatchiks who had lost or were losing their jobs under the new order. Some of the waving signs and red flags partially obscured Yocke's vision of the arriving dignitaries.

The lack of policemen and soldiers bothered Jack Yocke slightly, and he turned to his translator to ask a question about their absence when he heard the noise, a sharp popping audible even above the sounds of traffic from the street.

An automatic weapon!

There was no mistaking the sound.

The crowd panicked. People turned their backs on Yegor Kolokoltsev and his guards and tried to flee. The urge to leave hastily seemed to enter the head of every living soul there at precisely the same instant.

More weapons. The sharp popping was now the staccato buzzing of numerous weapons, but it was strangely muffled by screams and shouts.

Yocke grabbed a handhold on the rail of the speaker's platform and pulled himself up a couple feet so he could see better.

Four people with automatic weapons were shooting at the guards, most of whom were now on the ground. One or two gunmen were pouring lead into the middle limousine.

With all the guards down, two of the gunmen walked toward the car. They were dressed in the usual dark gray suits and wore hats. The crowd was dispersing rapidly now, everyone fleeing for their lives. Several of the elderly were sprawled on the pavement. One or two of them were struggling to rise.

One of the gunmen opened the car door and the other emptied a magazine through the opening from a distance of three feet.

Yocke looked around wildly. The stragglers from the retreating crowd were rounding the corners, probably running down the streets that led away from the square.

The gunmen dropped their weapons and walked away without haste.

No sirens. No more screams.

Silence.

Yocke looked around for the other reporters and their Russian stringers. Gone. He was alone, still clinging to the side of the speaker's platform.

He released his grip and dropped to the pavement. The

whole thing had been like a slow-motion film – he had seen everything, felt everything, the fear, the horror, the sense of doom descending inexorably, controlled by an unseen, godlike hand. Now if he could only get it down!

How much time had elapsed? Minutes? No – no more than forty or fifty seconds. Maybe a minute.

He looked at the backs of the fleeing people. The last of the crowd was hobbling around the corners. Some people had apparently been trampled in the panic; six or eight bodies lay around the square.

Yocke stood and watched the last of the gunmen disappear around the corner where the motorcade had entered the square. A half mile or so down that street was Red Square. The entrance to the metro, the subway that would take them anywhere in Moscow, was only a hundred yards away.

He was alone with the dead and dying. He walked toward the cars. The guards – he counted the bodies . . . seven, eight, nine. He walked from one to the other, looking. All dead, each of them shot at least six or eight times. Blood, one's man's brains, intestines oozing into congealing piles on the stones of the square.

The middle limo was splattered with holes, the door still standing open. Yocke looked in.

The big man was Yegor Kolokoltsev, or had been just a few minutes ago. Now he was as dead as dead can be. Two of the bullets had struck him in the head, one just under the left eye and the other high up in the forehead. His eyes were still open, as was his mouth. Somehow his face still seemed to register surprise. A dozen or more bullets had punched through his chest and throat. There was little blood.

Facing Kolokoltsev was another corpse. The driver of the limo sat slumped over the wheel.

The other two cars were empty. Empty shell casings lay scattered on the street.

Alone in the midst of the vast silence Jack Yocke bent and picked up a shiny shell casing. 9mm.

One of the weapons lay not five feet from him. He merely looked. He couldn't tell one automatic weapon from another.

He turned and looked again at Kolokoltsev. Then he gagged.

He staggered away.

His mouth was watering copiously and his eyes were tearing up. He paused and placed his hands on his knees and spit repeatedly. He had to write *this* too, capture all of it.

Now the sensation was passing.

He walked, working hard at walking without staggering, without succumbing to the urge to run, which was building.

The urge to run became dire. He began to trot. Faster, faster . . .

He saw a narrow street leading away from the square and ran for it. People were standing on the sidewalks looking into the square, but he ran by them without slowing down.

Telephone! He must find a telephone.

'Mike Gatler.' Mike was the foreign editor. He sounded sleepy, and no doubt he was. It was one-thirty in the afternoon here, but five-thirty in the morning in Washington.

'Mike, Jack Yocke. I just witnessed an assassination.'

'Terrific. Send me a story and I'll read it.'

'Right in Soviet Square, Mike. Right in front of Moscow City Hall. They gunned a big Commie weenie when he arrived for a political rally. Crowd there and everything.'

'You woke me up for this?'

'Gee, Mike. It's front page, for sure.'

Gatler sighed audibly. 'What happened?'

'They killed Yegor Kolokoltsev and eleven of his guards. Five gunmen with automatic weapons mowed them down.' The words came faster now, tumbling out: 'It was the god-damnest thing I ever saw, Mike, a cold-blooded execution.

First the guards, then the politician. I'm sure some of the bystanders in the crowd were shot too. Just their tough fucking luck. Like something from a movie. That was my first thought, like something from a movie. Something staged, unreal. But it was real all right.'

'Are you okay?' Gatler sounded genuinely concerned. The contrast between the irritation in Mike's voice at first being awakened and the concern he was now expressing hit Yocke hard.

'I guess so, Mike. Sorry I bothered you at home.'

'It's okay, Jack. Write the story. Take your time and do it right. Kolokoltsev, huh? The Russian nationalist?'

'Yeah. Bigot. Anti-Semite. Holy Russia and all that shit. A Nazi with a red star on his sleeve.'

'You write it. Do it right.'

''Night, Mike.'

''Night, Jack.'

He hung up the phone and stood in the lofty, opulent hotel lobby at a loss for what to do next. Over in the corner a pianist was playing, and the tune sounded familiar. Yocke's heart rate and breathing were returning to normal after the half-mile jog to the hotel, the only place he would find a telephone with a satellite link to call overseas. The Russian phone system was a relic of Stalin's era and couldn't even be relied upon for a call across town. But Yocke was still shook. The surprise of it as much as anything . . . damn!

Soviet Square . . . in front of that statue of Lenin as *The Thinker* . . . with a Pizza Hut restaurant just a block up the street where they serve real food to real people who have real money in their jeans. Hard currency only, thank you. No dip-shit Russians with only rubles in the pockets of their Calvin Kleins . . .

The clerk behind the counter was staring at him, as were several of the guests queued up at the cashier's counter. Now the clerk said something in Russian. A question. He repeated it. He seemed to have lost his English.

Jack Yocke shrugged, then headed for the elevator with the clerk staring after him. He should have made the call from the phone in his room. If he had thought about the effect of his conversation on the clerk, he would have.

As the elevator door closed Yocke recognized the music, Dave Brubeck's 'Take Five.' He began laughing uncontrollably.

At the American embassy Jake Grafton spent a few minutes with the ambassador, then was shown to a small office that was temporarily unused. There he began his report to General Brown on the conference today. He wrote in longhand and handed the sheets to Toad to type.

'It went well?' Toad asked.

'Maybe.' *Too Russian.* Jake, you could screw up a wet dream.

He had about finished the report when there was a knock on the door and Lieutenant Dalworth stuck his head in.

'Admiral, I have a message for you.'

Dalworth held out the clipboard with an envelope attached. 'Just fill in the number of the envelope and sign your name, sir.'

Jake did so. As Dalworth left the room Jake ripped open the envelope, which was marked with a top secret classification. It had of course been decoded in the embassy's message center.

FYI LTGEN A.S. Brown died last night in his sleep. News not yet made public.

FYI – for your information, no action required. Without a word Jake passed the slip of paper across to Toad Tarkington.

'Just like that?' Toad asked with an air of disbelief.

'When your heart stops, you're dead.' Jake Grafton folded the message and placed it back into its envelope. It would have to go back to the message center for logging and destruction. He tossed the envelope onto the corner of the desk. 'Just . . . like . . . that.'

'For Christ's sake, CAG, we've got to—'

'No!'

'We can't just—'

'No.'

Toad turned his back for a bit. When he turned around again he said in a flat voice, 'Okay, what are we going to do?'

'I don't know,' Jake said.

What could he do? Write a letter to the president?

'What did Herb Tenney do today, anyway?'

'He went out this morning after you left,' Toad told him. 'Came back about two or three.'

'He's got an office?'

'He's in with the other CIA types. They've got a suite just down the hall and their own radio equipment and crypto gear. They don't use the embassy stuff.'

'Who are the other spies?'

'Well, there are about a dozen, near as I can tell. Head guy is a fellow named McCann who has been here a couple years. I met him at lunch. One of those guys who can talk for an hour and not say anything. A gas bag.'

It was impossible, a cesspool of the first order of magnitude. 'Shit,' Jake whispered.

'Yessir. My sentiments exactly.'

'Have they got a safe in their office?'

'I suppose so. I haven't been in there.'

'Go in tomorrow morning. Look the place over.'

'If I can get in.'

'Tell Herb you want the tour. Gush. Gee-whiz.'

'Yes, sir.'

Toad threw himself into a chair. He sighed deeply, then said, 'Y'know, I really wish you and I had a nice safe job back in the real world – like bungee jumping or explosive ordnance disposal on a bomb squad. Something with a future.'

Jake Grafton didn't reply.

Albert Sidney Brown dead. Damn, damn and double-damn!

Well, it was time to call a spade a spade. The odds that Brown's ticker picked this particular time to call it quits were not so good. Ten to one he was poisoned. Murdered. By the CIA, or someone in the CIA. Christians in Action.

If the CIA really did it, he and Toad were living on borrowed time. Perhaps they had already been served half of the binary chemical cocktail. And any minute now Herb Tenney or one of his agents might get around to serving the chaser.

'You and I are going on short rations as of right now,' Jake told Toad. 'Go down to the kitchen and get us some canned soda pop and some food that we can eat right out of the can.'

'What do I tell the cook?'

'Tell him we're having a picnic. I don't know. Think of something. Tell him I'm sick. Go on.'

After Jake delivered his report to the message center for transmission, he went up to his room. The door that led to Toad's room was open and he was standing in it.

'Someone was in here today,' Toad said.

'You sure?'

'No, sir. But my stuff is a little different.'

Jake felt in his pocket for scratch paper. On it he wrote, 'Look for bugs.'

It took fifteen minutes to find it. They left it where it was.

'Are you hungry, Admiral?'

'No.'

Jake took off his uniform and lay down on the bed. He turned off the light.

Two minutes later he turned it back on, got out of bed and checked the door lock, then asked Toad to come in for a moment. With Tarkington watching, Jake took the Smith

& Wesson from his bag, checked the firing pin, snapped the gun through all six chambers, then loaded it.

No doubt the bug picked up the sound of the dry firing. Well, that was fair warning. If anyone came in here tonight Jake Grafton fully intended to blow his head off.

'Night, Toad.'

'Good night, sir.'

Sleep didn't come. Jake tossed and turned and re-arranged the pillow to no avail.

The problem was that he was totally alone, and it was a strange feeling. Always in the past he had a superior officer within easy reach to toss the hot potatoes to. Everyone in uniform has a boss – that is the way of the profession and Jake Grafton had spent his life in it. Now he had nowhere to turn.

He should have, of course. He should be able to just walk upstairs and get on the encrypted voice circuit to Washington. In just a few minutes he would be bounced off a satellite and connected with the new acting head of the DIA, or the Chief of Naval Operations, or even the Chairman of the Joint Chiefs, General Hayden Land. The problem was that the CIA might be monitoring the circuit.

Not the CIA as an organization, but whoever it was that had a grubby hand on Tenney's strings. The agency was so compartmentalized that a rogue department head might be able to run his own covert operation for years before anyone found out. If anyone found out. If the man at the top took reasonable care and kept his operation buried within another, legitimate operation, it was conceivable that it might never be discovered.

The more he thought about it, the more convinced Jake was that he had tripped over just such an operation. Who controlled it, what its goals were, how many people were involved – he had no answers to any of these questions.

So the encrypted voice circuits were out. A commercial line? Every phone in the embassy was monitored.

And if he found a circuit, who was he going to talk to? If

these people could casually squash a three-star general, no one was beyond reach. The ambassador? That Boston Brahman, that man of distinction in a whiskey ad? Yet he *had* to trust someone.

The military was built on trust. Trust and communications. In today's world of high-tech weapons systems and instant communications everyone in the system was merely a moving part. Amazingly, none of the moving parts were critical. As soon as one wore out, was wounded or killed, it was replaced. And the machine never paused, never faltered as long as the communications network remained intact.

Herb Tenney was a soldier too. Staring at the ceiling, Jake told himself he must not forget that fact.

As he began to go over it all for the third or fourth time, his frustration got the better of him. He climbed from the bed and went to the window. The sun hadn't set yet. He tried to visualize what the city must look like in the snow, for snow was the norm. The mean annual temperature here was minus two degrees centigrade. These long, balmy days were but a short interlude in the life of the city and those who inhabited it. In spite of the sun's golden glow he could see buildings in a gray winter's half-light amid the snow driven along by the wind. He could feel the cutting cold.

The Russian winter had killed tens of thousands of soldiers in the past three hundred years, he reflected. No doubt it could kill a few more.

CHAPTER SEVEN

He was going to have to take some chances, run some risks that were impossible to evaluate. As a young man he had learned to stay alive in aerial combat by carefully weighing the odds and never taking an unnecessary chance, so now the unknown dangers weighed heavily upon him. And back then he had only his life at stake, his and his bombardier's. Now . . .

But there was no other way.

When Toad came to the room this morning Jake sent him to get a car. 'You'll drive it,' Jake told him. 'Bring the blanket off your bed.' He put on his short-sleeved white uniform shirt and examined the ribbons and wings insignia in the mirror. All okay.

Three blocks away from the embassy Jake told Toad to stop. They searched the car as traffic whizzed by and the exhaust fumes wafted about them. Not much wind today, drat it.

They opened the hood and examined everything as a crowd of pedestrians gathered, probably attracted by their white uniforms. The two naval officers ignored the curious Russians. It took them five minutes to identify all the wires of the electrical system to their satisfaction. They opened the trunk and lifted out the spare tire and scrutinized every square inch and cranny. Toad put the blanket on the pavement and wormed under the car while Jake opened his pocketknife and took off the door panels. He probed the seat cushions and sliced open the roof liner. They peeled back the carpet on the floor.

Nothing.

When they started the car again they sat staring at the traffic zipping by and the onlookers on the sidewalk, who were drifting away one by one.

'You'd think if there was a bug in this thing we'd find it,' Toad said with disgust in his voice.

'Maybe.' You could never prove a negative to a certainty. All you could do was try to determine the probability.

'Miserable goddamn country,' Toad growled.

After a few moments Jake said, 'If anything happens to me, I'd like you to do me a favor.'

Toad waited.

'Kill Herb Tenney.'

'That,' Toad said with heat, 'will be a real pleasure.'

'Better be quick about it. I've got a feeling that if I die you're going to be knocking on the pearly gate very soon thereafter.'

Toad put the car into gear and pulled away from the curb.

They parked in front of the Hotel Metropolitan amid the taxicabs, right around the corner from Red Square.

Jake left Toad with the car and went inside. 'I wish to speak with one of your guests, an American named Jack Yocke.' And since the man nodded politely, Jake added, '*Pashah'lsta.*' Please.

'Yaw-key?'

'That's right.' Jake spelled it.

As the desk attendant consulted his files Jake surveyed the lobby. He had visited the embassy public affairs office earlier that morning and had gotten the name of Yocke's hotel from the file. He had looked it up himself so the clerk would not see what name he wanted. He felt foolish, paranoid.

'Here it is,' the desk man said, straightening from the files. 'I will telephone him.' The clerk looked natty in a dark suit and tie. Apparently these folks were going after those hard dollars with a vengeance. Jake nodded and went over to one of the plush chairs on the other side of the room to wait. Several of the tourists in line at the counters stared at him. A white uniform certainly had an effect.

Three minutes later the elevator door opened and Jack Yocke stepped out. He was visibly surprised when he saw Jake Grafton. He came over smiling and stopped in front of Jake with his hands held out to his sides.

'Clean and sober, Admiral. In the flesh.' He shook Jake's outstretched hand. 'How goes the war effort?'

'Off the record?'

Yocke laughed. 'You're the last man on earth I expected to see around here.'

'I came to see Lenin. I hear they're selling the body to some outfit in Arizona.'

'Yep. Gonna put the old boy on display right near the London Bridge in Lake Havasu City. Five bucks a head. Old ladies from Moline in stretch polyester and tennis shoes will be filing by the coffin whispering, "Well, I never!"'

'Toad's out in the car. How about coming outside for a minute or two for a chat?'

You had to hand it to Yocke. He didn't even blink. 'Sure,' he said.

'So how's the foreign correspondent gig going?' Toad asked Yocke when they were seated in the car.

'I don't know how I'm holding up,' Yocke said sadly. 'Every day three or four beautiful women, not less than a quart of vodka, meals fit for a czar or local party chief, a ballet or—'

'We've got a little problem,' Jake said firmly, interrupting the litany, 'that we thought you might be able to help with. It's an I'll-never-tell type of problem.'

'No story?'

'Not even a whisper.'

Yocke snorted. 'Do you know how damn tough it is to get a story in this Cyrillic borsch house? I've had exactly one, yesterday, when someone snuffed Yegor Kolokoltsev.'

'We heard about that. Five gunmen in Soviet Square?'

'I was there on the fifty-yard line, six rows back. Just lucky, I guess. I've been upstairs writing it up for the Sunday paper, three thousand sensitive, powerful words that would melt the heart of a crack salesman. The story is what I saw and a bunch of denials from the Russian cops. No, they did not know Kolokoltsev was going to speak. No, they did not keep the police away. That's about it. Lots of on-scene detail and a bunch of denials.'

'So,' Jake asked curiously, 'were they in on it?'

'Something smells, that's for sure. No police or military in the square. Five gunmen drill Kolokoltsev and all his bodyguards. They looked like they were shooting an army qualification course. Just pros punching holes in a professional manner. Then they dropped the guns and walked away. No haste, no waste.'

'It's the wrong feel,' Toad objected. 'The Russians don't do things that way.' He was about to add something when Grafton silenced him with a glance.

The admiral asked Yocke, 'What about that big story that you were so full of back in Washington? People stealing nukes and selling them?'

'Can't smoke it out. The people who were supposed to know something just laughed when I showed up with my letters of introduction and asked. All rumors. So I'm doing features and listening to would-be dictators preach anti-Semitic, fascist poison. I was just lucky to witness a rubout that would make a great movie. BFD.' Jake knew what that meant – Big Fucking Deal.

'Jack, I need to ask a favor. Call your editor and have him deliver a message in person to General Land.'

'This is supposed to make me laugh, right?'

'No joke,' Jake told him. 'Obviously I don't want to use any of the telephones at the embassy, encrypted or otherwise. Nor the embassy's message circuits. And I don't want General Land talking on a telephone in his office, home or car.'

'Why not?'

'Yes or no.'

'Want to tell me about it?'

'No, Jack, I don't. I just want you to say yes.'

'Who don't you want listening in? The overseas lines all bounce off the bird in the sky. Great connection – sounds better than the phone at home – but the people in the telephone office are undoubtedly KGB to a man. You can bet your ass they tape every call. Of course the KGB has a new name, the Foreign Intelligence Service, but a turd by any other name is still a turd. Ten dollars against a ruble they'll be routing a transcript in Cyrillic around Dzerzhinsky Square before you get back on the sidewalk.'

Jake said nothing.

'So you want to be overheard, huh? By the KGB. Or you don't care.' Yocke writhed in his seat. He glared at both of them. 'You knew I'd say yes. Admiral. Now figure out what I'm going to tell my editor.'

Jake Grafton pursed his lips. 'I'm assuming that this will be a tight little secret over at the *Post*.'

'Like Ted Kennedy's spring vacation plans,' Yocke replied sourly. 'You realize that if the KGB wants to know more they will pay me a visit and sweat me.'

'If you have your health . . .' Toad Tarkington said, and gave Yocke a wide grin. 'Jack, I'll never understand you. Where's your sense of adventure? The KGB might put you against a wall and shoot you. You'll be famous! If they just rip out all your fingernails and throw you out of the country the *Post* will probably give you a raise.'

'You macho pinhead! These Russians don't do walls or blindfolds or last cigarettes. No melodrama. They snatch you on the street, strangle you in the car and stuff you into a hole someplace out in the woods so no one else on God's green earth will ever know what became of you. Without muss or fuss you just cease to be. Cease to be *anything!* These people have ruled this country with terror for seventy years and they are real goddamn good at it. If you aren't pissing yourself when you think about them you're a congenital idiot. There ain't no rules but theirs and they keep changing them all the time. This ain't good ol' Iowa, Frogface.'

Toad grinned at the admiral and jerked his thumb at Yocke. 'You may find this hard to believe, but I'm beginning to like this guy.'

Yocke wasn't paying attention. Already he was trying to figure out how to explain this to his editor. He looked at his watch. It was 2 A.M. in Washington. He would call Gatler at home again. Mike was going to be thrilled.

'Let's get something to eat,' Toad suggested. 'For some reason I'm hungry.'

Jake nodded.

'Well, there's a good hard currency restaurant with big prices up the street at the Savoy and a slightly more modest one here at the Metropolitan. It's all Russian grub and the city water system is contaminated, unfit for human consumption. It's Russian roulette – radioactive beef and milk and vegetables full of heavy metals – spin the cylinder and pull the trigger.' He sighed. 'I know you want to treat, so you pick.'

'Here,' Jake said. Toad killed the engine and they climbed out. 'But we call your editor first.'

'Let me get this straight, Admiral. You want me to call Hayden Land right now, at two-twenty in the morning, and ask him to come to the *Post* to call you in the morning?'

Mike Gatler's voice was remarkably clear – the miracle of modern communications technology – and the amazement and disbelief seemed about to leak out of the telephone. Apparently Yocke's call had roused him from a sound sleep.

'No, sir. Tell him you want to meet him at the guard's shack in front of the river entrance to the Pentagon at 8 A.M. *There* you ask him to call me at this number in Moscow as soon as he can. He can use a phone in your office or a pay phone. This is important, Mr Gatler — *no other telephones*. Have him call me here at this number in Moscow. Have you got that?'

'Put Yocke back on the line.'

Jake handed the telephone to the reporter, who mumbled into the instrument and listened intently. After a bit he said, 'Admiral Grafton came over to the hotel this morning and asked for this favor . . . No . . . he hasn't said. He *won't* say . . . Yes.'

Yocke turned and eyed the two naval officers. 'Gotcha,' he told the telephone. 'I understand . . . how did you like my story about—' He bit it off and replaced the instrument on its cradle.

'I'm not to call him again at home in the middle of the night unless I'm dead. And I'm supposed to guarantee you absolute confidentiality.' He sat down beside Jake Grafton on the bed. 'You'll be deep background, never quoted or even referred to. I'm supposed to wring you out like a sponge.'

Jake Grafton grinned. He had a good grin under a nose that was a size too big for his face. When he grinned his gray eyes twinkled. 'Think Gatler will do it?'

'Yeah. The one thing you gotta have in the news game is curiosity — Mike Gatler is chock full of it. He's a helluva newspaperman. I don't know if Hayden Land will agree to see him, but I guarantee Mike will try.'

'He'll see him all right. If Gatler uses my name. Now let's go get some food. I'm starved.'

'Don't they feed you guys at the embassy?'

'Stove isn't working right,' Jake muttered and led the way through the door.

'Hayden Land, Chairman of the Joint Chiefs of Staff,' Yocke said cheerfully as he trailed the naval officers down the hall. 'This is big, huh?'

'So how long you guys been in Moscow?' Yocke asked after they had gone through the buffet line and were picking at the watery scrambled eggs and sampling the fatty sausage.

They had a table in the middle of the room and were surrounded by businessmen and here and there pairs of tourists. Over near the buffet line sat eight Japanese businessmen drinking orange juice and coffee and eating grapes. For twenty US dollars a head. The Russians, Jake Grafton decided, have capitalism all figured out. Charge every nickel the traffic will bear until they quit coming, then drop the price just enough to get them back.

'Couple days.'

'So what do you think?'

'I think a twenty-dollar breakfast is one hell of a way to start a morning,' Jake replied. He managed to choke down his first bite of fatty, greasy sausage and shoved the rest of it to the side of his plate. He tentatively sipped the coffee. It was hot and black, thank God!

'Twenty and ten percent tip,' Yocke said cheerfully. 'Twenty-two American smackeroos to get past that squat lady at the door.'

'These bastards bypassed capitalism and went straight into highway robbery,' Toad mumbled as he stared at the mess on the plate in front of him. 'No wonder Marx was appalled. Twenty-two fucking dollars! Jeeezus!'

Jake looked slowly around at the huge, splendid room in which they sat with the businessmen and tourists, eating nervously. There were just no Russian restaurants that served food a Western stomach could tolerate – none. 'This place is a boom town, like San Francisco during the gold rush. There's no price competition right now.' He shrugged. 'Maybe it'll come.'

Yocke tried to change the subject. 'What are you guys here for?'

Jake Grafton eyed the reporter and this time his gray eyes didn't twinkle. 'Give it up. Jack.'

'You gotta admit, Admiral, this whole thing is curious as hell. The embassy has gotta have enough communications gear to put you in touch with Slick Willie Clinton snarfing gut bombs in a McDonald's.'

Yocke shrugged, then leaned back in his chair and assumed his philosophical attitude: 'This whole darn country is curious. Everything is falling apart, nothing works right, yet everybody you meet is a literature expert, a music scholar, or an authority on eighteenth-century Russian poetry. Not a solitary one of them owns a screwdriver or a pair of pliers or even knows what they're for. So the commodes don't work, the light bulbs are burned out, the furnace in the basement crapped out last year, the pipes are busted – and they sit amid the rubble and talk about the nuances in Dostoyevski, the genius of Tolstoy. The whole place is a nuthouse, one giant pyscho ward, some psychiatrist's wet dream.'

'They must have something going for them,' Jake said as he smeared jam inside a croissant. 'They kicked the hell out of Hitler. They're tough, resilient people. They're survivors.'

Jack Yocke rubbed his head and thought about it. He was having trouble getting the right perspective, having trouble seeing the human beings hidden behind the body armor they all wore. 'Maybe,' he muttered. 'Maybe.'

'So what stories have you been working on while you've been here?' Toad Tarkington asked this question.

'Been wandering around trying to get a feel for the place, for the people. They're desperate. It's a scary situation. The people seem to just have no hope. And the Commies are playing to their fears. The anti-Semitism is right out in the open and it's ugly.'

Toad glanced at Jake Grafton, who was looking out the window at the street, now bathed in weak sunshine, as Jack Yocke rambled on about the more prominent Communists and their stump rantings. When the reporter finally paused Jake asked, 'How ugly?'

'What?'

'How ugly is the anti-Semitism?'

'They're prosecuting Jews for hooliganism, profiteering and hoarding. Throwing them into jail. Everyone is doing it but the only people being prosecuted are Jews charged before they changed the law. The persecution is even more blatant outside of Moscow, out in those little provincial towns nobody ever heard of where old Communists are still running the show. To hear some of the Commies tell it, they never had a chance to run this country right because the Jews screwed up everything. It's Hitler's big lie one more time.'

'It worked before,' Jake murmured.

He looked at his watch. Almost eleven. Five or six hours to wait. Maybe Toad could spend the afternoon with Yocke and he could get some sleep in Yocke's bed. He managed only an hour or two's sleep last night. Jet lag. He felt hot and dirty and tired. Or maybe he had caught a dose of that desperation that everyone here seemed to be infected with.

And this would be a good time to call Richard Harper, his private computer hacker, to ask if he had made any progress finding the money. If someone was buying nuclear weapons, then someone was getting paid.

But what will you do when you know?

Hayden Land was the first black man to hold the top job in the American military. A highly intelligent soldier and top-notch political operator, he also had the ability to think very straight when everyone else was panicking. This quality had served him well during the Gulf War several years ago when his sound leadership made him a national hero. Those in the know in national politics even mentioned him as possible presidential timber in 1996, when presumably he would be retired.

Jake Grafton had worked for Land in the past, so the general's calmness on the telephone was no surprise. Hayden Land *never* lost his cool.

'What did you want to talk about, Admiral?'

'Sir, I understand General Brown died a few days ago. I wonder if you have the autopsy results.'

'Well, I don't even know if an autopsy will be performed,'

General Land said. 'I thought he died at home of a heart attack.'

'One more question, sir. Have you seen a report from General Brown about listening devices being found in the DIA office spaces?'

Silence. It dragged for several seconds, 'No. Is there such a report?'

'The day I left to come over here General Brown said he was going to write one. We found the bugs a day or so before. Both he and I suspected they were planted and monitored by our friends at Langley, suspected for some very good reasons, but we had no rock-solid proof. One of the things my aide and I had discussed where it could be overheard by those bugs was the death a year or so ago of Nigel Keren, the British publisher. We thought we had some indications that someone from Langley might have killed him with binary poison.'

Jake paused for a moment. Land said nothing.

'Are you still with me, sir?'

'I'm here.'

'General Brown's death might also have been caused by binary poison. Since he apparently didn't write that report of those listening devices, I suggest you ensure that there will be an autopsy, a damn good one.'

'Just what were you and General Brown working on, Admiral?'

'We were discussing Nigel Keren, how he died, who might have killed him. I don't want to go any further into that on this telephone, sir. The KGB is probably eavesdropping. Still, this telephone was preferable to using the embassy communications systems. And I request that you don't use the telephones in your office, car or home to discuss this matter.'

More silence, then a slow, 'I think I see what you're driving at.'

'I don't know what is going on, General, but something is and I'm on the edge of it. So I need some help.'

'What?' That one-word response was pure Hayden Land. No beating around the bush, no questioning of his subordinate's assessment of the situation or demands for further information, just a straight, quick trip to the heart of the matter.

So Jake told him. The two officers talked for another twenty minutes before they spent a few minutes discussing what they were going to tell the *Washington Post* to explain this curious method of communication. Their answer – nothing at this time.

Jake straightened his uniform and put his shoes back on and locked the door behind him.

He found Toad Tarkington and Jack Yocke in the bar drinking espresso and gobbling pretzels. They both stood as Jake walked toward them.

'Thanks a lot, Jack,' Jake said.

'He called you?'

'Yes.'

'One word?' Yocke looked incredulous. 'That's all you're going to give me?'

Jake grinned. He extended his hand and the reporter took it.

As Toad and Jake were walking toward the main entrance, Yocke called, 'You owe me a steak when I get back to Washington.'

Jake lifted his hand in acknowledgment.

Out in the car Toad asked, 'Are you thinking what I'm thinking about that Yegor Somebody killing?'

'Not the Russians' style, you told Yocke. You can't hand Yocke a bone like that with meat on it, Toad – he's too smart.'

'Yeah. I'm sorry.'

'The whole thing looks like a classic in-your-face Mossad hit. Like Paris, Rome, Frankfurt, and a dozen others you could name. The KGB makes you disappear, the Mossad makes you a wire-service example.'

'Maybe the Russians are changing tactics.'

'Maybe.'

'Then again . . .'

For a while Grafton rode silently, looking out the window. Then he said, 'Say the Mossad decided to wipe a struggling young Hitler protégé and dropped a hint to someone in the Yeltsin government. Maybe some of Yeltsin's lieutenants thought the idea up. Whatever. Someone thought that Kolokoltsev's departure to Communist heaven wouldn't be an unmitigated disaster and called the cops off. That much is obvious, yet there's no way in the world to prove a damn thing on anybody. None of these clowns are ever going to breathe a word. Yocke is wasting his time asking embarrassing questions through an interpreter who is trying to keep from wetting his pants. All he'll do is irritate people who don't like to be irritated.'

Tarkington grunted. He was thinking about General Brown, smacked like a fly. 'Are you just speculating about the Mossad, Admiral, or was that a power think?'

Jake Grafton growled irritably. 'I don't know a damn thing.'

'I don't like any of this.'

'Write a letter home to mama,' Jake told him.

At least Judith Farrell is somewhere in Maryland, Toad told himself. She's mowing grass and watching baseball games on television and going to the theater on Friday nights. But even as he trotted that idea out for inspection he threw it back – he didn't believe it. He had seen her in action once, eliminating a terrorist in a Naples hotel. That memory came flooding back and he felt slightly ill.

'The Russians have their own rules,' Jake Grafton said. 'The language is different, the heritage is different, the mores are different, they don't think like we do. It's hard to believe this is the same planet we live on.'

Jake Grafton had listened for over twenty years to stories about all-male Russian dinners and vodka celebrations. They were always thirdhand or fourthhand, and the parties described sounded rather like something one might find in a college fraternity house on a Saturday night after the big football game.

And that, he thought ruefully, would be a good way to describe the festive atmosphere of which he was a reluctant part.

The problem was quite simple – he hadn't had this much to drink in years. He was sweating profusely and feeling slightly dizzy.

Across the table from him Nicolai Yakolev was telling another Russian joke, one about a high party official and a simple country girl. He had to tell it loud to be heard over the noise of the piano.

Jake had told a few of these jokes himself earlier in the evening, before the level of the fluid in the vodka bottle had gone down very far. He had never been very good with jokes – couldn't remember them long enough to find someone to tell them to – but he did recall several of those crude riddles that had been popular years ago, the so-called Polish jokes. So he transformed the bumblers into Communists and delighted the general and his guests with questions such as, How many Communists does it take to screw in a light bulb? Twelve – one to stand on the chair and hold the bulb, eleven to turn the chair.

Before dinner he had had a chance to meet the allied officers one on one.

Lieutenant Colonel West of the Queen's Own Highlanders was a deeply tanned trim man, about five feet six inches, with dark hair longer than US military regulations allowed. He seemed quite relaxed with the Russians and Jake heard him murmur a few phrases in the language.

'Delighted to see you, Admiral,' West said when they shook hands. 'Met you one time in Singapore years ago. No reason you should remember. Think you were a commander then.'

Jake seemed to think he did recall the man. 'A party with the Aussies?'

'Righto. About ten years ago. Jolly good show, that.'

Now he remembered. Jocko West, a specialist on guerrilla warfare, terrorism and jungle survival. 'You seem to have picked up a little of the local lingo, Colonel.'

West leaned closer and lowered his voice. 'Afghanistan, sir. A bit irregular, I dare say. Sort of a busman's holiday. These lads were the oppo.' He sighed. 'Well, the world turns, eh?'

The Frenchman was Colonel Reynaud, impeccably uniformed. He spent dinner chatting with two Russian officers in French. Prior to dinner, when he and Jake were introduced, he used English, which he spoke with a delicious accent. 'A pleas-aire, Admiral Grafton.'

'How did you manage to wrangle a trip to Moscow in the summertime, Colonel?'

'I am a student of Napoleon, sir, you comprehend? Think, had Napoleon arrived in the summer, perhaps history would have been so different, without these Communists. I came to see where it went wrong for him, for France. So I will do a little of work, a little of the seeing of the sights.'

'The people at my embassy told me you are an expert on nuclear weapons.'

Reynaud smiled. 'Alas, that is true. I study the big boom. In a way it is unmilitary, *n'est-ce pas?* The nuclear weapons will make *la guerre* so short, it will not be *la guerre.* They leave us without honor. It is not pretty.'

Jake managed to shake hands with Colonel Rheinhart, the German, and Colonel Galvano, the Italian, but he didn't get to visit with them until after dinner. They both impressed him as extremely competent officers of great ability. Rheinhart was the smaller of the two, a man whom the American embassy said had a doctorate in physics from the University of Heidelberg.

'Herr Colonel, or should I address you as Herr Doctor?'

The German laughed easily. One got the impression that Rheinhart would be a valuable officer in anyone's army.

Galvano was not as easy to read, perhaps because Jake had difficulty understanding his English. Still, he looked fit and highly intelligent, as all four of the colonels did. Their nations had sent the best they had, Jake concluded, and that best was very good indeed.

As he surveyed these officers at dinner he had wondered about his own selection. He was certainly not a weapons expert or diplomat. Could he get the job done? Looking at the foreign officers, he had his doubts. Then his eyes came to rest on Herb Tenney and the doubts evaporated. He had met a few slick bastards in his career and he thought he knew how to handle them, or at least get them sidetracked where they wouldn't do anyone any harm. He reached for his glass and had it almost to his lips when he remembered General Albert Sidney Brown. His hand shook slightly. He lowered the glass to the table without spilling any of the liquid.

Two hours after dinner General Yakolev still seemed fairly sober considering how much he had had to drink – at least two for every one of Jake's. He was sweating and having some trouble forming his English words, yet he looked pretty steady nonetheless.

A miracle.

Right now Jake Grafton felt like he was going to be sick. He excused himself and made for the rest room, where he found Toad Tarkington.

'What in hell do they put in that Russian moonshine anyway?' Toad demanded. 'It tastes like Tabasco sauce.'

Jake upchucked into a commode, then used his handkerchief to swab his face with cold water. His hands were shaking. Fear or vodka?

'You okay?' he asked Toad.

'About three sheets to the wind, CAG. I'm ready to blow this pop stand anytime you say.'

'A red hot night in Po City, huh?'

'I'm ready to go back-ship.'

119

'Give me another fifteen minutes or so. In the meantime get out there and mix and mingle.'

Jake led General Yakolev over to a corner where they wouldn't be so easily overheard. 'General, you impress me as a professional soldier.'

Yakolev didn't reply to that. His smile seemed frozen. God, his eyes seemed completely hidden behind those brows!

'I think you have brains and balls,' Jake added.

'The balls yes, but the brains? I have doubts. Others have doubts also.'

'I have a little problem that I need some help with,' Jake said as he fought the feeling that he wasn't handling this right. Why had he drunk those last two shots of vodka? This just wasn't going to work! He turned away with a sense of defeat, then turned back. What the hey, give it a shot. 'I'd like to ask a favor.'

Yakolev made a gesture that might have meant anything.

'I've had too much of your vodka. I'm having a little trouble saying this right. But I honestly need a favor.'

The general looked as foreign as an Iranian ayatollah. Jake pushed out the words. 'I want you to have a man arrested tomorrow.'

Now he could see Yakolev's eyes. They were locked on his own. 'Let's go into my office,' the Russian said. 'It's quiet there.'

The following day was overcast and gloomy when the contingent of foreign military observers gathered in the large room adjacent to General Yakolev's office where they had dined the night before. None of them looked the worse for wear, Jake thought as he surveyed them through eyes that felt like dirty marbles. He tried to slow the rate of blinking and swallowing, but he couldn't seem to affect it much.

The six aspirin had helped. At least he felt human again. Last night around midnight he had cursed himself for being a damn fool. After he and Yakolev had closeted themselves in the general's office, the old Russian had produced another vodka bottle from his desk drawer.

The last thing Jake remembered was a promise from the general that he would talk to the Foreign Intelligence Service, a name that gave the general a good laugh. Jake had laughed Like hell too because he was drunk.

Stinking drunk. God, how long had it been since he got so stinking, puking, deathly drunk? Fifteen . . . no, almost seventeen years. Make that eighteen.

Toad had driven him back to the embassy. He had passed out by then. He woke up in the bathroom hanging over the commode.

This morning he tried to pay attention as the Russian Army briefing officers used maps and charts to explain how the tactical warheads were being shipped to the disassembly site at an army base on the eastern side of the Volga river.

Herb Tenney was supposed to be here, but he wasn't. Jake and Toad had skipped breakfast and driven to the Kremlin in their own car, one of the black Fords the embassy used. Toad said Herb was coming on his own.

The briefing was an hour old when a soldier slipped into the room and handed General Yakolev a note. He read it, then interrupted the briefers and suggested a pause. He motioned to Jake.

'As you requested, your friend has been arrested.'

'Where is he?'

'KGB Headquarters. The soldier waiting outside will drive you there.'

KGB Headquarters on Dzerzhinsky Square was an imposing yellow building – the Russians seemed fond of yellow on public buildings. No doubt it made a nice contrast with the red flags that had hung everywhere in the not too distant past. Still, even with the cheerful yellow facade the building seemed to dominate the naked pedestal and traffic in the square below.

121

The driver steered the car to an entrance in the back and showed a document to the uniformed gate guard. Parked in the semidarkness under the building under the scrutiny of several armed soldiers, the driver remained behind the wheel of the car.

Jake and Toad were escorted through endless dark corridors by a slovenly man in an ill-fitting blue suit. The corridors had a smell, a light, foul odor. Jake was trying to place it when they went around a corner and there they were – the cells. They were small, dark. Some of them contained men. At least they looked like men, shadowy figures in the back of the cells who turned their backs on the visitors.

Terror. He had smelled terror, some evil mixture of sweat, stale urine, feces, vomit and fear. Looking at the forms of the men behind the bars and trying to see their faces, Jake Grafton felt his stomach turn.

He was perspiring when the guard opened a door at the end of the corridor, and unexpectedly they were in an office. There was a man in uniform behind the desk, the green uniform of the Soviet army, only this one wasn't in the army. He was a KGB general. He didn't rise from behind his desk, although he did look up. The escort left the room and closed the door behind him.

'Admiral Grafton.'

'Yes.'

'I am General Shmarov.'

Jake Grafton just nodded and looked slowly around the room. A large framed print of Lenin on the wall, which had once been green and was now merely earth-tone dirty. There was a window behind the general and it was even dirtier than the walls. Three padded chairs in poor condition. The desk. A telephone. And the KGB general.

Shmarov's bald head gleamed. Even with his mouth shut you could see that his teeth were crooked. Now he spoke again and Jake caught the gleam of gold. 'General Yakolev asked for a favor, so I was glad to help.'

Grafton couldn't think of a thing to say.

'Nicolai Alexandrovich is a friend.'

'Thanks,' Jake managed.

'Here is the passport.' The Russian held it out and Jake took it. It was a US diplomatic passport. He flipped it open. Herbert Peter Tenney. Jake thumbed the pages, which were festooned with entry and exit stamps. Tenney certainly got around. He passed it back to the general.

'Now if you'll just check it to see if it's genuine.'

'But of course.' A flash of gold.

The door opened and the escort in the blue suit was there waiting. Shmarov nodded his head. Grafton returned the nod and wheeled to follow the escort. Toad trailed along behind.

The room where the two Americans ended up contained only a table and a few chairs. On the table were clothes and shoes, a coat, a briefcase.

'His things,' Blue Suit said, and gestured.

'Everything?' Toad asked.

'Everything. He is being X-rayed. To see that nothing inside, then back to cell.'

'Thank you.'

Blue Suit gestured to the table, then pulled up a chair and sat down to watch. He took out a cigarette and lit it.

Jake took the briefcase while Toad started on the shoes.

The briefcase was plastic, with a plastic handle. It was unlocked, so he opened it and removed the contents, a legal pad, paper and pencils. Nothing else was inside. He examined the pens, cheap ballpoints, then disassembled them.

The padded handle of the briefcase showed wear but seemed innocuous. Jake used his penknife to cut it open. Nothing. Then he used the knife to slice out the padding that coated the interior of the case.

Their escort left the room for a moment, then returned with pliers, a screwdriver and a magnifying glass. Jake used the screwdriver to take off the tiny metal feet of the case.

Finally he turned his attention to the shoes. The laces, the heels, everything was examined closely and minutely with the magnifying glass.

When Toad began looking at the case, Jake turned his attention to the clothes – trousers, shirt, underwear, socks, tie, jacket and coat. He felt every seam and probed every questionable thickness with his pocketknife.

The suit wore a label from Woodward & Lothrop, a well-known department store in the Washington, DC, area. Jake shopped there himself on occasion. The belt was cut from a single piece of cowhide and had a hand-tooled hunting scene on it. The buckle was a simple metal one. A Christmas or birthday present, probably. After scrutinizing every inch of it as carefully as he could with the glass, he began leafing through the contents of the prisoner's pockets, which were contained in a cardboard box. A couple of keys, a wallet, a handful of loose ruble notes and American dollar bills, a fingernail clipper, a piece of broken shoelace, an odd white button that looked as if it was off a dress shirt, a key very similar to the one in Jake's pocket that probably opened Herb Tenney's room at Fort Apache – that was the crop.

Toad watched him examine everything under the magnifying glass, then helped him spread the contents of the wallet on one end of the table. Driver's license, credit cards, a library card, a folded *Far Side* cartoon torn from a newspaper, several hundred American dollars in currency, a receipt from a laundry in Virginia.

Toad perched on the edge of the table. 'Agent 007 always had a pocketful of goodies. I'm disappointed in our boy.'

'What should be here and isn't?'

Toad glanced at the Russian. 'What do you mean?'

'Is there anything you would expect to find him carrying around that isn't here?'

Toad surveyed the little pile, then shook his head. 'I can't think of anything. Except maybe an appointment or

124

memo book with some phone numbers. A bottle of invisible ink, a suicide pill, I don't know.'

'All his phone numbers are in his head.'

Jake picked up the keys, held them where the Russian could see them, then stuck them in his pocket.

'Let's go do the car,' he told Blue Suit as he handed back the magnifying glass and hand tools. 'We'll keep the keys and bring them back in a few hours.'

The man nodded and pulled the door open.

Back at Fort Apache one of the keys opened the door to room 402. The room number was right on the key. Jake Grafton turned on the lights. 'Go find Spiro Dalworth. I want screwdrivers, pliers, a magnifying glass, a big sharp knife from the kitchen. My pocketknife is too small.'

'Yes, sir.' Toad left.

Jake went into the bathroom and picked up all the toilet articles. He spread them out on a table and examined each of them.

The problem was that he didn't know what form the binary poison would be in, if it were here at all. A liquid would be the easiest to administer but the hardest to transport. Pills or powder would be easier to carry and almost as efficient. But any water-soluble solid would do, he thought, so even an object like a button or a pencil eraser might be the object he sought.

Now he sat looking at some tablets. A small plastic aspirin bottle with a child-proof lid contained the usual small white pills. He counted them. All of them had the word *aspirin* impressed into the surface. On one side. No, wait a minute. Some had the word on both sides. Huh! He separated the pills into two piles. Eight one-side-only and six both-sides, fourteen tablets total.

He put them back into the bottle and slipped the bottle into his pocket.

When Toad and Lieutenant Dalworth arrived, he put them to searching. 'I want to see any pills or powder or liquid you can find. Anything that might form a hidden container. Look carefully.'

Dalworth looked puzzled, but he asked no questions.

An hour later they decided that everything had been examined by all three of them.

'Mr Dalworth, thank you for your help. We'll sort of straighten everything out and lock the door when we leave. Of course, I'll appreciate it if you would keep this little adventure to yourself.'

Dalworth's eyes went to Toad, then back to Jake. 'I don't suppose this would be a good place to ask questions.'

'You're very perceptive, Spiro,' Toad said.

When the door closed behind him and Toad had checked to make sure that Mr Dalworth didn't have his ear against it, Jake removed the aspirin bottle from his pocket and spread out the tablets on the desk. 'Take a look at these, Toad.'

Tarkington used the magnifying glass. 'Well, they look like aspirin, but I dunno.'

'I have some aspirin on the bathroom sink in my room. Will you get them, please.'

They filled a tumbler with water and dropped one of Jake's aspirin in it. In twenty seconds the tablet had dissolved to a mound of white powder. After thirty seconds had passed they swirled it and the powder covered the bottom of the glass. After a minute it was still there.

Now Jake took one of the tablets with the double-sided label and dropped it into a fresh glass of water. It too dissolved rapidly, but without leaving the powder residue. The entire tablet went into solution.

'Thank God for the scientific method,' Toad muttered. 'When I was a kid I got a microscope one year for Christmas.'

Jake saved six tablets from his bottle and dumped the rest down the toilet. Those six he put in Herb Tenney's bottle. Herb's five remaining pills went into Jake's bottle.

As they folded clothes and replaced them in the suitcase

126

and dresser, Toad said, 'He's going to know someone was in here.'

'I suspect so.'

'Dalworth may blab.'

'He might.'

'You sure you got this figured out, CAG?'

'No.'

Toad touched Jake's arm. 'You're betting both our lives, you know.'

Jake just looked at him. 'I'm aware of that,' he said finally. 'If you have any ideas I'm always open to suggestions.'

Toad went back to straightening the closet. After a moment he said, 'I suggest we shoot friend Tenney and find a hole to stuff him and his aspirin bottle into.'

When Jake didn't respond, Toad added in a tight little voice, 'Of course you have carefully calculated all the possible reasons why there were two less of those pills marked on both sides than there were of the other kind.' His voice was sarcastic. 'No doubt you've weighed it, pondered on it, considered every possible aspect and come to some intricate, subtle conclusion that a mere junior officer mortal like me couldn't possibly appreciate.'

'What do you want me to say?' Jake replied patiently. 'That Herb probably took two for a toothache? We both know he probably fed them to us. Us and half the people in this embassy.'

'We really oughta take this guy out into the forest and make him dig his own hole. I kid you not.'

'KGB Headquarters must have really gotten to you.'

'Yes, sir. It sure as hell did. I admit it. I about vomited all over that fucking general's desk.'

'Hurry up. Let's get this done. We have to get back for the afternoon briefing.'

'How do you know,' Toad asked, 'that those are all the binary pills Herb has access to?'

'I don't.'

'He could have some in his desk in the CIA office, he

could have some stashed in any hidey-hole he thought handy. He can just ask Langley for more.'

'What a deep thinker you are! Let's hope he doesn't find out we took a few.'

'What if he runs short? What if he's embarked on a major urban renewal project?'

'You ask too many questions.'

'You and I are going to end up dead,' Toad said sourly.

'Sooner or later,' Grafton replied. What was there to say? Herb and his colleagues must have killed General Brown so that he wouldn't make waves. The job was only half done as long as Jake and Toad were wandering around upright.

'The whole fucking CIA can go to fucking hell for all I care,' Tarkington said crossly. When he got no reply, he muttered something to himself that Grafton didn't catch.

CHAPTER EIGHT

Butyrskaya Prison looked like something from a Kafka nightmare, Jack Yocke decided, and jotted the thought on a blank page of his notebook as he sat in the waiting room.

The Russian interpreter sitting on the bench across from him was as nervous as a pickpocket at a policeman's ball. He gnawed on a fingernail already into the quick, then stared at the sliver of nail still remaining. He pushed on the raw quick experimentally and grimaced. He crossed and recrossed his feet and stared morosely at the filthy paint on the wall and the dirty floor. He carefully avoided looking at any of the other people slumped on the wooden benches.

Yocke wondered about this desire to avoid even eye contact. After sweeping each of the other eight people in the room, his gaze returned to the uncomfortable interpreter, Gregor Something, Gregor followed by five or six Slavic syllables that sounded to Yocke's American ear like a pig grunting. Two days ago Gregor jackrabbited away from Soviet Square, yet the following morning he showed up at Yocke's hotel as if nothing had happened.

Still glowing with the virtuous warmth of his new-found heroism and curiously eager to make this gutless wonder squirm a little, Yocke asked, 'Why did you run?'

'My wife was ill.'

Gregor didn't blink or blush, didn't look away, even when Yocke sneered.

To be able to lie outrageously and shamelessly was an asset, Jack Yocke told himself, one that would of course stand Gregor in good stead here in this workers' paradise of poverty and desperation, but it would also be a cheerful bullet for his résumé even in brighter climes, such as the US of A. Across the pond in the land of the free and home of the brave he could lie like a dog to clients and customers, cheat on his spouse, steal from his employer, write creative fiction for the IRS, and in the unlikely event he ever got caught he could fool the lie detector and skip away with a happy smile. This multilingual grunter would fit right in, as red, white and blue as a telephone solicitor hyping penny stocks to shut-in geriatrics. Once he got his fastball high and tight he could even become a politician.

This morning in the waiting room of Butyrskaya Yocke asked Gregor, 'Have you ever thought of emigrating to America?'

'My wife's cousin lives in Brooklyn.'

Yocke stared.

'Brooklyn, New York.'

'I'm trying to recall if I ever heard of Brooklyn. It's out west, isn't it? With cowboys and Indians and tumble-weeds?'

'Perhaps,' Gregor said softly. 'I don't know. My wife's cousin drives a taxi and earns many dollars. He likes America.' He shrugged.

'America is a great country.'

'He drives a Chevrolet. Only five years old.' He glanced at the other people in the room to see who was listening. One or two had glanced up at the sound of a foreign language, but now all but one had retreated into their self-imposed isolation.

'Umm,' said Jack Yocke, looking hard at the young man who was looking at them. He had longish hair and an air of quiet desperation. His gaze wavered, then fell away.

'Petrol is cheap there, my wife's cousin says. Every day he drives many many miles. All the streets are paved.'

A door opened and a man passed through the waiting room. Jack Yocke caught a whiff of the prison smell. He had smelled it before in the jails of Washington, a devil's brew

130

of urine, body odor and fear. Yocke delicately inhaled a thimbleful as Gregor regaled his listener with the adventures of his wife's cousin in his Chevy on the paved boulevards of Brooklyn.

Two minutes after Yocke reached saturation, a man came through one of the doorways and spoke to Gregor, then led the way along endless dingy corridors. The warden's corner office was big and had a carpet. A dial phone straight out of the 1930s sat on the wooden desk.

The warden came around the desk to shake hands, then trotted back around the desk and arranged himself in his chair. He was a sloppy fat man with a heavy five-o'clock shadow that made his skin look dingy gray.

Gregor and the warden nattered a while in Russian, then Gregor turned to Yocke. 'He welcomes the correspondent for the American newspaper *Post* to Butyrskaya.'

'Thank him for taking the time to see me.' Of course Yocke had an appointment, arranged by an official with the Yeltsin government, but he was willing to pretend this was a social call.

More Russian.

'Ask your questions.'

'I am here today at the request of the editor of my newspaper, the most influential newspaper in the United States. Everyone in Washington reads my newspaper every day, from Hillary Clinton right on down. Everyone, including all the people in the Senate and House of Representatives. Tell him that.'

After an Uzi-burst of Russian, Yocke continued. 'I am here to interview Yakov Dynkin, a Jew who was convicted of arranging the sale of a private automobile for profit. I understand he was sentenced to five years in the gulag at hard labor.'

The warden's face lost its friendliness as Gregor translated. Yocke didn't understand the words, but he understood the tone. The interpreter said, 'Yakov Dynkin is not here. No Jews are here.'

'Has he been shipped to the gulag?'

'No,' was the answer that came back. Just no.

Yocke thought about it. Dynkin wasn't here and he hadn't been shipped to the gulag. 'Have they turned him loose with a pardon or probation?'

The warden merely frowned.

Yocke extracted a press clipping from his jacket pocket. He handed it to Gregor and pointed at the appropriate paragraph. 'Two weeks ago Tass said Dynkin was here. There it is in black and white.' Gregor stared at the clipping. 'Go on! Show him that and tell him I wish to see Dynkin and write about what wonderful treatment he is receiving here at Butyrskaya even though he was convicted of violating a law that was repealed a week before he was arrested.'

Slowly, as if this were costing him a major portion of his pension, Gregor passed the piece of paper across the desk. The warden refused to touch it, so it came to rest in the empty spot on the desk in front of him. He bent over and looked at the English words without showing the slightest glimmer of comprehension.

After a few seconds the warden picked up the offending paper and handed it back to Yocke, who accepted it. Another spray of words.

'He says you are wrong. Dynkin is not here. No Jews are here.'

'Where are they?'

'He doesn't know. Is there anything else he can help you with?'

'Couldn't he consult his records or something and tell me if Dynkin has ever been here? Or when he left. Or where he is.'

Gregor considered.

'These people do have records, I assume, something scribbled somewhere to tell them who is rotting in what hole . . .'

Gregor spoke to Yocke as if he were a small boy incapable of understanding the obvious. 'He is not here.'

'Who are you working for? Him or me? Ask him the question.'

'But he has told you the answer. What more could he possibly say? The warden is a powerful senior official. If he says the man is not here, then he is not. That is all there is to that.'

Jack Yocke smiled at the warden. He then turned the grin on Gregor. 'This fat geek is lying through his teeth. These greasy Commie bastards railroaded Dynkin for making an honest ruble just because he's a Jew. They've got him locked up somewhere in the large intestines of this shit factory. This pompous son of a bitch knows the whole prosecution was a farce to fuck Jews and embarrass Yeltsin and his people, make them look like lying hypocrites when they go begging in America and Europe for foreign aid. Dynkin sold a car for a profit and these old Commies are grinding him into hamburger.'

Gregor's face was frozen, immobile. Even his eyes were blank.

'Ask him if it's true that about a hundred and twenty thousand people are still imprisoned in labor camps for doing business that is legal in Russia today. Ask him.'

Gregor put his tongue in motion. After a few syllables from the warden, the translator told Yocke, 'He doesn't know.'

'Ask him how Russia can establish a free market-economy if it keeps all these people in prison for earning a profit.'

Gregor looked at his shoes.

'Ask him!'

The translator's head moved from side to side, about a millimeter.

Yocke flashed another broad grin at the warden. 'Come on, Gregor. There's a story here. These Commies ain't got religion. They're still the same filthy, diseased assholes they always were. They screwed Dynkin to get at Yeltsin. You can see *that*, can't you? They can't get away with it if we tell it to the world.'

Gregor's face looked as bad as Lenin's, who had been dead for over sixty years.

'Don't chicken out on me again,' Yocke pleaded. 'Think up something that will open up this pig's . . .'

But Gregor was leaving. He stood and nodded obsequiously to the warden while he jabbered away like a parrot with a hard on. The warden expended the effort to get to his feet. He tugged his jacket down over his gut and adjusted his tie. He grinned at Yocke and thrust out his hand.

At a loss for what to do next, Yocke closed his mouth, gave the warden's soft hand a token pump, then followed the retreating Gregor.

Going down the corridor Yocke demanded, 'What did you tell that fat screw?'

'Screw? What is a screw?'

'A prison guard. A power pervert.'

Gregor gave Yocke a look that was about an equal mixture of contempt and amazement and kept walking.

Outside in the street, Gregor exploded. 'You can't talk to a powerful person like you did in there. This is *Butyrskaya!* Are you *insane?* Do you know *nothing?*' He sprayed saliva.

'My newspaper sent me to get a story,' Yocke snarled. 'That asshole was lying! He didn't even look at the records. What a crock! You people have held your nose so long that you can't smell shit when you're in it up to your ears. You've been fucked by these people for seventy-five years because you bent over and grabbed your ankles and held the position. You gutless wonders will—'

Gregor spit at Yocke's feet. 'You are a little boy throwing pebbles at a great bear. The chain holding the bear is very rusty, very weak. If you arouse him you will end up in his belly and no one at your rich newspaper in Washington USA will ever know what became of you.' He snapped his fingers. 'Like that. You will be gone. You and your dirty words and stupid questions and your notebook where you write your words making fun of us. Gone forever, Mister Jack Yocke. Think about that if you have any brains to think with.'

They went to Gregor's tiny Soviet sedan and shoe-horned themselves in. Sitting there with his knees jammed against the dashboard, Yocke said, 'Why don't you drop the *kru-lak* act and stop feeding me bullshit?'

'Why don't you stop acting like stupid Yankee billion-aire looking down his nose?'

'I will if you will.'

Gregor inserted his key in the ignition, then glanced sideways at Yocke. 'Standing in Soviet Square while gun-men shoot bullets was the most grotesque' – he had to search for words – 'the most dumbest stupid thing I have ever in my life seen. Everyone ran because those who shoot don't want anyone to see their faces. We stupid Russians think of that real quick.' He bobbed his head once and snapped his fingers. 'Even if stray bullets don't kill you the gunmen will if you stand there like you are watching old men play chess. And *you* hung there on the side of the speaker's platform, an ape in the zoo. *You* weren't shot – a miracle, like an immaculate conception. Truly there is a God and he looks after grotesque stupidly Americans.'

Jack Yocke's embarrassment showed on his face. 'Well, that was sorta . . .'

Gregor pointed at the prison. 'In there, you shot your mouth.'

'Shot my mouth off.'

'Yes. Off. Shot mouth off. Can warden speak English?' Gregor shrugged grandly. 'Was the office bugged by people who tape and listen?' He shrugged again. 'Can the people who tape and listen speak English?' Another shrug. 'Will the warden tell something he has been told not to tell to *you*, an American reporter to write in your glorious impor-tant foreign newspaper God knows what?' He lifted his hands and raised his eyebrows.

'Rub it in.'

'Okay.' He used his knuckles to rub Yocke's head. 'There. It's rubbed in. You Americans!'

'So what happened to Yakov Dynkin?' Yocke asked as he tried to smooth his hair back into place with his fingers.

'We could spend the afternoon thinking possibilities. He is dead. Moved to another prison. Maybe sick. Maybe released. Maybe in Siberia. Maybe used to clean up mess at Chernobyl. Whatever, for us he is no more.'

'Then why did the warden say no Jews were here? Most liars don't expand the tale beyond what is necessary.'

'Oh?'

'Why tell a whopper if a little lie will do? If Dynkin's dead—'

'I don't know.' Another shrug.

'Let's try to find Dynkin's wife. I have her address written down here someplace.'

Gregor turned the key and the engine caught after only three seconds of grinding.

The apartment building was one of dozens in a sprawling area outside the second Moscow loop. They all looked alike, five stories high, splotchy plaster, flat roofs, not a tree in sight. They found the one they wanted because it had a number painted on one corner.

Yocke looked it over and began to compose his story in his head. The adjectives, nouns and verbs came effortlessly as he looked at the appalling, dreary buildings and tried to imagine what it would be like to call one of these concrete cell blocks home.

But he kept his thoughts to himself. Gregor probably lived in an apartment house like this. Or wished he did.

When Gregor parked and killed the engine, Yocke laid a hand on his arm. 'Let's see if we can reach an understanding between us. I'm a foreigner, a stranger. I'm here because the American people are interested in Russia and my newspaper wants to print the stories. All I want to do is understand. If I can understand what is going on, I can write it. But I need to get the truth. I need to get it anyway I can.'

Gregor stared straight ahead. 'In Russia there is no such thing as truth. There is only what you write, and it is good for someone and bad for someone else.'

That comment seemed to give Yocke no opening, so he attacked in another direction. 'Are you for democracy?'

Gregor considered. 'Maybe.'

Yocke frowned. Aloud he said, 'For democracy to work, people have to know what is really happening. My job is to find out.'

Come on, Jack! You sound like a candidate for county sheriff. Even you don't believe *that* treacle. You are employed by the owners of the newspaper to make them money, to write stories that sell newspapers. To keep the long green flowing they aren't too picky about who they screw, an attitude they share with hundred-dollar, have-a-nice-day hookers. Now that is *truth* as red, white and blue as a Harley tattoo.

'This isn't America,' Gregor explained patiently, damn him!

The reporter grasped his door handle and pulled. 'It's a hell of a lot closer than you think,' he muttered through clenched teeth.

Jake Grafton and Toad Tarkington sat in General Yakolev's car in the alley behind KGB Headquarters while they waited for the driver to return the keys. Toad was in the front beside the driver's seat. He stared at the cut-stone walls morosely. Herb Tenney was in the belly of the beast and that was a good place for him, he told himself. Unfortunately Herb would be out dancing in the sunbeams in about an hour.

Jake Grafton had properly rejected his spur-of-the-moment proposal to send Herb on to his next incarnation. The complexities of the proof problem troubled Toad not a whit: he *knew* Herb was guilty – but there undoubtedly were other people involved in Herb Tenney's slimy little mess; there *had* to be. Maybe as few as three or four others, maybe the whole damned CIA, all sixteen thousand of them slopping through kimchi right up to their plastic photo ID badges. As usual Grafton was right. Why trade the devil you knew for heaven knows how many you didn't?

And just what was Herb's mess? If the CIA were merely squashing billionaires like stinkbugs, that could be forgiven as some kind of kinky weekend sport, sort of like tennis with live grenades. If they switched to American billionaires they could probably get a TV contract and sell tickets. No, if that were the game they wouldn't be so twitchy.

So what *was* going on?

Keren was a newspaper mogul, wasn't he? Perhaps his papers had uncovered something the CIA didn't want uncovered. Now that made sense. Arms for Iran? Cocaine for guns? Maybe something to do with the last American election.

But all of this was pure speculation. He was trying to guess what the puzzle looked like after getting a fuzzy glimpse of one small piece.

Toad glanced over his shoulder at the admiral in the backseat. He too was looking at the grim secret police headquarters and the grotesquely ugly buildings across the street, but his face showed no emotion.

You're never gonna be an admiral, Toad-man. Never! You don't have the cool for it.

His mind turned from that happy subject to his serious contemplation of the murder of a fellow human being. He had been serious, he reminded himself guiltily. What if Grafton had said yes? Then it would have been his responsibility. No, Toad told himself, then it would have been the responsibility of both of you.

Are you that frightened of Herb? Toad asked himself.

Yes!

In spite of the mild temperature, Toad Tarkington shivered.

*

Toad almost went to sleep in the afternoon briefing, a technical seminar on how properly to dispose of nuclear warheads. The speakers were physicists and chemists and weapons designers, all of whom were in love with their subjects as far as Toad could tell.

When Herb Tenney slipped in and dropped into an empty seat, Toad came wide awake. Herb looked none the worse for his ordeal and sat listening as if he could actually understand this technical mumbo jumbo.

Toad tried to ignore Herb, which was difficult. He well knew that some people could sense when they were being watched, and he didn't want Herb to get the idea that he and Grafton were responsible for his recent unpleasantness, at least not for a while.

Still, when the break in the presentation came and he saw Jake Grafton angling through the crowd for Herb, Toad managed to be within earshot.

'Herb, I thought you were going to be here this morning,' the admiral said.

'I'm sorry, sir. Something came up unexpectedly.'

'*This* is important,' Grafton replied.

'I'm aware of that.' Toad thought this reply had just a trace of disrespect in it, which would be typical of the Herb Tenney he had come to know and love.

'We're supposed to be working together on this, Mr Tenney,' Jake said, his voice so low Toad had to step closer to catch the words. 'I don't know what else you have going on here in Moscow and I don't really care, but if you can't give this assignment the attention required then I'm going to have to report you to Washington. I expect you to be at official functions clean and sober and on time.'

'It won't happen again,' Tenney replied matter-of-factly, without a trace of rancor.

'Fine,' Jake said, and walked away.

That evening back at the embassy Toad Tarkington dug into his luggage. A couple years ago at a Virginia pawnshop he had purchased a Walther PPK, a slick little automatic in .380 ACP caliber. It had probably once belonged to a cop who had used it as a hideout gun because it had a spring-steel clip spot-welded onto the left side of the slide. The clip allowed the pistol to be slipped behind the waistband in the small of the back and hooked onto the top of the trousers. It rode there quite nicely, such a small package that it would usually escape notice, yet it could be drawn easily with the right hand.

He had brought along only enough shells to load the magazine once, so he did that now and slipped the magazine into the pistol. He cycled the slide to put a round in the chamber, then lowered the hammer. He tucked the pistol into the small of his back, checking carefully to make sure the clip engaged his waistband, then fluffed his shirt out over the protruding grip.

It wasn't much of a gun. Still, it felt good to have it.

He had brought more gun along, a 9mm Browning Hi Power, but it was too bulky to tote around unobtrusively. Toad got out the Browning and cycled the slide and sat on the bed thinking about Herb Tenney and his little white pills.

He pointed the gun at the mirror above the dresser and squeezed the trigger. The hammer fell with a metallic thunk.

He lay back on the bed and closed his eyes. Now he remembered the little square of paper he had found in the pocket of the shirt he was wearing when he unfolded it this morning. He fished it from his wallet and held it up where he could read it.

> *Your touch, your kisses*
> *open the pathways to my heart*

Rita was fond of writing little love notes and putting them where he would find them at a moment when he least expected it. He wondered when she had written this one.

Perhaps when she was ironing the shirts, the afternoon he was packing. Or days before.

Rita . . .

Funny, but when he was dating and playing the field he had never realized how much he could love a woman. Or how much a woman could love him.

Strange how life reveals its mysteries. Just when you think you have the game scoped out, that you know all the rules and all the intricacies, all it has to offer, a new rich vein of truth reveals itself.

Rita is what you have to lose, Toad Tarkington. Death is not the threat. That's coming sooner or later any way you cut the cards. The richness of life with Rita and the extraordinary gift of *what might be* – that is what Herb Tenney and his little white pills can deprive you of.

He held the Browning up where he could see it. Without realizing it he had eared back the hammer.

He pulled the trigger and listened again to the thunk as the hammer slammed down.

The embassy residents were at dinner when Herb Tenney dusted his bathroom sink with fingerprint powder. Yes, there were fingerprints there, most of them smeared but a couple fairly nice. He used tape to lift the best ones and placed the tape on a white file card.

Back at his desk he compared the prints to those on the fax he had received an hour ago on the CIA's private com equipment. One of them was a perfect match.

So Jake Grafton had personally searched the place. That dweeb Tarkington was probably with him when he did it. The fax also supplied him with a copy of Tarkington's fingerprints, but developing more raw prints for comparison hardly seemed worth the effort. Herb Tenney sighed and stowed the bottle of powder and the brush and tape in the fingerprint kit.

That arrest this morning had been a farce. They had stopped his car a block from the embassy and handcuffed him. Then a Russian had driven him and his car to KGB Headquarters. There he was escorted to a cell and stripped and X-rayed.

He had spent three hours sitting stark naked in an isolation cell before they returned his clothes. Throughout the entire experience no one had asked him a single question. Not when they picked him up, during the ride to the prison, nor while they were holding him.

After he was dressed, a man in a blue suit led him through the corridors to an office. Sitting behind the desk pawing through the stuff that had been in his pockets was General Shmarov.

'Find anything interesting?'

Shmarov held up the white button that came off yesterday's shirt and looked from it to the CIA officer. 'Maybe the cleverest transmitter I have yet seen, Tenney.'

Then he grinned and tossed the button on top of the currency and passport lying there. 'Sorry for the inconvenience today.'

'Was this supposed to be funny? Should I laugh now?'

Shmarov shrugged. 'You know how these things are. I was asked to do a favor by a very high officer in the Defense Ministry. He wanted your passport checked. How could I refuse? He had been asked to do this by an American naval officer.'

'Rear Admiral Grafton? He was here?'

'Yes. Grafton. With an aide. Did he leave any of your seams intact?'

Tenney found a chair and dropped into it. 'I think I caught a cold in your dungeon. I never realized how drafty these damned places are.'

'They searched your car and took the keys that were in your pocket. They brought them back a few minutes ago.' General Shmarov displayed the keys and placed them beside the button on top of the rubles and dollars. He lit a cigarette, took a deep drag, and filled the room with smoke. Then he said, 'Want to tell me what this is about?'

'I'm as mystified as you are, General,' Herb Tenney told him.

Shmarov displayed his gold teeth in a grin and puffed some more on his cigarette.

'Who rubbed out Kolokoltsev?'

The golden grin disappeared. Shmarov stubbed out the cigarette and stared through the dissipating smoke at his visitor. 'Someone who wanted to make a lot of trouble. They succeeded.'

'Hard to believe that something like that could happen here in Moscow, almost under your nose. Soviet Square is what, a half mile from here? A kilometer?'

'What do you know about it, Tenney?'

Herb Tenney got up and approached the desk. He picked up his things and placed them in his pockets. Then he put his knuckles on the desk and stared into Shmarov's face. 'I think it looks as if you people killed your own guys so you could set up Yeltsin. They'll think that over at the Kremlin. They'll think it in Washington too. Whoever pulled the cops out of that square really screwed the pooch.'

'We are not that stupid.'

'I'll tell them that at Langley. But if I were you I'd find someone to hang it on, and damn quick.'

The ringing phone woke Jake Grafton. He had thrown himself on the bed and just dozed off.

'Grafton.'

'Admiral, this is Jack Yocke.'

'Hey.'

'I was wondering if you could come over for a drink.'

'Well, I don't think—'

'See you within an hour, Admiral, in my room.' And Yocke hung up.

Jake cradled the receiver and swung his feet over onto the floor. He looked at his watch. Eleven at night. He was still fighting the jet lag and hangover and he felt lethargic, unable to concentrate. He put on his shoes and splashed some cold water from the sink onto his face.

Yocke's room was on the fourth floor of the hotel. He opened the door at Toad's knock. 'Come in.'

When he had the door closed Yocke said, 'General Land called a little while ago. You're to wait here with me.'

'For what? Another phone call?'

Yocke shrugged. 'I just take messages and deliver them.'

Jake sank into the one stuffed chair.

'How's the foreign correspondent these days?' Toad asked Yocke as he dropped onto the bed.

'He's right in the middle of the biggest story in Russia and he can't make heads or tails of it,' Yocke replied, staring at Jake Grafton. 'Can't print it either.'

'I guess assassins can be tough to interview if you can't find them.'

'That isn't the story I meant. Anyway, my editor took me off that and gave it to the senior man. I'm doing political stuff. Y'know, "Today the Russian Ministry of Economics announced a new stabilization policy for the ruble." Drivel like that.' He sighed. 'Other than that, the food here is barely edible and grotesquely expensive, the vodka tastes like rubbing alcohol, my bed is lumpy, the pillow's too big, and I had a devil of a time yesterday getting a roll of toilet paper from the maid. Had to give her a US dollar for it. I've got to find an apartment by next week and get out of this hotel or the bean counters at the *Post* are going to get testy. What's new with you?'

Tarkington just made a noise and stretched out on the bed. In a moment he said, 'This pillow is too big.'

'Would I lie to you?'

'I don't think the bed's lumpy though.'

Before Yocke could think of a reply, Jake Grafton asked, 'How would you like to tag along with me and Toad for a while?'

The question startled Yocke. Toad opened his eyes, sat

up and stared wide-eyed at Jake for a few seconds, then flopped back on the bed and groaned.

'Sort of like Washington a couple of years ago, eh?' Yocke said with a grin. 'Same rules?'

'Well, not exactly.' Jake frowned. 'I guess I don't know precisely what the rules should be. So I'd want some sort of promise that you won't print anything on any subject without my okay.'

'I assume that you're working with the Russians. Do they know I'll be there? A reporter?'

'I've talked to General Yakolev about it. I told him I could trust you.'

Toad groaned again. 'Spreading it a little thick, aren't you, sir? I'd trust Jack the Hack with parking meter money, but . . .'

'Yakolev? Isn't he the chief of staff for the new Commonwealth Army?'

'That's the guy. Nicolai Yakolev.'

'Soaks up vodka like a sponge,' Toad tossed in.

'I agree.' Yocke grinned broadly and offered Jake his hand. After the admiral shook it, he grabbed a steno pad and a pencil and plopped onto the edge of the bed, forcing Tarkington to scoot over. He flipped the pad open to a fresh page and said, 'Shoot.'

'No notes. None.'

'I *have* to take notes. I got a good memory but it ain't Memorex. Only way to ensure accuracy later on when I write the story.'

Grafton appeared unmoved, so Yocke steamed on. 'We're talking the *Washington Post* here, not the Alfalfa County *Clarion*.' Yocke added confidentially, 'I'll use my own private shorthand. No one can read it but me. Honest.'

'Not even if you write in Swahili.'

Tarkington chortled.

Yocke tossed the steno pad on top of the dresser. 'No notes.'

'The other part of it is that the CIA may try to kill you.'

145

Yocke's mouth fell open. He glanced at Toad, then back at Jake. 'The CIA? *Our* guys? You're kidding, right?'

'No.'

'I can't write a story if I'm dead.'

'That thought may occur to them too.'

'Them? The whole CIA or a couple of bad apples or who?'

'I dunno.'

Yocke lost his temper. 'Jesus Christ, Admiral! You don't give a guy much. What say we do this the conventional, tried-and-true traditional way? You tell me whatever you want to tell me and I'll write and publish it, just like a real working reporter. You'll be an anonymous, reliable source, an unnamed high government official. I won't reveal your name to another living soul, even if they throw me in jail. I'll stay alive and out of your hair. Anytime you want to talk, just give a shout.'

'Be like having your own psychotherapist on the cheap, CAG,' Toad said unctuously, 'but you could skip the messy details about your sex life unless you wanted our modern Dr Freud to make you famous.'

Jake Grafton shook his head. 'Won't work that way,' he told Yocke. 'You either come along for the ride on the chance that someday you may get to write a story or you stay at home. It's up to you.'

'Just what do you get out of this arrangement?' Yocke demanded.

'I get an independent observer who has the power to reach the American public. I'm not sure what that will be worth because I don't know how things will shake out. But . . . if Toad and I get killed and you somehow manage to live to tell the tale, it might make very interesting reading in some quarters. I don't know. Too many ifs. I just don't know.' He eyed Yocke. 'At the very least you're an unknown quantity added to the equation.' He shrugged.

A knock sounded on the door.

'Well?' Jake asked. 'Yea or nay?'

'I'm in.'

Yocke went to answer the door. The man who came in was wearing a suit and overcoat and had a hard case that looked as if it contained a videocamera handcuffed to his wrist. The case displayed a diplomatic tag.

'Admiral Grafton?'

'Yes.'

'I'm Master Sergeant Emmett Thornton. I need to see your ID, sir.'

Jake took out his wallet and extracted his green military ID card. Thornton gave it a careful look, then handed it back. 'Thank you, sir.' He extracted a piece of paper from his inside coat pocket and held it out. 'Now if you will just sign for this equipment, it's all yours.'

Jake scribbled his name. 'How much is this going to cost me if I lose it, Sergeant?'

'About a hundred grand.'

Toad snapped his fingers. 'We'll put it on our Amoco card.'

Thornton glanced at Yocke.

'He's okay,' Grafton told him.

Thornton laid the case on the bed and used a key to open it. They gathered around for a look as he began unpacking items. 'What we have here is a TACSAT – tactical satellite – com unit with built-in encryption device. The signal goes right up to the bird, which rebroadcasts it to the Pentagon com center. Ni-cad batteries and a universal recharger. All you do is set the encryption code and use it like a two-way radio. General Land wanted me to remind you that the codes were generated by the National Security Agency.'

Jake examined the switches and buttons on the device. 'We'll need a brief and the codes.'

'Yessir. I'll come to that. This other item is simpler. It's a tape recorder with an encryption device attached. You merely record a message, anything you want up to thirty minutes. Then you punch up a six-digit code in this window here. Find a telephone, call the party you want, and when they are ready, you hit the play button. The garbled sound goes out at high speed. Takes about sixty seconds to play a thirty-minute message. If the other party has a message for you, you then put your machine on record and hold it up to the phone. Later on you can play the message and the machine will decode it into plain English. This thing works with telephones or TACSAT.'

The TACSAT came with a set of codes on water-soluble paper. Since it was possible the codes could fall into the wrong hands, 'unauthorized personnel' was Thornton's phrase, each authentic message should start with a code word that the admiral was to make up. Now. After a moment's thought Jake wrote a word on a matchbook and showed it to the sergeant, who then burned the matchbook in the wastepaper basket.

'The code for the telephone encrypter is a little more difficult. If you other gentlemen would like to step out of the room for a minute?'

'No, Sergeant,' Jake told him. 'Let's you and I go for a walk.'

Out on the sidewalk in front of the hotel the evening breeze was picking up. The sergeant explained: 'General Land suggested this code. Take the date, multiply it by the year in which you were born, then divide by the hour of the day in which you sent the message.' He produced a sheet of paper. 'Try it. Today is the second of July here so write that as seven oh two. And use local time in the military format. It's now twenty-three fifty, so use twenty-three hundred.'

Jake got a pen from his shirt pocket and did the math. 'I get five nine three point six four seven – something.'

'You were born in 1945, right?'

'Yes.'

'Okay, Admiral. You would just punch that six-digit number into the encrypter and place the decimal in the proper place. Always start with a positive integer and carry

148

out any fractions so that you have six digits. Add zeros to the right of the decimal as necessary.'

'Who has this code, besides you and me?'

'Just General Land.'

'We'll always use Moscow time?'

'Moscow date and time.'

'Okay. Come upstairs and give Toad and me a complete brief on the gear and we'll be all set. Did you just get in from Washington?'

'I came here straight from the airport, sir. They're waiting to take me back.'

'Long flight.'

'I'm used to it. I sleep on the plane.'

Jake Grafton stared at the communications devices with a sinking feeling. After a moment he screwed up the courage to ask, 'Just how secure is this techno-junk?'

The sergeant faced him squarely. 'Admiral, this stuff is like a padlock on a garage. It'll keep honest people honest. But with a good computer a competent cryptographer could break any message in a couple hours.'

All Jake Grafton could manage was a grunt.

'The good news,' the sergeant continued, 'is that the ruskies don't have many good computers. They do most of their crypto work by hand, so it'll take them a couple weeks. Then one hopes the report will get routed here and there through the bureaucracy and a couple more weeks will pass before it lands on the desk of someone who may or may not decide to believe it.'

'A couple hours. With a good computer.'

'That's about the size of it, sir.'

And the CIA has the best computers in the world. Jake Grafton took a deep breath and thanked the sergeant for his trouble. Being an army man, the sergeant saluted.

CHAPTER NINE

The plane was the personal transport of the Minister of defense and still the rest room smelled like an outhouse and no water came out of the sink taps. No paper towels. So much for personal hygiene!

Jake opened the door and stepped out into the aisle that led to the cockpit. There was no cockpit door and he could see the instrument panel between the pilots.

The warning placards were in Cyrillic and the instruments had funny labels. He stood there looking over their shoulders for several seconds before the pilot realized he was there and looked over his shoulder. He said something in Russian and Jake replied in English.

'Good morning,' the pilot managed.

'Good morning,' Jake echoed. 'Nice plane you got here.'

When the pilot tapped his watch and made half a circle on the face with his finger, Jake nodded sagely and returned to his seat.

General Yakolev was in a seat across the aisle conferring with his aide. They were going over documents. Toad sat in the next row with Jocko West, who was broadening the American's horizons. Behind them sat the other foreign military representatives.

Today they were making a trip to a Russian nuclear weapons depot to see how warheads were disassembled. The name of the base they were going to was Petrovsk, on the Volga watershed. Jake glanced at the map again. The place was a hundred miles or so north northeast of

Volgograd, formerly Stalingrad, where the Soviet army shattered Adolf Hitler's ambitions.

Jake Grafton hadn't even been born then, but Yakolev was a young soldier in the Soviet army. Once again Jake pondered the twists of fate that had lifted Yakolev to the top, wondered again about the man who wore that uniform.

The window was scratched from being repeatedly wiped with dirty rags, but Jake managed to get a look through it at the land sliding by thirty thousand or so feet below. Forests, occasional small villages, roads that followed the contours of the land.

It just didn't look like America, or even western Europe. Those landscapes had their own distinct look that an experienced air traveler would recognize at a glance. Part of the problem, Jake decided, was that Russia was just too big. Great distances were the blessing that caused Napoleon and Hitler to founder and the curse that had stymied generations of Communist economic planners.

Soon Jake heard the power being reduced and felt the nose drop a degree or two as the pilot began his descent.

All this talk about weapons . . . it would be good finally to see some of the damned things.

The weapons were being disassembled in a makeshift clean room that didn't look any too tight. This was the scene of Yakolev's show-and-tell session. The Western visitors gathered in front of a plate-glass window and watched white-robed technicians use mechanical arms to manipulate the warhead parts while an interpreter translated Yakolev's comments, which were in Russian. Amazingly, when they entered the facility no one had offered them film badges to record the level of radiation to which they might be exposed, nor was anyone working here wearing one.

Beside the general stood a man in civilian clothes who looked nervous. Jake assumed he was the manager of this facility. Occasionally Yakolev asked him a question and pondered the reply, but the interpreter didn't translate these exchanges.

From the clean room an army truck took the party to a large hangar where row after row of missiles sat on their transporters. Against one wall were stacked wooden crates of pallets – nuclear warheads. The small party stood in silence taking it all in.

Yakolev stood beside Jake. Finally he spoke, in English. 'Impressive, yes?'

'That it is.'

'Russia shook the world with these missiles,' Yakolev said. 'And now we take them apart.'

Jake Grafton searched the older man's impassive face.

'We become another poor country without a voice in the world's affairs,' the general continued after a moment, still looking at the row upon row of missiles decorated with huge red stars. 'The television brings us news of the great things that are happening in Washington, New York, London, Paris, Bonn . . . We learn the thoughts of the great men of our age. The world's leaders ponder the future of mankind and debate how much money to give Russia while we eat our potatoes and borsch.'

Yakolev slapped Jake on the back. 'That is progress, no? No more bad old Communists! Now Russians buy televisions and watch CNN and the BBC and bet on world cup soccer and tennis matches at Wimbledon. They worry about stock prices in Tokyo and London and New York. No more bad old Russians! They are *just like us.*'

Yakolev turned away and Jake Grafton watched his retreating back. Then he stood looking at the missiles.

General Yakolev excused himself for a few hours' work, so Jake asked for a tour of the base. This disconcerted the civilian interpreter, but within a few minutes a military guide-interpreter was provided. 'What want to see?' the man asked with a heavy accent, wearing a perplexed look.

'The enlisted barracks, the mess hall and the hospital,' Jake told him.

The guide was in uniform, with a rank designation that Jake didn't recognize, and now he looked around in bewilderment. Jake guessed that he was in his early twenties. Seeing no one handy to voice his concerns to, yet unwilling to refuse the request of this important foreign visitor in the strange uniform, he slowly led Jake and Toad out the door of the hangar office and set a course across the packed dirt toward a distant building.

'What's your name?'

'Mikhail Babkin, sir.'

'You speak excellent English.' Jake Grafton mouthed the complimentary lie easily, without a twinge of conscience. English is different than all other languages, he reflected. Most Frenchmen listening to badly spoken French will pretend that they cannot understand or ignore the offender entirely. Yet any American meeting a goatherd in sub-Sahara Africa or on the windswept steppes of Mongolia who knows a word or two of pidgin English will compliment that worthy on his command of the language.

The barracks was of concrete construction, the usual Russian mix of too little cement, too much sand. The soldiers lived in one large, smelly, musty room with wooden bunks without springs. In the middle of the room stood a wood stove with an exhaust pipe leading to the roof. The bathrooms were communal, with no seats on the filthy toilets and one large shower with five drippy heads. There was no hot water heater. The smell . . .

'No hot water?'

'Hot? No.'

For an American naval officer who had spent half his adult life aboard ship where men were forced to live together in close quarters, this barracks was an appalling sight. The men who lived here must be constantly sick.

The mess hall was even worse. It was filthy, without refrigeration facilities or hot water. Jake asked how the

153

dishes were washed and was told that each man dips his plate into a large drum of cold water. He was shown the drums.

At the hospital he wandered the corridors and looked at the soldiers in the beds. They stared back at him. He peeked into one empty operating room with little equipment.

'Where do you sterilize the instruments?' They are boiled, he was told. There was a sink in the anteroom, the taps dripping. He turned them on full and let them run. Uh-oh.

'Hot water?'

'Hot? No. Want see X-ray machine?'

Stunned, Jake left the dimly lit building meekly when an officious person, presumably the administrator or doctor in charge, fired a volley of Russian at their escort and pointed at the door.

'The sewage treatment plant . . . I want to see the sewage treatment plant.'

The translator had great difficulty understanding the request. Toad got into the act. Finally Jake realized that there was no sewage treatment plant. Eventually it became clear that the sewage was piped straight to the local river. The translator led them to the bank where they could look down upon the discharge pipes.

And nearby was the garbage dump. Above ground. The wind brought a whiff of it to where Jake and Toad and the translator were standing. Some small creature darted toward the pile, birds wheeled above, clouds of flies . . .

For all these years, Jake thought savagely, we have been told about the vast capabilities of the Soviet military machine. And it's all a lie. The shiny missiles and pretty tanks are the whole show. The men who must operate these weapons are poorly housed, in ill health, live in unsanitary conditions and eat food a Western health inspector would send to a landfill. It's all a lie.

What was it General Brown had said? *The Soviet Union is*

a nation in total social and economic collapse. Nothing works. Nothing!

He was in a subdued mood when he boarded the plane for the return flight to Moscow. General Yakolev made some comment but he paid no attention.

Toad Tarkington had a drink in each hand, and he held out one to Jake Grafton, who looked but didn't reach.

'It's Scotch on the rocks,' Toad said. Seeing the look on Grafton's face, he added, 'I broke the seal on the bottle myself and poured it.'

Jake accepted the glass and tried to grin.

'I know,' Toad said.

Around them the Fourth of July reception at Spaso House, the United States' ambassador's residence, was in full swing. Jake Grafton estimated the crowd at four or five hundred people. They were everywhere, in every room, in every hall, bumping into one another, nibbling delicacies from the trays of passing waiters, and drinking champagne by the gallon. In one corner a combo played light music by American composers. The light from the chandeliers cast a warm, soft glow over everything.

Ambassador Owen Lancaster was mixing and mingling. Agatha Hempstead hovered discreetly, ready to whisper a name into the ambassador's ear yet far enough away that she was not a party to his conversations. It was a delicate balancing act but she seemed to pull it off without effort.

A few minutes ago Jake had seen Herb Tenney talking to the British Army officer, Colonel Jocko West. In rumpled civilian clothes that somehow didn't quite fit, West looked like the caterer's husband dragged away from the television to help with the snack tray.

On the other hand Colonel Reynaud, the French officer, looked like a millionaire standing in the casino at Monte Carlo waiting for the baccarat tables to open. He was impeccably turned out in full dress uniform with medals.

Just now he seemed to be discussing a wine with one of the embassy staffers – he was holding the glass up to the light, now sniffing it, paying close attention to what the State Department employee had to say.

Colonel Galvano, the Italian, was in a corner with a Russian diplomat. They were deep in conversation but weren't grinning.

'Jack Yocke here yet?' Jake asked Toad.

'Not yet, sir. Dalworth is waiting for him at the door.'

Toad reached out and flicked a piece of lint off the left shoulderboard of Jake's white dress uniform. With medals and sword. Toad was similarly decked out. He squared his shoulders and adjusted his sword.

'We look sorta spiffy, don't we, sir? What say you go stand over next to that South American general or policeman or postal inspector and let me get a photo for posterity.'

'Dalworth know what to do?'

'Yessir. I briefed him. Stick like glue all evening.'

'Even in the head.'

'All evening,' Toad repeated. Jake wanted Herb Tenney and his CIA colleagues to see Yocke and learn who he was, but he didn't want them moving in on him. So Spiro Dalworth had been carefully briefed.

'Okay,' the admiral said. Toad wandered off.

Dalworth seemed like a bright, capable junior officer. Just how the navy managed to keep attracting quality young people was one of the modern mysteries. It wasn't the pay or career opportunities, not in this era of red tape, budget cuts, politically correct witch hunts and reductions in force.

Jake was sipping his drink and musing about the hundreds of men like Dalworth he had known through the years when the ambassador rendezvoused on his right elbow. 'Good evening, Admiral.'

'Good evening, sir. Are all the Fourth of July whingdings like this?'

'Well, this is my first, and the staff said I was going to be surprised. I think for a lot of the Russians the invitations were a welcome relief from the ordinary. I don't think we'll have many leftovers, if you know what I mean.'

Jake knew. He had already glimpsed several Russians by the hors d'oeuvre table surreptitiously wrapping food items in napkins and pocketing them. He had pretended not to notice.

'Haven't had a chance to chat with you the last day or two. Everything going, okay?'

Jake Grafton nodded thoughtfully. 'So far.'

'Anything I or my staff can do . . . What do you think of General Yakolev?'

'I'm not sure yet.'

'He's as Russian as Rasputin. When you figure him out, I'd be interested to hear what you think.'

'Yessir. If I may ask, who are these four or five Americans that arrived this afternoon?'

'Eight of them, I think,' Lancaster said. 'They're investigators who are going to go through the files of the KGB, the Apparat . . .' Lancaster waved vaguely. 'When Yeltsin invited the Americans over to look at the files, we took him up on it. They're FBI, CIA, some military investigators, one each from the House and Senate Foreign Relations Committees.'

'Will there be anything left in the files to find?' Jake asked, musing aloud.

'Depends on how hard they look,' Lancaster said sourly. 'I doubt that shredder technology has arrived here yet but the Russians have matches and garbage dumps. Still, one never knows. A lot of these people thought they were in the vanguard of the march of history and wanted to preserve their place in it with written records. Then there's the bureaucratic imperative, what I believe you military types crudely refer to as CYA.'

CYA – Cover Your Ass. Jake Grafton knew about that!

'Is Yeltsin here yet?' he asked the ambassador.

'No. He didn't come last year either, which is a diplomatic faux pas that no European prime minister or president would ever commit. But this is Russia.'

Agatha Hempstead brushed against the ambassador's elbow, and he raised one eyebrow at Jake. Then he was on his way to the next group. Jake smiled at Agatha as she passed and got an expressionless nod in return.

He looked at his watch. What was the time in Washington? About ten in the morning. If it were not a holiday Callie would be at the university holding office hours. She had an eleven o'clock class this semester. Amy was on summer vacation, going swimming and flirting with the Jackson boy, who had long hair and pimples and a learner's permit. Since it was a holiday, they had probably gone to the beach. Jake wished he were there with them.

General Yakolev was here tonight with his boss, Marshal Dimitri Mikhailov. The head of the Russian military looked every inch a curmudgeon used to getting his own way. He was playing with a champagne glass and listening to an interpreter explain what the British ambassador was saying.

Apparently not that enthused with diplomacy, Yakolev wandered to the buffet table and helped himself. Soon Ambassador Lancaster had him cornered, but the Russian was eyeing Ms Goodbody Hempstead as he munched Swedish meatballs. Hempstead favored him with a demure smile. And there was Herb Tenney, handing them champagne from a tray. Herb Tenney, champagne waiter . . . Those CIA guys had all the social graces.

Jake looked at the drink in his hand. What if Tenney slipped his damned stuff into the embassy's water purification system? Spaso House's system? Moscow tap water was heavily polluted and the Americans ran it through a purifier before they made it available for human consumption. Perhaps the kitchen staff uses tap water to cook with. People brush their teeth with it. Ice cubes are made from it.

He had had what? – one or two sips?

Hell, Jake! Quit sweating it. This stuff is safe as holy water until Herb slips you the second half of the cocktail.

But it was no use. Even if he were dying of thirst he wouldn't touch it. He put the glass with its two ice cubes on the table behind him, on a magazine so it wouldn't leave a ring, and stuffed his hands into his pockets.

There was Yocke now, escorted by Spiro Dalworth. He came wandering over to where Grafton was parked and waggled his eyebrows in greeting. 'How's the booze?'

'Free.'

'Jack Daniel's and water, a double,' the reporter told Dalworth. 'And anything you want for yourself.'

After a glance at Grafton, Dalworth turned and headed for the bar.

'So what's new on the Soviet Square murders?'

'Damn if I know,' the reporter replied. 'They had me chasing human interest today. Tommy Townsend, our senior guy, took over the assassination since it's so hot, but the poor bastard is probably hanging out at the Kremlin waiting for a press release. The cops over here won't tell you diddley squat. I'm going to try to milk them tomorrow.'

'What human was of interest today?'

'Yakov Dynkin, a Jew that these enlightened democrats stuffed into a crack for selling a car for more than he paid for it. Funny thing, the warden of Butyrskaya Prison says he isn't there. No Jews are there, according to him. And I can't find Dynkin's wife.'

'You have her address?'

'Yeah. One of our people interviewed her a couple months ago. But the people at her apartment house say they never heard of her. Someone else has her apartment. No forwarding address. The people at the post office look at me like I'm a terrorist spy. The concept of giving a Russian's address to a foreigner doesn't compute.'

Jake Grafton rubbed his eyes.

Jack Yocke looked around at the expensive furniture and

original art on the walls and the cheerful people sipping champagne and Perrier. A sour look crossed his face. 'I wish to God I was back in Washington on the cop beat, back looking at street-corner crack dealers shot full of holes and interviewing their parents – even covering the District Building.'

'Well, look at all the material standing here tonight. Bring your notebook?'

'Tommy Townsend's here. Though maybe I can go down to the kitchen and get enough for a Style section piece on how they do the canapés with a Russian twist . . . Say, isn't that General Yakolev standing over there ogling that broad?'

'That's him.'

'I hear he wants to get rich. He signed a book contract the other day with a New York publisher to write a nonfiction treatise on the former Soviet armed forces. For a cool half a million. Dollars. That ought to keep the old fart in rubles until the middle of the next century.'

'Huh!'

'Yep. They've signed up Yakolev and about six other old Commies. One of them's in the KGB, one in the Politburo, a couple of Gorbachev's old lieutenants, a former ambassador to the United States and an ex-foreign minister. This time next year we'll know more about the goings on in the Kremlin than we ever knew about the Reagan White House.'

'Money talks.'

'It sings, but I don't have any to salt around. If I ever paid a nickel for an interview the *Post* would have my *cojónes*.'

'I didn't know reporters had ethics.'

'Ha ha ha and ha. I ask my little questions and smile brightly and these Russians look at me like I'm some sort of low-life slime.'

'Good luck.'

'Thanks.'

Dalworth returned with Yocke's drink, and with the lieutenant at his elbow, the reporter drifted off to mix and mingle.

Jake Grafton had just greeted the naval attaché, Captain Collins, when a face he recognized from *Time* magazine approached, Senator Wilmoth from Missouri. 'I thought I recognized you, Admiral. You're Grafton, aren't you?'

'Yessir. I don't believe I've had the pleasure of meeting you before, Senator.'

'You testified in front of one of my committees several years ago about the A-12 Avenger attack plane. We were never introduced. You were a captain then, I seem to recall.'

'Yessir.'

'Are you permanently assigned here to Moscow?' Wilmoth actually seemed interested, which surprised Jake a little.

'It's a temporary thing, Senator. I work for the DIA now.'

'Well, what's your slant on fledgling democracy?'

'Don't have one, I'm afraid, sir. Is this a working vacation for you or a business trip?'

'Business. I'm going to be digging through the KGB files too.' He looked at the crowd. 'I just wish there was some concrete thing America could do to help the Russian people. Our foreign aid is just a drop in the bucket and it's all we can afford.'

'I've got an idea,' Jake Grafton told him, then wished he hadn't. 'You'll think it's nuts,' he added tentatively.

Wilmoth eyed him speculatively. 'Well, I could always use a laugh.'

Oh, well. What's the harm? 'Buy Siberia. Russia could use the money and we could use the resources.'

Wilmoth looked slightly stunned. He was apparently trying to decide if Jake was serious when Tarkington appeared at the admiral's elbow.

'You have a telephone call from General Land, sir,' he

whispered. 'You can take it upstairs in the ambassador's office.'

As Tarkington retrieved Jake's attaché case from beside the credenza behind him, Jake said good-bye to the senator, who had decided to be amused at Jake's suggestion. The admiral followed Toad through the crowded room toward the stairs in the hall.

Three minutes later he picked up the telephone in the ambassador's office. The operator came on. 'Admiral Grafton? Please wait while I connect you with General Land.'

In seconds he heard Land's voice. After the usual greetings, Land asked, 'Got your gadget handy?'

'Yessir, but I don't have the code set.'

'You can do that afterward.'

'Just a moment, sir.'

The message took about twenty seconds to tape. The two men said their good-byes, then broke the connection.

Jake used a pocket calculator to compute the code, which he set into the device. Then he took it outside. A small garden in the back of the structure had some nice trees, some scraggly grass and flowers. No one was around. After a scan of the windows above him, he pushed the play button and held the device up to his ear.

Amazingly enough, the damned thing worked.

The second sentence was the essence of the message. 'Albert Sidney Brown was poisoned.' That thought was expanded and various chemical compounds were discussed, but there was no doubt. The corpse contained lethal amounts of a synthetic compound not found in nature.

When Jack Yocke got back to the Metropolitan Hotel that evening, he asked the desk clerk if he had any messages. Assured that neither his editor nor his mother had seen fit to invest in a call halfway around the world this evening, he strolled for the elevator.

He checked his watch. Only ten-thirty. What the hey, why not a cup of coffee before bed?

He detoured into the bar, nodded at Dimitri, the night barman, and ordered.

With his coffee in front of him, he sat contemplating the painting on the wall opposite the bar. It looked as if it were old and the varnish had darkened, but maybe it had been painted to look old. The wall of the Kremlin was on one side of the picture and St Basil's Cathedral on the other. But Red Square wasn't there — merely mud and a few shacks and a giant ditch along the Kremlin wall to make things tough for touring Mongols and visiting Poles. Just slightly left of center stood a nobleman listening to a peasant. Yocke looked at this painting at least three or four times a week and often wondered what the serf was saying.

His idle musings were derailed when he realized a woman had seated herself at the bar with only one stool between them. She greeted the barman pleasantly and ordered coffee in American English.

'A fellow Yank, as I live and breathe. What brings you to Sodom on the Moskva?'

She turned her head toward him and grinned. She had dark brown eyes, almost black, set wide apart. Dark brown hair tumbled to her shoulders. Her chin was the perfect size, her lips just right. With the exception of one prostitute who visited the hotel occasionally, she was the prettiest woman Yocke had yet seen in Russia, which was saying something since Russia had its fair share of beautiful women. Best of all, she was about his age and wasn't wearing a wedding ring. Or any ring.

'I live in Moscow,' she told him.

'Is that a Boston accent?'

'Actually Vermont, but four years at Brandeis ruined me, I'm afraid.'

'Name's Jake Yocke.'

'Shirley Ross.'

163

She wasn't cover girl *Cosmo* gorgeous, Yocke concluded, but she had perfect bones: the forehead, the cheekbones, the chin. Her face was a feast for the eyes.

She had been here over a year, she told Yocke, first as an interpreter for an American telecommunications company, then as a journalist for an English-language monthly magazine published here.

'Small world. I scribble for a living too. *Washington Post*.'

'The *Post*?'

'The one and only.'

'Do you know Sally Quinn?' Sally was a *Post* reporter, columnist and all-around original character. She had even written a novel or two.

'Uh-huh.'

Shirley Ross grinned.

Twenty minutes later they were sitting in the corner sipping Bailey's. 'So how is this borsch batch going to come out?' Yocke asked her.

'You want a prediction?'

He nodded.

'Yeltsin, democracy and where to place your bets for the coming civil war.'

Yocke tasted his drink again. She was working on her second but he was still nursing his first. After the whiskey at the embassy and the coffee here the liqueur was too sweet. And he was feeling the alcohol. This woman in front of him was also stimulating his hormones.

Her discussion of the political situation struck Jack Yocke as enlightened and well informed. She got her tongue around the names of these Russian politicians without a single slip. Jack Yocke felt slightly deflated. Shirley Ross knew more about Russian politics than he ever hoped to know. When she fell silent he told her that.

She grinned again. 'Not really. It's my job. You'll pick it up. Wow your friends back home when they get tired of talking about TV shows and movies. People will avoid you at cocktail parties.' She mugged with a suspicious glance out of the corner of her eyes, then joined him in laughter.

He looked into those deep brown eyes and felt completely at ease. American women are the very best. 'This Soviet Square killing – what are people saying about that?'

Her eyes flicked around the room and came to rest on him. 'Do you want Sunday op-ed bullshit or do you want the truth?'

Dimitri was loading the German-made dishwasher and making the usual noises. Jack and the woman were the only people in the bar. 'Without surrendering my right to later argue that op-ed pieces are an attempt to write the truth, I choose the second alternative. What truth do you know?'

She toyed with her swizzle stick while he studied her face. At last the eyes came up to meet his. 'The truth will never come out.'

'Perhaps,' he said, and relaxed. He looked at his watch. Tomorrow was going to be a long day hunting for cops willing to talk while he listened to Gregor's tales of Brooklyn. He took a deep breath, exhaled and scooted his chair back. 'Do you come here often, Shirley?'

'The KGB is setting up Yeltsin.'

'How do you know that?'

'I can't tell you.'

Yocke squared off to face her. 'What can you tell me?'

'Nothing that you can print.' She lay down the swizzle stick and hunted in her purse. She extracted a pack of Marlboros and a pack of matches. After she lit one she examined Yocke's face through the smoke.

'You came here tonight to meet me, didn't you?'

Her eyes stayed on his face. She smoked the cigarette in silence. The dishwasher behind the bar lit off with a rumble.

'Anything you tell me I have to confirm. Someone else must confirm every fact or I can't print it.'

'If you ever tell anyone where you got this or who I am you will ruin me.'

'We never reveal sources who request anonymity.'

'This is Russia.'

She didn't know anything. Perhaps she thought she knew something, but what the hell could it be? She's an American, for Chrissake!

'Three KGB officers . . .' She stubbed out the cigarette and looked at Dimitri, who was working on receipts on an IBM computer terminal. Her eyes came back to Yocke.

'Three KGB officers . . .' He had to lean forward across the table to hear her voice above the noise of the dish-washer.

She swallowed and fumbled for another cigarette.

'Three KGB officers went to police headquarters a half hour before the assassination. They ordered the police away from Soviet Square.'

'How do you know this?'

A whisper: 'The order was transmitted over the radio. The police in the square heard it on their little radios. You've seen those little radios they wear, haven't you?'

'I've seen them.' The police here were wired up just like the cops in Washington and Detroit.

'Kolokoltsev was a pawn sacrifice. It's the king they want.'

'Who's they?' To his chagrin, Yocke's voice came out a whisper. He raised it a notch and repeated the question. 'Who's they?'

She just shook her head.

'I need some names.'

She leaned back and sucked fiercely on the cigarette. Her eyes went to Dimitri and stayed there.

'He can't hear us.'

'He's KGB. All these hard-currency hotel people are.'

'He can't hear us over that dishwasher,' Yocke insisted. 'You're going to have to point me in the right direction. Give me a name. One name. Any of them. Any one of them.'

She stabbed the cigarette out in the ashtray and drained her drink.

'I have to have someplace to start looking, Shirley, or your trip down here was a waste of time. You must know how goddamn tough it is to get Russians to open up to an American reporter. It's like asking a dope dealer if he's got a load coming in anytime soon.'

Her lips twisted into an attempt at a grin as she stood up. Now the lips straightened. Gripping her purse tightly she leaned across the table and whispered, 'Nikolai Demodov.'

'Was he one of the three?'

But she was walking out. She went through the door and turned left and was gone.

Up in his room Jack Yocke wrote the name on his computer screen and sat staring at it. Nikolai Demodov.

Well, it was a pretty story. No getting around that. A pretty story. He didn't know enough to even guess how much truth there might be to the tale, if any, but his instinct told him some truth was there. You develop that instinct in this business after you have listened to a lot of stories. Maybe it's their eyes, the body language.

He tapped aimlessly on the keyboard for a few moments, then turned the computer off.

He brushed his teeth and washed his face and hands and stared at his reflection in the mirror over the sink while he thought about Shirley Ross and the three KGB agents.

If only he could have gotten more out of her. How should he have handled it? She must have known all three of the names. At the minimum she knew how the hell Nikolai Demodov fits in. Where had he lost her? And where did she get her information?

Aaagh! To be tantalized so and have the door slammed in your face! Infuriating . . .

Most people are poor liars. Oh, every now and then you meet a good one, but most people have not had the practice it takes to tell a lie properly. Cops can smell a lie. So can some lawyers and preachers. And all good reporters. Even if you can't put your finger on why it plays right, you know truth when you find it.

Just now Jack Yocke decided he had seen some of it. And the glimpse excited him.

CHAPTER TEN

Sergi Pavlenko was dozing in the guard shack when the noise of a helicopter brought him awake. He was nineteen years old, a conscript from a collective farm, and he was not used to helicopters. He came immediately awake and went outside where he could see better.

It was one in the morning, the middle of the summer night, which was still short here three hundred miles southeast of Moscow at the Serdobsk Nuclear Power Plant.

The lights of the helicopter were curious, a red, a white and a light that flashed and made the machine look like some unearthly thing, some vision from a vodka-drenched nightmare. When it became obvious that the machine was going to land here, Sergi Pavlenko straightened his uniform tunic and resettled his hat on his head at the correct angle. He eased the strap that held his rifle into the correct position and stood erect with his heels together, as a proper soldier should.

Now the helicopter's landing light came on, a spotlight that shone downward and slightly ahead. Pavlenko started. He had never before seen a helicopter flying at night and the landing light was unexpected.

As the light moved toward him, the thought suddenly occurred to him that he might be in the place where the descending machine was going to alight. Galvanized, he scurried back toward the guardhouse at the entrance to the power plant.

Safe in his refuge, he looked across the enclosure at the

guard kiosk at the main gate, where he could just see his friend Leonid under the light pointing with one hand and covering his mouth with the other. Leonid would laugh and tease him; he must have looked like a frightened rabbit running from the helicopter.

And now it was there in front of him, roaring like an enraged bear and stirring up a hurricane as it settled onto the grass.

The engines died immediately. The pilot obviously had no fuel to waste.

Five men climbed out. One of them, wearing a dark suit and dark tie, came toward him. Sergi straightened to attention.

'Where is the manager?'

'I don't know. No one said you were coming.'

'I'm accustomed to being met by the manager of the facility.'

'The telephone from the outside is out of order. It has not worked all night.'

'Well, tell the manager I am here.'

Sergi was at a loss for words. *Who* was here? Should he ask for identification? The panic must have shown on his face, for the man's expression softened and he growled, 'Just get him out here.'

There was a telephone in his guardshack, a little wooden building that looked as if it had been added as an afterthought right by the concrete wall of the reactor building. It was a rotary dial instrument. Sergi wiped his hands on his trousers before he picked up the handset and checked the list of telephone numbers taped to the wall. The list was so dirty as to be almost unreadable. Control room, number 32. That was the only place in the complex where there would be people this time of night.

The first time Sergi dialed nothing happened. No ringing in the earpiece. The equipment was old and the electrical switches were worn out, like every other telephone system in the former Soviet empire. Still, the only telephone on Sergi's collective farm had belonged to the manager, an important person, and Sergi had never used it. Having a telephone waiting for him to pick up to call someone – just within the facility, this instrument could not be used to call elsewhere – made Sergi proud. To complain about the quirks of the instrument was an impulse that had never crossed his mind.

Now he used his thumb on the hook to break the circuit, then lifted it and listened for the dial tone. There it was. He carefully dialed the number again. This time he heard the ringing. As he waited he turned and looked at the helicopter and the big red star on the fuselage. One of the passengers was over at the kiosk at the main gate talking to Leonid: Sergi could see them standing together under the light.

A man's voice answered the telephone.

'This is the main door guard,' Sergi Pavlenko said loudly into the mouthpiece. 'A helicopter has arrived. An important person wishes to see the manager.'

'The manager is home in bed. I'm the watch officer.'

'Yes, yes. He is waiting here to talk to someone in authority. It is a big helicopter with many rotor blades.' This fact impressed Sergi; it should impress the man inside too.

Apparently it did. 'I'll be right out,' the voice told him.

Sergi Pavlenko hung up the telephone and turned to report to the man from the helicopter. As he did so the man used a silenced pistol to shoot him once in the head, killing him instantly.

The five men worked fast. The main door had a lock that worked only from the inside. When the watch officer opened it they herded Leonid from the main gate, the watch officer and everyone in the building into an empty office and gunned them down with silenced submachine guns. They didn't bother to pick up the empty brass cartridge cases strewn about.

171

They blocked the front door open with a piece of wood and carried in bags from the helicopter.

The reactor was operating at 50 percent power. The man who had shot Sergi examined the control panel carefully, then led the way through the lead-lined door that led to the reactor space.

A nuclear reactor is, when explained to schoolchildren, a very simple piece of machinery – a large tea kettle is the common analogy. True, the first reactor, Enrico Fermi's pile under the University of Chicago's football stadium, was indeed simple. But there was nothing simple about the Serdobsk reactor, a liquid-metal-cooled fast breeder. The core was made up of five tons of metallic oxides of uranium-235, plutonium-239, and uranium-238, the breeding material that would be converted into plutonium during the course of the reaction. This material was fashioned into twelve thousand long pins, each less than six millimeters in diameter and arranged with extraordinary precision inside a small core, a hexagonal container only three feet across each face.

The core sat in a cylindrical stainless-steel pot filled with molten, liquid sodium that was cycled through the core by three pumps. Unavoidably the sodium flowing through the core absorbed some neutrons and was converted into sodium-24, a highly radioactive gamma ray emitter, so the radioactive sodium was run through an exchanger where it gave up some of its heat to the secondary cooling system, also liquid sodium. The unpressurized stainless-steel vat that contained the core and the primary and secondary cooling systems was forty feet high and forty feet in diameter. Between the surface of the liquid sodium and the top of the vat was a cloud of argon, an inert gas. Lead shielding surrounded the entire vat. Surrounding the lead was a concrete vault with walls about three feet thick.

Pipes brought the secondary sodium out of the vat near

the top and took it to a second heat exchanger, where it was used to boil water for steam to turn turbines, then returned it to the vat. The pipe holes in the vat and the lead and concrete shields were all above the level of the liquid sodium.

The nuclear reaction itself was controlled by dozens of graphite rods that absorbed radiation. These rods were withdrawn from the core to start the reaction and pushed into it to kill it.

The men from the helicopter began with the rods. Standing on top of the concrete vault, they planted a series of small explosive charges designed to shatter the rod mechanisms before they had a chance to slide down into the core. This job took about half an hour.

Still on top of the concrete biological shield, they used tape measures and chalk while the man in charge consulted a sheet of paper in his hand. When the chalk marks were precisely where he wanted them, he personally began placing six shaped charges that would vent their explosive force down into the vat. While he was at it several of the men climbed up the ladder and wandered out into the hallway for a smoke.

One of them came running back. 'Colonel, the helicopter is starting!'

'What?'

'Listen.'

Yes, he could faintly hear the whine as the engines spooled up. He stumbled and almost fell running for the ladder. He hurried up and raced along the catwalk toward the control room. He arrived outside just in time to see the helicopter transition into forward flight and move away into the darkness.

Two of the men came out behind him and one aimed his submachine gun at the departing machine.

'Nyet,' the colonel cried. 'That won't do any good.' The fool! If he successfully shot down the helicopter the noise of

173

the crash would bring everyone in the army camp over here. And it would be damned hard to fly out of here in a crashed helicopter.

The colonel stood listening to the noise of the machine as it faded. When all he could hear were the night noises of frogs and insects, he still stood undecided. He had expected problems, but not this – to be abandoned by the helicopter pilot! Betrayed!

The pilot was a Ukrainian. He should have demanded a Russian pilot. The colonel choked back his rage and frustration and wondered what to do. He had, he well knew, miserably few options.

'What do we do now, Colonel?' one of the men asked.

The query decided him.

'Let's set the charges.' He was surprised at his own voice. It sounded calm, in control, which wasn't the way he felt at all. Usually when he was enraged his voice became a hoarse croak.

'If we hadn't cut the telephone lines we could call for another helicopter,' one of the men said disgustedly. 'We certainly can't blow this damn thing up unless we have transport out of here.'

'Back inside,' the colonel said. 'Let's finish the job while I think.'

They were reluctant but the habit of obedience was strong. The colonel followed them back into the building.

It took forty-five minutes to finish setting the charges atop the biological shield. Forty-five minutes of sweating an impossible situation.

He should have had a backup chopper, should have brought a two-way radio. But there was no time. *'No! Do it now! Do it tonight!'* the general had said.

All the careful planning, all the preparations that didn't get done, all the backups that weren't quite ready. That was the trouble with the Soviet system – the remorseless pressure to make 'it' happen always forced shortcuts, compromises in quality and safety. It was infuriating when you saw the disasters everywhere you looked but goddamn catastrophic when it was your life on the line. How easy it was for a bureaucrat or general to shout 'Now!'

He forced himself to work slowly, with meticulous care, as he set the shaped charges. There would be no second chance. This had to be done right the first time, which, he told himself furiously, would be the only recorded instance of the accomplishment of that feat in Russia since the czar impregnated his bride on their wedding night.

He was perspiring heavily when he finished. He stood back and used a rag to wipe his face and hands. 'Insert the detonators.'

'Colonel, how are we going to get away from here?'

'I said insert the detonators. Wire them up but don't arm the triggering device. I'll go find us some transport. Give me a submachine gun.'

One of the men passed his weapon over.

'Get busy.'

The colonel slung the weapon over his shoulder and climbed the ladder.

When he left the cavernous room two of the men were inserting detonators and wiring them to the firing device as the other two watched.

The army camp was three kilometers up the road. The colonel cooled off as he walked in the darkness. He was unwilling to use the flashlight, so he stumbled occasionally over uneven places in the road. Still he walked quickly. Only two hours until dawn.

He stopped when he was still fifty meters from the circle of light above the gate and looked the camp over. It was surrounded by a sagging, rusted wire fence. A guard kiosk stood by the open gate. No doubt a sentry was there, the only man awake in the camp. He hoped that no one else was awake.

There, by that building in the back, wasn't that a truck? Yes. It had grass growing around it to the top of its wheels. Perhaps there was a car or another truck in the garage.

The colonel moved toward the sentry's kiosk, staying in the shadows, making as little noise as possible. He kept the submachine gun over his shoulder but held the pistol with the silencer in his right hand.

He was still fifteen feet from the kiosk, just coming into the light circle, when the sentry inside the unpainted wooden shack saw him and jerked in surprise.

The colonel pointed the pistol at the soldier and said, as calmly as he could and just loud enough to be heard, 'Don't move. Just stay exactly as you are and you won't get hurt.'

The man froze. He was young, in his late teens.

'Now very carefully, step outside.'

The soldier complied. He was trembling.

'Where is the other sentry?'

The soldier merely shook his head.

The colonel pointed his weapon and repeated the question.

'I'm the only one, sir.'

'If you are lying you will be the first to die. Do you understand?'

'Yes, sir.'

'Let's go look at the truck.' The colonel snapped on his flashlight and used it to point the way. He followed the soldier, who had now decided to raise his hands a little.

The truck was a rotting hulk. The tires were flat, the glass was broken from several windows, weeds peeked through the radiator grill.

'Where is the other truck?' he demanded, his voice a forced whisper.

'In the garage.'

'Open it, quietly. If anyone wakes up . . .'

The truck in the garage was fairly new, painted olive drab and had air in all the tires. Keeping the weapon pointed at the soldier, the colonel eased the driver's door open and shone the flashlight on the instrument panel. No ignition key was required. Merely switch on the electrical

176

system and push the starter button. The colonel reached in and flipped the electrical switch. The proper lights came on. He examined the fuel gauge. The needle rested on the left side. Empty! The colonel flipped the switch off.

'Where's the gasoline?'

'We haven't had any gas for a month.' The young soldier's hands were down and his voice unnaturally loud.

The colonel lowered the barrel of the pistol and fired a round into the dirt at the soldier's feet. The report was merely a soft pop. 'You'd better find some.'

'Over there.' The gesture was quick, jerky.

There were some cans against the wall, beside a motorcycle. The colonel hefted one. Half full. The others were empty – all eight.

'This motorcycle – does it work?'

'Oh yes. The captain rides it every day over to the reactor. And into town on Sundays. He—'

'Shut up!'

The colonel quickly checked every other fuel can in the garage. All empty. He examined the controls on the motorcycle, the tires, then opened the cap on the fuel tank. At least half full. He made the trembling soldier fill the tank from the only can containing fuel.

'Okay, push it out of here and down to the kiosk at the gate.'

Under the light at the gate the colonel examined the machine. He turned the petcock and let gasoline flow to the carburetor, twisted the throttle, checked the chain and the clutch.

The only way to see if it would run would be to start it. But not here.

'Start pushing.' He gestured to the northwest, toward the reactor facility. The soldier did as he was told.

It was hard work pushing the motorcycle along the dirt road in the darkness. The machine fell once and the soldier went on top of it. The colonel waited while he righted the thing and got it going again.

When they had gone about half a kilometer the colonel told the soldier to stop and put down the kickstand. Then he shined the flashlight into the soldier's eyes and shot him while he stood blinking helplessly.

The man went down without a sound. The colonel dragged the corpse off the road into some weeds.

With his gun in one pocket and the flashlight in another, he climbed aboard the motorcycle and eased the kick starter down until he felt compression. Then he raised himself up and gave a mighty kick.

No.

Again.

Nothing.

Again.

The fourth time the machine chugged once, but he fed it too much gas and it died.

This time he got all of his body weight into the downstroke of his leg and the machine gurgled into life. As he sat astride the saddle and waited for the engine to warm, the colonel used the flashlight to check his wristwatch. Almost an hour gone. One hour of darkness left.

Carefully he disengaged the clutch, popped the transmission into gear, and eased the clutch out. The engine almost died but he caught it with the throttle and let the clutch engage. The sound the engine made was well-muffled since the machine was fairly new.

The colonel brought it to a stop a hundred meters short of the gate to the reactor facility. He walked from there.

Two of his men were waiting by the door.

'We thought we heard an engine a few moments ago,' one told him.

'You did. A car. I parked down the road in case someone comes by. Are the detonators set?'

'Yes, sir. All you need to do is set the timer. Do you want us to go on down and sit in the car until you come?'

'Okay. I need maybe ten minutes. I'll send the others along.'

When these two were about twenty-five feet away with their backs to him, he used the silenced submachine gun.

It wasn't fair, but there it was. He had transport for one. The reactor had to be destroyed. After he had shot them he walked over to where they lay and put a bullet into each man's skull.

One of his men was in the control room. 'I've got a car parked down the road out of the light,' he said. 'Go sit in it until I get the device armed.'

'How much time are you going to give us?'

'What's the maximum possible time?'

'One hour.'

'Then that's what we have.'

'That would be a lot if we had a helicopter,' the man objected reasonably, 'but we don't. What if we have a flat tire or this car breaks down?'

The colonel wasn't in the mood. 'We take our chances. Where's Vasily?'

'In the reactor space checking the wires and detonators one more time.'

'Go wait in the car.'

Just before the man reached the door the colonel took the submachine gun off his shoulder and shot him. As he was lowering the weapon the door to the reactor clicked shut.

He heard a noise, running feet. Damn! Vasily.

The colonel popped the magazine from the weapon and replaced it with a full one. After he had checked to ensure it was seated properly, he opened the heavy, lead-lined door to the reactor space and slipped in.

A bullet smacked into the wall.

What else can go wrong? Sweat broke out on his face. A more dangerous place for a gunfight would be hard to imagine. One stray bullet could sever a critical wire or punch a hole in a pipe carrying molten sodium or water or steam or . . .

179

He was inside against the wall, the door on his right side. Another bullet whapped against the wall.

The silenced pistol was in his left hand, the submachine gun in his right. Where was—

A bullet caught him in the hip and half turned him around. He tossed the submachine gun and fell heavily on his face, his right hand palm up at an odd angle.

The trick was old and hoary and he was a fool to try it. If he had had a moment to think he wouldn't have. If Vasily kept his wits about him or used a smidgen of sense . . . But he didn't. He didn't even shoot the colonel a second time, a mistake the colonel certainly wouldn't have made.

The colonel lay like a sack of very old potatoes. He felt the catwalk vibrate from Vasily's footsteps and he even got a glimpse of one foot. Still he lay absolutely motionless, muscles slack, scarcely breathing, his left hip on fire as the numbing shock of the bullet wore off. When he heard the door begin to open beside him he moved – rolled and instantly triggered the pistol into Vasily's foot, then his leg, then as the man fell, into his body. He fired again and again as fast as the pistol would work. When it was empty he stopped shooting.

Vasily sighed once as the spent cartridges tinkled on the concrete far below. He didn't inhale again.

The colonel got slowly to his feet and examined the location of the bullet hole in his clothing. Blood was oozing out. The catwalk where he had lain was smeared with it.

He put his weight on the injured hip. Well, the bone wasn't broken, although the wound hurt like hell. He looked at Vasily to ensure he was dead, then popped the empty clip from the automatic and inserted a full one from his jacket pocket. When that was done he retrieved the submachine gun. He hung it over his shoulder on its strap.

He made his way along the catwalk and descended the ladder onto the top of the reactor shield.

Thank God the charges were there, still properly

installed and wired up. He got out his dirty handkerchief and wiped his face and hands as he examined the timer mechanism.

One lousy hour.

He pushed the test button on the battery, verified that the green light came on, then released the button.

One stinking, tiny, miserable little hour.

For it came to him then that his luck had gone very bad. Everything had gone wrong. All of his experiences in life had taught him that luck runs in cycles – sometimes good things happen for a while, then bad. And he was deeply into the bad just now. Was this hole in his hip the last of the bad things, or only the next to last?

He was not a religious man. Nothing in his forty-four years of life had even suggested possible resources other than his own skill, courage and endurance. Yet just now as he stared at the detonator he sensed that his own resources probably weren't going to be enough.

He twisted the knob that turned the needle on the clock face. He turned it to the maximum reading, sixty minutes. He consulted his watch.

Now he looked about, again tested his weight on his injured hip, savored the sharp edge of the pain, wiped his hands one more time.

This was necessary. They would not have sent him if it weren't.

Oh, hell. Everyone has to die sooner or later and he wasn't afraid of it. Dying is the easy part, like going to sleep. Getting to that moment can be a real bitch, though.

He looked again at the sweep second hand on his watch. When it swung by the straight-up position he pushed the button to start the timer on the detonator. Exactly one hour from now, at 5:07 A.M. If this clock keeps good time.

He watched it tick for a few seconds, then crossed to the ladder and went up it, favoring his bad hip only a little.

In the control room the colonel scanned the dozens of gauges and dials. With a sure hand he reached for the master control and began inching the rods out of the core while he kept a careful eye on the temperature gauges. Another five minutes passed before he was satisfied with the new stabilized readings. The reactor was now at almost 80 percent power.

When he left the building he removed the wooden doorjamb and let the outside door close and lock.

Fifty-three minutes.

He limped past the bodies sprawled near the gate and turned right on the road. The breeze cooled the sweat on his face but he didn't notice as he hurried along.

He got on the motorcycle and checked that the fuel was on. When he tried to shift his weight to his left hip and push up to get some leverage for the kick start lever the pain was so bad he almost fell over.

Gritting his teeth, he tried again. This time he managed to kick the bike through but it didn't start.

Again with no luck.

The third time it fired and he gave it just enough gas to keep the engine going. He almost collapsed onto the seat. His leg was wet with blood. How long before he passed out? He fumbled for the headlight switch. There. But the headlight didn't come on.

He hadn't checked the headlight. Burned out, probably.

Somehow he got the bike into motion.

This road led off to the northwest, he remembered, upwind, so he stayed on it. When he went by the gate to the reactor facility he got a fleeting glimpse of his watch from the light on the pole. Forty-one minutes to go.

Riding a motorcycle on a rutted dirt road on a dark night takes intense concentration and high physical effort. The colonel found that even at a slow speed he was always on the verge of losing control. Still, with every minute he gained confidence. When his eyes were fully adjusted to the darkness he could see the road easily enough, so he eased on more throttle and shifted to a higher gear. This meant he was going faster when he fell. The nose wheel hit a rut, the handlebars twisted violently and he was instantly flying through air.

The impact with the ground stunned him.

When his wits returned he levered himself upright and groped for the motorcycle. He *had* to put some miles between himself and that reactor. He tried to see the hands on the watch but it was impossible. He felt for the flashlight. It didn't work. Broken by the fall.

The submachine gun on his shoulder was gouging him, so he took it off and threw it away into the darkness.

Getting the bike upright took all his strength.

Kick. No start. Kick again.

He lost count of the number of times he tried to start the motorcycle.

How long had it been? How much blood had he lost?

Flooded. He had probably flooded the damn thing.

He sat wearily on the bike gathering his strength.

Are you beaten?

No!

Throttle off. Kick, a real high arch off the bad hip so all his weight would come down on the kick lever under his right foot.

The engine caught. Slowly he twisted the throttle and brought the engine up to a fast idle. Now the shift lever.

He kept the bike at a slow pace, maybe four or five miles per hour. The wind in his face was the only bright spot. If he could just get a little distance and get behind something solid, some earth perhaps, he could survive the blast. The wind would carry the radioactivity in the other direction.

He was climbing a hill. He could tell by the amount of throttle necessary. And the sky was getting lighter to the northeast. He realized then that he could see the road and the ruts better, so he eased on more throttle.

How much time?

Couldn't be much. If he could just get over the hill. There on the other side, with the hill between him and the reactor, there he would be safe.

Every bounce, every jolt was another second past.

How many more did he have? He took his left hand from the handlebar and tried to see the watch. The bike swerved dangerously and he grabbed the handlebar again.

How far had he come? Was he far enough . . . ?

The shock wave almost knocked him off the motorcycle. Then intense heat. He felt intense heat on his neck, on the back of his head, even through his jacket. And he wasn't under cover, wasn't . . .

Behind him a cloud of dirt and debris blown aloft by the explosion formed in the darkness above the reactor. In seconds it began to glow. The radiation intensified. The sensation of furnace heat was the last thing the colonel felt as a virulently radioactive ball of fire rose from the melted remnants of the steel, lead and concrete shielding.

In seconds he was dying even as the motorcycle continued away from the blast, dying like the sleeping soldiers at the army base on the other side of the reactor, dying like every other mammal within four miles of the now-glowing nuclear plant. Four miles, that was how far the colonel had traveled. The motorcycle continued upright with his dying weight for a few seconds, then the front wheel kicked against a rut, and the machine and the corpse upon it skidded to a stop in the road.

The engine of the motorcycle choked to a stop as a mushroom cloud formed over the reactor and the wind on the ground strengthened markedly as air rushed toward the intense heat source.

People and animals a few miles farther away from the reactor had several minutes of life left, amounts varying depending on the amount of material shielding them from the runaway nuclear inferno. By the time the sun came up in the northeast only a few insects were still alive within seven miles of the plant. Other people were also dying as a cloud of ferociously intense radioactivity drifted southeast on the prevailing wind.

CHAPTER ELEVEN

As Jack Yocke dressed the following morning his mood was gloomy. The euphoria he felt last night had completely evaporated. He had managed only two hours' sleep and spent the rest of the night tossing and turning.

At about four in the morning the implications of being sought out by Shirley Ross finally sank in. Why Jack Yocke? He wasn't a famous personage, not a known face. And how had she known to find him at the Metropolitan? Now the significance of her evasion of that question grew. Maybe this was a setup.

He was in way over his head, chasing an impossible story. He didn't speak the language, he didn't have an ongoing professional relationship with a single, solitary soul in this goddamn hopeless Slavic morass. He was a foreigner in a country deeply suspicious of all foreigners. He didn't know the politics in a capital where politics was the staff of life, played for blood and money. Nobody would talk to him. Nobody would trust him to tell the truth. Nobody.

Except Jake Grafton, and he didn't count. He wouldn't know beans about the Soviet Square killings. Even if he did and were willing to share it, Yocke couldn't print it. He needed something he could publish.

Gregor was standing beside his battered tan Lada when Yocke came out of the hotel. The sixty-degree morning air was heavy with pollution and the sky looked like rain. The best the reporter could manage in reply to Gregor's cheerful hello was a nod. He sagged onto the passenger's seat and stared morosely though the windshield at a beggar woman arranging herself for a day on the sidewalk while Gregor got himself situated behind the wheel and coaxed the car to life.

'Sleep well?' Gregor asked.

'Not really.'

'Where would you like to go this morning?'

Yocke sighed and ran his fingers through his hair. 'Police headquarters.' No, on second thought, the district attorney was the place to start. What did they call the prosecutor over here? 'Make it the public prosecutor's office.'

'No interview with Yeltsin? Well, maybe tomorrow.'

'Boris will have to wait. Tomorrow we do Gorby's proctologist.'

'Procto . . . ?'

'Can the corn and drive.'

The foyer was crowded with reporters. Yocke's heart sank. He looked around for Tommy Townsend, the *Post*'s senior correspondent, and didn't see him. At least a dozen people from the international press crowded around the desk man, who was grunting surly Russian and scowling. A television team had lights on and a camera going. What a way to start a day!

Gregor elbowed his way to the desk, and in two minutes came back with the word. A press conference in fifteen minutes. Jack Yocke stared at the TV reporter putting the final touches on his hair and nodded. If Townsend showed up, Jack was going to have to make a critical decision since the Soviet Square Massacre was now Tommy's story. Should he share the Shirley Ross tip with Tommy?

Thank heavens he didn't have to. Tommy never showed, even though the press conference started late, as do most things in Russia. It went about as Yocke expected. In the glare of the television lights the prosecutor's spokesman made a statement about the ongoing investigation – no leads yet on the identities or whereabouts of the killers that could be announced publicly, no arrests imminent, the

Russians had asked for Interpol assistance. The questions from the floor were asked in a respectful tone, merely for clarification of the spokesman's points. No one asked about anything he had not mentioned. Yocke edged toward the door behind the podium and pulled Gregor along.

When the farce was over he buttonholed the spokesman on his way out, a husky man who tried to breeze by.

'I need to speak with the prosecutor for one minute.'

Through Gregor came the answer: 'He is busy. He cannot see you.'

'The *Washington Post* has a story about why the police left the square that the prosecutor needs to confirm or deny.'

The spokesman eyed him suspiciously. 'Wait,' was his answer.

Yocke waited. The other reporters drifted out, the television crew packed up lights and extension cords and cameras and departed, Gregor lit a cigarette and lounged against the podium. Yocke looked at his watch.

Fifteen minutes had passed when he looked again. Gregor was on his third cigarette.

The prosecutor bustled into the room. '*Washington Post?*'

'Yes.'

'What is your story?'

Yocke took a deep breath and stared the man straight in the eye. He had but two lousy bullets to fight the war with and here goes shot number one: 'The police were pulled out of Soviet Square by a transmission over the police radio system.' He paused for Gregor to translate.

The prosecutor's eyebrows knitted, but that was his sole reaction.

Yocke continued: 'The police left because three KGB agents appeared in police headquarters and demanded that the police be removed from the square.'

Now the prosecutor's eyes widened in surprise. He spewed Russian. 'Where do you get this story? We announce nothing. Who talk to you?'

Yocke had counted on the man being a novice at dealing with Western reporters. He was new at the game, all right. Yocke decided to try a shot in the dark.

'Why have you relieved the police chief from his duties?'

The attorney's face darkened a shade. He chewed on the back of his lower lip while his eyes scanned Yocke's face. The reporter tried to remain deadpan, but it was difficult. 'We are investigating,' the prosecutor finally said.

Jack Yocke bit his own lip to keep from smiling. 'Will he be prosecuted?'

The man shrugged. 'Maybe.'

'For obeying the KGB?'

'Who has talked to you? No one should talk during an investigation.'

'Was the police chief in conspiracy with the killers?'

'Certainly not.'

'But he should not have obeyed the KGB?'

The prosecutor took a deep breath and adjusted the jacket on his shoulders. He frowned. 'This is a complex matter with many facets. We want no stories written just now. Surely you can understand that an accusation not later supported by facts would do great damage. To people's rights. To human rights. To right to a fair trial. Surely you see that, *Washington Post*.'

Jack Yocke couldn't believe his luck. He had expected stony denials and the prosecutor had denied nothing. And he had implicitly confirmed that the police chief had obeyed the orders of KGB officers, technically now Ministry of Security officers. The reporter decided to fire his last bullet and pray for a hit.

'Was Nikolai Demodov one of the KGB officers?'

The reaction was an explosive '*Nyet*.' Gregor translated the rest of it. 'That's a lie. Who told you this lie?'

'It was just a rumor. But you deny it?'

'Absolutely. It's a lie.'

'Who is Nikolai Demodov?'

189

But the prosecutor was leaving. He turned his back and stomped away.

Jack Yocke whipped out his steno pad and furiously began taking notes.

In the car he asked Gregor, 'Who is Nikolai Demodov?'

'Big man in KGB. Deputy to General Shmarov.'

'And who is Shmarov?'

'Number two man, I think. Little is printed about top Ministry of Security officers. They are Old Guard, old Communists loyal to the past. No-goodniks, most of them.'

'Shmarov is a no-goodnik? That means he's anti-Yeltsin, antidemocratic, doesn't it?'

The Lada squealed loudly as Gregor braked to a stop at a red traffic light. He sat hunched over the wheel staring at the red light on the pole. 'I want more money,' he said with finality. 'You told me you wished to write stories about life in Russia. Human being interest. You must pay me more.'

Jack Yocke rolled down the passenger window and dragged a half-bushel of pollution down into his lungs.

'You have no idea what it means to be Russian,' Gregor remarked.

The light changed and he popped the clutch and revved the tiny engine of the little sedan. Beside the car an army truck kept pace and poured noxious fumes through Yocke's open window. The American gagged and hastily spun the crank.

'Where are we going?' he asked Gregor.

'I don't know. You haven't told me.'

Soviet Square, Yocke decided, and informed his colleague. Gregor just nodded.

It was a broken-down car with the hood up that gave Yocke the idea. Cars with open hoods and the drivers bent over engines that refused to run were commonplace in Moscow. In a society without spare parts, without mechanics, without garages, without service stations, you either fixed it yourself on the side of the road with parts from

190

junked vehicles or you left it there to be mined for parts by other motorists.

He explained what he wanted to Gregor, who again demanded more money. Yocke explained about his editor's parsimony and getting the expense approved in Washington, Moscow on the Potomac. Reluctantly Gregor agreed to help.

As they neared Soviet Square on Gorki Street Gregor turned the ignition off and let the car coast to the curb. Both men got out and raised the hood. Gregor disconnected the spark plug leads and took the top off the air filter. They put their elbows on the fender and their butts in the air and waited.

A policeman in gray uniform and white hat, carrying a white traffic baton and wearing a brown leather holster from which the butt of a small automatic protruded, arrived in three minutes. Yocke got busy under the hood and Gregor did the talking. Two minutes later, when the policeman wandered away, Gregor summed it up in a short sentence. 'He was on duty in Red Square the day of the assassination.'

They tried it again around the corner. The cop this time smoked one of Gregor's cigarettes and offered mechanical advice. They finally got the engine running and drove away waving.

'He heard the transmission over the police radio. He was one of the ones that left. The name of the policeman in charge of the radio is Burbulis.'

'We'll make a reporter of you yet. Police station.'

It took a lot of talking and cigarettes all round from the Marlboro carton, but Gregor and Yocke got in to see Burbulis. He was a chain smoker with steel teeth. He eyed Yocke suspiciously.

'I write for the *Washington Post*, a great American newspaper,' Gregor translated. 'I am following up a report that your chief is in trouble with the prosecutor because of the Soviet Square killings.' While Gregor translated this, Yocke tried to decide how much Burbulis liked the chief of police. He was praying for a little professional loyalty even if Burbulis loathed the man personally.

'Not his fault. I know the men. Good KGB men. We have worked together many times.'

'Names and addresses,' Yocke told Gregor, trying to keep the excitement out of his voice. 'Get names and addresses.'

They got three names and one address. And a lecture about the duty of the police to cooperate with the proper authorities. 'This questioning of police doing their duty by the prosecutor would never have happened in the old days,' Burbulis summed up, and sneered. 'Yeltsin has no courage. No respect. He understands nothing.' Burbulis smashed his fist on the table and glowered.

Out on the street Yocke carefully wrote down the names as Gregor spelled them in English. The address was merely a street. 'Do you know this street?'

'Yes. Off Arbat.'

He had it! A sure-fire page one barn burner that implicated the KGB in the murders of Communist ultra-nationalist Yegor Kolokoltsev and his henchmen! He jabbed his fist in the air and let out an exultant shout. The story would be picked up by the wire services and papers that reprinted *Post* stories and run worldwide. By Jack Yocke. Send the best, fire the rest!

He ignored the staring pedestrians and did a little hot-damn shuffle.

He had it all right, but first he had to write it. And if these KGB Commie assholes got a whiff of what was going down, he would write it ten years from now when he got out of the gulag in the middle of the Siberian winter.

He dove into the passenger seat of the Lada. 'Back to the hotel, James, and don't spare either of your beasts.'

Up in his room he packed the laptop in its padded case and confirmed that he had his passport and travel papers. He added a change of underwear to the case and his toothbrush and razor. He decided an extra pair of socks wouldn't hurt and stuffed them in. Then he zipped the case closed and stood staring at the rest of his stuff, taking inventory. His wallet and credit cards were in his pocket. He had a couple hundred on him. The rest of his cash and travelers checks were in the hotel safe; they could stay there.

He made sure his two suitcases were unlocked. If and when those guys came to look, he didn't want them breaking the locks.

He looked at his watch. Ten minutes before two. He had had no lunch. He wasn't hungry. Too excited.

He rode down in the elevator with a smile on his face. He even sang a few bars to himself in the mirror, a little James Brown: 'I feel good, da da dada dada da, like I knew I would, da da dada dada da.'

Gregor unlocked the trunk and Yocke laid the computer on top of a pile of engine parts and fan belts.

'We gotta go find these three KGB guys and see if they'll finger Demodov.'

Gregor sat behind the wheel and stared at him. 'Then what? Will you want to go see Demodov? In Dzerzhinsky Square?'

'I'll just call him, or try to anyway. He'll deny everything. Not worth the wear and tear on your car.'

'Idiot.'

'His denial in the last paragraph of the story will be the icing on the cake. Every last living soul will know he's guilty as hell.'

'Idiot,' Gregor repeated.

'Hey, this is the *Washington Post*, not the Slobovia *Gazette*. We always run the denials. About one time in a hundred the asshole is telling the truth, then we're covered. The lawyers like it like that.'

Gregor put both hands on the wheel and sat staring stonily ahead.

'Come on. Let's go.'

'I don't know what hole you will dive into when the story is printed, but I live here. I don't have any holes.'

'I told you I would talk to my editor about a raise. I meant that.'

Gregor snorted.

'What are they going to do to you? Is this your fault? Are you a reporter? You just drove me around and translated, for Christ's sake! Yeah, they may sweat you a little, and you can tell them everything. You have absolutely nothing to hide or apologize for. You're an interpreter! Then what? They'll let you go. You know that and I know that. The world has changed. Joe Stalin is rotting in some hole in the ground.'

Gregor started the car and put it in motion. 'I wish I were driving a taxi in Brooklyn with my wife's cousin.'

It took an hour and a half to find the only address they had, one for a KGB agent named Ivan Zvezdni. His apartment was on the top floor of a ten-story building and they had to walk up. The smell of grease and dirt and cabbage hung like a miasma in the crumbling concrete stairwell.

The woman who opened the door was in tears. Gregor had barely gotten out Yocke's identity and profession when she began to wail. 'They took him away. Just minutes ago,' Gregor muttered to Yocke. 'Men from the public prosecutor's office.'

Yocke eyed the only soft chair and eased himself into it. He wasn't leaving until he had it in spades.

It took half an hour to get the whole story, but it was worth it. Two mornings ago Zvezdni received a telephone call from Nikolai Demodov ordering him to go to police headquarters and tell the chief to pull the officers out of Soviet Square. Zvezdni knew it was Demodov because he knew his voice. Demodov specialized in political matters.

Although Demodov didn't explain the order, Zvezdni told his wife that the boss probably didn't want the police presence tarring the Old Guard with the wrath that

Kolokoltsev's message usually brought forth from Yeltsin's aides, especially since Yeltsin's people had denied Kolokoltsev a rally permit. Mrs Zvezdni didn't pretend to understand any of it, and she claimed her husband didn't. Ivan was a good officer, a loyal servant of the state. He always did as he was told, she said.

Whatever Ivan Zvezdni thought of Demodov's reasons, he obeyed orders this time too. He did, however, take two other agents along to protect himself. Mrs Zvezdni named them. Now he was under arrest. For doing his duty. For obeying orders. Life was just not fair. Mrs Zvezdni was reduced to silent tears.

It was damn thin, Yocke thought, but looking at Mrs Zvezdni he bought it. Well, if you were a KGB agent and your boss called and gave you an order, wouldn't you obey it?

The apartment was crowded but neat. There was no refrigerator. The family's food supply sat on a sideboard under a window. The furniture was old, scarred and spotlessly clean. The carpet was clean and threadbare.

'Make sure,' Yocke told Gregor, 'that she understands I write for an American newspaper.'

'She knows that. She does not care.'

He wanted to touch her arm, pat her head, but he refrained. She was using a scrap of white cloth to wipe her tears. 'Tell her I am sorry,' he said.

He was going to have to work fast. This story was too hot to wait. On the way to the car he told Gregor, 'Find a phone.' Gregor didn't protest.

Gregor made the call to the KGB. After repeated waits and spurts of Russian, he motioned to Yocke and handed him the receiver. They were standing at a pay phone on a sidewalk somewhere near Arbat Street. The phone was mounted on a wall and had a little half booth arranged around it.

'Hello. My name is Jack Yocke. I'm a reporter for the *Washington Post*.'

The voice on the other end said 'wait' in a heavy accent. At least it sounded like 'wait.'

Another minute passed before a guttural voice pronounced a name: 'Demodov.'

'Mr Demodov, do you speak English?'

'Yes.'

'My name is Jack Yocke. I'm a reporter for the *Washington Post*. We have a story that we are going to run that says that three National Security agents went to police headquarters this past Tuesday and asked the police chief to pull the police out of Soviet Square. The chief complied and Yegor Kolokoltsev was murdered minutes later. According to our information, you were the person who sent them to police headquarters. Do you wish to comment?'

Silence. Finally the voice again. 'I did not do that.'

Yocke scribbled the answer in his private shorthand.

'Have you been questioned by the public prosecutor about this matter?'

'No.'

'Are you aware that Ivan Zvezdni, one of your subordinates, was arrested by men from the public prosecutor's office just about an hour ago?'

'No. How do you know all this?'

'Do you wish to make any other comment about this story?'

'I know nothing about it. What more can I say?' And the connection broke.

Yocke replaced the phone on the hook and turned to Gregor.

'We got it. He denies everything.'

CHAPTER TWELVE

'Admiral Grafton, this is Jack Yocke. I've got a little problem and need your help.'

'What kind of problem?' The tone of the admiral's voice on the telephone made it clear that he didn't have time for a social call.

'It's a long story, sir, and I'd like to tell it to you in person.'

'I'm really swamped right now. Where are you?'

'Down here in the little reception office in front of the embassy compound.'

Grafton sighed. 'Okay. I'll send Toad down.'

'Thanks.'

Yocke hung up the telephone and went back outside. Gregor was sitting in the car, double-parked in the street. The reporter bent down so he could talk through the passenger window. 'I'll need the computer out of the trunk.'

Gregor killed the engine and climbed out. He opened the trunk without a word and let Yocke reach in and get the computer case. 'So it's good-bye then.'

'You're still on the payroll, Gregor. And I will talk to the editor about that raise.'

Gregor closed the trunk, locked it, then got back into the car. Yocke pulled a roll of bills out of his pocket and peeled off five twenties. He stood by the driver's door. 'Here. This is for you.'

Gregor stared up at him. He tried to smile but it didn't come out that way. 'No.'

'This isn't charity, Gregor. You've earned it. Feed your family.'

The Russian started the car and put it in gear. Yocke tossed the bills in his lap as the car got under way. 'I'll call you,' he shouted.

He adjusted the strap of the computer bag and watched the Lada go down the street trailing a thin blue cloud of exhaust fumes. After it disappeared from sight he turned toward the embassy gate. Toad Tarkington was standing there watching him.

'What have you been into this time?'

Yocke glanced at the gate guard, a Moscow policeman wearing the usual gray uniform. He went past him into the reception office and turned to face Tarkington.

'The KGB was waiting for me at my hotel.'

Toad snorted. 'You sure?'

'We drove by. There were a dozen police cars out front, a dozen or so guys in dark suits around the entrance. Three or four at every other door. It looked like Al Capone's garden party. I tripped over a hornet's nest.'

Toad snorted. 'Kicked it over, you mean. Then you come charging over to the Hotel Grafton with your hair on fire and a rat in your mouth.'

'Dammit, Toad, I've got to write this story and file it.'

'Story on what?'

'The Soviet Square killings.'

Toad pursed his lips as he examined Yocke's face. 'Better come up and tell it to the admiral,' he said, and made a hi sign to the receptionist behind the safety glass. After she pushed her button Toad opened the door for the reporter.

Jake Grafton was surrounded by computer printouts and maps. He was curt. 'Let's hear it.'

So Toad told it. Quickly and concisely. When he had completed his recitation the admiral glanced at Tarkington, who was leaning back against the wall with his eyebrows up as far as they would go.

'So the KGB set up their stooge, Kolts-something,' the admiral said. 'Why?'

'Well, there are several possible reasons why they might have done it, like—'

'You're going to write this story without *knowing* why they did it?'

'Yep.' Yocke glanced at his watch. 'It'll run on tomorrow's front page.' Seeing the look on Grafton's face, the reporter went on: 'Gimme a break, Admiral. If we had waited to get Lee Harvey Oswald's reasons before we reported Kennedy's assassination, we'd still be waiting.'

'That's a real argument stopper, but it's hardly germane to this case.'

'Facts are facts.'

'If you've got any.'

Jack Yocke's face flushed. 'Jesus! You're worse than my editor.'

'I'm just pointing out the obvious. If I were a reporter I'd want it in spades before I accused someone of murder. But you're the guy they pay the big bucks.' Grafton cleared his throat while Jack Yocke figured out how to handle his face.

When the reporter spoke his voice was carefully under control. 'I'm not accusing anyone of anything. I've got a story about how the police were pulled out of that square and in my professional opinion, it's solid. I—' He stopped speaking because Jake Grafton had waved his hand, cutting him off.

The admiral toyed with a pen, clicking the point in and out a few times. 'Yeltsin is going to be one happy man when he hears about this,' he said finally.

'I suppose.'

Toad cleared his throat. 'How about describing this woman you met in the bar.'

'Now wait a minute. It doesn't really matter who she is. She merely gave me a tip and I verified it by an independent investigation.'

Yocke hadn't given the woman's motives a thought and

Toad's question irritated him. In America people routinely sought out reporters to put them onto a story. Reporters knew these people were driven by a variety of motives, including revenge. Yet if the story checked out as true and newsworthy, the tipster's motives didn't really matter. And Jack Yocke knew damn well he had latched onto a big, true story. A huge story. The dimensions of it slightly awed him. And it was solid. There was no way in hell those people today were acting, feeding him a line. After questioning a few thousand people, he knew the truth when he heard it. If he heard it. And by God, today he had heard it.

The problem was Tarkington. He was a good man, but at times he was tough to swallow. Jack Yocke took a deep breath and added, 'The public prosecutor has the three KGB agents who went to the police station locked up right now. They want to jug me.'

'Yeah, yeah, I know all that. You've scooped everybody and you're gonna be famous. Now tell me what this broad looked like.'

'Well, she was about five eight or so, dark brown shoulder-length hair, dark brown – almost black – eyes set wide apart, a classic bone structure.'

'Good figure?'

'Well, I suppose so.'

'You queer or what?' Tarkington asked sharply.

'She was wearing modest clothes, a good wool suit. Underneath it all she was probably built like a brick shithouse. Is that what you want to hear, sailor boy?'

Toad met Jake Grafton's gaze. His eyebrows went up and down once in reply to Grafton's silent question.

'You know her?' Yocke asked Toad.

'Just curious, Jack. What I'm trying to figure out is why you.'

'Because she knew I was a reporter.'

'This town is full of reporters. Why you?'

'You two sailors are a real pair. I thought you'd let me hole up here.' His voice rose: 'But no, Jack, you might write

200

something that embarrasses the good ol' US of A. and we probably can't handle—'

'That's enough,' Jake said disgustedly. 'You can sleep on the couch. Right now you go into Toad's room' – he nodded toward the bedroom door – 'and write your story. When you're ready to send it in let me know. In the meantime don't pick up the phone even if it rings.'

Jack Yocke stood and hoisted the computer. He had half a mind to tell these two clowns where to go and what to do to themselves when they got there, but . . . He mumbled his thanks, then his eye fell on the maps and computer printouts. 'Say, what is all this paper?'

'Not a word to your editor about this one,' Jake told him. 'But you ain't the only guy with problems. The Russians just had another nuclear power plant meltdown.'

'*Holy* . . . ! Like Chernobyl?'

'Maybe worse.'

'Where? Around here?'

'Someplace called Serdobsk, about three hundred miles southeast of here. Now go in there and shut the door and let us work.'

After the door closed Toad turned on the radio. Classical music came out.

'Judith Farrell?' Jake asked.

'I'd bet the ranch, CAG.'

Jake Grafton went to the window and stood looking out. He rubbed the back of his neck, then moved his shoulders up and down. Finally he stretched.

When he turned around he told Toad, 'The Israelis sure get their money's worth out of that woman.'

'Uh-huh.'

Toad was looking at the map spread upon the floor. The wind was going to spread that radioactivity over hundreds of square miles. He was looking now at the villages in the fallout zone. He couldn't even pronounce the Russian names upon the chart. A great many people from a culture he didn't know were about to die, and it sickened him.

'Do you believe in God?' he asked Jake Grafton.

'Only on Sundays,' the admiral replied.

'There's a military base here in this footprint, sir. Petrovsk. Here, take a look. Wasn't that the base we visited a couple days ago?'

Jake Grafton looked. 'Yes. Petrovsk. Missiles with nuclear warheads.'

'They'll have to evacuate that base, if they haven't already.'

Evacuate. That meant airplanes, fuel. And what percentage of the base personnel could be carried on the planes?

'Wonder if Moscow will even tell those people that a lethal cloud of radioactivity is coming their way?'

'If only five or ten percent of them could possibly escape, would you tell them?' Jake Grafton mused, his voice so low that Toad almost missed the comment. '*What* would you tell them?'

A little later he muttered, 'A lot of that radioactivity is going to go into the Volga.'

He looked again at the predicted radioactivity levels. The numbers were two or three times worse than Chernobyl. How did people manage to make such horrible messes on this tiny, fragile planet? His finger moved on the map, down the Volga past Saratov and Engels, past Kamyshin, all the way to Volgograd, formerly Stalingrad. The water supplies of those cities would be grossly contaminated. The land. The food supply. Jake Grafton picked up the estimate of the various isotope levels and their half-lives and stared at it, trying to take it in.

And on down the Volga to the Caspian Sea. How much radioactivity could that closed inland ocean tolerate before it became a dead sea?

This was worse than a disaster – it was a nightmare. When the Russian people finally learned the truth, what would be their reaction?

The telephone rang and Toad picked it up. After saying 'Yessir,' several times, he replaced the receiver and told

Jake, 'The ambassador wants you to go with him to the Kremlin. In a couple hours our president will announce that the United States will assist Russia any way it can.'

Jake Grafton took a deep breath and let it out slowly. 'So when is the Yeltsin government going public on this?'

'The ambassador's aide didn't say. Soon, apparently.'

Yeltsin had no choice. Gorbachev had waited for days to tell the world of Chernobyl and had been excoriated for it. But Gorbachev had been a Communist and Yeltsin swore he no longer was. 'Umm,' Jake Grafton said.

'Maybe you'd better wear your uniform, sir,' Toad said gently. 'It looks like it's going to be one of those days.'

'Jack Yocke has just been had by a pro. She conned him good and he's so anxious for a story – any story – that he swallowed it without even tasting it.'

Toad Tarkington nodded. 'I'll buy that.'

'She may try again.'

'Naw. She's not that stupid. Too big a risk.'

'When the stakes get this large any risk is justified. *Any risk!* We've got to get to her before Jack Yocke does.'

Captain Herbert 'Tom' Collins was the naval attaché. As the senior naval officer he supervised a staff of just three other officers: one a marine lieutenant colonel, one a navy commander, and the other the politically impure lieutenant, Spiro Dalworth. A surface warfare officer with a destroyer command behind him, Collins had acquired a degree in Russian from the US Naval Postgraduate School in Monterey, California, while he was still a lieutenant. Tonight Jake recalled with a jolt that Collins' first assignment after the Naval Academy had been to nuclear power school. After graduating, he then spent his first tour tending a reactor aboard a nuclear-powered frigate.

These days Collins tried to keep track of what was happening in the former Soviet Navy as the ships, planes and sailors were divided between the newly independent republics. The job was impossible. In the past the naval officers had subsisted on a mere trickle of information, mainly what the Soviets wanted them to see and hear – now they were drowning in it. The Russians were showing them everything, telling everything, talking openly about weapons capability, maintenance problems with ships, engines, radars, planes, problems with personnel, training, recruitment, supply, food . . . everything. If there were any secrets left in the new Commonwealth, Collins had yet to bump into one of them.

Two nights ago he told Jake Grafton, 'Today the Russian Navy would lose a fight with the Italians. Honest to God, since the collapse they can't get food or fuel to steam with. They can't feed the sailors; they can't maintain the ships; they got 'em tied up rusting at the pier. A couple more years of this and most of those ships will be beyond salvage.'

Tonight in the courtyard Tom Collins turned up the volume on his portable radio, which was tuned to a Russian station playing American jazz. They were standing in the shadow of the new embassy complex, empty and condemned because it was hopelessly infested with bugs – the electronic kind.

'Isn't one of your chiefs a communications specialist?' Jake asked.

'One of my two, sir. Senior Chief Holley.' Collins was eyeing Jake's uniform and the ribbons displayed there. The admiral had just returned from the Kremlin with the ambassador.

'I need to borrow him for a while. Holley and Dalworth.'

'We're drowning in my shop, Admiral. I've got them working twenty hours a day.' Collins and the other military people were using every contact they had to try to discover what the Russian military knew about the extent of the damage from the Serdobsk meltdown. Jake had spent the day helping, trying to analyze information received in dribbles from all quarters.

'I understand. This is important.'

'Aye aye, sir.'

Jake Grafton felt like a jerk. He merely needed two people he could trust – anyone really – and Collins had an important job to do. Still, if he could get to Judith Farrell . . .

'So what are the Russians saying?' Jake asked.

'Same old story. It's all Yeltsin's fault.'

'Is it?'

'Well, there's no money to maintain reactors and they're all in terrible shape. An American inspector from the Nuclear Regulatory Commission would have a heart attack if he saw one of those plants, but they've been like that for years. This country is too poor to properly build or maintain or operate nuclear power plants. They just don't have the technical expertise or the trained people.' Collins' shoulders sagged. 'They're like monkeys with a computer.'

'Nobody over at the Kremlin will even hazard a guess about why that thing melted.'

Collins grunted. 'There are meltdowns and there are meltdowns,' he said. 'The accidents at Three Mile Island and Chernobyl could be classified as radiation leaks. This one was a real whing-ding, snap-doodle of a meltdown – there isn't much left out there. The satellite sensors show unbelievable temperatures. The first reading they got was thirty minutes after the thing went. We got a fax of a satellite photo half an hour ago and you wouldn't believe it. Looks like the damn thing was hit with a ten-ton block-buster. The structure is gone – steel, concrete, everything. Nothing left but some rubble and a hole in the ground.'

After a bit Collins added, 'Of course, there's not a chance in a zillion that anyone survived it.'

Grafton whistled. 'You're saying it's almost like it blew up.'

'That's precisely what it did. In the argot of the trade, "a power excursion," or a runaway. In lay terms, the son of a bitch blew up.'

Jake was stunned. Today no one had mentioned an

explosion, nor had the word passed the lips of anyone at the Kremlin. 'I thought nuclear reactors couldn't explode.'

'A popular misconception. Fast breeders can. This one did.'

Jake was still trying to take it in. 'Exploded?'

'The core exploded.'

'A nuclear explosion?'

'Boom.'

'How could that happen?'

Collins rubbed his face. He looked around, then by reflex turned up the volume on the radio. 'Serdobsk was a liquid metal fast breeder reactor, one of the first ones the Russians built. The core is made up of uranium-235, which is surrounded by rods of uranium-238, which breed into plutonium. In a water-cooled pressure reactor, bleeding off the water causes the core to melt and fission to stop. Of course the hot core can melt the containment vessel and release radioactivity, but fission stops. In a breeder, loss of coolant has the opposite effect: the fission reaction increases. The more rapid the coolant loss, the worse the effect. As the temperature rises the core melts and fills the spaces between the rods. When the material is compact enough, it can detonate in a nuclear explosion.'

Collins waved a hand impatiently. 'It's been years since I studied this stuff, but as I recall, theoretically you could get an explosion about the equivalent of ten tons of TNT if the core is really cooking when the coolant goes. That looks to me about what they had. An explosion like that would blow maybe half the core material into the atmosphere – that's tons of really filthy uranium, plutonium, iodine, strontium-90, that kind of crap.'

Jake Grafton felt like a sinner listening to God's verdict. 'Tons?'

Collins was merciless. 'If you want all the trade words, a liquid-metal-cooled breeder is autocatalytic – it's its own catalyst for manufacturing power excursions. The process of compaction and excursions that result in more compactions is a little like what happens in a collapsing star at the end of its life. Power melts the core, it crashes down, more power, more rebound or crashdown, poof! Think of it like a little supernova. The nuclear reaction stops only when the core disassembles – blows itself to smithereens.'

'What could cause this . . . core compaction?'

'Well, I'm no expert, but—'

'You're as close to an expert as I've got.'

'As I recall, there are a bunch of theoretical possibilities. Basically any event that causes the core to be compacted can start the process. The reactor is cooled by liquid sodium, which is hotter than hell: molten steel could cause the sodium to vaporize and explode. A sodium vapor explosion is the most likely way, but fuel vaporizing could trigger it. Or an external explosion that damages the core and compacts it, or coolant loss or surges that damage the core—'

Jake had had enough. He stopped the recitation with a raised hand. 'So how bad is it?'

'Bad?' Collins stared at him as if he were a dense child. 'This reactor was old, full of plutonium and really raunchy crud. Plutonium is the deadliest substance known to man. It has a half-life of twenty-four thousand two hundred years. One would have to wait for about ten half-lives, call it two hundred and fifty thousand years, for the stuff to cool off to the tolerable level.'

'Forever.'

'Essentially forever.'

'How much land will have to be permanently abandoned?'

'I dunno. They're trying to figure that out in Washington. And I'm trying to make some estimates. Depends on the winds and how much atmospheric mixing there was, how much rain, all that stuff.'

'So guess,' Jake Grafton said.

'Maybe fifty thousand square miles. Maybe twice that.' Collins shrugged.

'Yeltsin's fault,' Jake Grafton said slowly.

'It's somebody's.' Collins weighed his words. 'You know, I got out of nuclear power after my first tour. Oh, I was a gung-ho little nuke all right – had my interview with that troll Rickover and did my time in Idaho and thought we had the fucking genie corked up tight. But this stuff' – he looked around again, searching for words – 'God uses fusion to make the stars burn. We use fission now and we're working up to fusion. We're playing God . . . toddlers sitting in the dark playing with matches. The consequences . . . I just decided I wanted no more of it.'

'Serdobsk blew. Man's hubris? Or did someone help this supernova compaction along?'

'What do you want, Admiral? Probability theory?'

'Yes.'

'Never bet on God. Go with the main chance. Men build 'em, men screw 'em up.'

'If you were going to blow a breeder, how would you go about it?'

Collins was in no mood for what-if games, yet a glance at Grafton's face made him concentrate on the question. 'Shaped charges on top of the vessel. Blow down and in. Put some hot molten steel into that sodium stew. The charges wouldn't have to be very big since the containment vessel is unpressurized. With luck I'd get a little sodium vapor explosion that would send a shock wave down into the core. The first shock wave would lead to a power excursion and another – bigger – shock wave, and so on. If I were willing to meet my maker with that on my conscience, that's the way I'd do it.'

Jake Grafton just grunted.

The telephone rang at midnight. 'Admiral Grafton.'

'This is Richard, Admiral. I've got it.'

Jake came wide awake. Richard Harper, 'This isn't a secure line, Richard.'

'Okay.' Two seconds of silence. 'It was a hell of a trail

and they were damn cute, but I *got it*. How do you want it?'

'I'll have someone call you. Can you write it out?'

'Sure.'

CHAPTER THIRTEEN

The storm broke in Russia the next morning. The speaker of the Congress of People's Deputies managed to call the house to order, but that was the last thing he accomplished. While the world watched on television the deputies brawled. Finger pointing and shouting gave way to shoving and fists. Before the camera was turned off several deputies were seen to be on the floor being kicked and pounded with fists by their colleagues.

A huge, angry crowd gathered in Red Square. Conspicuous today were the red flags, the ugly mood. Then, as if someone struck a match, the crowd exploded. A truck was overturned and set on fire. Policemen were beaten, several to death. Then the rioters spilled out of the square and headed for the nearby hard-currency hotels and restaurants, which they looted. One hotel was set ablaze. Foreigners were attacked on the streets and beaten mercilessly. Somehow CNN managed to televise most of the riot live to a stunned, angry, frightened world.

Although the sense of fear and betrayal was strongest in Russia, the rest of the world felt it too. Nuclear power plants stood throughout the Western world. Their safety had long been an issue, but the debate seemed esoteric to electorates concerned with the mundane issues of jobs, wages, education and housing. The massive, catastrophic pollution from the Serdobsk accident was something the public could understand. They were seeing the consequences of an accident that advocates of nuclear power said would never happen.

In Italy the coalition government fractured and the premier resigned. The French president addressed a crowd estimated at ten thousand people and was forced to stop speaking when a riot broke out on the edge of the crowd. Across the channel the British prime minister was questioned sharply in Parliament from both sides of the aisle about the dangers of Britain's nuclear reactors. Here too a significant percentage of the lawmakers were immediately ready to shut down all the reactors.

By the time Americans began to wake up with their coffee, newspapers and morning television shows, the fat was in the fire. The television played scenes of rioting in Russia and the political crises in Europe while people read the front pages of their newspapers with a growing sense of horror. Jack Yocke's story on the KGB's involvement in the Soviet Square massacre – it was dubbed a massacre by an inspired headline writer and the name stuck – made the front page of the Washington *Post*, at the very bottom. The rest of the page was devoted to the Serdobsk meltdown.

Experts were stunned by the extent of the disaster. It was as if none of the redundant safety systems in the reactor had functioned. Initial estimates on the level of radioactivity at ground level where the reactor had stood were hastily developed from satellite infrared and other sensors. 'It will be three hundred thousand years,' one physicist declared, 'before an unprotected human can safely walk upon that site.'

In the Capitol in Washington congressmen elbowed one another vying to get in front of the cameras in the press briefing rooms. Every one of them swore he would support a critical review of the American nuclear power program. A significant minority was ready to shut down all the reactors right *now*. Among this minority were several of the legislators who had fought hardest on behalf of the utilities that operated reactors – the same people, incidentally, who had accepted the most PAC money from those utilities.

The antinuclear lobby was having a great day. Triumphant

211

and exultant as the tide lifted their boat, they excoriated senators and congressmen who had consistently pooh-poohed safety concerns. They damned the Nuclear Regulatory Commission as an industry puppet, vilified every public official who ever said that nuclear power was safe, and demanded the immediate resignation of the secretary of the Department of Energy.

While the antinukes danced and pranced in television studios in New York and Washington, a huge crowd gathered outside the Capitol and were harangued by impromptu speakers. After an hour the crowd became unruly and police used tear gas to break it up.

When the sun rose in Japan the antinuclear, anti-technology forces arrayed in helmets and plastic body armor were ready to do battle with club-wielding riot police. The battle surged through downtown Tokyo, commuter trains were literally overturned, power lines were dragged down while still hot, and a mob broke through the fence at Narita airport. Outnumbered riot police turned and ran as the demonstrators charged for the Boeing 747s at the terminal gates. Most of the giant planes suffered minor damage, mostly to their tires, but two were set on fire.

The chaos brought the city to a choking halt while legislators in the Diet crafted a hasty plan to shut down Japan's nuclear power plants. The power loss would stun the economy, but in a small nation that had never forgotten Hiroshima or Nagasaki, this was the only possible political choice. As uncomfortable, perspiring physicists sat before television cameras and tried to assess the Serdobsk melt-down damage based on fragmentary information, Japan got out of the nuclear power business.

At stock exchanges around the world the value of stocks in electrical utilities that owned nuclear power plants fell disastrously before trading was halted because of the huge disparity between buy and sell orders.

But Serdobsk was in Russia, and it was there that the situation got completely out of control as the evening shadows lengthened. The development 'at any price' mentality of the post-World War II years was revealed for what it was – a grotesque miscalculation that had bankrupted the nation, left the people paupers on the brink of starvation, and now had made huge portions of the nation uninhabitable. Raging mobs roamed the core of Moscow and no foreigner was safe. Three hotels were now ablaze. The entrances to the Kremlin were blocked with barricades, and police hid behind them to fire into the enraged crowds. Several tanks appeared on the streets, only to be surrounded and disabled. The crews were dragged out and beaten to death as television camera crews broadcast the scenes from the safety of the rooftops.

A mob surrounded the American embassy complex and probably would have stormed it if the ambassador hadn't ordered the marines to use live ammunition and shoot to kill. They did. By the time the summer sun had set, over a dozen bodies lay on the streets around the embassy. One of the bodies was of a young woman who had tried to get close enough to the wall to hurl a Molotov cocktail. When a corporal shot her, the bottle shattered beside her and her corpse was immolated. This vignette would have made great television, but unfortunately the CNN crew on the rooftop across the boulevard was having trouble with their satellite feed.

Jack Yocke saw the incident and used it to lead off a story for the *Post*. He knew he had something. The woman's hair blowing in the wind as she lay dead in the street, the burning gasoline igniting the asphalt, her clothing, and finally that wispy brown hair – he could still see the scene in his mind's eye as he tapped on the laptop and tried to capture the insanity of infuriated, berserk people charging marines behind a brick wall armed with M-16s. Blood and guts were what he did best, so he wrote quickly and confidently.

As he wrote he could still hear the occasional sharp crack of an M-16. Now and then through the open window he got a whiff of the acrid smoke of a burning car that the locals had torched this morning. It was a Ford with diplomatic plates – just which embassy employee it belonged to Yocke didn't know. When he was finished he checked his work over for spelling and punctuation, then called the *Post* on Grafton's telephone and sent the story via modem.

After Yocke had sent off his story, he locked the door of the apartment and went looking for Jake Grafton. He found him against the southwest corner of the compound wall busy with the TACSAT gear and encoder. The admiral merely glanced at him and continued to punch buttons, so Yocke sat down beside him.

Above them, standing on some empty furniture crates so he could see over the wall, was a marine with a rifle. He was scanning the windows of a Russian apartment house just across the alley. Fortunately no rioters had chosen to get up there and shoot down into the compound, probably because none of them had guns. The Communists had made damn sure that the civilian inhabitants of their workers' paradise were unarmed and stayed that way.

'Hell of a day, huh?' Yocke said.

Grafton finished with the number sequence. He diddled a bit with the dish and high-gain antenna on top of the box and finally got the voice echo in sync with his voice. He pushed another button, then leaned back against the wall with the telephone-style handset cradled on his shoulder and glanced at the reporter. 'Yeah,' he said.

After a moment be spoke into the mouthpiece. 'General Land, please. Admiral Grafton calling.'

More waiting. Grafton nodded at Yocke's trousers. 'Toad loan you those?'

'His are too small. He bought me some stuff at the embassy store.'

Grafton merely nodded and played with the handset cord.

Almost a minute passed before he spoke again:

'Admiral Grafton, sir. Calling from the embassy compound in Moscow ... Yessir ... Ambassador Lancaster talked to Yeltsin about a half hour ago on the satellite phone. Called Washington and they called Yeltsin and patched him through ... I think the local phone system is overloaded, everybody calling everybody ... Yessir ... Yeltsin told the ambassador that the generals won't bring in troops to put down the rioting. They want him to resign and appoint a junta ... That's right, a junta – seven of them ... Marshal Mikhailov, General Yakolev, a KGB guy named Shmarov – those three I've heard of. There're a couple more generals and one admiral. The seventh guy is some civilian ... Yessir.'

Grafton eyed Yocke, who had raised his eyes and was watching the marine on the crates.

'I don't know,' Grafton said, then listened some more.

Grafton was in civilian clothes – Yocke noticed that the trousers were none too clean. Neither was the shirt. Then he realized the clothes were Russian, not American. So were the shoes.

'I wonder if you could order some photos for me. I want satellite photos of the Russian base at Petrovsk.' He listened a moment, then spelled the name of the base. 'That's right. It's in the footprint of the Serdobsk fallout. Should be too hot for humans. I want a shot at least a month old, one maybe last week and one now. And some of that Serdobsk nuke plant.'

The admiral listened a moment, then went on. 'Well, I would like about six antiradiation suits ... No, better make that ten suits, with oxygen-breathing apparatus. Fly them in on a C-141. We'll get out to the airport somehow ... Ten ... Yessir ... Self-contained breathing apparatus, the whole shooting match. Geiger counters, film badges, everything ... Yessir, I'd like to get down to Serdobsk if I can.

'Well, I don't think Yakolev is going to lift a finger. He's busy trying to take over the government ... Not a soul, sir. No, I don't think he'll do anything to obstruct us, but the worse this gets the worse Yeltsin and the democrats look . . . I know, that occurred to me too. That's one reason I want to get to Serdobsk.'

Grafton fell silent for a moment and eyed Yocke. It wasn't a pleasant look. 'We'll steal one,' he told General Land. 'Send me a couple pilots that can fly anything, and I mean anything. And just to be on the safe side, could you send a marine recon team with all their gear and hot suits?'

They talked about that for a moment, then Jake said, 'And one more thing, sir. I've had a man named Richard Harper trying to find the money trail to whoever it is here in Russia that is selling weapons. He called last night and said he has it. I asked him to write a report. He's supposed to mail it to my wife, but I wonder if you could send someone from your office over to his house in Chevy Chase to pick it up? Make a copy for yourself and send me a copy.' Jake gave him Harper's address.

'Thank you, sir,' he said finally and hung up the receiver. He punched buttons and the lights on the gadget went out.

'Needless to say, you don't want me to print a word of that,' Yocke said conversationally.

'Needless to say.'

'What are you going to steal?'

'A helicopter.'

'Can I go too?'

'I'll think about it.'

Yocke nodded. Grafton packed the com gear into a soft carrying bag. He was zipping it closed when Yocke asked, 'Think Yeltsin will resign?'

'Maybe.'

'Well, by God, after—'

'He may not have a choice,' Grafton said. 'In case you haven't noticed, Russia is a Third World shithole. The rule in Third World shitholes is that the head of government serves at the pleasure of the guys with the guns.'

Jack Yocke wasn't paying much attention. His mind was in high gear ruminating on Nikolai Demodov and the KGB general, Shmarov, who it turned out wanted to be one of the magnificent seven. And Demodov denied he had been involved in the Soviet Square rubout . . . Shit! Those assholes must have been biding their time, waiting for just the proper moment to dump Yeltsin. They just didn't want that xenophobic neo-nazi Kolokoltsev around to embarrass them when the puck went down. But how could he tie those Commies to Kolokoltsev's killing?

Grafton stood and arranged the strap of the com gear bag over his shoulder. He looked up at the marine. 'Did you hear anything, Corporal Williams?'

'Not a word, sir.'

'Fine.'

Grafton took a couple steps, then paused and looked back at Yocke. 'Well, you coming or are you going to sit there in the dirt contemplating your navel?'

The reporter got up and dusted his trousers. 'You oughta see my navel. Got a ruby in it. Arab belly dancer gave it to me when I was sixteen. She was my first piece of ass.'

Yocke's attempt at humor fell flat with Jake Grafton. He too had seen the girl shot and her corpse burned. And he was trying to understand what must have moved her to pick up a bottle filled with gasoline with a burning rag stuck in the mouth and run across that street at the American embassy.

Betrayal? The Russian people had been betrayed by the Communists, all right, who had promised much and delivered little.

But the American embassy?

Perhaps she felt a profound anger at a system that for fifty years had paid any price to acquire technology, yet in the end the technology betrayed them all. The Americans were the gurus of high-tech, the master alchemists.

Musing thus, Jake was still unsure. A great disgust at technology and technicians was motivating much of the political unrest worldwide, he thought, but still . . . Ser-dobsk was a Russian reactor. Perhaps mixed with those emotions was the age-old Russian suspicion of all things foreign. The Russians weren't as bad as the Chinese in that regard, but they did fear the outside world, some sort of a national inferiority complex that they soaked up with their mother's milk.

He would like to have asked that young woman, but that chance was gone forever. She was a heap of charcoal and bone now, out there on a spot of melted, charred asphalt.

Jake Grafton wondered if the dead woman had had any relatives at Serdobsk or out there in that radioactive footprint.

He was opening the door to the apartment building when Jack Yocke asked, 'Did General Land say what America's response to the meltdown was going to be?'

Now Jake saw it. He let go of the door handle and turned to face Yocke. He could almost hear her voice. *You are America. You are not stupid and venal and corrupt, yet you did nothing to help us. You let the stupid, venal, corrupt men tell their lies and build their poisonous monuments to our ignorance and so destroy us, the helpless. You, America.*

Jack Yocke repeated his question.

'No,' Jake Grafton muttered, shaking his head. 'He didn't.' And he turned back for the door handle.

Upstairs in the apartment, which of necessity was also Jake's office, Yocke had more questions. 'Just how much nuclear material was in that reactor, anyway?'

'About four and a half tons.'

'Tons?'

'Yeah. Maybe three or so tons of uranium and a ton and a half of plutonium.'

'Gee, that sounds like a lot. I guess I always thought those things used just a couple of hatfuls.'

'This was a fast breeder. A typical water-cooled reactor would have maybe three times that amount.'

'So this time they got off lucky?'

Jake Grafton snorted. 'Not hardly. The goddamn stuff

blew up, went nuclear. Probably half the core went into the atmosphere. We don't know enough yet to even make an intelligent estimate. And a breeder like that – it figures they had three or four tons of plutonium in the pipeline, just lying around. Some of that probably got swept up into the atmosphere and scattered all over too. No, these Russians just had no luck at all.'

After a bit Yocke asked, 'So how bad is it?'

'Bad?' Grafton looked perplexed.

'Compared to Chernobyl.'

Grafton shrugged. 'A hundred times worse? Two hundred times? "Bad" is a ridiculous understatement. The stuff that went into the air is really filthy . . .' He groped for words, then gave up. 'Really filthy,' he repeated. 'Serdobsk is way the hell and gone away from everything, so no cities were poisoned immediately, but by the time all that fallout hits the rivers and streams and lakes . . .' He shrugged. 'I wouldn't be surprised if this incident ultimately kills a million people.'

Jack Yocke just stared.

'*Another million,*' Jake Grafton roared savagely. 'God in heaven, when will it ever stop?'

Yocke got out his laptop and pecked aimlessly until Jake suggested he do that in the bedroom, so he went in and closed the door. The muffled crack of a rifle penetrated the room and Jake half-rose off the couch before he thought better of it.

He needed time to think. One of the most trying things about a military career, he thought, was that so many decisions had to be made immediately with the best information available, which used to be precious little and fragmentary at best. Then came computers and the highly touted information age; the trickle of information became a raging torrent of facts and numbers endlessly pouring from laser printers that no one had time to look at. Who could drink from a fire hose?

Jake Grafton knew that if he merely picked up a telephone

and asked, he could have more information in an hour than he could read in a year. Better to go with what he had. He leaned his head back onto the couch, closed his eyes and tried to assess his meager collection of facts and impressions.

The most important fact . . . impression maybe . . . was one he wasn't sure he had right. Most people automatically assume that people everywhere are all alike – *'they think like we do!'* Jake knew better. But he thought he could see the viewpoint of the professional soldiers like Yakolev who saw their place in Russian society slipping out from under them. Without the American enemy to stimulate the allocation of damn scarce resources and keep the ranks filled and people motivated, the military was crumbling. They had tried to fashion a new mission to protect ethnic Russian minorities wherever they might be and had been out-maneuvered by Yeltsin and his allies. The nukes were being taken away while the Americans and Europeans kept their conventional forces, there was no money, not even to feed the troops, the industrial establishment necessary to support a modern military was disintegrating, all at a time when the values the leaders had devoted their lives to were belittled or rendered politically meaningless. The Soviet Union was gone. Mother Russia was collapsing from within, there were no more secrets to guard, there was no place for men of integrity and honor. So the generals were going to save Russia in spite of politicians.

How far would these men go?

How far had they already gone?

Yakolev: *'I serve Russia!'* A uniform for a patriot or a bloody rag to hide a tyrant's nakedness?

Someone was shaking him. He opened his eyes with a start. It was Tarkington, holding a finger to his lips for silence. He seized Jake's arm and nodded toward the hall door, which was partially open. His lips moved, a silent word: 'Come.'

When they were in the hallway Toad eased the door

shut behind them until it clicked, then led Jake down the hall. He passed Jake his pistol, which was sheathed in its shoulder holster. The gun had been under the pillow in Jake's bedroom, and Toad had retrieved it before he woke the boss.

'Yocke has an outside call,' he whispered. 'The senior chief stalled and told her he's trying to find him. When we get back to the switchboard he'll ring the phone. Yocke's in there, isn't he?'

'Uh-huh.' Jake glanced at his watch. Almost two in the morning.

Toad broke into a trot.

'Is it her?' Jake wanted to know.

'I didn't hear her voice. But I got this feeling.' After all, Toad thought, how many women could there be in Moscow who want to talk to Jack Yocke?

When the two officers came through the door, Senior Chief Dan Holley flipped a switch on the switchboard. 'Still there, ma'am?' he asked. Then he said, 'He's staying with some folks. I'll ring now.' Then he toggled the switch again and handed the headset to Jake Grafton.

'The mike won't work, but you'll hear everything.'

Jake donned the headset and listened to the ringing. The telephone in the apartment was in the small living room and Yocke was probably asleep, so this was probably going to take a moment.

The phone rang and rang.

Oh, damn. Two nights ago when Yocke arrived at the embassy, he had told him not to answer the phone. What if he doesn't?

Toad and the senior chief were watching. More ringing.

C'mon, Jack. You're supposed to be a curious reporter!

'It's ringing,' Jake told his audience. And then the door opened and Spiro Dalworth slipped into the room. Jake had had Spiro, Toad and the senior chief alternating shifts on this switchboard since Captain Collins gave his approval.

The regular operator supervised and gave them directions, but the navy men listened to the voice of every caller and waited for someone to ask for Jack Yocke.

Now it had happened.

Ten rings. Eleven. *Dammit, Jack! Answer the phone!*

'Hello.' Yocke was still half asleep.

'Jack?' A woman's voice. An American woman. Was it her?

'I think so.' He sounded almost petulant.

'This is Shirley Ross. I'm glad I reached you. I tried half the hotels in town and was about to give up when I thought of the embassy.'

'Hmm. What time is it?'

'It's late I know, but I just had to talk to you.'

'Glad you called.' Yocke's voice was crisp and alert. He was wide awake now. 'How are you weathering the riot?'

'I heard about your story,' she gushed. 'I'm so thrilled! It's so important that people know the truth.' She was laying it on too thick, Jake Grafton thought, and he bit his lip. 'I never thought you would get it,' she finished.

'Luck.'

'And . . . I don't know just how to say this, but . . . I didn't think you had the courage to write it.'

'Balls like a bull. What's on your mind tonight, Shirley?'

'There's more. A *lot* more. They're counting on the fact that no one will ask the right people the right questions.'

Yocke merely grunted.

'They're playing for keeps, and they don't really care who gets hurt.'

'Shirley, I'll never get inside that place, even if anyone inside would talk to me, which they won't. Oh, I could do some follow-up on the guys who followed orders and got arrested – when they get out of the can – if they ever get out – but the story has hit the wall. These things happen.'

'It's something else.'

Silence as Yocke digested it.

When the silence had gone on too long, she said, 'Something really important . . .'

'I'm listening.'

'The Rizhsky subway station.'

'Gimme a fact, Shirley. One little fact and the promise that you know more.'

'Have I lied to you?'

'Jesus! How many times have I heard that line! Yeah, baby, I love you no shit.' Yocke sighed audibly. 'A subway station. Are the subways still running?'

Jake Grafton's eyes widened in surprise. He hadn't thought she could pull it off.

'Amazingly enough, yes. An hour from now. Come alone. And be careful.'

'Where is that, anyway?' Yocke asked, but she had already hung up.

Jake pulled off the headset and tossed it on the table.

Geez, she calls on the local phone system, which is only working because it's the middle of the night, and she tells him where to meet her! She might as well have put it in the newspaper. So it'll be Judith Farrell, Jack Yocke and enough KGB agents to arrest the Presidium.

'She told him he had courage,' Jake reported to the little group. 'He told her he had balls like a bull.'

Toad Tarkington grinned broadly.

She'll meet him on the way. Or someone will. That's the way she'll work it. She just wants him out on the street and moving in the right direction. That means she'll probably pick him up quick, not long after he leaves the embassy.

'She set up a meet at the Rizhsky subway station,' Grafton told his audience. He rubbed his face to ease his fatigue. 'As curious as Yocke is, it's hard to see how the sucker lived this long. Unbelievable.'

He had three guys plus Yocke. No radios. Clandestine surveillance in a foreign city was Judith Farrell's game, her profession, how she lived – none of his people had any training or experience, including Jake.

223

'Okay,' Jake said finally. 'Toad, go see how many of those rioters are still outside and figure out how we can get out of here without getting beaten to death. Then get back here quick. Spiro, go get Yocke. Senior Chief, go find the marine captain and get a couple more pistols, three M-16s, four of those infrared binoculars, and some ammo. Go.' He shooed them out.

There was no way he could trap Judith Farrell. He was going to have to send Yocke out into the streets and pray that Farrell found him before the KGB did, and that the reporter could somehow convince Farrell to play the game Jake's way.

'Amateur night in Moscow,' he muttered disgustedly.

The switchboard lights were blinking again. Jake went into the office next door to find the regular operator and ask him to return to the board.

CHAPTER FOURTEEN

Jake was in the empty office next to the switchboard when Toad Tarkington returned. 'Looks pretty deserted out there, Admiral, all things considered. A few people gawking at the bodies but that's about it.'

'They haven't picked up the bodies?'

'No, sir.'

'Any Russian cops around?'

'Not a one in sight. They split early this morning.'

'Go get a car. Open the gate and bring it into the compound. No, get two cars. Go.'

Toad went. One of his great virtues was that he never had to be told anything twice. Nor did he ask foolish questions or want directions clarified. He just grabbed the ball and ran with it.

Spiro Dalworth came in leading Jack Yocke, who looked grim.

'Go help the chief with the maps and weapons,' Jake told the lieutenant, who closed the door behind him.

Yocke glanced at his watch. 'What's up?' he asked.

'Sit down.'

Yocke did so. 'Dalworth said you wanted to see me.'

Jake just nodded. Yocke was wearing jeans, moderately dirty tennis shoes, and a nondescript sweater. Jake dimly recalled seeing Tarkington in that sweater a few days ago. Yocke must have helped himself. He still looked as American as a ball park hot dog. Jake Grafton pulled out the lower drawer of the desk he was sitting behind and parked his feet on it. A muffled report of a gun penetrated into the room. Jake closed his eyes and massaged his forehead.

'Admiral,' Yocke began impatiently, 'I really—'

'How long do you think you'll last out there before the KGB picks you up?'

Jack Yocke's face first showed surprise, then darkened into anger. 'You were listening! Damned if I will—'

'*Shut up!*' Grafton's voice cracked like a whip. He softened it a little and continued, 'You aren't naive enough to think it's possible to have a private conversation on a telephone in this country, are you? They tell me that sometimes there are so many eavesdroppers on the line that there isn't enough juice left to ring your phone.'

Yocke leaped to his feet, grabbed a bound report off the desk and hurled it against the far wall. He planted his feet in front of the desk where Jake sat and glowered down at the admiral. 'I'm about fed up to here with this cra—'

'Sit down and we'll talk this over.' Jake nodded at the chair Yocke had vacated.

When Yocke was back in his chair, Jake continued. 'You're a good reporter, Jack. Somewhere deep inside that polished chrome *Post* ego I think you really do give a teeny-tiny damn about the people you write about. But, honest to God, when are you going to see that you are in about ten miles over your head?'

Yocke merely stared at the admiral.

'I want you to keep your date with Shirley Ross. We're going to help you.'

'Thank you, thank you, thank you. The US government wants to help *little ol' me*, praise the Lord! I don't know whether to shout hosannas or just let the pee trickle down my leg.' He took a long deep breath and exhaled slowly while he examined his hands. Finally he said, 'What do you think she wants to talk to me about?'

'I don't know.'

Yocke thought that over. 'Her name isn't Shirley Ross, is it?'

'No.'

'Why don't you level with me, Jake?'

'I am leveling with you,' Jake Grafton said, the soul of reason. 'The truth is that you can't tell the wrong people what you don't know. I suggest you take a little comfort from that fact. There are people in Russia who could make a stone sing – they've had a lot of practice.'

'Boy, they'd be wasting their talents on this kid. You still haven't even told me why you want me to go out there tonight. For some strange reason I have this sneaky suspicion it ain't got nothing to do with writing stories for the *Washington Post*.'

'I want to have a private chat with Shirley Ross. You're going to get her for me.'

Jack Yocke didn't reply. He worried a fingernail and glanced at Jake Grafton from time to time, but he had nothing more to say.

Senior Chief Holley and Spiro Dalworth returned carrying maps and guns. Jake Grafton selected a map of the city and spread it out on the desk. Then Toad came breezing in. 'Cars are ready,' he announced and glanced at Yocke, who ignored him.

'Gather around.' Jake leaned over the map. He pointed out the embassy and the Rizhsky subway station, which was a transfer point for the adjoining train station.

'The first assumption is that the KGB listened to the call. They monitor all calls to the embassy. Shirley Ross knows that. So she will have to pick Jack up before he gets to the rendezvous. Now there are two ways to figure the KGB – either they think Shirley and Jack are who they seem, two neophytes playing games, so they merely go to the subway station and wait for them to arrive, or they figure that these are two pros and the meet will occur on the way, so they try to follow Jack from the embassy. My guess is they'll play it both ways, try to follow Jack and have people at the station, just in case.'

'Third possibility, sir,' Toad said. 'Maybe they'll think

the subway station was just a blind and the meet is on for someplace else.'

'So they follow Jack,' the admiral said. He looked at the reporter. 'The second assumption is that they really want Shirley. Want her alive or dead. You're just bait.' Jake Grafton shrugged. 'I may be wrong. They may try to grab you as soon as they lay eyes on you. Are you in?'

'Want her alive or dead? Why?'

Jake thought about it. How much could he tell Yocke? 'By this stage of the game the folks in Dzerzhinsky Square may have gotten an inkling or two that Ms Ross is the source of some of their painful difficulties.'

Yocke's face was flushed. 'You've assumed all along that I was going to help you. I haven't decided.'

Jake Grafton had had enough. 'Don't get pissy with me, kid. You've got ten seconds to decide. Yes or no.'

The pistols that the senior chief had put on the desk were 9mm automatics. Jake picked one up, popped out the magazine and reached for a box of cartridges on the desk.

'Why do you want Shirley?' Yocke asked.

Jake Grafton's open palm descended onto the desk with a vicious smack. 'In or out?' he snarled.

'Fuck! I'm in.'

'We'll meet you here.' He stabbed his finger at the map and everyone bent over to look. 'It's that park on the south bank of the Moskva River where the statues are, about four hundred yards east of the entrance to Gorky Park.' He looked at the reporter. 'You're going to have to find it in the dark. Study this map carefully. When Shirley picks you up, you bring her here. If you're followed there will probably be shooting. I want Shirley Ross alive and uninjured. She's *your* responsibility.'

'What if she doesn't want to meet you?'

'Make sure she does. Tell her anything you want.'

Jack Yocke looked from face to face. He swallowed once. 'I don't get paid anywhere near enough to do this shit.'

'When this is over we'll get you a tattoo.'

Toad Tarkington slapped Yocke on the back. 'Relax, Jack. Everybody has to contribute their mite. And under our enlightened system of government you only have to die once. That's right in the Bill of Rights along with all the freedoms – freedom of religion, freedom of the press, freedom of sexual satisfaction, freedom from ex-wives, free—'

'Kiss my ass, you silly son of a bitch.'

'Do this right and I'll kiss your ass at high noon on the front steps of the *Washington Post*.'

'I want a story out of this,' Yocke told Grafton.

'You know the rules,' the admiral replied mildly. 'If and when I say.'

Jack Yocke bit his lip. He was going to write a story about this whether Jake Grafton liked it or not. Grafton knew damn well who Shirley Ross was – probably an American agent: he had known from the moment Yocke first mentioned her name. And Grafton didn't even cheep. And Tarkington – always with the smart mouth and shit-eating grin because he knows something you don't. Yocke's slow burn began to sizzle.

Jesus, what if that story she gave him about the Soviet Square killings wasn't true? Could it have been a setup? The possibilities swirled in Yocke's mind as he examined the admiral through narrowed eyes. He looked at the nose a touch too big, the short salt-and-pepper hair, the cold gray eyes. *Grafton could have set it up!* Sure.

Say Shirley's story was all true except for the identity of the person who made the telephone call to the KGB agents. Say the agents thought they were talking to Demodov and it wasn't really him. What if Demodov was the fall guy? What if Demodov's denial was *true?*

Was Jake Grafton capable of a stunt like that?

Like what? Faking the phone call to set up Kolokoltsev? Or killing that neo-Nazi and his aides? Kolokoltsev was no great loss to anybody. In fact, his demise was one of the few bright spots in a Russia trying to come to grips with a

sordid past and an uncertain future. That bigoted demagogue . . . was . . .

Staring at the admiral now, Jack Yocke felt the cool hard
shape of truth as rigid as steel. Jake Grafton was capable of
doing whatever he thought was right. God help the poor
bastard who wandered into the way! Jake Graf—

'You want a gun?' Jake was holding out an automatic.
Dalworth and the senior chief were loading M-16s.

The reporter stared at the pistol, his train of thought
broken. A gun. He shook his head. 'If I get caught with a
gun the *Post* will fire me.'

Toad was incredulous. 'I knew civilian jobs were hard to
get, but . . . You'd rather be dead than unemployed?'

'If I'm unarmed they may not shoot me. Killing reporters
is damn poor PR. Sooner or later they'll get tired of feeding
me and ship me home to the bony bosom of my editor.'

Jake Grafton shrugged and tossed the pistol on the table.
'Your choice.'

'And I thought you'd decided to get into the game,' Toad
Tarkington said.

'Been a lot of reporters buried because they knew too
much,' the senior chief remarked.

Yocke flipped a hand in acknowledgment but refused to
change his mind.

Jack Yocke walked out of the embassy with nothing but his
passport in one pocket and a wad of rubles in another. He
had studied the map for fifteen minutes and thought he
knew where he was going. He had exactly six minutes to
make the subway station rendezvous and there was no way.
He had pointed out to Grafton that he was going to be very
late, but the admiral said, 'They'll wait for you,' and made
him take the time to study the map carefully.

He scurried out the main gate past the bodies lying in
the street, pathetic little piles of rags with all the life
smashed out. His course inadvertently took him by the
body of the woman incinerated by her own Molotov

230

cocktail. He tried not to look, looked anyway and almost vomited.

Moscow was not lit up like an American or European city. Occasional weak streetlights enlivened the gloom and gave enough light to see, but they offered little comfort.

Yocke wasn't alone on the street. People were watching from doorways and alleys, people staying well under cover. Yet they made no move to interfere with him. There was no traffic at all.

He walked as fast as he could and had to resist the urge to break into a trot.

If his editor ever heard about this evening's expedition he would be fired within two heartbeats for taking foolish risks. So why had he agreed to this anyway?

Grafton had laid out the route, the most direct way to the rendezvous. His course took him north on Tchaikovsky Street, through Vosstanija Square and onto Sadovaja-Kudrinskaja Street, which was really the same boulevard as Tchaikovsky Street. The names of the streets of Moscow changed at every major intersection, a European tradition designed to baffle tourists and keep taxi drivers fully employed.

He was getting into the rhythm now, his heart and lungs pumping as he swung along with a stride that ate up the distance.

Once he heard running footsteps and ducked into a doorway. The street was empty. Trying to stay calm, he stood stock-still for several seconds as his heart thudded like a trip-hammer.

Were they watching? Waiting for him?

'Someone will meet you long before you get there,' Jake Grafton had said.

Of course someone is watching.

For the first time that evening Jack Yocke felt the icy fingers of true fear. Unsure of what he should do now, he finally stepped back onto the sidewalk and resumed his journey. Where in hell was Shirley Ross?

His head was swiveling uncontrollably. When he realized that he was really seeing nothing because he was trying to see everything, he locked his head facing forward. Still his eyes swept nervously from side to side and he couldn't resist an occasional glance behind him. But he wasn't being followed.

They *must* be watching. Of course!

They. Whoever *they* were. Watching him hump along like a bug scurrying across a stone floor. Any second the shoe would come smashing down and—

He could smell himself. He was perspiring freely and he stank. He wiped the sweat off his forehead and rubbed his hand against his trousers, which left a wet spot.

A little car came around the corner and drove past him. The two heads – two male heads – didn't turn his way. The car went up the street and turned right at the next corner. A black car.

He was tiring. The nervous energy was burning off and the pace he was making was too fast. He slowed to almost normal speed.

Ahead of him on the right a door opened. Unconsciously he swerved left toward the street and picked up his pace.

God! He should have accepted that pistol Grafton offered. Grafton knew what the score was and offered it – why didn't he have the sense to—

'In here, Jack.'

It was her voice, a conversational tone.

'Don't just stand there,' she said. 'Come in here *now!*'

He went through the door into a darkened hallway. She was there, with a man. The man closed the door and she took his arm. 'Through here, quickly. We have a car out back. Hurry.' She broke into a trot.

'Jake Grafton wants to see you.'

'Where?'

'A park on the south side of the Moskva. He said—'

'Quiet.' She went through a door and they were in an alley. 'Into the car.' She dove into the passenger seat and

232

Yocke climbed into the back. Before he could get the door completely closed the car was in motion. He opened it partially and slammed it shut.

'Lie down,' she said.

He did so.

The car swerved and accelerated with a blast from the exhaust.

'Jake Grafton said that—'

'Wait.'

With his head against the seat Yocke tried to look out the windows. The car was accelerating down a narrow street, now braking and swerving around another corner.

'When the car stops,' Shirley Ross said, 'I want you to quickly get out. The same side you got in on. Be sure to close the door. There will be a panel truck right beside the car. You go into the truck and I'll be right behind you.'

'Okay.'

And almost immediately the car swerved sideways again. In seconds the driver applied the brakes.

'Now.'

He sat up and grabbed the door handle and got out as fast as he could. There were four vans there, but only one with the rear doors open. Shirley pushed him toward it. He scrambled in and she followed and someone closed the door and the vehicle began to move.

'Where?' she said.

'A park on the south side of the river four hundred yards east of the entrance to Gorky Park. They put the statues there after they tore them down.'

'I know where it is.' She moved forward in the van's interior and said something to the driver in a language Yocke didn't know.

When she returned to his side she devoted her attention to a small device she held in her hand. Then she held it up to her ear. A radio. Yocke could hear the voices.

'Are we being followed?'

'They are following three of the vans.'

'This one?'

She held up a hand to silence him. After a minute she went forward to confer with the driver.

How in hell had he gotten himself into this mess anyway? Hurtling though the streets of Moscow in a van that smelled like a garbage truck, being trailed by the KGB – he braced himself against the swaying of the vehicle as it darted around a corner.

She was back beside him. 'In a few minutes we will switch vehicles again. Stay with me.'

'Okay.'

She listened intently to the radio.

'What's your real name?'

She didn't reply.

'What did you want to tell me?'

'You? Nothing. I need to talk to Jake Grafton and the telephones are all tapped. He figured it out.'

Jack Yocke opened his mouth again but now her fingers were against his face, feminine fingers that brushed his cheek and remained against his lips.

Jake Grafton sat in the grass with his back against one of Felix Dzerzhinsky's bronze legs, facing in the direction of Gorky Park. About seventy-five yards to the north, his right, was the south bank of the Moskva River. Farther ahead on the right, between where he sat and the boulevard in front of the Gorky Park entrance columns, was a vast low building, a cultural institute, with its empty parking lots. Farther to the west the Grecian columns of the park entrance gate were visible behind streetlights on the boulevard. Several hundred yards away to the south, on Jake's left, were block after block of drab apartment buildings. Behind him to the east the park went for a quarter mile until it reached a street.

Toad Tarkington was on Jake's left lying on his belly amid some scrub trees and weeds. Spiro Dalworth was against the corner of the cultural building. Senior Chief

Holley was behind Jake, watching his back. All three men had M-16s.

The city seemed abnormally quiet tonight, Jake Grafton thought. Perhaps the day of rioting had drained the energy from the Moscovites and they were home in bed worrying about their future. They certainly had a bucketful of troubles to fret about.

Ambassador Lancaster had telephoned as Grafton was walking out the door of his apartment, five minutes after dispatching Jack Yocke. Toad took the call and made some excuse. Whatever was on the ambassador's mind would have to wait a few hours.

Tonight Jake's .357 Magnum revolver lay beside him in the grass. All he had to do was drop his hand to it. In his hands he held a stick that he had picked up before he sat down. He was whittling upon it with his pocketknife while he speculated about what Lancaster had wanted. Lancaster didn't seem the type to invite him to Spaso House for an evening of poker.

No stars tonight.

Another high overcast that might or might not bring rain.

How long had it been? Twenty minutes?

Over on the boulevard in front of Gorky Park several trucks rumbled by. The noise carried oddly, sounding abnormally loud. The city was too quiet.

Looking the other way, toward the northeast, Jake could see the turrets and spires of the Kremlin, lit up tonight as usual. It was eerie, in a way, how for centuries that old fortress had housed czars and czarinas in extraordinary opulence. Favored by accidents of birth, they had lived out their lives in that palace and the one in St Petersburg while the mass of Russians struggled just to stay alive. When the Communists came along they moved right in. Yet like the czars, the days of the Reds were over, so tonight Yeltsin and his allies were in there trying to figure out how to ride the tiger. And out here amid the discarded, smashed statues

235

the Russians were still struggling to stay alive, just as they always had.

Bracing his elbows against his knees, Jake scanned the area again with what appeared to be heavy binoculars. Unlike regular binoculars, this set picked up infrared light.

He could see Spiro against the corner of the building. He had told the lieutenant to stay down, but he was up against the wall, peering this way and that.

Do the Russians have infrared binoculars?

Toad was nearly invisible – all Jake could see was the faintest indication of a glow where he must be lying. The senior chief seemed equally well hidden.

No one else in sight. Not a dog, not a prowling cat, not a drunk or pair of lovers. Well, it's not a good night for drunks or lovers.

Jake raised the glasses and scanned the buildings to the south and east.

Somewhere in the city Yocke was playing secret agent. That guy! Always sure he knew everything when in reality he was just stumbling along in the dark with everyone else.

Maybe he shouldn't have let Yocke go. If something happened to him . . .

Finally he lowered the glasses and zipped up his jacket. The evening was getting chilly. Wondering about Yocke, worrying about Yeltsin and his grand experiment, Jake Grafton went back to his whittling.

Jack Yocke couldn't see any of the features of the man behind the wheel of the van, even looking in the rearview mirror. He had dark hair and wore a dark jacket and whispered with Shirley Ross in a foreign language that Yocke tried in vain to identify in the deep silence that had fallen once the van's engine was turned off. This was the third van he had been in tonight. Shirley Ross apparently had access to a motor pool.

The driver and the woman consulted a map, made more whispered comments, stared out the window to the left.

The driver had a hand-held radio that now sounded start-lingly loud. He turned down the volume and held it close to his ear.

Finally she turned back to Yocke. 'The statues are over there about a hundred yards or so, through the little trees.'

'Who are you?'

'You and I will get out and walk across the grass. Stay with me. If anything goes wrong, just fall down on your stomach and stay there.'

'If what goes wrong?'

'Anything.'

The man in the front seat handed back a submachine gun. Shirley Ross put the strap across her left shoulder, tucked the butt under her right armpit and grasped the pistol grip and trigger assembly with her right hand.

The driver got out of the van and closed the door. In seconds the rear doors of the van opened.

'Let's go,' she said, and went first.

Jack Yocke took a deep breath, then followed.

The van was sitting in front of a huge slab of apartments. Across the street was the park. She was already moving. Yocke followed. As they crossed the sidewalk and entered the weeds and longish grass, it occurred to him that he had never even got a glimpse of the driver's face.

There was just enough light for him to pick up the vague outline of tree trunks and bushes. He tripped twice, then had to take several long strides to catch up to Shirley Ross, who was just a vague black shape moving quickly away from him.

Once she stopped and he almost bumped into her, then she was moving again, though in a slightly different direction.

Just as Jack Yocke was beginning to wonder if she knew where she was going, she slowed down and spoke softly: 'Good morning, Admiral.'

'Hello, Judith. Come sit over here by Stalin's head.'

'I don't think we were followed, but they might have

fooled me. They've been running spot surveillance on you since you arrived and they're hunting really hard for me.'

Yocke almost fell over the marble statue that lay on its side. He sat down with his back against it. Shirley sat on his right. Sitting facing them, with his back against one of the huge bronze statues, the reporter recognized Jake Grafton. He had a pair of heavy binoculars in his hands.

'I brought your reporter back,' Shirley told Jake. 'Where can we put him so that you and I can have a private conversation?'

'Oh, I think he's earned a little piece of the truth. He won't print anything without my permission.'

'You trust him?'

Jake Grafton chuckled. 'Beneath that polished, ambitious facade beats a pure and noble heart.'

'Shmarov blew up the Serdobsk reactor.'

'Sure,' Jake Grafton said. 'And the KGB killed Kolokoltsev in Soviet Square. If we're going to tell each other fairy stories, Judith, let's go find a warm bar that serves good whiskey.'

'Oh, you know we killed Kolokoltsev. After we did it the KGB breathed a collective sigh of relief – the man was an embarrassment to the Old Guard heavy hitters – and so I thought why not get some PR mileage out of it, muddy the water.'

'How do you know about Serdobsk?'

'The helicopter pilot that flew them down there is one of ours. He helps us pay off the authorities and smuggle Jews out. Then a few nights ago he was called at home and told to come in for a priority flight. Five men and their equipment to the nuclear power plant at Serdobsk. When he got there he realized things weren't going right when his passengers shot one security guard and herded the other inside. So he waited a bit, then started the engines and got out of there. The reactor blew up about two hours later.'

After a few seconds of silence, Jake Grafton asked, 'Who does your man work for?'

'KGB.'

'And the passengers?'

'Also KGB. The man in charge was a Colonel Gagarin.'

'How do you know Gagarin blew the thing up?'

'Obviously I'm adding two and two.'

'Where's Gagarin now?'

'I don't know. He never came back.'

'He blew himself up?' Jake asked incredulously.

'Well, he didn't shoot the guard at the front gate for sport, then carry bags full of equipment inside to equip the local baseball team. But he and his men could have gotten out somehow and the KGB then eliminated them. I don't know.'

'And Shmarov?'

'Gagarin was one of his lieutenants. He didn't do anything that Shmarov didn't know about and approve.'

'It's damn thin, Judith.'

'Admiral, in this business you are never going to get sworn affidavits.'

Jake Grafton could see her silhouette but not her face. She sounded tired. How many years had it been since he last saw her? He counted. Five. Five years running clandestine, covert operations, five years of false identities, deceit, risks calculated, chances taken, five years of stalking enemies of the Jewish state, five years of secret warfare . . . and she had been a covert operations professional when he first met her in Italy.

'Let's talk about Nigel Keren,' Jake Grafton said.

'You guarantee that this reporter . . . ?'

'If he writes a word that I don't approve of, you can shoot him anywhere you find him.'

Jack Yocke didn't think that was a joke.

The woman was answering Jake: '. . . Keren was financing our efforts to get Jews out of Russia. He gave us about a billion dollars.'

'A *billion?* That much money—'

'Bribes,' she told him. 'Expenses. We had to pay off the

239

authorities, pay for everything.' She turned slightly, toward Yocke. 'You were looking for Yakov Dynkin? He's in Israel now. We'll get his wife there as soon as we can. We bought him out of prison, bought a false passport and visa. He left from Sheremetyevo.'

'Keren was a Jew,' Jack Yocke said.

'Keren wanted to help. The CIA finally found out about it through the KGB and decided to stop Keren's contributions. The Arabs want Jewish immigration to Israel stopped and the CIA was trying – is trying – to play all sides in the Middle East. Iraq and Syria are buffers against Shiite fundamentalism, but they are bitter enemies of Israel. Give everybody a little, preserve the status quo. They—'

A shot rang out. Then another.

A stream of muzzle flashes from the darkness. Jack Yocke threw himself sideways as a surge of adrenaline shot through him and tried to burrow under the marble statue of Stalin. Vaguely he was aware of a silenced, guttural buzzing beside him, more shots, then a weight fell across his legs. A heavy report sounded just beside him. More shots.

And as suddenly as it began, it was over. In what, ten or fifteen seconds?

'Judith? Judith?' Jake Grafton's voice.

Yocke tried to move but the weight on his legs held him. It was a body. 'I've got her,' Jake Grafton said. 'Get up, Jack.'

Grafton had a small penlight. 'She's been shot. Judith, can you hear me?'

Someone else was there. 'Two CIA guys from the embassy.' Toad Tarkington's voice. 'They're both dead. We've got to get the hell out of Dodge.'

'Judith's been shot,' Jake told him. Now Toad saw the revolver in his hand. 'You and Yocke take her to the car and I'll get the other guys.' He took the M-16 from Toad and slung it over his shoulder.

She was heavy. Jack Yocke got her legs and Toad her shoulders. Toad wanted to go faster than Yocke could manage. 'Come on, you son of a bitch,' Toad swore. 'Move it!'

They had to carry her a hundred yards. She seemed to weigh a ton and several times Yocke thought he might drop her. She was limp, unconscious. Somehow his savage grip on her bare, shaved legs seemed obscene, an invasion of her womanhood that added embarrassment to the stew of emotions surging through the reporter.

'What happened?' Yocke asked Toad between breaths as they stumbled along.

'Two men. I got one with the first shot and the other charged and exchanged shots with Judith. I think they shot each other or else Grafton or somebody drilled him. Hell, maybe I got him too, not that it matters a damn. I got a look at their bodies. Both CIA guys from the embassy.'

CIA? Jesus, Yocke swore under his breath, he thought that story this Shirley or Judith or whatever her name is had told was all crap!

'What did you say?' Toad demanded.

'Jesus!'

She groaned once, just before they maneuvered her into the backseat. Toad jumped in back. 'You drive, Jack. Keys are under the floormat.'

Yocke got behind the wheel and fumbled with the keys.

'Come on, Yocke! Let's get her to the embassy before she bleeds to death.'

Somehow Yocke got the right key into the ignition and the engine started. He pulled the lever into drive and tried to resist the urge to floor the accelerator.

In the backseat Toad was trying to see where she was hit. Three bullet holes, as near as he could tell, all into the left lung area. He had his arm around her and could feel the warm, sticky wetness. Damn! One of them must have punched into her heart.

241

She whispered something. He put his ear almost against her lips. 'Hello, Robert.'

'We'll get you to the doc at the embassy, Hannah.' Without thinking, he had used her real name. He almost bit his tongue.

Her pulse was fluttering, her muscles slack.

And Toad knew. She was dying. Fury welled in him, all the frustrated bitterness accumulated through the years from loving a woman when the love wasn't returned, couldn't be returned – now it washed over him as a wave of pure rage, then as suddenly dissipated, leaving an emptiness in its place.

'Judith Farrell,' he whispered, his lips right next to her ear. 'I have loved two women in my life. You were the first.'

Whether or not she heard him he didn't know. A moment later he realized she had no pulse. He hugged her tighter and sat watching the buildings as the car sped through empty streets.

CHAPTER FIFTEEN

'Somebody sold us out.' Toad Tarkington was in a fine fury, his face dark, his eyes narrowed to slits. Unconsciously Jack Yocke took a step backward.

Senior Chief Holley and Spiro Dalworth took the full brunt of Tarkington's anger. They stood their ground as Toad continued in a low, intense voice: 'Someone here in this room told the CIA where the meet was, who was going to be there. They didn't get it over the phone, they didn't get it from a wiretap, they didn't follow anybody there. Someone talked, whispered into a spook's ear, and because of that, Judith Farrell *died*.'

Spiro Dalworth's face was a study as he tried to keep it under control. Toad Tarkington zeroed in, put his face inches from that of the lieutenant. *'Somebody broke the faith.'* He said the words slowly, like an Old Testament prophet pronouncing the doom of a king. 'Somebody betrayed his shipmates, sold out to the spook fucks playing power politics. Why don't you tell us about it, Dalworth.'

'Commander, I—'

'You *shit!*'

'Listen, we're on the same team. I—'

The back of Toad's hand flicked across Dalworth's face with a whiplike smack. Dalworth staggered and almost fell.

'That's enough, Toad,' Jake Grafton said.

Tarkington stepped back and stood glowering at Dalworth, who rubbed the side of his face and looked at the admiral. 'Sir, I'm *sorry!*' the lieutenant said. 'I thought—' His voice broke. He was near tears.

'Who'd you tell?' the admiral asked in a tired voice.

'Herb Tenney. We've talked before about an agency job when I get out. My naval career—'

'When did you tell him?'

'Before we left to go to the park.'

Jake Grafton looked out the window at the fountain in front of the complex cafeteria. On the other side of the square was the empty new embassy riddled with electronic listening devices. KGB bugs, CIA bugs, maybe Mossad, MI-5, German bugs, you name it. Was there anybody anywhere in this uncertain world who was willing to sleep in blissful ignorance of what the US ambassador said to his aides? Or his assistant? Or his wife?

'Admiral, I—'

'No.' Jake Grafton thought he knew what Tarkington was going to say. Toad would desperately love to go find Herb Tenney and shoot him dead.

Let's assume Judith was telling the gospel truth. The CIA learned of the Nigel Keren operation through the KGB. And the KGB has just blown up the Serdobsk power plant, contaminating thousands of square miles and killing thousands of people, thereby triggering a leadership crisis that might result in a new dictatorship of the Old Guard, some of whom lead the KGB. Assume also that this development would not be frowned upon by the rogue clique in the CIA that controlled Herb Tenney. In some crazy way it fitted. Jake Grafton got that hollow feeling in the pit of his stomach again.

The Middle East, eastern Europe, the horn of Africa, southeast Asia . . . Every major event affects every person in this interdependent world. The collapse of communism in the Soviet Union upset the equilibrium. No, the collapse of the shah in pro-Western Iran was the triggering event. Like shock waves radiating from the epicenter of an earth-quake, these events triggered other events, upset the bal-ance of power that kept a world with too few resources and too many greedy men from coming apart at the seams. And now the seams were ripping.

He turned from the window. 'Toad, you and Jack take Farrell's body back to the park.'

'Why not the Israeli embassy, sir? She ought to have a decent funeral and burial. She deserves that.'

Jake Grafton thought the white-collar crowd at the Israeli embassy would be extremely embarrassed if they received the body of a covert soldier killed in an operation that the government of Israel would deny all knowledge of. He merely repeated his order: 'Take her to the park.'

'Aye aye, sir. Come on, Yocke.'

'Senior Chief, go to bed.'

Jake Grafton and Spiro Dalworth were standing alone in the room when Toad Tarkington closed the door.

Out in the car Judith Farrell's body lay under a pile of jackets on the backseat. Toad got behind the wheel and Jack Yocke got in beside him.

The sky was just beginning to gray when Toad turned the corner and sped south on the wide, empty boulevard that ran toward the river.

Jack Yocke was still trying to fit together all the pieces. 'How well did you know her?' he asked Toad.

Toad didn't answer immediately. 'Pretty well,' he said finally.

'Shirley Ross, Judith Farrell . . . aliases?'

'Yep. And she had others.'

'Do you know her real name?'

'She told it to me once.'

'To die like that . . .'

'In her line of work it was bound to happen sooner or later.'

As they crossed the Moskva bridge, Jack Yocke asked, 'Do you think her team really killed Kolokoltsev in Soviet Square?'

Toad said, 'You told me that one of the gunmen held the

door to the limo open and one stood there cool as a cucumber squirting bullets into the people inside? Well, the shooter for the *coup de grâce* was undoubtedly Judith Farrell. That was the payoff – those people were putting their lives on the line to kill that anti-Jewish hate merchant. You can bet your last kopek that Judith Farrell was right there at the trigger to make damn sure there was no slipup. That was the way she operated.'

Jack Yocke glanced into the backseat, then looked back at Toad. 'She was an assassin?'

'She fought for her people.'

'Well . . .'

'*Asshole!*' Toad roared. '*I* killed a man tonight. *I* am not in the mood for moralizing from the editorial page pulpit. This ain't a cocktail party in Georgetown! They slaughter people by the millions on this fucking continent! Mass murder is the European sport. Got a social problem, kill another million!'

'Sorry,' Yocke said contritely.

Toad snarled, 'They oughta make you the fucking wine editor at the *Post*.'

The two men sat in the car looking at the park as the night faded into a gray dawn. They had nothing else to say to each other. Each was occupied with his own thoughts.

If there was anyone watching, Toad didn't see them. Finally he opened his door and stepped out. 'Help me with her,' he muttered to the reporter.

They left Judith Farrell under the nearest tree. Toad tried not to look at her face. As he straightened up he could see the body of the man he had shot still lying just as he had fallen.

On the way back to the car Jack Yocke glanced over his shoulder at the body of the Israeli agent. Toad Tarkington didn't.

A Russian army detail was picking up the bodies around the American embassy compound when Toad and Jack returned. The soldiers were piling the corpses in a large truck. They weren't carrying weapons.

A marine opened the gate and Toad drove through. As he got out of the car he saw her walking toward him. She wore khakis and a leather flight jacket and her hair was in a bun. When he held out his arms she broke into a run.

'Rita!'

'Hello, Toad-man.' She gave him a fierce hug, then stepped back. 'I brought you a present,' she said. She unzipped the jacket and held it open. 'Me!'

He took her in his arms. 'When did you get here?' he asked finally.

'An hour ago.'

'Why?'

'Admiral Grafton asked for three pilots. I volunteered.'

Toad tried to frown. 'I told you never to volunteer.'

'Ah, Toad-man, you do it all the time.'

'Yeah. And look at me. God, I'm glad you're here.'

The marine recon team commanding officer was Captain Iron Mike McElroy. His broad shoulders tapered to a trim waist and a flat stomach that was probably corrugated like a washboard under his camo shirt. He saluted crisply and introduced himself. He and Jake had just started to get acquainted when Agatha Hempstead came marching across the sidewalk straight at them.

'Ambassador Lancaster didn't know or approve of this decision to bring in a marine recon team.' She ignored Captain McElroy.

'General Land talked to the president about it,' Jake Grafton said mildly. 'The president approved it.'

'Owen – Ambassador Lancaster should have been consulted. This request should have gone through the State Department. We can't have the military making foreign poli—'

'Ms Hempstead,' Jake said firmly, cutting her off. 'I apologize to Ambassador Lancaster. I did not intend to cut

247

him out of the loop. But time and urgent operational considerations required that I communicate directly with General Land in the Pentagon.'

'What considerations? What considerations do you consider to be nonpolitical? Here in Russia everything is political! Everything! I don't think you understand Ambassador Lancaster's position!'

Jake cocked his head and eyed Ms Hempstead. 'You're the one who seems to be having the difficulty understanding who is responsible for what, ma'am. I suggest we stop this little turf war before it goes any further and start cooperating.'

'What considerations?'

Jake Grafton was ready to use a dirty word or two, but he swallowed it and rammed his fists into his pockets. 'The situation here in Russia is a bit out of control. I'm sure you've noticed.'

'The marine guard is quite capable of defending the embassy compound from a riot, Admiral.' Jake had never heard a flag officer's rank pronounced quite this way. Antipathy, derision, disrespect – Goodbody Hempstead got a lot of mileage out of one little word. 'The decision to augment the marines is for Ambassador Lancaster to make. A reconnaissance team armed to the teeth is *not* going to help matters very much!'

She paused, so Jake said, 'The team is not here to augment the marine guard.'

But she was merely marshaling her arguments, not entertaining replies. 'I'm sure the Yeltsin government will be making a diplomatic protest within hours. A recon team ready for combat strikes me as a very serious stretch of the military cooperation agreements that we have been operating under these last few weeks. Ambassador Lancaster—'

'Maybe I'd just better have a talk with the ambassador.'

'What *are* you going to use the team for?'

'I'll tell it to the ambassador.'

So seven minutes later he was standing in the ambassador's office. Boris Yeltsin was on television addressing the nation. Jake and Hempstead stood silently while the ambassador listened to a translator. When the broadcast was over, Lancaster muttered, 'Well, at least he's not resigning.'

'These seven people that want to take over, this junta, any mention of them?' Jake asked as the translator left the room.

'No. That's a good sign, I think. But the situation is very fluid.' Lancaster sat down behind his desk and turned to Jake again. He went straight to the point: 'What's the recon team for?'

'I haven't decided yet, sir. I thought they might come in handy.'

'Admiral, I don't want you or Hayden Land starting a war. Before any of those gung-ho special warriors dons his warpaint or steps outside of this compound, I want a complete briefing. In writing.'

'Yessir.'

'We'll put them in the gymnasium. They can sleep there. But so help me, Admiral, the secretary of state is not going to be a happy little camper. Foreign policy is the prerogative of civilians under our system of government. It's a tried and true system and we're going to ensure the United States sticks with it. If Land shoved the president out onto thin ice the shit is going to hit the fan.' The cuss word sounded weird coming from the New England Brahmin. Jake would have bet money the old man had never even heard the word.

'Before you even scratch yourself,' the ambassador continued, 'I want a complete briefing.'

'I should have discussed my concerns with you, sir, but the press of events didn't seem to allow the time. I apologize. In a few hours I'm going to steal a couple helicopters from the Russians and fly down to Serdobsk for a look. I want to see that power plant.'

Lancaster sat back in his chair. 'They tell me that site is too hot for humans.'

'The marines brought some antiradiation suits. And we probably won't land. But I want to see what the place looks like and we need to get some better data on radiation levels.'

Lancaster digested that with a sour look on his face. Apparently he came to the conclusion that the less he knew the better. '*Steal* helicopters?' he asked mildly.

'Steal.'

Jake reached across the desk for an envelope, turned it over and wrote: Today I will steal two helicopters and fly to Serdobsk.

He signed his name, wrote the date, then passed the envelope to Lancaster, who looked at it and sighed. He ran his fingers across his scalp. 'You don't let much grass grow under your feet, do you, Admiral?'

'One other thing you should probably be aware of, sir. I would suggest you and Ms Hempstead keep this to yourself, not report it to Washington, not discuss it with anyone else on the embassy staff.'

'The ambassador will make that decision,' Agatha Hempstead said tartly.

Jake Grafton shrugged. 'Last night my aide and I had a little shooting scrape with a couple armed men near Gorky Park. They were killed. I think they might have been CIA agents.'

'Who were they?' Lancaster asked.

Jake gave him the names.

Owen Lancaster and Agatha Hempstead just looked at each other, then transferred their stunned gaze to the admiral.

'If you'll excuse me, sir,' Jake said and got to his feet. 'I have to go see about those helicopters.' The diplomats watched him go without recovering their voices.

Jack Yocke tapped listlessly on his computer. He had found

that having the keyboard under his fingers was therapeutic. When his mind was wandering his fingers merely tapped out disjointed phrases, but when he was thinking about something specific his fingers strung words together into sentences as his thoughts rolled along.

The secret is to think in logical, coherent sentences, which most people don't do. Yocke did, most of the time. As he witnessed an event or thought about a subject the words scrolled through his mind. If he had a keyboard under his fingers the words became text.

Now he glanced at the screen. 'Nigel Keren' was written there.

Ah yes. The headline flashed through his mind and the words appeared on the screen. 'British billionaire Nigel Keren murdered by CIA.' That headline could get him a story in every newspaper in the world.

And he couldn't write the story.

Frustrated, he got up from the computer and went to the window. He was still in Admiral Grafton's apartment in the embassy complex, and unless he was willing to head straight back to the land of Diet Coke and hot dogs, he was going to have to stay here.

A great end to your first foreign correspondent assignment, Jack! Write one good story that blames a political murder on the wrong crowd, the local secret police, who promptly jump on your case like stink on Limburger.

Maybe he should call his editor. He glanced at the phone and even took a step in that direction, then returned to the window.

Yocke knew his editor. Gatler would pretend to be incredulous, thunderstruck: you're hiding out and missing the *great* stories, the big, stupendous, attack-on-Pearl Harbor, war-declared stories – world's worst nuclear accident kills zillions, democracy collapses in Russia, military dictatorship ousts Yeltsin? If you don't get a piece of those stories, his editor would shout, you'll go back on the cop beat for the rest of your natural, miserable life.

Jack Yocke had no intention of informing his editor that he had made a tiny little mistake on the Soviet Square Massacre story. That the KGB were innocent lambs, victims of a foul Israeli plot to besmirch their honor. He wasn't going to call that one in, even if Grafton gave him permission to print the truth, which he wouldn't.

The fact is that he had been set up by someone who knew just how much truth he could uncover and how to twist it into the story she wanted told. *Now* he knew, and he couldn't tell. Wouldn't tell, even if he could.

But everyone manipulates the press, don't they? Politicians and cops, athletes and movie stars do it all the time.

Moscow seemed quiet out there beyond the brick wall topped with two strands of barbed wire. Yocke could see the marine opening the front gate and letting cars go in and out.

As he watched he saw Toad Tarkington, Rita Moravia and Spiro Dalworth pile into a car with a couple of marines armed with M-16s. Two more marines and the other two pilots got into a second car. Away they went, out the gate. His curiosity piqued, Yocke wondered about their errand and destination.

When the second car turned the corner and was out of sight, Yocke turned back to his computer.

No, the story he wasn't getting was *KGB blows up Serdobsk reactor! Zillions Die!* Now that would be a story that would make Jack Yocke as famous as Michael Jackson, a story to launch a hell of a career, a story to get him his own column, maybe even an investigative team like Bob Woodward had. And what did Woodward dig out from under his rock? Richard Nixon with a coverup dripping from his fingers – a popcorn fart compared to this little beauty.

But he hadn't missed it yet. Oh no! Jake Grafton had it and no other reporter was going to get a sniff. Sooner or later Jack Yocke would mine that ore. He could feel it in his bones.

Zillions die. Not zillions, but maybe tens of thousands.

The import of those words struck home as Yocke stared at them on the computer screen. Tens of thousands, men, women, children – the lame, the halt, the blind, the virtuous, the guilty, the oh so very human. All. Everyone in the fallout zone.

And that Mossad killer Judith Farrell told Jake Grafton the KGB did it intentionally. On purpose. Murder. Political murder. The ends justify the means. Kill them all.

Was she lying again?

Suddenly Yocke had had enough of the computer. He turned it off and went to the window and looked out for a while.

Then, since he was tired, he laid down and tried to sleep. After a while he did.

Jake Grafton was also thinking about the people in the fallout zone, thousands who were already dead or dying or sick as a human could be. If this were America or western Europe there would be no helicopters to steal. Those machines the networks hadn't commandeered to carry their insta-cams, satellite feed gear and blow-dried reporters would all be in use for evacuation and relief efforts. If this were America or western Europe.

One of the interpreters was watching Russian television and periodically summarizing what she heard, and she had not gotten a single hint that any relief efforts were under way.

'It's too early,' Captain Collins said uneasily. 'It'll take them a while to figure out what they need to do, then another while for anyone to decide he has the authority to set things in motion, then a third while for anybody to get off his ass and actually do something. The only certainty is whatever they do will be too little, too late, and completely ineffective.'

Jake nodded. He had had only an hour's sleep last night and was very tired. He tried to concentrate.

'How hot is the fallout zone?' he asked Collins.

The nuclear engineering officer just shrugged. 'At one of these Russian nuke facilities a few years ago,' he said, 'they didn't know what to do with the hot waste, so they dumped it into a pond a hundred feet deep. Kept doing that. Then one summer the pond partially dried up and the mud turned to dust and blew away. Contaminated an area of four hundred eleven square miles. Contamination level of six hundred roentgens an hour, which is a fatal dose. Spend one hour anywhere in that area unprotected and you're history.'

'So what did the Russians do after Chernobyl?'

'They lied about the extent of the accident, they lied about the radiation dosages people got and the number of victims, they ordered in troops to clean up the mess and lied about the dosages they got, they lied about the extent of food contamination, the relief money was stolen by corrupt officials, they misdiagnosed the cancers . . . they basically fucked it up from end to end.'

Collins searched for words. 'Maybe lie is the wrong word. These people have always operated on the premise that no one should ever be told bad news, so they are incapable of effectively dealing with any problem at any level. Bad news doesn't go up the ladder and doesn't come down, which means that *no one ever knows the truth*.'

On that note Collins felt silent. When Jake failed to ask any more questions, Collins had a question of his own. 'What do you want me to do with Dalworth, Admiral?'

'Did he tell you about the fracas in the park?'

'Yessir. And about whispering to Herb Tenney.'

It was Jake's turn to shrug. 'Don't do anything.'

Collins picked at a discolored place on his uniform trousers.

'Did Dalworth tell you those two guys we killed were CIA?'

'Uh, yessir.'

'I may need Dalworth,' Jake said slowly. 'I don't know what the hell Herb Tenney is up to, but whatever it is, it's going to get him burned. I intend to light the fire.'

CHAPTER SIXTEEN

What was Herb Tenney up to? Jake worried the question as he lay inert on a couch with a throbbing headache. He had downed four aspirin and now had a wet washcloth draped across his forehead. Droplets of water trickled through his hair and wet the miserably thin pillow.

It was hard to keep the proper perspective. Somehow, some way, a group within the CIA was embedded in this Russian mess up to its hidden microphones. Perhaps Toad's reaction was the proper one – absolute outrage. But Toad would surrender to that emotion and lose sight of the other aspects. That was the thing about Toad . . . passionate sincerity was the steel buried under that flippant shell he wore to ward off the bumps and abrasions of everyday life.

He still loved Judith Farrell, Jake was positive of that. Toad had given himself to her once, years ago, and he was the type of man for whom there could never be any emotional retreat. Love once bestowed could never be withdrawn. Oh, he could love another woman, and did – he was desperately in love with Rita Moravia. Now he must hide the hurt of the loss to avoid injuring another – only the Toad-man would get himself into that pre- dicament. And Jake could only guess how badly he was hurting.

Yakolev, Shmarov . . . He had met those two and come away confused. Yakolev at least wore the face he thought the foreigners wanted to see: maybe all he did was wear it. Shmarov looked like some hideous apparition from a Boris

Karloff movie, ready to jerk out fingernails and slice off testicles.

Money. Somehow he had missed the money connection between Nigel Keren and the Mossad, and it was right there in plain sight. *Billionaire* publisher and industrialist Nigel Keren . . . Money, money, money . . .

Richard Harper said he had *it*. But what did he have? Is money the connection between the CIA and the KGB?

The salient feature of communism that made it different from every other system of government man has yet devised was that it made everyone poor. All one could hope for under communism was access to more perks, to the right schools, a dacha in the Lenin Hills, a car, shopping in the party stores, party hospitals, and a plot in a party cemetery when the party doctors could do no more. But money? No. Today Boris Yeltsin was only paid the ruble equivalent of a hundred dollars a month.

What do desperate comrades do when the tide goes out and leaves them stranded on a mud bar?

What have they done?

Everyone must be dead at the Petrovsk Rocket Base. Collins said it was in the center of a fallout pattern, a mere eighty miles downwind. The men and women there must have died quickly, almost in their tracks. Perhaps the people in the clean rooms lasted a little longer. Perhaps not.

But the missiles and their warheads would be unaffected. They would be sitting there in the hangars on their transports and the clean room would be full of partially disassembled warheads.

How do you dispose of plutonium warheads? This was the question that had bedeviled the foreign experts and the Russian military. Simply taking them apart wasn't the answer – they could be assembled again by anyone with the know-how.

Atomic weapons were the ultimate curse, Jake told himself once again. Their very existence warped space and time and human affairs like little black holes.

There must be some solution, something that rendered the warheads incapable of harming anyone. But what?

'Admiral. Admiral Grafton.'

It was Senior Chief Holley.

'Commander Tarkington called on the scrambled hand-held.' At least the marines had brought com equipment! 'They've found some choppers. He said to tell you it'll be a couple more hours before they're fuelled and checked out.'

'Thanks, Senior Chief.'

He tried again to turn off the muscles, to relax completely into sleep. So Toad found some choppers . . .

He was drifting in a late afternoon sky filled with giant white clouds over a blue landscape, clouds with tops shot with fire and bases hidden in deepening shadow.

He saw the clouds the other day from the window of the jet as they flew back to Moscow from the missile base, saw them from above, from the angle that God sees them. What does *He* think, watching the clouds drift across the landscape, watching the humans grapple in the mud, poisoning one another in the deep purple shadows?

The question flitted across a tired mind, then was gone, leaving only the clouds and the blue land below and the dark shadows of the coming night.

They looked like garbagemen in the one-size-fits-all baggy NBC (nuclear, biological, chemical) suits. American servicemen called these things hot suits because there was no provision to cool the wearer. Britain's Jocko West helped the French and German officers into their suits, then donned his own. The Italian officer, Colonel Galvano, couldn't be reached at this hotel or the Italian embassy.

Although normally the suits merely provided filtered air, these were the latest models with a limited self-contained oxygen supply. When the oxygen was gone they would have to go on filtered air, and in an environment as hot as the one Tom Collins predicted, the filters were going to get quickly contaminated.

Before they came out to the airport, a heliport on the southeastern side of the city, Jake had spent twenty minutes talking with General Hayden Land on the scrambled telephone. 'Do what you think best,' Land said. What else could he have said?

'Can you fly this . . . thing?' Jake asked Lieutenant Justin 'Goober' Groelke, one of the pilots who came to Russia with Rita and the marines. Goober was already decked out in his hot suit.

'I think so, sir. I got a couple thousand hours in big choppers.'

'How much fuel do we have?'

'Not enough. We'll all ride in this one. Toad's loaded the other machine with fuel in drums. All we could find was a hand pump. We'll fly in formation as far southeast as we can, land the other machine in a clean area. Then we'll refuel this chopper and fly on. When we come back from the hot zone we'll fuel up again.'

'Or abandon this machine.'

'Yessir. If it's too contaminated.'

'What kind of condition are these machines in?'

Here Groelke paused. 'These are fairly new machines, Aeroflot Mi-8s, with very low times on the tachs. They've been sitting outside without engine covers for a couple months, apparently. We cleaned the dirt and bird shit out of the intakes as best we could, drained the sumps, checked all the systems we could, all the fluid levels, the hubs . . . The hydraulic fluid may have some water in it and the engine oil doesn't look good on either machine. The batteries were dead. We used a power cart to start the engines and we hovered both machines. There's no telling how much dirt was in the engines before we turned them up. I assumed that you were willing to run some risks . . .' His voice trailed off as Jake's head bobbed once.

Both men were professional aviators – they well knew

the risks of flying in unknown machines that had been essentially abandoned. The weeds were now flattened by the rotor downwash where Goober hovered, but they had been up to the belly of the machines when the Americans found them. One of the tires of the helicopter carrying the fuel had been flat. A half hour was spent getting an air compressor from the hangar to start. A family of birds had nested in one cooling intake, but Goober didn't think that worth mentioning.

'How are you going to get these engines started out there' – Jake nodded toward the southeast – 'if they run long enough to get us there?'

'We loaded two power carts into the other chopper, sir. That cut the amount of extra fuel we could carry.'

'I don't want to walk back.'

'I think we'll be all right, sir.'

Well, Goober was his pilot. He could go over the figures with him or take his word for it. 'Okay,' Jake told him and turned to his little group. 'Let's get out of these suits after Captain Collins checks each one. Be careful with them. These are the only hot suits we have.'

'How did you get permission to borrow these machines, Admiral?' Colonel Rheinhart asked as he worked his zipper down.

'It's a standard midnight requisition, Colonel,' Toad put in, but his smile never arrived. Jake Grafton saw that and wondered if Rita did. She was helping Captain Collins check the suits. 'Common procedure in the American Navy,' Toad assured him.

'Oh, you're stealing them?'

'We showed the guards at the gate a personal note from Boris Yeltsin.' The colonel looked at him askance, so Toad added, 'An interpreter at the embassy wrote the note. We gave it to the sergeant of the guard as a souvenir, along with two cartons of cigarettes and a bottle of bourbon.' Actually Spiro Dalworth had done the talking and Toad had watched. Dalworth was trying hard to please Tarkington, who had little to say to him. Just now Dalworth stood watching this exchange. He wasn't trying on a hot suit since he was going to remain with the fuel chopper.

'What if the Russians shoot us down?' Jack Yocke whispered to Jake Grafton, who pretended not to hear him. The admiral walked over to Rita and had some final words with her.

'If I may, gentlemen,' Colonel Reynaud offered, 'I believe it is time to "mount up"? As zhey say in ze western movies, we are burning ze daylight.'

Jake rode beside Goober Groelke in the copilot's seat for the first leg. He was impressed by Groelke's flying ability: he handled the large Russian helicopter like he had flown it for years. Jake examined the faces of the instruments that were telling him God-knows-what and watched the pilot at work for the first five minutes, then his mind wandered.

More puffy clouds this afternoon. And they had a late start.

They soon left the heavily industrialized suburbs of Moscow behind and followed a two-lane road for a while, then the road turned more to the east and the helicopters flew across wood lots and fields and here and there small villages. The land didn't look prosperous, Jake decided. From a thousand feet the fields looked weedy and unattended, the occasional house just a shack, the villages collections of shacks. At random intervals the machines crossed above power lines and railroad tracks, incongruous fixtures that ran across the gently rolling countryside from one hazy infinity to the other.

The helicopter flew from sunlight into the random cloud shadow, back to sunlight again while Jake Grafton thought about radioactivity and nuclear warheads.

The noise was loud but not painfully so. Oh, to be able to fly on forever and never have to arrive. His eyelids grew heavy. To fly on and on and never have to arrive at the radioactive hell embedded in the haze and puffy clouds somewhere beyond the horizon, beyond the blighted promises and twisted dreams . . .

Fueling the helicopter that was to take them on to Serdobsk and Petrovsk was a nightmare. The hand pump leaked and took the best efforts of two men. Everyone took turns. Three or four minutes of intense effort reduced most of them to puffing. The marine captain was in the best shape, but after five minutes even he needed a break.

They were in a pasture several miles from the nearest village, but no one came to see who they were or why they had landed. Two scrawny steers watched from the safety of some trees at the far end of the field.

'How's the machine flying?' Jake asked Goober.

'Left engine is running a little hot,' he was told, 'but the oil levels seem okay. And the pressure in the primary hydraulic system fluctuates occasionally, but it's nothing we can't live with.'

'And the other machine?'

'A bunch of circuit breakers popped. The stab aug is out. Several hydraulic leaks.'

The refueling took over an hour while Tom Collins rigged his radioactivity detection equipment, which he described to Jake as advanced Geiger counters. The sensors were on small winches so they could be lowered from the open rear door of the chopper to get readings at ground level. In the meantime Groelke and the other pilot climbed all over the two helicopters, checking everything.

When fueling was complete, everyone stepped behind the helicopter to relieve themselves, then took long drinks of water. The party that was flying on donned the hot suits.

'Toad,' Jake said, 'you ride with Goober in the cockpit.' Toad would do the navigation. He had several charts which he got out and stacked in the order in which he would need them. Most of the officers had cameras. They checked them carefully before they donned their helmets and zipped the gloves into place.

They were going to breathe filtered air as long as the radiation levels were not too high. Collins would tell everyone when to switch on their oxygen systems.

Jack Yocke walked over to Jake and said, 'If anything goes wrong, we're dead men. You know that?'

Jake Grafton was tempted to make a flippant reply, but after a look at the reporter's face, he refrained. 'I know, Jack,' he said patiently, and pulled his helmet on.

He knew the dangers better than the reporter did. No one in the other machine had hot suits and the machines would be too far apart for radio reception. If this machine had a serious mechanical problem and was forced down, everyone abroad was doomed. Even in well-maintained helicopters with excellent equipment and thorough, careful planning, this mission was too dangerous for anyone but a desperate fool. Which was, he told himself scornfully, why the Russians weren't here and he was.

He had given the other pilot explicit orders: if we don't come back after six hours, you are to return to Moscow.

The hour-and-forty-five-minute flight from Moscow had put a sufficient charge on the helicopter's batteries that Goober got a start without using the external power cart. They had wrestled one of the carts into the passenger bay and Spiro Dalworth was outside standing beside the other, just in case.

Jake strapped himself into the crewman's seat by the rear door. He surveyed the compartment. Some of the other people had strapped in, some hadn't. Yocke was playing with his buckle, toying with the adjustment catch. Perhaps each of them in his own way was pondering his karma.

Jake looked forward and saw Toad looking back at him. He gave Tarkington a thumbs up.

When the engine RPM had stabilized, Goober lifted the tail and the machine left the ground.

All that remained of the Serdobsk fast breeder reactor was rubble arranged around a shallow hole in the ground. From a hover two hundred feet above the plant it was obvious that no one had survived the blast. Jake Grafton lay on his belly with his helmeted head poking out the open helicopter door. Seventy-five feet below him the radioactivity sensor was inscribing little circles in the air. Beside him people were taking turns snapping cameras.

Jake felt a hand pulling him. It was Collins. They put their helmets together and Collins shouted, 'We can't stay here more than a couple minutes. It's hotter than holy hell down there.'

'What's that stuff over there?' Jake pointed to the wreckage of a building several hundred yards away from where the reactor had stood. Numerous drums were visible amid the concrete rubble, some of them split open. The contents looked dark, almost black.

'Plutonium. They probably had tons of the shit stored there.'

'The containers have ruptured.'

'Yeah, and the stuff is going to get blown away on the wind or washed into the creeks and rivers or soaked into the soil. Come on, Admiral, let's get the hell outta here.'

Jake went forward to the cockpit and tapped Goober on the shoulder. The pilot eased the stick forward and the helicopter left the hover.

'Circle over that KGB troop facility.'

Groelke did so. One of the buildings had burned and several bodies were visible, but nothing moved. Nothing.

The helicopter flew in a gentle circle until it was pointed southeast toward Petrovsk. Goober Groelke climbed to several thousand feet to minimize their radioactivity exposure.

Now the noise of the engines became mesmerizing, Jack Yocke thought. One listened carefully, anxious not to hear any change, any burble or hiccup or unexplained sound. With your life depending on the continued smooth running of these two engines, the sound captures your attention and holds you spellbound. The ruins of the reactor had been horrifying, but the sound of these engines was the promise of continuing life, a drug more powerful than anything a doctor could prescribe.

Yocke tried to put his emotions into words, tried to string the words together as he sat with closed eyes and concentrated on that perfect humming.

On the floor of the passenger compartment Tom Collins fiddled with his equipment and made notes of radioactivity readings from which he could extrapolate estimates of the levels present on the surface. Jake Grafton watched him. At times Collins shook his head. Finally he folded up the notebook and sat hunched, staring at the needles on the dials in front of him

The helicopter flew over a village, then a small town, then farther along another village. Cattle lay dead in the fields. Not a sign of life below, not even buzzards. They were dead too.

All those people went to bed one evening and at dawn, or just after, the radioactive fallout arrived, an invisible rain that fell without noise, without beauty, without warning, and brought quick, gentle death. Most of the victims probably died in their sleep.

Is that the fate of civilization? Is that the end that awaits our species? No bang, no warning, just death for every last man, woman and child as they lay sleeping on the dawn of the last day?

Jake Grafton felt his eyes tearing over and blinked repeatedly.

Collins had given up on the instruments and was standing beside Grafton looking aft, out the open door, when they saw the river, the Volga, broad and deep, the water reflecting the blue of the sky and the white of the clouds.

'Let's go down and hover just above the surface.'

Goober turned the machine and went back. After twenty seconds of hovering, Collins signaled to fly on. Toad saw him and waved his hand at Groelke.

Jake bent down to where Collins was making notes.

He was not writing down radiation levels, but a sentence: 'The Volga is now a river of radiation carrying poison to the sea.'

They circled the Petrovsk Rocket Base while Collins took more readings. Jake looked out the window. The barracks and offices and hangars were all intact, but nothing moved. From this altitude the scene reminded Jake of a model railroad setup, complete with cars, trucks and several airplanes parked on the mat just off the runway, and a locomotive and flatcars near the biggest hangar.

But his attention was captured by the empty transporters parked on the mat. There were three of them, green tractors with green flat trailers hooked behind them, all empty.

Jocko West and the two European officers stood in the door looking at the transports, then Rheinhart began snapping pictures.

'I think we can land, Admiral,' Collins shouted.

'How long?'

'As little time on the ground as possible.'

'How hot is it?'

'Unprotected, you'd be fatally ill in a half hour. Maybe less.'

Groelke put the chopper near the main hangar and killed the engines to save fuel. Breathing pure oxygen, the people got out of the machine carefully, gingerly, conscious of anything that might rip or damage their antiradiation suits.

'Goober, stay with the machine. Toad, stay with him.'

Jake Grafton led the little party toward the open hangar door.

The giant missiles riding on their transporters were stark, functional sculptures with the red star prominent upon their flanks.

There was open space near the door, apparently enough for the three transporters that sat a quarter-mile away across the concrete. Impressive as the missiles were, the little group was soon standing gazing at medium-size wood crates arranged on pallets.

One of the boxes had been ripped open, revealing a cylindrical-shaped device about twelve inches in diameter. Wires and electronic devices covered it like spaghetti. Yet just visible between some of the wire bundles was a dull black substance arranged in the shape of a ball. This black stuff, Jake knew, was the conventional explosive trigger. Upon detonation it would squeeze the plutonium in the core – the center of the ball – into a supercritical mass. There in that tiny space the plutonium atoms would have their electrons stripped away, an instantaneous rape that would release stupendous amounts of energy. $E = MC^2$.

Jake Grafton counted quickly. Four warheads on each pallet, how many pallets? Almost a hundred.

The visitors were wandering away from the warheads when they saw the bodies stacked in one corner. Jake went over for a look, then found that only Jack Yocke had followed him.

Blood everywhere. Blood? Jesus, these people were shot! Lined up and gunned down.

Now he saw the spent cartridges that lay scattered around. He picked one up. Soviet. Not that that meant anything. The Soviets sold military equipment all over the world, just like the Americans, Germans, French and British. Superpowers do that, right? To keep the factories humming and the diplomats employed.

How many people? Fifteen or so.

There was a telephone on the wall and he went toward it. He held the handset against his helmet and tried to hear a dial tone. Nothing. He played with the buttons. Finally he replaced the instrument on its hook.

He left the building and headed for the clean room.

More bodies, all with bullet wounds. Some had died quickly, others bled a lot. There were bullet holes in the protective shield that sealed the room from the raw plutonium on the other side of the window. Even the flies were dead on the floor. Jake Grafton looked, then turned to find Jack Yocke staring at him through his faceplate. Yocke had a camera but he wasn't taking any pictures. Jake brushed past him and headed for the door.

He had seen all he wanted to see. The others were ahead of him, walking toward the helicopter. Yocke trailed behind. Jake counted. Everyone here.

He climbed through the door and found Goober and Toad in the cockpit. 'Crank it up,' he shouted. 'Let's get outta here.'

Goober manipulated switches. Nothing happened. 'Battery's dead,' he announced.

It took all of them to manhandle the power cart out of the helicopter. After looking all the controls over carefully, Toad Tarkington set the choke, turned on the battery, and pushed the start button. Nothing happened.

'Fuck,' Toad said, loud enough for Grafton to hear. 'Nothing in this fucking country works,' he announced, then turned back to Jake.

Grafton looked at his watch. They had been on the ground for fourteen minutes. 'Those transporters probably have jumper cables and some hand tools. Maybe. Go see.'

Toad went trotting off, a silver figure laboring through the heat waves rising from the concrete.

Time passed. Jake Grafton stared at the sky.

There was a jet up there. He could see the contrail. There it was, a silver gleam coming out from behind that cloud.

The mirror was in his pocket. Inside the hot suit.

Well, there was no other way. He gingerly unzipped the suit enough to admit his hand, reached inside and snagged the mirror. Then he zipped the suit closed.

The mirror was rectangular, about two inches by four inches, with a hole in the middle. Jake looked above him for the jet, then raised the mirror and tried to get the refracted spot of sunlight to come into the crosshair. Then he realized that a cloud had drifted between him and the sun. He put the mirror down and studied the clouds.

A few minutes.

'Those people were murdered.'

Jack Yocke was beside him.

'Everyone southeast of Serdobsk was murdered,' Jake Grafton said. 'Those folks in there just happened to be shot.'

'Why?'

Jake flipped a hand at the empty transporters.

'Somebody stole some missiles?'

'Looks that way, doesn't it?'

'How are we going to get this helicopter started?'

'I don't know that we can.'

Then the sun came out. And there was the jet, still high up there against the blue. Jake raised the mirror to his eye and moved it carefully to focus the light.

Yocke began to understand. 'Is that Rita up there?'

'Maybe. I hope so.'

'Goddamn it, Grafton,' Yocke began. 'Why didn't—'

'We'll get out of this or we won't, Jack. That's the whole story.' He was working the mirror. The sunspot was right on the crosshair. 'Those people in there look like they are at peace.'

'That's a peace I'm not ready for yet.'

'They probably weren't ready either, but it came regardless. The one thing I can promise you – this is going to be one of the most peaceful spots on this planet for a couple hundred thousand years.' Jake removed the mirror from his eye and turned to face the reporter. 'The peace that death brings is all any of us can count on.'

Yocke was watching the jet high in the sky above. 'I think maybe she saw you,' he said.

One of the transporters rumbled into life. With diesel smoke pouring from the exhaust pipe, it slowly rolled toward the helicopter. 'There's a set of jumper cables in it,'

Toad told Jake when he got down from the cab, 'but no tools. The fucking Russians stole 'em or never put them in.'

'Try to hook the cables up and get that power cart started. Rita's coming but we may still need this chopper.'

The jet was a three-holer, a Tupolev 154 with Aeroflot markings, a Russian ripoff of the Boeing 727 design. It wasn't until it turned off the runway that Jake realized there was no hot gas coming from the center engine exhaust.

Rita taxied up and gestured to him from the cockpit.

'Everyone, we're taking the jet,' Jake roared. 'Help Captain Collins with his gear. Then get on the back of the transporter. Toad, when everyone's on it, back that thing up to the door of the jet.'

Two US marines opened the door for them and they scrambled aboard. Toad came in last. 'Do we need to move the transporter?'

Rita was standing there. 'No,' she told him. 'I'll back us out with thrust reversers. Close the door and let's go.'

They took off the hot suits and threw them into the back of the passenger cabin. Jake made his way to the cockpit and dropped into the copilot's seat. 'You got an engine out?'

'Yessir. It was overheating. Maybe a bad thermocouple, but I don't know. We got a heck of a takeoff roll without it, but I think we can make it.'

'How much runway we got?'

'About nine thousand feet. We're light, nowhere near max gross weight. We'll make it if the tires don't blow. There's no tread left and I could see cord in a couple places.'

Jake Grafton looked down the runway at the trees beyond. Relatively flat terrain, thank the Lord! 'Well, I guess we'll find out soon enough.'

Toad stuck his head in. 'Rita, you get more beautiful every time I see you.'

She flashed him a wide grin.

'Did you see the mirror okay?' Jake asked.

'Yessir. I had a little trouble finding this place. Most of the Russian nav aids don't work. I circled for about a half hour and had about decided you were going out on the chopper.' She was all business, relating it crisply, a matter of fact just to be reported.

'There's the gear handle and the flaps.' She touched each lever. 'We'll begin our takeoff roll with the flaps up so we'll accelerate a little faster. I'll call for takeoff flaps at about a hundred eighty kilometers per hour – the airspeed is calculated in clicks so don't get excited. You put them down to the first detent, takeoff. When we're airborne I'll call for the gear, then the flaps.'

'Let's do it.'

She taxied to the very end of the runway and held the brakes while she ran her two good engines up to full power. Then she released the brakes.

The jet accelerated slowly. Jake could hear the thumping as the wheels passed over the expansion joints.

Rita Moravia made no attempt to rotate, merely sat monitoring the engine instruments and the airspeed indicator between glances at the end of the runway, which they were stampeding toward at an ever increasing pace.

'Flaps,' she called.

Jake moved the handle to takeoff. The indicator moved. 'They're coming!'

The airspeed needle kept rising, but oh so slowly. The end of the runway came closer, closer.

Jake was reaching for the control wheel to rotate the plane when Rita eased it back and the nose came off, then the main wheels just as the end of the runway flashed by. 'Gear up,' she called, and Jake Grafton raised the handle.

When the gear was fully retracted the plane accelerated better. Still Rita kept the nose down and let the airspeed increase. 'Flaps up,' she said at last, and Jake moved the handle.

When they were climbing through three thousand

meters – the altimeter was calibrated in meters – Rita told Jake, 'This is the biggest plane I've flown. Handles better than I thought it would.'

CHAPTER SEVENTEEN

When the airliner was level at cruising altitude, Captain Collins checked everyone for radiation. Jake had to part with his shirt. Colonel Rheinhart lost his trousers. 'As soon as we get to Moscow,' Collins told them, 'I want each of you to take a long shower. Wash your hair thoroughly. The stuff you want to get rid of is radioactive dust and dirt. Stay in the shower as long as you can stand it and don't come out until you're as clean as a new penny.'

When Jake had settled into a seat, Yocke came over and sat beside him. 'Where'd you guys get this airliner?'

'Aeroflot.'

'Who'd you have to kill?'

'Nobody. Toad told them we wanted to charter an airliner and waved American money. He got this one full of gas for seventeen hundred dollars cash and two bottles of mediocre whiskey that he stole out of Spaso House on the Fourth of July. The Aeroflot man insisted a Russian pilot come along, but he came down with something and got off when Rita gave him a hundred. She flew it out of Sheremetyevo.'

'What about air traffic control?'

'One of the enlisted marines speaks tolerable Russian. He's up in the cockpit with Rita now.'

Yocke shook his head. 'It's amazing what real money will buy.'

'Ain't it, now.'

'Think that's what happened to those missiles?'

'Your guess is as good as mine.'

'Now, Jake! Don't start that crap! I've risked my butt this afternoon right along with you and Rita and all these other military heroes. It wouldn't hurt an iota for you to come clean and tell me the whole truth. For once.'

Jack Yocke got the gray eyes full face. There was no warmth in them. 'That's the second time you've called me Jake. You aren't old enough or wise enough. Don't do it again.'

'Yessir. No offense. But I mean it about leveling with me. I feel like a kid in a haunted Halloween house. I've paid my buck and I keep getting the shit scared out of me even after it ceases to be fun. How about telling me what you know?'

'I don't know what happened to those weapons. I was as surprised as you were when I saw those empty transporters and the bodies.'

'The story I heard that got me over to this country was that the Iraqis were trying to buy some nuke weapons. I heard they had three billion to spend for the right toys.'

'Where'd you hear that?'

Jack Yocke scratched his nose, then rubbed his face good. It went against the grain to reveal a source but he didn't see any way out of it. Finally he said, 'One of the ICB executives told me, off the record. He was sitting in a New York jail awaiting trial when I interviewed him.' The International Commerce Bank had recently been shut down worldwide for money laundering on a stupendous scale, that and a garden variety of other financial crimes.

'Did you believe him?'

This was the crucial question. A professional reporter hears a lot of stories, every now and then a true one. The good reporters can smell a lie a block away. 'I thought he was telling the truth,' Yocke told the admiral. 'Or what he believed to be the truth. It had the right feel.'

'I don't mean to insult you, but did you get that feel when Judith Farrell told you her Soviet Square tale?'

'Yeah, I did. I've been thinking about that. In the first place she was a professional liar and damn good, and second, most of the story was true, in fact all of it except who was ultimately responsible. So it played well. There was nothing fancy or hyped. I bought it.' He shrugged.

Jake Grafton visibly relaxed. 'Don't feel like the Lone Ranger. I bought one of her stories one time too.'

Jack Yocke got the feeling he had just passed some kind of test. 'Well, the ICB tip didn't pan out over here. I had the names of two former ICB execs who had run to earth in Moscow that my source swore knew the ins and outs — if they could be persuaded to talk. These two birds supposedly shuffled the money every which way to Sunday to make it impossible to trace. That made sense, so I looked for them for four straight days but couldn't get a sniff. Not that I'm any great shakes at finding people in Moscow, but still . . .'

'I heard about the money going through ICB too,' Jake said softly. 'Maybe from Iraq. Maybe from an Iraqi working for Iran.'

'Heard any names? Which Russian might have gotten the dough?'

'A name or two. That much money, it's impossible to keep it secret. Oh, they've tried. But that much money . . .' He had repeated the rumors to Richard Harper in the hope that he could find the trail. Did he?

He heard the power being reduced. 'I'd better go talk to Rita,' Jake said. 'We'll land at another airport and Toad can call Aeroflot. No use letting the manager see who was on his chartered airplane.' Yocke got out of his seat, then Jake maneuvered himself into the aisle and walked forward to the cockpit.

Three billion dollars. That wasn't pocket change anywhere, but in Russia it was a stupendous amount of money. Too much, really. Jack Yocke moved to the window seat and sat staring out, wondering where the money could be, what a Russian could use it for. In Russia there were no stocks to buy, no bonds, no office buildings to invest in, no art masterpieces for sale, no private oil syndicates setting

275

out to drill up Siberia or the Gulf of Mexico. It was amazing, really. Here was a whole nation with not a god-damn thing to invest money in, unless you were looking to throw your bucks into worn-out factories producing ob-solete, shoddy goods that no one on the planet except starving, penniless Russians wanted.

However, one possibility did come to mind. He looked toward the cockpit, started to get out of the seat and go that way, then decided against it. If he thought of it, the idea must have already occurred to Jake Grafton.

He sighed and scratched himself and turned his attention back to the window.

It was dark when the Tupolev 154 landed at Domodedovo, a huge field for domestic airliners thirty miles southeast of Moscow. Rita taxied to the corner of the airport most remote from the terminal and shut down the engines. Jake went back to find Captain Collins. He wiggled a finger at Iron Mike McElroy, the marine captain, who came over. 'I want this airplane washed before we call Aeroflot. I don't want any radioactivity overdoses on my conscience.'

McElroy agreed to use his people to find some tank trucks and hoses and to do the washing, and Collins agreed to use his equipment to ensure they got the hot spots and diluted the runoff as much as possible.

'Do the best you can,' Jake told them, and left it at that.

An hour later Jake was in Ambassador Lancaster's office in the embassy complex. Ms Hempstead sat on the couch with a notepad on her lap.

'Yeltsin refused to resign,' Lancaster said. 'The anti-Yeltsin forces have forced a no-confidence vote in the Congress of People's Deputies. The best Yeltsin could do was get it delayed until Friday.'

This was Monday evening. Jake glanced at the calendar on the ambassador's desk to make sure. Three days.

'Yakolev and Shmarov have been on television,' the

ambassador continued. 'They and the rest of the junta seem to have a lot of support. People are hungry, unemployed, the factories don't have raw materials or markets, this Serdobsk disaster may have been the last straw.'

'Yeltsin was popularly elected. I didn't know the legislature could throw him out.'

'Technically they can't. But over here they're still making up the rules as they go along. If he loses on the no-confidence vote he can either call for a new election of deputies or resign and let the congress choose a successor. The problem is that his support is melting away.'

'What's the American position?'

'We've got to let the Russians sort it out for themselves. We'll recognize any government that gets in without resort to violence.'

'How about blowing up the Serdobsk reactor? Would Washington classify that as a violent act?'

Lancaster goggled. Hempstead came off the couch and floated toward the desk. 'Blew it up? Who?'

'I'm not accusing anyone of anything. I'm merely asking a question.'

'This isn't the time for soaring hypotheticals, Admiral,' Hempstead said acidly, 'or cute questions about when someone stopped beating his wife.' She stalked back to the couch and snatched up her notepad.

'I assume you do have some basis for your question,' Owen Lancaster said uneasily. 'Exactly what did you find out on your helicopter trip to Serdobsk?'

'The reactor and containment vessel are gone, sir, nothing left but a crater and some rubble. The entire control building was destroyed. A storage building a hundred yards or so from the reactor was severely damaged and the plutonium containers that were inside ruptured.'

Lancaster merely nodded. Like most people, he had only the vaguest idea of what a meltdown was or what the physical effects might be. He expected something terrible of course, but just what was rather hazy. This description sounded properly catastrophic, so he murmured 'horrible' and shook his head. 'Nobody survived, I suppose?'

'No, sir,' Jake Grafton said, and paused for a few seconds to gape at the vastness of the great man's ignorance.

Then he continued: 'The fallout zone is huge and extraordinarily hot. Collins will have some numbers in a few hours. We won't know the exact dimensions of the fallout zone until aerial surveys are conducted. But to return to my question – I guess I didn't phrase it right. Please excuse me. I'm just curious about how willing the United States government might be to get into a shooting scrape over here if the junta looks like it might be coming out on top.'

'That's a decision for the president,' Hempstead piped from her ringside seat, her tone suggesting Grafton was a few cards short of a full deck.

Lancaster spoke more slowly. 'I seriously doubt if anyone in Washington will be very enthusiastic about a military adventure in Russia, Admiral, even if Yakolev himself personally blew up a dozen reactors and CBS News has a videotape of him pushing the plunger. Speaking hypothetically, of course.'

Jake Grafton wondered what the administration's reaction would be to medium-range ballistic missiles armed with nuclear warheads in Iran or Iraq. He didn't ask the diplomats though. He wanted to talk to Hayden Land before he set Lancaster's pants on fire.

While Senior Chief Holley was checking the navy's minuscule office for bugs and rigging the telephone scrambler, Jake went to find Jack Yocke. 'I want you to write a story about what you saw today. Get the radiation numbers and isotopes and all that from Collins when he gets back. Write an eyewitness account, just what you saw. Leave out the bit about the transporters and the missiles. And let me see the story before you call it in.'

Jack Yocke had just completed his shower. He was tired and looked longingly at the couch in the small apartment

278

that Grafton and Tarkington shared. Now Grafton was ordering up journalism like a fried-to-order hamburger. Yet he barely paused before he said, 'Yessir. I'll have the story for you in about an hour. When Collins gets back I can just insert a few paragraphs.'

'I'll be down in the office.'

Back in the office Holley was still looking for electromagnetic fields that shouldn't be there. 'What did Herb Tenney do today?' Jake asked.

'He left the embassy about eleven, sir, and returned in time for dinner.'

The admiral grunted and began to think about what he was going to say to Hayden Land. When Holley pronounced the office clean, Jake punched his code into the scrambler and placed his call. It took seven minutes before the Pentagon operator got them connected.

'Let's go secure,' Land told him after he heard Jake's voice.

Jake pushed the proper button and waited while the two encrypters talked to each other with chirps and clicks, then he heard Land's voice. 'Richard Harper is dead.'

'How?'

'Apparent heart attack.'

'Do you have the report?'

'No. The house was ransacked.'

Jake didn't wait for the effect of that to numb him. He immediately began to report the events of the day.

While Jack Yocke tapped away on his laptop in the small living room, Toad and Rita took a long shower together and then crawled into bed. With the lights out and her head cradled on Toad's shoulder, Rita said, 'On the ride over here from the airport Yocke was telling me some wild tale about some women he met, a Shirley Ross and a Judith Farrell. I listened for about five minutes before it dawned on me that he was talking about Elizabeth Thorn.'

'She had a lot of names.'

'And she's dead.'

'Yes.'

'You loved her, didn't you?' Rita whispered.

'Yes.'

'Yocke needed someone to share it with.'

'Uh-huh.'

'He's a good guy underneath.'

Toad Tarkington didn't want to talk about Jack Yocke. Judith Farrell was on his mind, and this extraordinary woman beside him. 'It wasn't—' Toad began.

'Hush,' she told him. 'I'm not jealous. I know what I mean to you.'

He thought about that, tried to get the round peg into the square hole. Women are really amazing creatures – just when you think you've got their brain structure figured out, they stun you by revealing a feature of genetic engineering that you never expected, not in your wildest –

'Still,' she added, 'I think you should have told me about her. Oh, you married me and all that, but I didn't realize that you had all these torrid romances stacked in the closet that I am going to have to keep dealing with.'

It dawned on Toad that the peg wouldn't fit. 'You aren't the first woman I ever shook hands with.'

'You did a lot more than shake Elizabeth Thorn's hand, or Judith Farrell, or whatever her name was. Don't sugar-coat it and don't deny it.'

'Rita, I'm not denying anything! And I'm not going to lie to you about Judith. She was one hell of a fine woman. I loved her very much. She went her way and I went mine and eventually I met you. And I'm damn sorry she's dead.'

'Just how many more of *these women* are out there?'

The ol' Horny Toad knew the ice was damn thin. He carefully weighed his answer. 'You're the woman I married. You're the woman I want to spend my life with. Why are you jealous?'

'I am *not* jealous! Answer the question.'

'What question?'

'How many?'

'I dunno for sure. I didn't carve notches on the bedstead. Not counting you, let's see . . . maybe ten thousand, more or less.'

'Go ahead and count me, Romeo,' she growled. There was acid in her voice.

'Well, I'd have to consult my little black books. All of us Romeos have those. I did ratings, on a one-to-ten scale. I can probably use those records to come up with a fairly accurate count, although of course I didn't rate casual encounters. As I recall you scored a ten. It's sorta sad, but there weren't many tens, not more than one a month. All those books . . . it'll be a big job.' He took a deep breath and exhaled audibly, laced his fingers across his chest and stared at the ceiling, apparently contemplating the vast quantities of time and effort that were going to be involved in rooting through his voluminous files.

When she remained silent, he decided to take the offensive. But carefully. 'How many of your old boyfriends are you gonna torture me with?'

She thought about that. Finally she began counting on her fingers. At last she said, 'One hundred ninety-three. The first was a boy named Freddy that I had a crush on in kindergarten. He had blond hair and dimples and I desperately wanted him for my very own. The second was—'

'I missed you,' Toad told her.

'Oh, Toad, I missed you too.'

And then she sat up and he could see her whole face, her eyes, her nose, her mouth spreading into a smile. 'You're going to be a daddy,' she said softly.

'*What?*'

'It's too early to be absolutely sure, but I think so.'

He was horrified. He shoved her out to arm's length. 'You're pregnant and you flew that jet into that radioactive hell this afternoon? Are you out of your mind?'

One of her eyebrows arched. 'Not so loud. Let's not discuss this with Jack Yocke.'

'Rita,' he hissed, 'if you're pregnant you can't—'

'I can do what has to be done. Like every kid ever conceived, Toad Junior is going to have to take his parents as they come. Flying is what I do.' She stroked his eyebrows with a fingertip. 'Relax. I'll be careful. I pulled his father out of the fiery furnace today. Someday the Toadlet will understand and thank me.'

Toad needed time to digest it. After a while he said, 'Do you think it's a boy?'

Rita grinned and shrugged.

'Well, you ought to go back to the States. You shouldn't even have come over here. This place is too goddamn polluted for a pregnant woman.' Herb Tenney and his binary poisons crossed his mind. 'And—'

She wrapped her arms around him and pushed him backward. With her face just inches from his, she told him, 'Toad Tarkington. The women you fall in love with aren't housewives. If I become one I risk losing you. That's a risk I have no intention of taking.'

'But—'

'But nothing! This baby is mine too. You just stifle your male instincts and start thinking up names. I'll handle the rest of it.'

Toad tried to sort it out. Perhaps she was right, he decided. Probably. Women! If it floats, flies or fucks, rent – don't buy! Great advice but impossible to follow. After a bit he asked, 'Can you still make love?'

This question drew a giggle from the mother-to-be, who grasped him in a very intimate way and lowered her mouth onto his.

Senior Chief Holley woke Jake at five in the morning. The sun was already up. 'The helicopter made it back a couple hours ago. The guys just got here.'

'Fine,' Jake said, and the senior chief closed the door behind him. Jake had left orders that he be awakened when they returned, now he had trouble getting back to sleep.

He couldn't eat, not with Herb Tenney in the same city, and he was only getting a few hours' sleep a night. This regimen wasn't good for him – he would soon have trouble concentrating. Maybe he was already feeling the effects.

He lay in the darkness staring at the ceiling. Soon his thoughts were on Callie and Amy. What time was it in Washington? What would they be doing today?

When he came awake again the chief was shaking him. 'Admiral, we have a call from General Land. I've set up the encrypter in the living room.'

Jake got out of bed and pulled on his pants. In the living room Jack Yocke was drinking coffee.

'What time is it?'

'Almost noon.'

'Toad up?'

'Still in bed.'

'Let him sleep.'

'Want me to leave?'

'You can stay, but everything you hear is classified. You can't print anything.'

'I know the ground rules,' Yocke said mildly and sipped at the coffee. 'Take your call. I'll get you a cup.'

'Admiral Grafton, sir.'

'Land. I got yesterday morning's satellite photo and the one the bird got at seven local time this morning over Petrovsk. How many empty transporters were there outside when you were there?'

'Three, sir.'

'This morning there were four. There were also two bodies there this morning.'

'Dead bodies?'

'They're lying down. The photo interpreter's labeled them dead. They look dead to me. One is right by a transporter, the other is near the abandoned helicopter.'

'Much cloud cover at Petrovsk this morning?'

'About thirty percent or so. There was a decent hole over the field when the bird went by.'

'We're lucky.' Jake had asked for the daily satellite shoot, but he hadn't expected anything this dramatic. 'Sounds like someone went back to the gold mine.'

'The morning after the meltdown was overcast, so nothing that morning. The next day the transporters were there. And yesterday. This morning four.'

'Who was it?' Jack Yocke handed Jake a cup of coffee and sat down on the couch.

'An AWACS bird over the Persian Gulf picked up three transports leaving a military airfield near Samarra, northwest of Baghdad, at a few minutes after nine last night. They tracked them flying just a little west of north until they departed the area. Then three transports came back this morning a few minutes after dawn. One crashed fifty miles north of the air base, the other two landed there.'

'They didn't have the right gear to withstand the radiation.'

'Looks that way.'

'General, somebody is going to have to destroy those missiles before any more of them are carried away. Those missiles are too big a temptation.'

'I'm going over to the White House in about fifteen minutes. I've already talked to the secretary of defense. He and the national security adviser will meet us there. Why don't you be in Ambassador Lancaster's office an hour and a half from now? Someone will call you.'

'Aye aye, sir.'

Jake hung up the phone and switched off the crypto device.

'Someone went back?' Yocke asked.

'Apparently. They carried off at least three missiles before the meltdown. That night. The radiation was supposed to cover up the fact the missiles were missing, for a while anyway. But someone got careless and left the transporters outside.'

'Why didn't they take the transporters too?'

'Too big. Too heavy. Oh, maybe they took one or two,

but they opted to leave at least three behind and take the missiles instead.'

'And someone went back last night?'

'And maybe got a couple more missiles. Left at least two dead people on the mat and one more empty transporter.'

'Satellite?'

'Uh-huh.'

'Just how good are those satellites?'

'They can see something the size of a pack of cigarettes. The problem is that we only have so many satellites. Right now we're trying to monitor every base in Russia where nukes are stored.' Jake started to add something, then just shook his head.

'So what are we going to do?'

'If you mean the United States, Land is going to see the president now.'

'Who got the missiles?'

'Saddam Hussein.'

'Oh, hell.'

'That isn't the worst of it. Remember all those warheads stacked around? Those are highly portable. Odds are that for every missile they carried away, they took half a dozen warheads.'

Jake Grafton headed for the bathroom to shower and shave. He decided to put on his uniform. It looked like it might be that kind of day.

'What?' said Ms Hempstead, her brows knitted.

'I expect the ambassador will be getting a call in a little while from the White House. General Land asked me to be here when it comes.'

'Have a seat, Admiral. I'll talk to the ambassador. He's on the telephone right now with Yeltsin's aide, trying to arrange an appointment.' She whirled and marched for the door to the inner sanctum.

Jake Grafton picked a seat and settled in. The secretary thought she could spare him a smile, then thought better of it and went back to pounding the keyboard of her computer terminal. Jake picked up a three-month-old copy of *Southern Living* and began to leaf through it. There were articles there on a couple of houses he wouldn't mind living in if he ever inherited five million dollars.

Ten minutes later he tired of the magazine. He checked his watch. The ambassador's door was firmly closed. The secretary was pretending to work on something on her desk.

He was examining the paintings on the wall thirty minutes later when the door opened. 'Would you come in, please, Admiral Grafton,' Hempstead said. She stood aside and he walked in.

The ambassador was on the telephone. He was listening. Every now and then he said, 'Yessir.' Finally he said, 'He's here now with me, sir . . . Yessir . . . If you think . . . I'll let you know immediately. Yessir. Good-bye.'

Lancaster hung up and looked around blinking. His eyes settled on Grafton, then moved to Hempstead. 'Agatha, please use the telephone in the other room to get me an appointment with Yeltsin. Tell the aide I have an oral message from our president that I must deliver immediately. Have a seat, Admiral.' Jake did so.

When Hempstead was gone, Lancaster said, 'It would have been nice if you had given me some warning about this last night.'

'I thought I'd better talk to my boss first, sir.'

'So you didn't level with me. I've been an ambassador on and off for over twenty years. I was talking to presidents about affairs of state when you were a lieutenant filling out fitness reports on drunken sailors. I was helping prevent World War III when our new president was smoking pot without inhaling.'

Owen Lancaster got out of his chair and walked around the desk. He leaned against the mantel of the fireplace, then half-turned so he could see Jake.

'I'll tell you right now that the United States has no

business taking sides in the Russians' political battles. We have no money to offer them. We have no bottled cure for all the problems they face. All our crowd knows how to do is jack the interest rate up or down a half a point and hire another ten thousand bureaucrats to manage the social problem de jour. These people are going to have to solve their own problems.'

When Jake said nothing, Lancaster came over and dropped into the adjacent chair. 'The president wants me personally to brief Yeltsin on the goings on at the Petrovsk military base. I am to give him two options. A – he may order an air strike on the missiles and warheads still in the hangars at Petrovsk. The weapons must be destroyed by noon tomorrow, or B – the United States will do the job for him. His choice.'

'I doubt if he will accept either option,' Jake murmured.

'That is also my opinion. He doesn't have enough clout with the Russian military to enforce an order telling them to blow up their own base, and it would be political suicide to allow American warplanes to fly across Russian territory to make an attack on a Russian military installation. The president and national security adviser see this the same way. So . . . if he refuses both options, I am to give him a third, a compromise. He will supply two airplanes and weapons and two of your test pilots will fly to Petrovsk and destroy the base.'

'I see.'

'I wish you did, Admiral.' Owen Lancaster levered himself from the chair and went to the window. With his back to Jake he said, 'The Russians are a proud people. We are going to force Yeltsin into doing something that will probably sink him politically. To get rid of what? – a hundred or so nuclear warheads? – we are going to run a serious risk of putting a military dictatorship into the Kremlin. A hundred weapons – a drop in the bucket. Our president made this decision in less than an hour after talking with only Hayden Land and the national security adviser, who six months ago was preaching the big ideas to pimple-faced fraternity boys at a college in New England, kids who are still carrying their first condom in their wallets.'

'Yeltsin is no liberal Little Rock Democrat, sir. He's half dictator. Any government Russia gets will be a dictatorship to some degree.

'Admiral, I quit listening to that isolationist apologia when my hair started falling out. The Russians have gone from tyrant to tyrant since the dawn of time. They *like* tyrants – someone to do the thinking for them. But Yeltsin . . . he's trying to force these isolated wood hicks into the world economy, the world culture. Boris Yeltsin may be Russia's last hope. And ours.'

Lancaster headed for the door. As he went he muttered, 'You knotheads don't seem to understand that you can't go off half-cocked when the whole goddamn planet is at risk.'

CHAPTER EIGHTEEN

It was three in the afternoon when Lancaster informed Jake by telephone of Yeltsin's decision. 'He'll make two Su-25s available at the Lipetsk air base.'

'Where is Lipetsk?'

'About two hundred miles south. There will be a helicopter waiting for your pilots in two hours at Domodedovo. It will take them there.'

'Yes, sir.'

'And, Admiral . . . I don't know what story he is telling the air force.'

'Uh, are you trying to say we're on our own?'

'Precisely.'

Jake hung up the telephone and looked around at his little staff. 'Okay, gang. Here's the plan. Rita and I will catch a chopper in two hours at Domodedovo that will take us to a Russian air base. They'll make two Su-25 Frogfoots available. Rita and I will bomb the base at Petrovsk. Any questions?'

'Uh, CAG,' Toad began, glanced at Rita and cleared his throat. 'Why Rita?'

Jake was genuinely surprised. Toad was not in the habit of questioning Jake's decisions. 'Well, she flew F/A-18s for several years before she went to test pilot school. Goober Groelke has a helo background, and Miles' – the third test pilot – 'came out of antisubmarine warfare. This job is dropping bombs and getting hits the first time around.'

'Oh.'

Jake looked expectantly at Toad.

'Just curious, that's all.'

Rita was looking at her husband through narrowed eyes. A domestic matter, Jake decided, and forgot about it.

'Frogfoots. Those will be good planes for this job,' Groelke said.

'Should be,' Jake acknowledged. 'We'll find out.' He knew the Frogfoot from its reputation. A Russian close-air support and antiarmor weapon, the plane was a close copy of the Northrop A-9, which had lost the US Air Force's competition for a tank killer when flying against the A-10 Warthog. The Soviets used Frogfoots in Afghanistan and supposedly they were good airplanes.

'Brunhilde Tarkington,' Toad said to Rita when they were alone.

'What?'

'A name for the kid. If it's a girl.'

'Don't you ever, *ever* do that to me again, Toad. I don't question your professional assignments. Don't you question mine.'

'I'm not pregnant. Nor am I ever likely to be.'

'And don't get cute with me, Bub!'

'I just love it when you talk dirty.'

She gave him her coldest stare. 'I wear the uniform, I got the training, I take the pay – I *will* fly the missions when they come.'

'Brunhilde.'

'Not on your life.'

He watched her walk away with her shoulders slightly hunched, her head down, as if she were walking into a strong wind.

This fatherhood bit . . . it was awful sudden. Of course, when you're married and do all the conjugal things, parenthood is one of the risks. Or rewards. Whichever. Still, it would have been nice to have a few years to think about it before it became a fact. Why didn't she say, Maybe we ought to think about being parents? Why didn't she say that?

Perhaps, he thought, she assumed I was thinking about it all along. Women are big assumers. The biggest assumption of all is the one they routinely make, that men think just like they do. And they are tortured by disappointment when it is proven for the umpteenth jillion time that men *don't*.

Because he hadn't been thinking about it. In fact, the possibility had never once crossed his mind. Kids are little people who wail in supermarkets, get beaned by baseballs at Little League, and ride in the back end of station wagons making faces at people in other cars. Other people have them. Usually other older people. The fact that he had been a kid once upon a time had never inspired him to want one of his very own or to even contemplate the prospect.

Of course he knew the theory that sex causes kids, but he had assumed Rita was taking care of everything. After all, she never got pregnant before.

Surely Rita would not have made a decision like that on her own. Would she?

Maybe there had been an accident. Toad Tarkington, professional naval flight officer, knew a great deal about accidents. A little dollop of carelessness could cause you to crash, burn and die. Sometimes even without the carelessness you crashed, burned and died – at a level too deep for philosophers, luck was involved. Life is a grand game of chance. This kid must have been an accident, he decided. Not that it mattered.

Diapers. They were extremely messy and smelled to high heaven. Of course he had never actually seen or smelled a loaded diaper or wiped a baby's bottom – he knew from listening to adults who had taken the parental plunge. As he contemplated the messy prospect now, he shuddered. And washing clothes in the same machine used for diapers! Do people get two washing machines? His mom had never owned but one . . . Funny, he had never thought of that before. He would have to ask somebody.

291

He wondered if Rita would want to nurse. There's something . . . not obscene . . . jarring, yes, jarring, about watching a woman open her blouse and do something to her bra and plug a kid in. Seeing a woman nurse gave Toad the same sensation he got watching a sword swallower: the sight jolted him right to his toenails. These modern women have waited so long for kids they do it everywhere – in cars, restaurants, theaters, stores, hair places – not just in the ladies' room like their grandmas used to do.

And somebody once said that babies don't just eat three square meals a day – they are hungry every two hours. That seemed like a lot, and he frowned. Every two hours couldn't be right. That guy must have had a fat kid.

His kid wouldn't be fat. He would speak to Rita about that. Eat right and get plenty of exercise, throw the ol' ball around, climb trees and play tag and all that stuff. He would see to it.

Boy or girl, he would raise this kid right. Help with the homework and stories at night, lots of sports . . .

How in the heck had his parents done it?

He recalled some spankings and flashes from holidays and picnics, and some run-ins with the little girl who lived next door – Becky or Rebecca or something like that – but it was precious little when he tried to add it up. That stunned him. Shouldn't he remember more? God, he hadn't tried to dredge up this stuff in years, not since . . . well, he had never tried.

And now he needed it. Slam bam thank you ma'am and he was going to be a father.

Maybe he ought to write to his mom and get some sort of operator's manual, something in writing.

Rita wouldn't like that, might get all huffy.

Did she remember more about being a kid than he did?

Probably not, but she would confidently assume that since she wasn't cursed by the Y chromosome she would instinctively know the right things to do.

Why couldn't he remember?

Jake Grafton used the phone in the office after the senior chief had rigged the scrambler. He reached General Hayden Land at the Pentagon.

'The real problem is Iraq,' Land told Jake after he had related Ambassador Lancaster's little speech. 'Missiles armed with nuclear warheads in Saddam Hussein's arsenal is something these people in Washington don't want to face.'

'The Iraqis only took a few missiles,' Jake informed him. 'Apparently they elected to take warheads instead.'

'I think so too. The president didn't have any problem putting the wood to the Russians to destroy Petrovsk. He was ready to use US assets to bomb it if the Russians refused. Almost too ready.'

'What do you mean, General?'

'He hasn't got burned yet by one of these military adventures blowing up in his face. So he's ready to damn the torpedoes and full speed ahead.'

'What did CIA say to all this?'

'They told the president to go slow. That he risked making an enemy of Russia. They were about to threaten World War III but he shut them up before they got it out.'

'General, now is the time to go get those weapons in Iraq. Every day that passes means we are one day closer to a desert Armageddon.'

'I'm listening,' Land said.

'We're going to have to go into Iraq. An airborne assault. We'll go into Hussein's backyard, take or destroy the missiles and warheads, and leave as quick as we can. We're going to have to do it before he uses those weapons.'

Silence. 'That won't be easy.'

'Yes, sir. I know that.'

'Saddam may bag the whole lot of you.'

'That's a possibility. But we'll destroy the missiles first. General, we're going to have to pay a little now or pay a lot later – there are no other options. Any way you cut it, we've got to get the jump on him. We *have* to take the initiative while there is still time.'

'I don't like it. It's too risky. Too many things can go wrong, then you'll be stuck on the ground with a lot of casualties. The Iraqis may bag the whole lot of you, then we have a political prisoner situation. No, the way to do this is an air strike. We'll bomb that base into powder and that will be the end of Saddam's nuclear arsenal. We might lose a few pilots, but not a whole bunch of people.'

'If destroying the missiles were the only objective, I would agree with you,' Jake told the chairman. 'But it's not. We must prove to the world that Saddam has the weapons. We've got to show the world these missiles and warheads. Here's what I want to do.' Jake laid it out. His explanation took almost five minutes.

When Jake was finished, Land didn't say anything for several seconds. Finally he said, 'Well, maybe. I'll think about it. Present it to the president. As a soldier, I'll tell you right now that all that is too complicated.'

'It's our best shot, sir.'

'I'll think about it. What time frame are you thinking about for this operation?'

'As soon as humanly possible, sir. As soon as we can plan it. The sooner the better. I'm going to be flying one of these Russian jets down to Petrovsk tomorrow. We're flying out of the Lipetsk air base. We leave here in about an hour. I figure we'll get a checkout on the planes tonight, then fly first thing in the morning. Tomorrow night I can go to Arabia.'

'The weather people say that you can expect scattered to broken stratocumulus in the Petrovsk area, maybe fifty percent coverage, bases around three or four thousand feet, occasional rain showers.'

'That'll be good enough.'

'Who is the other pilot?'

'Lieutenant Commander Moravia, sir.'

'Okay. Take your scrambler with you and call me from Lipetsk before you take off. I'll go back to the White House and see what they think about Saddam Hussein.'

'Yessir.'

'Good luck, Jake.'

'Thanks, General.'

Only two options left to stop Saddam Hussein – an air strike or an airborne assault. Jake thought about that after he broke the connection. When you are down to just two options in this dangerous world, you are in deep and serious trouble. He knew that and Hayden Land knew it, but did the president?

She was in the apartment rolling her hair into a bun, with her mouth full of bobby pins. She was already wearing her flight suit and steel-toed flight boots.

'Gertrude Murgatroyd Tarkington,' Toad told her. 'Or Tarkington-Moravia or Moravia-Tarkington. Do you want the kid hyphenated?'

'Tarkington is okay,' she said, grinning around the bobby pins and eyeing him in the mirror.

He rammed his hands into his pockets and stood looking at this and that, avoiding meeting her eyes. 'Have you told your folks?' he asked finally.

'Of course not. Just you. We'll wait until the rabbit dies before we tell anyone.'

'Does a rabbit really die?'

'Not anymore. Used to though.'

Toad thought about that for a moment, about rabbits giving their lives to let women know they were pregnant – really! There was a *whole lot* about this baby business that he didn't know.

He glanced at her reflection in the mirror and said, 'You be careful out there.'

'I will.'

He came over and stood right behind her. 'This is supposed to be a little day jaunt down to Petrovsk, roll in and make a couple of runs with live ordnance, then back to the barn. But it may not go like that.'

'What do you mean?'

'The other night we were sitting in a park when people started shooting. Some people here and there would probably like to see Jake Grafton dead. Somebody wants those missiles pretty badly. Keep your head on a swivel. Watch your six. If anybody looks cross-eyed, blow 'em out of the sky.'

Rita got her hair the way she wanted it and inserted bobby pins.

'Grafton's been shot at by experts,' he told her. 'Anybody that straps him on is in big trouble. Just stick to him like glue. Stay with him. No matter what, fly your own airplane.'

'I will, Toad.'

She finished with her hair and turned around to face him. He put his hands on her shoulders. 'I want you back in one piece.'

'I know, lover.'

'We're in a helluva fix when we send pregnant women to fight our battles.'

'Shut up and kiss me.'

Jake took Spiro Dalworth along because he spoke Russian. Unfortunately he knew next to nothing about aviation or airplanes or weapons, so the terms didn't translate very well. Yet somehow Jake and Rita found out what they had to know. They took turns sitting in the cockpit of an Su-25 asking questions. Dalworth translated and a Russian pilot supplied the answers.

The pilot was young, a lieutenant. He was in culture shock. 'Who flies?' he asked Dalworth.

Spiro pointed to Jake and Rita.

'The woman?'

'Yes, she will fly.'

'A woman? *She* will fly?'

'Yes.'

When Rita asked a question, the answer was short, curt. When Jake asked one Dalworth had trouble finding a pause to translate amid the Russian's verbal flood. Rita saw the problem and addressed her comments to Jake, who then asked the questions. The process seemed to work better that way.

The olive-drab airplane with a red star on the tail seemed an excellent piece of military equipment. With two internal engines generating over eleven thousand pounds of thrust each, ten external weapons pylons under a wing designed to haul a big load of ordnance, an adequate fuel supply, and a twin-barrel 30mm cannon mounted internally, the airplane seemed just what the doctor ordered for ground attack. The avionics were not state-of-the-art, however. The plane lacked a radar and had no computer to assist the pilot, who had to do his own navigation with a minimum of electronic help. Jake and Rita would have to find the target with their Mark I, Mod Zero eyeballs and attack it with dumb weapons. The plane contained a laser ranger and could deliver laser-guided weapons, but it lacked a laser designator. The bombsight was strictly mechanical.

The cockpit and pilot chores were straightforward enough, yet the switches and gauges were scattered throughout the cockpit with apparently no forethought given to ease of operation or minimizing the pilot's work-load.

Visibility from the cockpit wasn't great either. Although the pilot sat well forward of the wing, the view aft was nonexistent and the view downward was restricted by the sides of the airplane.

The electronic warfare (EW) panel was simple and passive. Lights illuminated when the plane was painted by radars on certain bandwidths, but after receiving that quiet warning the pilot was on his own.

'It's no A-6 or F/A-18,' Rita remarked.

'More like an A-7,' Jake muttered.

The only officer they met was the lieutenant who had led them to the hangar for their briefing. The CO of the base and the CO of the air wing were conspicuously absent. They were cooperating on orders from Moscow, but that was all.

The officers' quarters were a barracks. Rita tossed her stuff on a bunk and stared back at the Russian pilots, who were whispering among themselves.

They were offered food. Jake declined for everyone – he didn't want to risk a case of the trots. Hunger was preferable.

After Jake had used his satellite com gear for another long talk with General Land in Washington, he sat on a bottom bunk with Rita and examined the charts they had brought from Moscow. With only these charts they had to find the Petrovsk base, then find their way back here. Most of the Russian nav aids were inoperable and the Su-25 might not reliably receive the ones that were transmitting.

There was a minor flurry in the bathroom when Spiro insisted all the Russians depart so that Rita could use it, but the lights went out without fanfare after Rita disappointed a little knot of onlookers by crawling under her blanket fully dressed.

Jake Grafton lay under his blanket staring into the darkness, tired but not sleepy. The hangar where the missiles and warheads were housed was priority number one tomorrow morning. Then, if there were any bombs or cannon shells left, they would attack the clean room with its warhead parts stacked everywhere. And they had to do it on the first flight. There was no way they could ask Yeltsin to let them fly another mission, not with the outstanding cooperation and friendly attitude these uniformed folks here had displayed.

And then there was the problem of the missiles in Iraq. Just how long did mankind have before Saddam Hussein decided his new arsenal was operational? Had the dictator reached that point already? How could the Americans plan an airborne assault into Iraq that minimized the hundreds of possible things that could go wrong and yet gave them a reasonable chance of grabbing or destroying the weapons before the Iraqi military massively retaliated? Were the odds good enough to order people into action, or should they be asked to volunteer? They would volunteer to a man, Jake was convinced, but he wanted no part of asking anyone to commit suicide. Nor did he plan on doing it himself.

What was Herb Tenney up to these days? Did the CIA tell him of this bombing mission? What could he do about it? Why would he do anything? More to the point, what could Yakolev and his cohorts do, assuming they were so inclined?

Dozens of questions, no answers. But first things first. The mission tomorrow – Jake knew how tough it would be. Using contact navigation to get to Petrovsk would be tough enough. Flying there in a type of aircraft he had never flown before was a helluva challenge. The task would be huge even if he were current on jet aircraft, which he wasn't. How long had it been since he had flown a tactical aircraft? Three years? No, four. Actually four years and three months.

And Rita had never been in combat. Oh, this wasn't supposed to be combat, but what if someone started shooting? How would Rita handle it?

Maybe he should have said something to her.

What? Knowing Rita Moravia, anything he could come up with would wound her pride. Oh, she wouldn't let on, would say yessir and nosir with the utmost respect, but . . .

So what could go wrong tomorrow?

Only a couple million things. He began to list them, to sort through the possibilities and try to decide now what he would do if and when he was faced with real problems.

He was still mulling contingencies an hour later when he

finally drifted into a troubled sleep filled with blood and disaster.

He was preflighting the ejection seat and removing the safety pins when he realized that one pin was already out. This one here, attached to the others with this red ribbon, that went where? He looked. Must be somewhere here on the side of the seat, to safety the drogue extraction initiator mechanism.

He found the place. A steel pin protruded from the hole. He tried to pull it out with his fingers.

Nope. It was in there to stay.

Someone hammered this steel rod into that hole. Oh, the ejection seat would still fire, but the drogue chute would not deploy and so the main chute would stay in its pack as he sat in the seat waiting, all the way to the ground.

Jake Grafton climbed back down the ladder to the concrete. Spiro Dalworth was standing there with the Russian lieutenant, the only officer on the base who had talked to them.

'Spiro, tell this clown to take me to the base commander.'

Dalworth fired off some Russian. When it didn't take, he repeated it.

The Russian pilot's eyes got large, but he whirled and started walking. Jake Grafton and Spiro Dalworth stayed two steps behind him.

The base commander had his office in a crumbling concrete building with the Russian flag on a pole out front. He was a rotund individual with a lot of gold on his epaulets. A general, probably.

'Someone sabotaged my airplane, hammered a steel pin into the ejection seat so that it will not function properly. Tell him.'

Dalworth did so. The general looked skeptical.

'I want two different airplanes. And I want his people to arm them while we watch.'

This time the general fired off a stream of Russian and gestured widely.

'He says that you are mistaken. You know nothing of this airplane, which is a fine airplane. Combat-tested in Afghanistan. His men are all veterans and take excellent care of their equipment. This is a front-line fighting unit, not—'

'Pick up his telephone. Call the Kremlin in Moscow. Ask for Yeltsin.'

To his credit, Dalworth didn't hesitate. He reached for the telephone as if he were going to order a pizza. When he asked the operator in Russian to get him the Kremlin operator, the general came out of his chair with a bound.

Jake was ready. He pulled the .357 Magnum revolver from his armpit holster and fired a round through the top of the general's desk. The gun went off with a roar that the walls of the room concentrated into a stupendous, soul-numbing thunderclap. The bullet punched a nice hole in the top of the wooden desk and a long splinter came loose. Dalworth almost dropped the telephone.

The general froze, staring at Jake, who looked him straight in the eye as he returned the pistol to the holster under his leather flight jacket.

The door flew open and a soldier with a rifle appeared. Dalworth said something to the general and made a shoo-ing motion to the soldier, who finally backed out of the room and closed the door.

Dalworth started talking on the telephone. After three or four sentences and a wait, he looked at Jake expectantly.

'Tell them that this general doesn't understand that he is to cooperate.

'Tell them that the two airplanes he wants us to fly have been sabotaged.

'Tell them that I want two good airplanes armed to the teeth, and I want them *now*, as President Yeltsin promised the president of the United States.'

Dalworth translated each sentence in turn and listened a

moment, then held out the instrument to the Russian general, who accepted it reluctantly.

When the general finally hung up the phone, he stood, straightened his uniform jacket as he snarled something at Dalworth, jerked his hat on and headed for the door.

'We are to follow him, Admiral. From what I could tell, he was bluntly told to cooperate or face the music.'

Jake grunted and strode after the general.

The Russian general stood in the middle of the parking mat and gave orders fast and furiously. He pointed, first at the planes Jake and Rita were to fly, then at the row of Su-25s still sitting in their revetments.

The general was in fine form, with officers and enlisted saluting and trotting obediently when Rita approached Jake. She held out her hand. In it were five coins, rubles.

'I found these glued to the stator blades inside the intakes of the plane I was to fly.'

Jake nodded. The coins would have stayed glued while the engines were at idle, but when the engines were accelerated to full power for the takeoff roll the coins would have come unstuck and been sucked through the compressors, which would have started shedding blades seconds later. The predictable result would be catastrophic engine failure and perhaps fire just as the aircraft lifted from the runway with a full load of weapons. It would be a spectacular way to die.

The airplane switch took an hour. New planes were pulled forward with a tractor and topped off with fuel. Two arming crews took the 250-kilogram bombs off the sabotaged planes and manhandled them onto the racks of the new ones. Another arming crew serviced the 30mm cannon on each plane with belts of ammo. While all this was going on, Rita inspected each aircraft, examined the fuses on the bombs, looked at each arming wire.

She was still at it when the general told Dalworth the planes were ready, and he translated this message for Jake.

Grafton turned his back on the airplanes and stood looking toward the office building. The telephone lines went to a pole that also carried the lines from the hangars. These lines went off to the east until they disappeared behind some buildings that looked like enlisted barracks.

Above them clouds floated southeast. Patches of blue were visible in the gaps. The clouds were puffy, full of moisture.

When Rita was finished, she came over to Jake. 'Whenever you're ready, sir.'

The Russians had G-suits, torso harnesses, oxygen masks and a variety of helmets arranged upon the hood of a tractor. The two fliers donned the flight gear carefully and tried on helmets until they found ones that fitted snugly.

'I'll lead,' Jake told Rita. 'You follow me as soon as I begin my takeoff roll and rendezvous in loose cruise. I want you above me. We'll spend the day below two hundred feet and only climb when the target is in sight. The radio has four channels – we'll use channel one. Get a radio check on the ground and then stay off the radio except for emergencies.

'When we're airborne, I'm going to arm my gun and shoot out the telephone box on the edge of the base. Once you arm your weapons, don't de-arm them. Our old equipment would always chamber a round on arming and leave the round in the chamber when you disarmed it, so the gun jammed the second time you hit the arming switch. I don't know how these guns are wired but let's take no chances.'

'Yessir.'

'Got any advice on how to fly this thing?'

'Be smooth,' Rita Moravia said. 'Let the plane fly itself. No sudden control inputs – don't force it to do anything. Stay in the center of the performance envelope as much as possible. Visually check every switch before you move it. Be ready every second. Don't ever relax.'

'You got your mil setting for the bombsight?'

'One hundred ten mils.'

'Okay.'

'Rita, if anything happens to me, bomb that missile storage hangar. No matter what.'

'Aye aye, sir.' She said it matter-of-factly, without inflection.'

Jake Grafton wanted to ensure that he was properly understood. 'I guess what I'm trying to say is, do whatever you have to do to destroy those missiles.'

'I understand.'

He examined her face. She was a beautiful woman, but right now she wore a look of confidence and determination that would have set well on any man Jake had ever flown with. Satisfied, Jake turned to Dalworth.

'Stay with the helicopter. Don't let the pilot wander off. Wave money at him if you have to. And don't let anyone here touch that machine. If we aren't back in three hours, get the hell out of Dodge.'

'Aye, aye, sir.'

'Let's get at it,' Jake Grafton muttered to Rita as he pulled his helmet on.

'Oh, Admiral,' Rita said. 'Thanks.'

Jake looked at her, not quite clear on what she meant. She drew herself to attention and saluted.

He nodded at her and a puzzled Spiro Dalworth and, with his charts in one hand and his oxygen mask in the other, walked toward his plane.

CHAPTER NINETEEN

Jake's aircraft didn't want to come unstuck from the runway. With the engines at full power it was accelerating nicely, but the nose wheel remained firmly planted. He tugged experimentally on the stick.

The trim! He had guessed at the takeoff setting. He blipped the trim button on the stick with his thumb and eased the stick back. Now the nose came up. And the mains were off. He was flying. The wings rocked and he over-controlled with flaperons as he reached for the gear handle.

It wouldn't move. He pushed it in, then pulled it out. *Now* it moved. Had to be pulled.

Trimming nose down, airspeed increasing. Gear indicates up. When he felt comfortable he looked for the flap handle, then moved it to the up position. Here they come . . .

At a thousand feet he retarded the throttles some, lowered the nose a little and dropped the left wing about fifteen degrees. The plane stabilized in a level left turn. No warning lights, no gauges with pegged needles. He hit the switch to segment the hydraulic system.

He glanced over his shoulder and caught sight of Rita's plane.

His aircraft was decelerating. Not enough power. He added a little, readjusted his nose attitude, cursed himself for being so far behind the plane.

His oxygen mask didn't fit right. It was leaking oxygen around his cheeks, making flatulent noises that he could hear above the background roar of the engines. He tried to tighten the retaining straps with his left hand, and finally gave up.

Another glance at Rita, who was turning with him and closing.

She's a good stick. Don't worry about her. Fly your own plane.

When Rita was stabilized behind him and out to the right side, Jake began looking at the ground. The base was small by US standards, the buildings grouped tightly together, probably to keep everything within walking distance. Surrounding it were miles of forests.

There was the telephone line leading off, and there by the road intersection, wasn't that some kind of junction box mounted on that pole?

He reversed his turn, and when the plane stabilized, reached for the master armament switch. He lifted it. There was no locking collar like US planes possessed. Now the gun switch.

As he turned it on he felt a thud. That would be the gun charging. He hoped. Bombsight on, reticle lit. What had that Russian pilot said? Ten mils deflection for the gun? He twisted the adjustment knob.

Now into a left turn, looking again for the road intersection. It was several miles away off the left wing, slightly behind it, so he turned steeply to get the nose around.

More power in the turn, as the wings come level back off some. This will be a nice slow pass, plenty of time to aim.

He was too fast. Throttles back more, nose down a smidgen and trim.

He concentrated on finding the pole in the bombsight.

Small target. Too goddamn small . . .

There!

Damn, he was too close. He slewed the nose a tad with rudder, adjusted the nose attitude with stick, then quickly centered the rudder and squeezed the trigger.

The gun vibrated hard and he saw the muzzle flashes through the sight. At night the muzzle blast would be blinding.

Now off the trigger and stick back smartly. With the nose well above the horizon he rolled the plane ninety degrees and looked. *Careful, boy*, you're carrying a hell of a load low and slow!

Pole and box down!

Level the wings . . . raise the nose. More power. Safely away from the ground, let's turn on course 130.

He craned his neck. Rita was back there, stepped out and up. As he watched she eased in a little closer and gave him a thumbs up.

Okay!

Airborne and still alive. *Okay!*

The two Su-25s soon left the last of the forest behind and found themselves over the steppe. Jake had descended to about two hundred feet above the rolling terrain, which meant that he was constantly jockeying the stick and adjusting the trim as the plane rose and fell with the land contours. Below them the grass spread from horizon to horizon, broken only by stands of wheat and an occasional dirt road.

This broad valley of the Volga had been peopled since ancient times, yet now the fallout would deny it to future generations. The enormity of the Serdobsk tragedy intruded into Jake's thoughts even as he worked on holding course and altitude.

Farther south, below the radioactive fallout zone, stood the city of Volgograd, formerly Stalingrad, the city built in the 1920s and 1930s as a civic monument to the new Communist way of life. In the last half of 1942 it had been the site of the stupendous battle with the German army that marked the turning of the Nazi tide. The battle destroyed Stalin's city, of course, and nearly everyone in it. When the Red Army counterattacked and trapped the German Sixth Army, Hitler sacrificed over a quarter million men rather than give up that pile of rubble. Stalingrad, that shattered monument to a generation sacrificed in a titanic struggle between two absolute despots, was rebuilt after the war. Soon the radioactive particles and mud carried by the Volga would make the city a deathtrap once again.

He had loved this type of flying when he was younger. Racing low across open country, working the stick and throttles to make the airplane dance gracefully, sinuously, in perfect rhythm with the rise and fall of the land – this was flying as it ought to be, a harmonious mating of man, machine and nature.

Today the magic of it never occurred to him. He was thinking of shattered dreams and tyrants and a people poisoned as his eyes scanned the terrain ahead and occasionally flicked across the instrument panel. On one of these instrument checks his eye was caught by a light, a small bulb that flicked on, then off, then on again.

He looked carefully, identifying it. He was being painted by a fighter's radar. Perhaps they had not located him yet, but the fighters were looking.

Damn!

He and Rita were flying two subsonic attack planes, and somewhere up there above the clouds fighters were stalking them. *Oh, yes, they're after us.* Jake Grafton assumed the worst. That was the only way to stay alive. Automatically he tugged at the straps that held him to the ejection seat, tightening them still more.

Without warning the warplanes crested a low rise and the great river lay before them, with clouds and swatches of blue sky reflecting on its wide, brown surface.

The planes cleared a power line and then shot out over the water. The sky reflections on the water drew Jake Grafton's eyes upward. He scanned, and saw contrails . . . two pairs. In seconds the eastern shore swept under the nose and Jake Grafton eased into a gentle climb to stay just above the rising land.

Contrails in pairs . . . they could only be made by fighters in formation. Fighters. Looking for . . . ?

This eastern shore of the Volga was heavily eroded into

corrugated ravines and streambeds. Jake Grafton picked a decently large creek and dropped into the valley it had cut flowing west toward the river.

He was down here in the weeds hiding from radars that sat on the surface of the earth. These radars would provide vectors to the fighter-interceptors when they found him. If he stayed below their horizon, they couldn't.

But fighters aloft – the new generation of Soviet fighters possessed pulse Doppler radars that allowed them to look down and identify a moving target amid the ground clutter. And the new missiles would track a target in the ground clutter. 'Look-down, shoot-down' the techno-speak guys called it.

The light blinked on and off several more times.

What's the worst airplane that could be up there? The MiG-29? It was sure deadly enough, but no. The absolute worst plane that he could think of was another masterpiece from the design bureau of Pavel Sukhoi, the Su-27 Flanker. Designed in the mid-1980s to achieve air superiority against the best planes the West possessed, the Su-27 was thought by some Western analysts to be able to outfly the F-14, F-15, F-16 and F-18, plus every fighter the French, British and Germans have – all of them.

If those were Flankers up there, they were probably carrying AA-10 'fire and forget' antiaircraft missiles with active radar seekers.

And a missile could be on its way down right now.

He lowered the nose and dropped to fifty feet above the rocky creek. Rita was still with him, in tighter now, only forty or so feet away and a little behind.

The warning light was on steady.

They've found us. Missile to follow. Or a lot of missiles.

The land was a rough wilderness devoid of trees. Rock outcroppings, meandering creeks in rocky draws, sandy places – Jake Grafton was working hard holding the attack plane in the draw. Several times he couldn't make a turn and lifted the plane across the rim with only several feet of clearance, then banked hard and slipped the plane back into the draw.

Vaguely he was aware that Rita had slipped into trail behind him where she could ride just above his wash.

'We have fighters above us,' he told her on the radio.

No response. Radio silence meant radio silence to Rita Moravia. If she heard—

A flash on his left. He glanced over and saw a rising cloud of dirt and debris as it swept aft out of his field of vision. A missile impact!

'They're shooting,' he announced over the radio.

He lifted the nose of the plane and cleared the little valley, then dropped the left wing. Throttles to the stop, stick back – the Gs tugged him down into the seat.

Another flash, this time on his right side.

Jesus, each Flanker can carry up to *eight* missiles! How many have they fired?

When he had completed about ninety degrees of turn he rolled wings level, eased the nose back down. He was running only twenty feet above the high places in the lumpy ground, which gave him a tremendous sensation of speed. The warning light was blinking.

A pulse Doppler radar identified moving targets by detecting their movement toward or away from the radar. If he could fly a course perpendicular to the searching fighter, its radar could not detect him. When it lost him the searching fighter would probably turn to alter the angles and try to acquire him again. Still . . .

Trying to ensure he didn't inadvertently feed in forward stick, he craned his head to see aft.

The missiles will be coming at three or four times the speed of sound, fool! You'll never see them. But you will kill yourself looking for them.

He concentrated on the flying. After twenty seconds on this heading, he rolled into a right turn, then leveled the wings after ninety degrees of heading change. Back on his original course, southeast. The warning light went out.

A small miracle. A temporary reprieve. Jake Grafton was under no illusions — he was flying a plane designed to destroy tanks and provide close-air support to friendly troops: those Sukhoi masterpieces above were designed to shoot down other airplanes. The Russians couldn't make a decent razor or even an adequate toothbrush, but by God they could built great airplanes when they put their minds to it.

He looked for Rita.

Not there.

Did they get her?

How much fuel have those guys got? He and Rita were late getting off. Maybe the fighters were already airborne and are running out of fuel. There's a maybe to pray for.

The warning light was blinking again.

He rolled into enough of a turn that he could look behind him. Visibility was truly terrible out of this Soviet jet! Clear right. He rolled left and twisted his body around. Uh-oh. Up there at the base of that cloud, coming down like an angel on his way to hell — a fighter!

And Jake was still toting ten 250-kilogram bombs, about 5,500 pounds of absolutely dead weight. He was going to have to get rid of the bombs or he would be meat on the table for the fighters.

He turned hard left to force the fighter into an overshoot, make him squirt out to the right side because he couldn't hack the turn. As he did so, Jake worked the armament switches. In a strange plane he had to look to check each one, all the time pulling Gs and hoping the fighter was doing what he wanted him to do.

He couldn't just pickle off the bombs, not this close to the earth: they would hit the ground almost under him and might detonate. If they did the shrapnel and blast would destroy his aircraft, and him with it.

When he had the switches set, he rolled hard right and stabilized in an eighty-degree bank, four-G turn. Then he pickled the bombs. The G tossed them out to the left. The instant the last one went he tightened the turn to six Gs.

Where was that fighter?

There – crossing over above in an overshoot.

And Lord, there's another one at eleven o'clock honking around hard.

These guys weren't first team – they came in too fast and scissored the wrong way. Pray that they don't learn too fast!

He checked the compass. He was headed southwest. He brought the nose more west and punched the nose down. He wanted to run right in the weeds until he found those ravines and valleys that led down to the Volga. If he could just hide in those . . .

The fighter high on his left was pulling so hard vapor was condensing from the air passing over his wing – he was leaving a cloud behind each wing. Damn – it *was* an Su-27! He had to be in afterburner. That guy was aggressive enough, no question about that.

And the other one – Jake twisted his body halfway around, risked flying into the ground just to get a glimpse – at six-thirty, thirty degrees angle off, nose already down, accelerating.

How much fuel do these clowns have?

The rough ground ahead was his only chance. These guys could go faster, accelerate faster, and probably out-maneuver him. A stand-up dogfight with two of them would be suicide.

Jake was down to fifteen or twenty feet above the ground now, going flat-out with the throttles against the stops, doing maybe five hundred knots – the damn airspeed indicator was calibrated in kilometers and only God knew the conversion factor.

He was too close to the ground to look behind him. In fact, he was too close to the ground – he was sure he had hit a rocky outcrop but somehow managed to avoid it by inches. To kiss the ground at this speed would be certain death, yet his only hope to stay alive was to fly lower than those two fighter pilots would or could.

There — on the right! The ground dropped away into an eroded valley.

Quick as thought he had the stick over and was skimming down into the valley. Turn hard — pull, pull, pull! — to keep from hitting the sides that rose steeply above him.

Well into the winding valley, Jake Grafton eased over to the left side as he pulled the power levers back and deployed the speed brakes.

His speed bled off quickly. If one of those guys came into the gorge after him . . .

Cannon shells went zipping across the top of his right wing like orange pumpkins.

The right wing fell without conscious thought. Speed brakes in. Throttle full forward.

The fighter slid by on his right side, the pilot climbing and trying to slow.

As the sleek fighter went in front Jake pulled up hard and squeezed the trigger on the 30mm cannon. No time to aim! Just point and shoot!

The cannon throbbed and Jake hosed the shells in front of the twisting fighter, which flew into them. A piece came off the Su-27. Fuel venting aft. A flash.

Jake released the trigger and rolled away as the fighter exploded.

Where was the wingman?

A blind turn to the right coming up. Jake pulled hard to make it and got the nose coming up. As he went around the turn he climbed the side of the little valley and popped out on top. He swiveled his head.

There! Coming in from the left side, shooting.

Nose down hard. Back toward the valley.

The second fighter was going too fast and overshot. That's the problem when you've got a really fast plane: you want to use all that speed the designers gave you and sometimes it works against you.

313

This guy pulled Gs like he had a steel asshole. The fighter tried to turn a square corner, the down wing quit flying and the plane flipped inverted. In the blink of an eye the Su-27 hit the ground and exploded.

Jake got into the valley, retarded his throttles to about 90 percent RPM and stayed there.

He examined the electronic warfare panel. Goddamn light still blinking.

He rammed his left fingers under his helmet visor and swabbed the sweat away from his eyes.

They would find him again. How many more? He had seen four up there when he and Rita crossed the Volga a lifetime ago. Two were down, two still flying, perhaps off chasing Rita, perhaps now up there somewhere in the great sky above examining their track-while-scan radars and looking for him, perhaps calling on the radio to their comrades who would never answer again.

Could they find him in this valley, which was fast ceasing to be a steep gorge and was spreading out as the creek flowed its last few miles to the Volga?

There − on the left − another valley coming into this one. Jake dropped the left wing and pulled the plane around. He went back up the new valley, still seeking shelter as the EW light blinked intermittently.

Jake Grafton had flown his first combat mission in Vietnam over twenty years ago. He knew the hard, inescapable truth: in aerial combat the first pilot to make a mistake is the one who dies. The two men who had died in the Sukhoi fighters had each made fatal mistakes. The first man pursued too fast, so he had overshot when his victim unexpectedly slowed down. The second was overanxious, had pulled too hard and departed controlled flight too close to the ground. He was dead a half-second later, probably before he even realized what was happening.

The next time Jake might not be so lucky.

He swabbed more sweat from his eyes as he examined the fuel gauge. Still plenty. Like the A-6, the engines of this

Russian attack bird were easy on fuel and the plane carried a lot of it. That was the only advantage he possessed when compared to the fighters, which sacrificed fuel economy to gain speed and range to gain maneuverability.

Where were the other two fighters? Chasing Rita?

A flicker of concern for Rita crossed his mind, but he forced it away. Rita was a professional, she had been an F/A-18 Hornet instructor pilot for two years before she went to test pilot school – she could take care of herself.

He hoped.

No time to worry about her. If only he knew where she was . . .

They came in shooting from the rear quarter on each side. His first inkling that they were there was the sight of glowing cannon shells passing just in front of the nose, from left to right. He rammed the stick forward and his peripheral vision picked up shells passing just above the canopy from right to left. Just streaks really, but he knew exactly what they were.

The negative G lasted only for an instant before he had to jerk the stick back to avoid going into the ground. But it was enough. Even as he fought the positive G he saw the pair of fighters flash across above his head and arc tightly away for another pass.

He wouldn't survive another pass.

Slamming the throttles full forward, he kept the nose coming up and topped the cliff on the right side of the valley, then ruddered the nose down. He pulled hard in a tight turn, trying to turn inside the faster fighter.

And the fighter pilot wasn't looking!

The idiot had his head in the cockpit – he was worried about flying into the ground. That was a serious threat this close to the earth, the brown land whirling by at tremendous speed just scant feet below the right wingtip.

The nose of Jake's plane passed the fighter and he began to pull ahead. Range closing as the aspect angle changed. The fighter was turning into Jake. Angle off about seventy degrees, now eighty, ninety as the two planes flashed toward each other. Jake eased out some bank. A full deflection shot –

Now!

He triggered the cannon. The tracers passed in front of the fighter's nose, then in an eyeblink the fighter flew through the stream, which stitched him nose to tail. His nose dropped and his right wing kissed the earth.

Jake raised his nose a smidgen to ensure he didn't share the same fate, banked and pulled.

If he could get around quickly enough, he would present the second fighter with a head-on shot, and if that guy had any sense he would refuse the invitation and pull up into the vertical, where Jake lacked the power to follow.

And that is what happened as the two planes flashed toward each other nose to nose. Jake wanted to take a snapshot but couldn't get his nose up fast enough. He slammed it back down and was pulling hard to get the plane's axis parallel to the canyon when he flashed over the rim. He let the plane descend on knife edge until the rock wall shielded him.

His heart was threatening to thud its way out of his chest. Talk about luck! Three mistakes, three dead men who would get no wiser.

But this last guy – he was no overeager green kid who thought he was bulletproof. He had pulled his nose up the instant he saw the head-on pass developing. This guy would take a lot of killing.

And Jake Grafton didn't know if he had it in him. Somehow he got his visor up and swabbed away the sweat that poured into his eyes when he pulled Gs, this while he threaded his way up the valley and looked above and aft to see what the Russian was up to.

What would you do, Jake Grafton?

I'd slow down to almost coequal speed and follow along, getting lower and lower, and when my guns came to bear I'd take my shots. And he would fall.

316

Jake got a glimpse of his opponent. He was high up and well aft, on a parallel course, his nose down. He must have lost sight for a moment and allowed Jake to extend out. But now he was closing.

You've had a good life, Jake. You've known some fine men, loved a good woman, flown the hot jets. Maybe your life has made a difference to somebody. And now it's over. That man up there is going to kill you. He's going about it just right, slowly and methodically; he isn't going to make any mistakes. And you are going to die.

The Russian was throttled back, coming down like the angel of doom.

What's ahead? I'll out-fly the bastard. I'll fly that son of a bitch into the ground.

Even as the thought raced through his mind, he knew it wouldn't work. This guy wasn't going to make any mistakes unless Jake forced the action. If he were allowed to play his own game he would win.

Jake Grafton risked another over-the-shoulder glance to see if he had room. Maybe. It was going to be tight.

He kept the wings level and pulled the stick straight aft. The throttles were up against the stops. A nice four-G pull so he would have something left on top. If this guy were wise and had plenty of fuel, he would light his burners and climb, avoid the head-on that was developing. A head-on pass that gave each guy a fifty-fifty chance – that was the best Jake could play for when the other pilot had every performance edge.

But the Russian pilot accepted the challenge!

Upside down at the top of the loop, Jake fed in forward stick and placed the pipper in the reticle high to allow for the fall of his shells, then pulled the trigger. The Russian was already shooting. Strobing muzzle blasts enveloped the nose of the opposing fighter as Jake pulled his trigger.

Jake felt the trip-hammer impacts as cannon shells ripped into his plane. Then the Russian blew up.

Jake knifed through the falling debris and tried to right his machine. Fuel was boiling out the left wing and the left engine was unwinding. He shut it down. A big red light on the left side of the bombsight was illuminated – fire. He needed a lot of right rudder to control his plane.

Now he was level. And alive.

For how long?

That depended on the fire warning light. It flickered several times, then went out. Maybe he had a chance after all.

He glanced at the compass. He was heading east. He dropped the right wing into a gentle turn and let the nose drift down as he juggled the rudder to maintain balanced flight. He had to get low again, avoid the radar that was probing this sky.

He steadied up heading south, descending. One of the Russian's cannon shells had impacted the second weapons pylon on the left wing, shattering it and twisting it so badly fuel was coming out of the wing. Even as Jake stared at the damaged pylon the last of the wing fuel rushed away into the slipstream. Primary hydraulic pressure was on its way to zero. If that was the primary system gauge.

The warning lights seemed predictable. The damaged engine hadn't blown up – if it did there was nothing he could do but die. His heart was still beating, thud, thud, thud. He was still *alive!*

That Russian must have been low on fuel. In a hurry. Too bad for him.

Jack Yocke tapped aimlessly on his laptop computer and from time to time glanced at Toad Tarkington sitting in the big chair. Toad had a pistol in his hand and kept looking at it, turning it this way and that, wrapping his fist around the grip and hefting it.

Herb Tenney lay on the couch with his hands taped together behind his back, his ankles taped together, and a strip of tape over his mouth. Herb seemed calm.

Jack Yocke had done the taping with a roll from the first aid kit when Toad brought him into the room at gunpoint.

Now the three of them sat – Herb calm, Yocke full of questions, Toad playing with that goddamn pistol.

'Did he come willingly?' Jack asked, breaking the silence.

'Uh-huh.'

'Where did you find him?'

'In the cafeteria. Waited until he had finished his coffee and followed him out.'

'Would you have shot him if he didn't come along?'

Toad merely glanced at Yocke, then turned his gaze back to the pistol in his hand. The reporter saw the same thing that Herb Tenney must have seen fifteen minutes ago. Toad would have pulled the trigger with all the remorse he would have had swatting a fly.

Jack Yocke had another question, but he didn't ask it. Did Jake Grafton tell you to corral Tenney? Toad didn't do anything unless Jake Grafton told him to, Yocke told himself, and once told, Toad would do literally anything. The asshole was like a Doberman, ready to rip the throat out of the first man his master sicced him on.

Yocke sighed and went back to tapping. He was listing what he knew about Nigel Keren, about the Mossad bribing Russians to get Jews out of the country and assassinating Russian politicians, about the KGB blowing up the Serdobsk reactor, about a hangarful of nuclear-armed mobile missiles and warheads that were going south into Iraq a planeload at a time. He was sitting on at least four huge stories, any one of which would win him a Pulitzer prize, and all he could do was tap on this frigging keyboard and pray that someday soon he could telephone something to the *Post*. If he still had a job!

He felt a little like the prospector who has spent his whole life looking for traces of color when he finally stumbles onto the mother lode. And doesn't know where the vein leads.

All he really had were pieces of stories. Jack Yocke had

spent five years chasing stories and he knew that he didn't have all of any one of them. Oh, he had some great pieces, but he didn't know where the roots led.

Jake Grafton knew. Of that he was convinced.

Damn, he was getting as goofy as Tarkington. Toad sat there playing with his pistol and if you asked, he would tell you that Jake Grafton knows everything. What's your problem? Grafton will tell you what he wants you to know when he wants you to know it. If that time ever comes. And if it doesn't, then you shouldn't know.

Jack Yocke didn't think Jake Grafton knew all the answers. He thought Jake was feeling his way along, examining the trees, trying to size up the forest. Jack Yocke didn't have Toad's faith.

The truth, he decided, was probably somewhere in the middle.

He jabbed the button to save what he had written and then turned off the computer. He closed the screen over the keyboard and pulled the plug out.

'You done?' Toad asked.

'What's it look like?' Yocke snarled. He was extremely frustrated, and Toad marching in a big CIA weenie at gunpoint hadn't helped.

'Would you like to help me?'

'Do what?' Jack asked suspiciously.

'Well, you gotta sit here with this pistol and watch our boy Herb. I have an errand. If Herb twitches, blow his fucking head off. If anybody comes through that door besides me, blow their fucking head off. Think you can handle it?'

'No.'

'You ought to be the pro-choice poster child, Jack. If your mother only knew how you were going to turn out she would have grabbed a rusty old coat hanger and done it herself.'

'Any time you get the itch, Tarkington, you can kiss my rosy red ass. I am not about to get mixed up in the middle of a war or shoot anybody. And no more goddamn cracks about—'

Toad tossed the gun at him. Yocke snagged it to prevent it from hitting him in the face.

Toad stood up. He looked over the items from Herb's pockets that were spread on the low coffee table and selected a ring of keys, then faced Yocke. 'Anyone besides me comes through that door, they'll kill you if you don't kill them first. And you can bet your puny little dick that Herb would cheerfully do the job if he had his hands free. Think about it.'

With that Toad went to the door and carefully opened it. He looked out. Now he checked to ensure the door would lock behind him, passed through and pulled it closed.

Jack Yocke looked at Herb Tenney to see if he had any big ideas. Apparently not. He then examined the pistol in his hand. This thingy on the left side looked like the safety. Is it on? Yocke kept his finger well away from the trigger, just in case.

He had had a journalism professor who once told the class that the problem with the profession was the company a reporter had to keep to get his stories. Truer words were never spoken, Jack told himself ruefully.

'If I get out of this alive,' he informed Herb Tenney, 'I'm going to get a job washing beer mugs in a bikers' saloon. Associate with a better class of people. Keep better hours. Make more money. Get laid more.'

Out in the hallway Toad slowed to talk to the marine sergeant sitting at the head of the stairs with an M-16 across his knees. He also wore a pistol in a holster on a web belt around his middle. 'Everything okay?'

'Yessir. Not a soul's been around.'

Toad glanced down the hall at the marine on the other end, who was looking his way.

Satisfied, Toad said, 'He's in there with Jack Yocke. If he

comes out shoot him in the legs. Whatever you do, don't kill him.'

'Aye aye, sir.'

When he was inside Herb's room, Toad scanned it, then went straight to the bathroom and Herb's shaving kit above the sink. Yep, the shit still had that plastic pill bottle with the child-proof cap. Toad glanced at them to ensure they were what he wanted, then pocketed them. He considered taking Herb his toothbrush. Naw. His fucking teeth could just rot.

Out in the bedroom Toad got Herb's suitcase and opened it. Well, ol' Herb was a neat packer. His mother would be proud.

Toad dumped everything into a pile in the middle of the bed and examined the lining of the suitcase. He and Jake Grafton had been through Herb's stuff once before, but it wouldn't hurt to do it again. Carefully and thoroughly.

Underwear, socks, shirts, trousers, a sweater. A spare can of shaving cream. Toad squirted some onto the carpet. Yep, shaving cream.

The closet held several suits, ties, white shirts and a spare pair of shoes. Toad examined the shoes. He got out his penknife and pried off the heels. Nothing. He felt the suits carefully and threw them on the floor. Except for a spare pen and a pack of matches that Herb had overlooked, the pockets were empty.

Now he turned his attention to the room, systematically taking everything apart. As he worked he thought about Rita.

Pregnant. Refusing to stop flying.

If he were her, he would . . . But he wasn't Rita. Rita was Rita and that was why he married her.

You just have to take women as they come. It's hard to do at times, considering. Amazing that hormone chemistry could make such a big difference in the way men and women's brains worked. It was like they were a different species, or creatures from another planet.

He threw himself into the chair and sat staring morosely at the mess in front of him. There was nothing here to be found, of that he was sure. So he thought some more about Rita in the cockpit of that jet, flying through a strange sky over a radioactive landscape, nursing the stick and throttles and dropping bombs and fighting the Gs.

There were so many things that could go wrong. And a Russian jet for chrissake, designed, built and maintained by a bunch of vodka-swilling sots.

She can handle it, he told himself, wanting to believe. She'll get back all right. She's with Jake Grafton. I mean, she's good and he's great. They're a good team. They'll make it.

Fuck, they'd better! He wasn't up to losing Rita just now. She had damn near died in a crash a few years back – just the memory of those days made him nauseated.

And he didn't want to lose Jake Grafton either. Grafton told him to snag Herb Tenney, and if Grafton didn't come back, Toad was going to have to figure out what to do next. Not that he had a lot of options. One thing sure, though – Herb was going to be finishing off his supply of happy pills if Jake Grafton didn't make it.

When he opened the door to the apartment, the first thing he saw was Jake Yocke's pasty face, then the Browning Hi-Power which he held with both hands. It was pointed askew at nothing at all.

Toad locked the door behind him and took a look at Herb, who was pretending to sleep.

Yocke held the pistol out to Toad butt-first. Toad took it and stuffed it into his waistband. 'Thanks,' he said. 'I kept waiting to hear the shots.'

Yocke didn't think that comment worth a reply.

'Would you have used this?' Toad wanted to know.

'I don't know.'

After they had sat Herb Tenney on the ceramic con-venience in the bathroom, then fixed a can of chili for lunch, Yocke asked, 'How can you just walk around sticking pistols in people's faces?'

Toad looked mildly surprised. 'I'm in the military. Jake Grafton gives orders, I obey them.'

'This isn't a movie, you know. That's a real gun with real bullets.'

Toad helped himself to another spoonful of chili. When it was on its way south he said, 'You keep looking for moral absolutes, Jack. There aren't any. Not in this life. All we can do is the best we can.'

'But how do you know you're doing the right thing?'

'I don't. But Jake Grafton does. It's uncanny. He'll do the right thing regardless of the consequences, regardless of how the chips fall. I'll take that. I do what I'm told knowing that the CAG is trying to do right.' Even as he said it his mind jumped to Rita. He had bowed to Rita's decision to fly while pregnant based on faith in her judgment. Now the chili made a lump in his stomach. He dropped the spoon into the bowl and shoved it away. 'You gotta believe in people or you're in a hell of a fix,' he said slowly.

'You answer a question, Toad, by evading it. What is *right?* Why do you think Grafton knows what *right* is?'

Toad was no longer paying attention. He was staring at his watch, watching the second hand sweep. They should be on the ground by now . . . if they were still alive. Why hadn't they called? Did he really trust her judgment, or was he a coward not to assert himself? If anything happened to her . . .

Jake Grafton saw the smoke column twenty miles away. The black smoke towered like a giant chimney at least three thousand feet into the atmosphere. As he got closer he could see that the wind had tilted the column, which was visibly growing taller, mushrooming into the upper atmosphere.

Creeping up to two hundred feet to avoid the dust being sucked into the inferno raging at the base of the smoke, he bounced in turbulence even here on the up-wind side of the fire. The turbulence made his bowels feel watery: that damaged wing might have a broken spar. As the plane bucked the stick felt sloppy and the secondary hydraulic system pressure dropped. He must be oh so careful.

The hangar was ablaze. Rita.

Ten or fifteen minutes ago?

Something silver on the mat? A wing?

It couldn't be a wing from Rita's plane, could it? *Could it?*

He edged in for a closer look. No. It was a big wing, attached to a transport that was also on fire. She caught someone parked on the mat and shot them apart.

He turned away from the blaze and consulted his fuel gauge. Fuel would have been okay plus a bunch if he hadn't spent all that time maneuvering at full throttle and let that jerk shoot up his plane. Going to be tight.

Right engine was still alive and pulling hard – no more warning lights. The slop in the controls when operating on the backup hydraulic system was acceptable as long as he didn't have to defend himself, as long as the secondary pump held together, as long as he could make his aching right leg work. The plane flew okay on one engine if he held in forty pounds or so of right rudder. The rudder trim wasn't working. Sorry about that!

He had about forty miles of radioactive terrain to cross before he could get out and walk. It was a little like flying over a shark-infested ocean – you prayed for the engine to keep running, counted every mile, watched the minute hand of the panel clock with intense interest.

Jake Grafton's eyes scanned the vast distances between the horizon and the bottom of the cumulonimbus clouds. He gazed up into the gaps between the clouds, searched behind him and out to both sides. The sky appeared to be empty. Because he knew how difficult another aircraft was to spot in a huge, indefinite sky, he kept looking. And occasionally his eyes came inside to check the clock.

So she made it to here and took out the hangar and that transport on the mat. He hadn't seen any craters on the mat that would mark misses. Apparently she put all her ordnance into the bucket, a neat, professional job.

Thank you, Rita, wherever you are.

He listened to the engine. He watched the clock hand sweep. He unhooked his oxygen mask and swabbed the sweat from his eyes.

Forty miles of terrain required about ten minutes of flying to cross. When the ten minutes had passed Jake began to relax. His right leg was hurting since he had to maintain constant pressure on the rudder, but he felt better. It was goofy when you thought about it – Captain Collins said *about* forty miles, and of course the fallout zone had no definite boundary. The intensity of the radiation would just decrease as the miles went by. Knowing all this and feeling slightly silly, Jake still felt better with each passing mile.

If this shot-up jet would just hold together . . .

When the city of Lipetsk appeared in the haze at ten or twelve miles, Jake Grafton eased the nose of his Su-25 into a climb. He went across the city at several thousand feet and made a gentle turn to line up for the northwest runway about eight miles away.

Nothing happened when he lowered the gear handle. He found the little emergency switch and held it in the down position. The gear broke free of the wells and fell into the slipstream – he could feel the drag increase.

His numb right leg refused to put the right amount of pressure on the rudder. The nose wandered a little from side to side. Carefully playing his single engine, Jake Grafton tried to keep the speed up and fly a flat approach. Only when he was sure he could make the field did he use the electrical switch to drop ten degrees of flaps.

He cut the engine immediately after he felt the tires squeak. Without brakes this thing would roll forever; he had no idea how to engage the emergency system. He had tried turning the parking brake handle ninety degrees and it didn't want to rotate.

When the jet was down to about twenty mph it began to drift toward the edge of the runway. There was nothing he could do. It rolled off the edge and came to rest in the grass.

For the first time in over an hour, Jake Grafton relaxed his right leg. It was numb, shaking.

Jake used the battery to open the canopy. As the huge silence enveloped him he took off his mask and helmet and wiped the sweat from his hair. He was drained.

Somehow he managed the energy to get his gloves off and begin unstrapping. When he got the fittings released he sat there massaging his right thigh.

'Admiral! Admiral Grafton!' It was Rita, running across the grass toward him.

'Hey, kid. Am I glad to see you!'

She slowed to a walk, just fifty feet or so away. She glanced at the shattered wing pylon, then looked up at Jake. 'I got the hangar, sir.'

'I know,' Jake said, and wiped his eyes with his fingers. 'I know.'

CHAPTER TWENTY

The helicopter's two radios were mounted on a shelf on the bulkhead between the cockpit and passenger compartment. The leads had a collar that allowed them to be unscrewed when the radio needed to be removed for servicing. Jake Grafton used his fingers to twist the collars and pull out the plugs. Then he told Spiro Dalworth to tell the pilot to land at the Lipetsk railroad station.

Not a single Russian had come out to look the Su-25s over when Jake landed at the army airfield fifteen minutes ago. He climbed down from the cockpit and followed Rita toward the helicopter.

'What happened at Petrovsk?' Jake asked.

'There was a four-engine jet transport on the mat, sir, and they were loading a missile aboard. I looked on the first pass and shot on the second. On the third the transport caught fire. I then bombed the hangar and it caught fire. I fired out the gun on the clean room.'

He wondered what thoughts went through Rita Moravia's mind when she saw live humans and knew they couldn't be allowed to get on that plane and leave. What had she thought when she lined up the cargo plane in her sight and pulled the trigger? All things considered, it was probably better not to ask. 'Did you see any markings on the plane?'

'Arabic script, sir. They must have wanted those missiles pretty badly to risk a trip in daylight.'

'Lot of cloud cover. They might have pulled it off.'

'Saddam sent his people on a suicide mission. One man I saw on the ground wasn't wearing a hot suit.'

The wars of the kings were much more civilized, Jake reflected. No wonder Churchill preferred the nineteenth century over this one.

The Russian chopper pilot was already in the cockpit and started the engines as they climbed aboard. Within a minute he lifted the machine from the parking mat.

Staring now at the disconnected radio leads, Jake concluded he needed a knife. He didn't have one. He wedged the lead between the hammer and frame of his revolver and used that to strip off the collar. Now the lead could not be reconnected. He did the same with the lead to the second radio.

Someone wanted him dead. Perhaps those dead fighter pilots had orders to concentrate on the lead plane or were so ill with buck fever that they lost track of Rita at a crucial moment. Whichever, both he and Rita were fortunate to be alive. Still, with only a telephone call more fighters could be launched to shoot down this unarmed helicopter and convert their earlier escape into an alarmingly brief reprieve.

A prudent man would find another form of transportation. Jake Grafton was a prudent man.

Very prudent. After the chopper settled into the street in front of the railway station, he asked Dalworth, 'What's the pilot's name?'

'Lieutenant Vasily Lutkin, sir.'

'Tell him to fly on to Moscow after we get off.'

He watched the helo pilot lift the collective and feed in forward cyclic. The pilot glanced once at him, then concentrated his attention on flying his machine.

Jake watched the helicopter until it crossed the rooftops heading just a little west of north.

Vasily Lutkin might make it. Maybe. If his luck was in.

Those four fighter pilots were trying to kill you, Jake, but not this guy.

Okay, so now you know how Josef Stalin did it. Just give the order and watch them go to their doom.

329

With sagging shoulders he followed Dalworth and Rita into the cavernous station.

And how much luck do you have left in your miserable little hoard, Jake Grafton? *Not much, friend. Not much. Guilt and luck don't mix.*

There was a vending booth inside the terminal building selling Pepsi in tiny paper cups, about an ounce of the soft drink for a ruble. Jake laid a ten-ruble note on the counter and while Dalworth went to buy tickets, he and Rita each drank five cupfuls of the sticky sweet liquid. Then Jake wandered off for the men's room, burping uncontrollably.

The train was full to bursting. There were no empty seats in the car they found themselves in so the three Americans wedged themselves into a little space on the floor. Men, women, and children with everything they owned filled the car. One man had a goat. Several women had baskets that contained live chickens. A man lay in the floor between the aisles vomiting repeatedly while a woman periodically gave him something to drink from a bottle.

'Radiation sickness, I think,' Dalworth whispered.

Jake just nodded. After a half hour Rita went over to help, dragging Dalworth along to translate.

The air was thick with a miasma of odors. Smoke from Papirosi cigarettes made a heavy haze.

The train stopped about once an hour for ten minutes or so. Each time Jake stayed seated in his corner with his hand under his jacket on his gun butt watching the people fighting their way aboard. The scrambler was wedged under his legs.

No one got off the train. Moscow was the universal destination. Some of the people who clamored aboard were soldiers in uniform, but they were wrestling bags of person-al articles. No one in uniform or out paid any attention to the Americans. Finally the train got under way again and all the struggling humanity somehow found a place to ride.

330

These Russians had endured so much, yet there was so much still to endure. When he had replayed the morning's flight for the twentieth time and the adrenaline had finally burned itself from his system, Jake sat looking at his fellow passengers, trying to fathom their stories and their lives as snatches of Russian swirled on the laden air. Finally his head sagged onto his knees and he slept.

Every minute passed slower and slower for Toad Tarkington. He paced, he stood at the window from time to time and stared out, occasionally he turned on the television and stood gazing at the images on the screen for minutes at a time without seeing them, then snapped it off. He paced some more.

When he could stand it no longer he picked up the phone and dialed. 'Captain, this is Toad. Heard anything?'

Then he hung up and went back to pacing, and fidgeting, and gazing gloomily at Herb Tenney and Jack Yocke.

'What did Collins say?' Yocke asked.

'Nothing.'

'What are you going to do if Grafton and Rita don't come back?'

Toad didn't answer. He didn't want even to acknowledge the possibility out loud, let alone discuss it with Jack Yocke. Jake Grafton and Rita Moravia were the two most important people in his life. He felt as if he were teetering on the edge of a dark abyss. Every minute that passed made the gaping horror more probable, and more unspeakable.

After a while Yocke said, 'Surely we ought to discuss it.'

'They'll be back.' End of conversation.

They were on the ground somewhere. Tactical jets carry a limited supply of fuel, and when it's exhausted . . . no one ever ran out of gas and floated around up there unable to get down. So where were they? In the fallout zone? Shot down! Why *hadn't* they called? Any way you figured it, something had gone seriously wrong. And our boy Herb probably had something to do with that something.

Toad found himself glowering at the CIA agent asleep on the couch. Sleeping! He forced himself to look away.

By six o'clock in the evening Toad had reached the breaking point. For lack of something better to do, he decided to go find Collins. 'I'm going out,' he announced to Jack Yocke, who looked up from the paperback novel he was reading. 'Keep an eye on Herb.' Toad hoisted himself erect and walked toward the door.

'Aren't you going to give me your pistol?' Yocke asked.

'Nah. There's marines outside.'

'Outside?'

'In the hallway. You have any trouble, just shout and they'll come running.'

The reporter was speechless.

Toad pulled the Browning from his waistband. 'This thing wouldn't do you any good anyway.' He thumbed off the safety and pulled the trigger. Click. 'It's empty.'

Yocke found his voice. '*Empty!*'

One of Jack Yocke's endearing qualities – and he had precious few, in Toad's opinion – was that sometimes he was extraordinarily slow on the uptake. Maybe it was an act. Whatever, Toad Tarkington savored the moment. 'You don't think I'm stupid enough to give a loaded gun to a trigger-happy thrill-killer like you, do ya? If you didn't shoot off your own toe, you'd probably go berserk and murder everybody north of the Moskva.'

'You dirty, rotten, slimy, retarded stumblebum, you—'

That was the high point in a long, dreary day of merciless tension and uncertainty. Toad stepped through the door and pulled it shut behind him before Jack Yocke got really wound up. He mumbled a greeting to the marine sitting at the top of the stairs as he went by.

It was after 7 P.M. when a pale, exhausted Rita Moravia sagged onto the floor beside Jake. Her flight suit reeked of vomit.

'How is that sick man?' Jake asked.

'Dead. Radiation poisoning, dehydration I think – oh, I don't know. His heart stopped and we just . . . gave up.' She brushed a wisp of hair out of her eyes and hugged her knees.

Several platitudes occurred to Jake, but he held his tongue.

'How did you evade those fighters this morning?' Rita asked. 'This morning! God, it seems like another lifetime ago.'

'One guy stalled and went in, I shot down the others.'

'You were lucky.'

'That's all life is: luck – some good, some bad, most indifferent. Some of it you make yourself, most of it you just have to take as it comes.'

'What's going on here, Admiral? Why did the Russians blow up their own reactor?'

'To hide the fact that nuclear weapons were gone.'

'You aren't serious?'

'Oh, but I am. Somebody – let's postulate a small group of somebodys – collected a lot of money from Saddam Hussein for some nuclear weapons. Saddam took delivery at Petrovsk the evening before the reactor blew up. Everyone there who wasn't in on the sale was killed. Then the reactor exploded and the usual prevailing wind delivered a lethal concentration of fallout on Petrovsk. Eventually someone would visit Petrovsk, but the way things work in Russia, that visit was a long way off. Maybe years. When it eventually came to pass, our small group of somebodys were sure they could control the dissemination of the news of what happened at Petrovsk because long before then Boris Yeltsin would be driven from power. And they would be in.'

'How could they be sure of that?'

'The reactor explosion would cause a political crisis. They would escalate the event to a crisis if it didn't happen naturally. And they had done their homework with

Saddam's money. A lot of money. Real money, hard currency. The people at the top in Russia are just like the people at the top everywhere else – they want good food, nice clothes, adequate housing, an education for their kids, decent medical care. The Communist party used to deliver all that, but those days are gone. Whoever can deliver that life-style to the people in power will rule.'

'Money.'

'Hard currency – US dollars. For bribes. To dole out to the faithful. To buy votes in the legislature. There's a flourishing dollar economy in Moscow – just how on earth does an honest Russian come by dollars?'

'Oh, my God,' Rita whispered. 'To murder all those people! I can't believe it.'

'This is *Russia*,' Jake told her, his voice low. 'Even the stones are guilty. See that old man over there, the one with the campaign ribbons on his lapel? He's a veteran of World War II. He probably has a hundred stories about how he and his fellow soldiers fought to the last ditch and saved Russia from Hitler. What he won't tell you about are the penal battalions – every division had one. These were unarmed battalions of political prisoners – Russians who had said something unwise about Stalin or the NKVD, people who appeared to be less than happy living in the new Communist paradise. The men in the penal battalions were herded ahead of the tanks before every attack to step on the land mines and clear the way. And German machine gunners slaughtered them and revealed their positions to the Red Army troops. Then the tanks and gallant soldiers like that old man killed Nazis and won glorious victories. They saved Mother Russia. Ah yes, that old man is proud of his ribbons.

'Yet this is the amazing part – *the Commies never ran out of recruits for the penal battalions.* That maniac Hitler gassed and shot and starved his domestic enemies – all at his cost. Stalin killed his enemies just as dead but he turned a nice profit doing it. And Stalin didn't bother cremating the

334

corpses: he let the body parts rot right where they lay to fertilize the soil.

'Yes, Rita, a group of ambitious people intentionally blew up the Serdobsk reactor. If a half million humans had to die to get them to the top, so be it. Like that old man over there with the ribbons, these people have paid their dues. *They have created a hell on earth and they are going to rule it.*'

'Stalin's children,' Rita murmured.

Twenty minutes later the train entered the outskirts of Moscow. 'Where's Dalworth?' Jake asked Rita.

'I don't know. He wandered off when that man died.'

'Find him. We're going to have to hop off this train fast and try for a taxi. If our luck is in, no one will be looking for us at the railroad station.'

She was very tired. 'You sent that helicopter pilot off to be shot down.' It was just a statement of fact, without inflection.

Jake Grafton merely glanced at her. 'Go find Dalworth,' he told her patiently.

If there were any security men scrutinizing the crowd, Jake didn't see them. The three Americans went through the station unaccosted, found the exit with Dalworth's help, and walked out onto the sidewalk. There were taxis. Jake and Rita climbed into the backseat of one while Dalworth negotiated the fare.

The streets looked normal to Jake's eye with the usual traffic and strolling pedestrians, here and there a policeman. At ten o'clock in the evening the sunlight, diffused by a thin layer of cirrus, came in at a very low angle and gave the city a soft, almost inviting look.

Dalworth sat in the front seat chatting with the taxi driver, and in a few moments he turned around and said to Jake, 'This fellow says that troops have road blocks around the embassy. They're checking everyone's papers.'

The taxi proceeded for several blocks before Jake spoke. 'We need to find something else to ride in.'

'Like a tank,' Rita said gloomily.

About a quarter mile from the embassy they passed a line of armored personnel carriers parked by the curb. 'One of these might do,' Jake said. 'Could you drive one, Rita?'

'It doesn't have wings,' she pointed out.

'Yes or no?'

'Yes.'

'Spiro, tell the driver to pull over.'

He dropped them at the head of the line. One soldier with a rifle stood on the curb. There were at least a dozen APCs in the line and another soldier lounged at the far end, almost two hundred feet away. Apparently the concept of vehicle theft hadn't caught on here yet.

'Walk by this guy,' Jake told his companions, and the three moved. Jake kept talking. 'Rita will drive. Dalworth will take the soldier's rifle and I'll assist him into the vehicle.'

The Russian soldier remained relaxed as they approached, his rifle held in the crook of his left arm. He watched them disinterestedly. As the trio passed him Jake drew his revolver and stuck it into the Russian's ribs as Dalworth neatly seized the rifle. The door to the APC stood open, so Rita merely climbed in.

Jake nodded toward the vehicle and the soldier, wearing a look of uncertainty and fear, went willingly enough. Jake glanced toward the other sentry. He was facing in the other direction. Really, these kids shouldn't be guarding anything more valuable than a garbage dump!

When everyone was inside, Dalworth closed the door and dogged it down.

'Any time, Rita.'

'Give me a minute, sir.' She was looking at the controls.

The seconds dragged by. Finally she adjusted a lever and pushed a button. The engine turned over but didn't catch.

More fiddling.

'Maybe our guy here knows how to drive,' Dalworth suggested.

'Ask him.'

Dalworth did so. The soldier's eyes got big, but he held his tongue. He was young, about twenty. Not a trace of beard showed on his face.

Rita ground some more with the starter. Then the diesel caught. She wrestled with the shift lever, ground the gears, then engaged the clutch. The thing lurched, then got under way.

'Empty his rifle,' Jake told Dalworth, 'and throw it in the back.'

Dalworth popped out the magazine and handed it to Jake, who tossed it into the back of the vehicle. The rifle followed.

The APC lumbered along at a stately pace. Rita steered it toward the center of the street. Two blocks later they saw a line of cars waiting in front of a roadblock with several dozen soldiers milling about.

'Drive right through,' Jake told his pilot. 'And don't run over anybody.'

'Admiral!'

'They'll get out of your way.'

She floored it and the soldiers ahead scattered. Amazingly, no shots were fired.

'Maybe they would have let us through,' Dalworth remarked.

'Maybe,' Rita agreed.

Jake kept his maybes to himself.

The APC rumbled the two blocks to the embassy along an empty street. She turned the corner from the boulevard and dropped down the street to the main entrance of the embassy, where she braked to a stop.

At least the stars and stripes were still flying.

The Russian soldier sat glued to his seat staring dumbfounded as the trio walked past four armed US marines in battle dress and entered the little brick reception building.

The marine on duty behind the desk punched the button to let them in and spoke through the window. 'The ambassador wants to see you, sir, and so does Captain Collins. And welcome back!'

He was rewarded with a grin from Rita.

The security door hadn't even closed behind the trio as the sergeant at the desk dialed Toad's telephone number. Lieutenant Commander Tarkington had been down here three times this evening – the sergeant was delighted that he had some good news to deliver for a change.

Toad came thundering down the stairs as Rita started up.

'Hey, Babe!'

'Hello, Toad-man,' she said as she was lifted from her feet in a fierce bear hug.

CHAPTER TWENTY-ONE

'General Shmarov is dead,' Tom Collins told Jake.

'Are you kidding me?'

'Nope. Apparently had a heart attack last night. Died in bed. At least that's what I hear from the Defense Ministry and Yeltsin's office. Of course, someone might have taken him for a ride last night and pumped a lead slug into his chest. Lead poisoning is a leading cause of heart attacks among the upper echelons in this neck of the woods.'

'Humph,' Jake Grafton replied, trying to visualize how Shmarov's demise fitted in. 'So what is CIA up to today?'

'Nothing, as near as I can tell. Toad escorted Herb Tenney upstairs right after breakfast this morning. Harley McCann' – McCann was the ranking resident CIA officer – 'went to his office and did the usual. I think he's still there.'

'At nine-thirty at night? He's got to know we have Tenney under lock and key.'

'Well, even if he's the worst spy we have, you'd think he'd find an event like that hard to miss. We've had armed marines guarding your apartment all day.'

'Shmarov had a heart attack.' Jake Grafton shook his head. 'What's the ambassador want?'

'He's been on the phone to Washington all day. Probably has some instructions, wants to know what happened at Petrovsk . . .'

'I'll have a little visit with Herb first. Then you and I will go see the ambassador.'

'Yes, sir.'

'In the meantime get the marine, Captain McElroy, and

have him stand by outside my apartment. Have him wear his sidearm.'

Herb Tenney's color wasn't good when Jake entered the apartment. His shirt was wet with sweat and his forehead was shiny. He looked as if he hadn't shaved in days.

'Where's Toad?' Jake asked Jack Yocke.

'In the bedroom with Rita.'

'Ask them to come out here, will you please?' Jake pulled a chair around to face Tenney, who was still on the couch.

While the reporter knocked on the bedroom door, Jake ripped the tape from Herb's mouth, wadded the strip up and tossed it toward a wastepaper basket. He missed. Rita and Toad came out of the bedroom holding hands.

'I want to go to the bathroom,' Herb said belligerently.

Jake weighed it for two seconds, then nodded. Toad and Jack hoisted him to his feet and carried him. When they got their guest settled on the throne with his pants down, Toad came out and shut the door.

'It went okay today. He hasn't said a word, we haven't questioned him. He's eaten a little and had a couple naps. Maybe I misread him, but I thought he looked slightly stunned when the gate guard called and said you and Rita were back. I told Yocke, and Herb had trouble controlling his face, I thought.'

'No questions today even when you had the tape off?'

'No, sir. The man knows how to keep his mouth shut.'

'A truly rare talent in this day and age. Find anything in his room?'

Toad took the pill bottle from his shirt pocket and handed it to Jake. 'There's four of each left in the bottle – eight pills.'

'Get my pill bottle from my bag.'

Rita asked, 'Admiral, do you want me here?'

'Yep. You and Toad and Jack and Spiro Dalworth. But everyone keeps their mouth shut, no matter what. Toad, take Jack into the bedroom and tell him if he says one word, he'll be ejected. Then rig up Jack's cassette tape recorder just out of sight under the couch.' Toad went and Jake turned to Rita. 'Call Captain Collins and ask him to send Dalworth up.'

'Aye, aye, sir.'

In the bedroom Toad delivered the message to Yocke, who merely nodded. Toad popped the magazine from the Browning and removed a handful of cartridges from his pocket. He pushed the shells into the clip one by one.

'Why didn't you have your pistol loaded today?' Yocke asked.

Toad was tired, emotionally drained. His mind wasn't working fast enough to come up with a quip, so for once he told Jack Yocke the unvarnished truth. 'Jake Grafton wanted him alive. Sitting there looking at him with a loaded gun, waiting . . . I don't know if I could have resisted the temptation to kill him.'

Yocke watched as Toad finished loading the magazine and snapped it into the handle of the pistol. He worked the slide, thumbed the safety into position. Then he slid the pistol into the small of his back.

'Why are you loading it now?'

'Maybe I'll get lucky.'

In the bathroom Jake filled a dirty glass of water and examined the white tablets from Herb's bottle. He selected one marked Aspirin on one side and dropped it into the water.

It all came down to this. If Herb knew Jake had sub-stituted aspirin for half the binary cocktail, he was too many steps ahead for Jake to catch him now.

He held the glass up to the light and swirled the water as the tablet slowly disintegrated. Into a pile of white powder.

Aspirin.

Thank God!

*

Out in the living room Herb Tenney was back on the couch. Jake Grafton emptied the pill bottle onto the table. He picked up each tablet and examined the markings. When he was finished he had two small piles of tablets.

'General Shmarov died last night,' he remarked conversationally. 'Tell us about that.'

Herb had watched Jake examine the white tablets. Now he looked at the faces of the other people in the room, then back at Jake. 'I don't have anything to say.'

'Tenney, I don't think you understand how tight the crack is that you're in. You are going to talk or we're going to force these pills down your throat. All of them.'

'Now you listen, Admiral. I don't know what the fuck you think you're doing, but I know my rights. I have the right to an attorney and I have the right to remain silent. You're an agent of the government.'

'You think there's going to be a trial? You're joking, right?'

Jake Grafton hitched his chair closer to Tenney and leaned forward so his face was only a foot or so from Herb's. 'Let me say it again – either you answer my questions with God's truth or I'm going to stuff these pills into your mouth and tape it shut. The pills will dissolve in your mouth even if you don't swallow.'

Herb Tenney looked at the tablets and he looked at Jake Grafton. He was perspiring. Everyone was looking at him except Jack Yocke, who was staring at the tablets on the table.

Herb cleared his throat. 'Get these other people out of here.'

'They stay.'

'All this is classified.'

'Yeah, and if you tell me your pals will have to kill me. I've heard that crap before.'

'What do you want to know?'

'Who made the decision to kill Nigel Keren?'

Herb Tenney licked his lips. Sweat formed a little

342

rivulet down his cheek and a drop coalesced on his chin. Then it fell away.

'Who?' Jake repeated. He picked up a tablet and examined it. Finally he placed it back on the table and stood up.

'Toad, Spiro, hold him down. Rita, get the tape and tear off a strip.'

Toad came flying across the room like a linebacker. He slammed into Tenney and knocked him flat on the couch, then sat on his chest. Dalworth was just a step behind. Rita charged for the bathroom to get the tape roll.

Herb tried to scream. He couldn't get air with Toad sitting on his chest. Then Jake held his nose until his mouth popped open. Herb's skin was slippery with sweat and he was still trying to scream. Jake stuffed the tablets in as Herb bucked and writhed, even with Toad on his chest and Dalworth on his legs. Jake used both hands to hold his jaw shut.

'Where's the damn tape?'

'Jesus H. Christ, Grafton!' Yocke's voice, from somewhere behind.

'Let me in there,' Rita said, elbowing her way into the pile. She slapped a strip of tape over Tenney's mouth. Then they released him.

The naval officers stood back, breathing hard. Herb was snorting through his nose, his eyes wild.

'Can you feel them dissolving, Herb?' Jake leaned over until his eyes were only a few inches from those of the CIA agent's. 'The poison will be absorbed through the sides of your mouth into your bloodstream. You know more about the effect than I do. How long will it take? How long before your heart stops? An hour? Five hours? Twelve? Maybe you have a whole day. I hate to see you die like this, Herb, but it was your choice.'

Tenney was moaning in his throat.

Jake let him moan. Now Herb managed to get into a sitting position. He was bobbing his head.

'You want to talk now?'

343

Tenney's head bobbed vigorously.

Jake reached over and ripped the tape away from Herb's mouth.

Herb spat the pills onto the floor. He sobbed convulsively. Then he vomited.

'Who?'

'Let me wash my mouth out.'

'*Who?*' Grafton roared savagely.

'Schenler.'

'Harvey Schenler? Deputy director of the CIA?'

Herb Tenney nodded.

'*Answer me, goddamnit!*'

'Yes.'

'Why?'

'I don't think—'

'I don't give a fuck what you *think!* Why?'

'Keren was giving the Israelis money to get Soviet Jews to Israel. The Arabs don't want them there. We're trying to stabilize the Mideast.'

'So you poisoned Nigel Keren. How'd you do it?'

Tenney rubbed his mouth, then bent at the waist and wiped his tongue on his trousers. When he straightened he looked from face to face. 'It was in his aspirin bottle,' he said finally.

'You murdered a man and stabilized the Mideast. Everything's okay down at the corner gas station. Congratulations.'

'Now look here, Admiral,' Tenney said heatedly. 'The world is a cesspool and you know it. We need oil. The Arabs have it. We have enough troubles with the ragheads without idiots like Nigel Keren using their fat wallets to cause more. The situation is volatile.'

'Albert Sidney Brown? Did he stick his fat wallet somewhere it didn't belong?'

'I don't know anything about General Bro—'

'*Don't lie to me!*' Jake thundered. He could really roar when he wanted to; this time he rattled the windows. 'You

344

are one answer away from the grave. I've killed four men today, maybe five, and believe me, I won't lose any sleep if I have to kill you.' Jake Grafton paused, then shook his head with annoyance. 'In his aspirin bottle! Well?' he demanded.

'Brown was about to cause serious problems.'

'What kind of problems?'

'He sent a written report of the bugs to Schenler. Demanded an investigation. There was no other way to cork him.'

Jake changed direction. 'General Shmarov — why'd you kill him?'

'I am not—'

'Sit on him, Toad.'

Tarkington stiff-armed Tenney on the shoulder and he toppled. 'No,' he sobbed. 'For Christ's sake, no!'

'Answer the question.'

'Shmarov set up the weapons sale to Iraq. He arranged everything, the transfer of the money, the reactor explosion — everything. He was in the junta but he was hedging his bets, showing the American delegation KGB files, files that they shouldn't see, just in case Yeltsin came out on top after all.'

'Didn't he bribe the deputies?'

'Yeah, but you know how it is. Those kind of swine won't stay bought.'

'What kind of files?'

'You're so fucking smart, you tell me.'

Jake opened his mouth to say Toad's name, but he refrained. Another episode with the pills and Tenney might indeed die, even if one-half the binary cocktail were aspirin. Perhaps he already had the missing chemical in his system.

'Okay,' Jake said slowly. 'The CIA and the KGB have cooperated on numerous matters in the past. Those were the files Shmarov was going to hand to the senator and the people with him. Those files would inevitably lead the

345

Americans to Harvey Schenler and his cronies, people like you, people who have been running their own foreign policy within the CIA. So Shmarov had to die. And all along I thought you were just trying to poison me. Ha! You were sent here to make sure Shmarov didn't spill the beans either. How many people in Moscow were on your shit list, Tenney?'

'Kiss my—'

'Richard Harper.'

'Who?'

Jake Grafton bent down and began picking up the tablets from amid the vomit on the floor. Several of them were soft but intact.

'Don't fuck with me, Tenney. I'm out of time and patience.'

'We caught Harper in some of the computer files and tracked him down,' Herb Tenney said, his voice rising slightly. 'He wasn't a very good hacker, nowhere near as good as he thought he was.'

'He found the money trail, didn't he?'

'What money trail?'

'*The* money trail, you simple shit.' Jake Grafton unzipped a large chest pocket on his flying suit and extracted an envelope. He removed the contents. 'Here is a letter to me written by Richard Harper. Look at it. It's in Harper's handwriting. Look at it!'

Tenney looked.

'Harper sent it to my wife,' Jake continued, his voice like broken glass. 'She took it to Hayden Land and he sent it here by diplomatic pouch. You got to Richard Harper too late!'

'I don't know what you are talking about.'

'I'm talking about Saddam Hussein's three *billion* dollars. I'm talking about the Mideast Palm Oil Import Corporation, a CIA front. I'm talking about J. W. Wise Organic Commodities, Inc., another CIA front. I'm talking about seven more corporations controlled by the CIA that shuffled Saddam Hussein's money back and forth all over the world until it ended up in Moscow – in the hands of General Shmarov and his allies in the military and in the legislature. Money for nuclear weapons. Money to buy friends. Money to overthrow Yeltsin. Blood money! Tell me about *that* money!'

'I don't—'

'If you tell me you don't know just one more time we're gonna do the pills. This time the tape stays on.'

Tenney shook his head and sweat flew. 'I didn't know he wrote a letter.'

'I guess not. If you had, my wife would be dead now, huh?'

'Listen, Admiral. We—'

'So now Saddam Hussein has nuclear weapons? Is *that* right?'

'We helped possible friends in high places in crucial nations with money! Okay? We've done it before. We'll do it again. Jesus, where do *you* think you are? Oz? Never-never land? We—'

'Answer my question!' Jake roared. 'Saddam Hussein has nuclear weapons?'

'Israel has them. Russia is in meltdown. We need a stable government in Russia or the world is facing a new dark age. Hussein wants to be a regional power. A couple dozen nuclear weapons – shit! We have tens of thousands. He knows that. So he can be a big frog in a little pond and we can make damn sure he doesn't get out of line.'

'You think you can control him? What about the Gulf War?'

'Let's call a spade a spade, Admiral. We can control him or kill him. America needs a stable government in Russia. That's priority number one. With Russia on its feet and in our corner, the two of us can keep Saddam on a short leash or knot the noose.'

'So you let Shmarov and Yakolev murder a half-million Russians. No, let me rephrase that – *you helped them murder a half-million Russians!*'

347

'We *didn't*—'

'Harper found that the money went through CIA dummy corporations, didn't he? *That's* why you killed him.'

'You make it sound as if we're the bad guys. We aren't. We're trying to keep the peace in an unstable world. Surely you can see that? We had no choice. Yeltsin is failing: he's doomed. He can't possibly succeed, not a chance in a million. Either we have an in with his successors or we get the door slammed in our faces. *That's* the only goddamn choice we have.'

'How long have you and Schenler been running your own foreign policy?'

'Huh?'

Jake's voice was almost a whisper. 'How long has the CIA been running its own foreign policy? That's a simple question.'

Tenney looked bewildered, as if he didn't understand what was being asked. And then the truth dawned on Jake. Presidential administrations came and went but the professional spies soldiered on regardless. The CIA had been doing what the CIA leaders believed necessary for as long as there had been a CIA, almost fifty years. It still was.

'All you people, you bottle-sucking lollipop *amateurs* – fucking around in national security matters,' Herb raved, becoming more and more infuriated. 'You're all gonna *die!* This ain't a fucking football game. This is real, for keeps. *America* is at stake here.'

He's coming apart, Jake Grafton decided. He's been through too much.

Jake averted his eyes as Tenney ranted on: 'Those ten-cent codes you use on the scramblers – they've been reading the messages thirty minutes later. They even fax me hard copies. *They* know what the fuck you traitors are up to. *They know!*'

Jake and Toad taped Herb Tenney's mouth and put him in the bedroom. When the door was closed, Toad asked, 'So he wasn't trying to poison us?'

'Sure he was,' Jake muttered. He put the tablets into the bottle and dropped it into his shirt pocket.

'What are those tablets, some kind of suicide pills?' Spiro Dalworth asked.

'Binary poison,' Toad told him. 'It's medicine for people you don't want to see anymore.'

Jack Yocke sat over in the corner with his chin resting on one hand. He glanced at Jake Grafton, who was staring at the floor, then leaned back in his chair and closed his eyes.

Toad reached under the couch for the cassette recorder and pushed the rewind button. When the rewind was complete, he placed the recorder on the table and pushed the play button. He thumbed up the volume. Several minutes went by as they listened to feet shuffling, someone coughing, then finally Jake Grafton's voice: 'General Shmarov died last night. Tell us about that.'

The little machine had caught it all. The confusion and muffled comments as they poisoned Tenney were brutally plain, as was the sound of Tenney retching afterward. The listeners studiously avoided looking at one another.

When Tenney got out Harvey Schenler's name, Jake motioned to Toad to turn off the tape. 'Get the senior chief and fire up the TACSAT,' Jake told him. 'Send that tape to General Land.'

'You heard Herb, CAG. They'll crack the code.'

'Send it. Use the TACSAT. In the meantime we'll deliver a message of our own to Harley McCann.'

'What about the ambassador? He wanted to see you.'

Jake glanced at his watch. 'The night's young.'

Jake was still in his flight suit when he entered the ambassador's outer office and encountered Agatha Hempstead. She sniffed gingerly, no doubt slightly appalled at Jake's aroma, then opened the door to Lancaster's office.

The ambassador looked coldly across the top of his glasses at Jake Grafton and said, 'I asked to see you when you returned to the embassy, Admiral.'

'Yessir. I apologize. I didn't have much to tell you two hours ago, except to report that Lieutenant Moravia destroyed the weapons at the Petrovsk facility and a transport that was probably Iraqi. We were intercepted by four Russian fighters on the way down there.'

'But you evaded them. Obviously.'

'Yessir. Is Senator Wilmoth still in Moscow?' Wilmoth was the US senator who wanted a peek at the KGB files.

'He's staying at the embassy, but he's leaving tomorrow. The KGB slammed the door today after Shmarov died. I'm afraid Yeltsin doesn't have a lever big enough to pry it open.'

'I might be able to help. Could you ask the senator to come here to your office now? I have a tape I would like for you both to listen to. Then we're going to have to have a lengthy chat.'

Lancaster looked dubious, but he picked up the telephone. Jake took the cassette player from his pocket and sat it on the desk. Hempstead helped him find a plug.

When Wilmoth arrived, Jake started the tape. He had to stop it at numerous places and explain. Lancaster wanted to know what in the world Admiral Grafton was forcing into Herb Tenney's mouth, so Jake displayed the two pill bottles, even dumped the tablets onto Lancaster's polished mahogany.

After the first run-through, Jake played the tape again without interruptions. Then a third time at Senator Wilmoth's request.

It took some digesting. The fact that the Old Guard junta had blown up the Serdobsk reactor infuriated Wilmoth, who swore in a manner that Jake Grafton found most gratifying. Finally he said, 'Wait until the president hears this!'

'I suspect he's listening to it right now, sir,' Jake told him. 'I've already sent this via a TACSAT unit to General Land at the Pentagon. He said he would take it to the White House immediately.'

'What about Harley McCann?' the ambassador said. 'Was he in on this?'

'Captain McElroy has him outside in your waiting room. Why don't you ask him?' McElroy had taken four marines with him to the CIA spaces. They had found McCann and his deputies merely sitting at their desks, waiting. 'Apparently after Toad snatched Herb Tenney this morning, they talked it over and decided that they didn't want any part of whatever was going down. They appear to be quite ready to talk.'

'I have a few questions to ask them,' Wilmoth said heatedly.

'I suggest, Senator, that you send a team of your investigators to the CIA office and impound the files. I don't know what the CIA puts on paper, but some of that stuff might be interesting reading.'

Wilmoth grabbed for the telephone.

Lancaster reached for the white tablets on the desk and examined them. Finally he put them back on the desk next to the pill bottle.

When Wilmoth got off the phone, Jake said, 'Perhaps, Mr Ambassador, tonight would be a good time for President Yeltsin to call on the American Embassy. We can made a duplicate tape for him to keep. He might be able to find a good use for an artifact like that.'

Lancaster nodded. 'And?'

'Well, I need a plane to get to Saudi Arabia. I need to get there without being intercepted and attacked by Russian fighters. Perhaps after Yeltsin listens to the tape, we can discuss that problem with him.'

'On the tape you said you killed four men today. Who?'

'We were intercepted by fighters. Rita and I are still alive.' Jake Grafton shrugged.

Lancaster grinned wolfishly. 'I'm beginning to understand why General Land holds you in such high regard, Admiral. Agatha, while we're talking to Mr McCann, would you see if you can get President Yeltsin on the telephone?'

'Start scribbling.'

'Scribble what?' Jack Yocke was down on his hands and knees with a sponge and a bucket trying to clean Herb Tenney's vomit from the carpet. He leaned back on his heels and looked up at Jake Grafton.

'How the Old Guard blew up the Serdobsk reactor and murdered a half-million human beings. How the Old Guard sold nuclear weapons to Saddam Hussein. How they used the money to bribe elected Russian politicians to vote Yeltsin out. *That* story. Write it.'

'An agent of the US government tortured for information can hardly be quoted as a "reliable, high-placed government source,"' Yocke pointed out acidly. He dabbed at the wet place in the rug. 'I don't know if there was a single word of truth in what he said.'

'I thought you were a red-hot reporter.'

Yocke threw the sponge in the bucket and got to his feet. He sat down in the chair he had occupied during Tenney's interrogation. He dried his hands on his trousers. 'I don't want to write it.'

Grafton gazed at Yocke for a moment, then found a chair. 'Maybe you'd better explain.'

'The world is full of bad people. I write about them every day. They rob, steal, cheat, take drugs, bribes, beat their kids to death, kill their spouses in drunken rages or gun the bitches on the courthouse steps when they're stone-cold sober. Those people I can understand. They're human. These people here, people like Tenney, Shmarov, Yakolev . . .' Yocke's voice trailed off.

'They're human too. Their crimes are just worse.'

'No. They aren't human. They are *evil*. They have no humanity.' Jack Yocke shuddered.

'They're human all right,' Jake Grafton told him. 'If anything, too human. What you don't want to face is that everyone has a little Hitler, a little Stalin in him. Given the means and motive, a lot of people could become absolutely corrupt. What's the difference between killing a man and ordering his death? What's the difference between ordering one death or a half-million? Or a million? Or five million. Or ten million. With a stroke of a pen you can kill all the Jews – all the educated people – all the rich people – all the poor people – all the homosexuals . . . whoever. Evil and sin are exactly the same thing – you just need to convince yourself that the ends justify the means. *Every human alive is capable of that little trick.*'

'I don't want to write it.'

'You don't have a choice. I'm making the decisions around here. Get out your computer and plug the damn thing in. If necessary, I'll write the story for you.'

'Just who the fuck do you think you are, Grafton?'

'I'm a public servant trying to do his job. You are a newspaper reporter who wants to get famous by writing the truth. We've got a bucketful of truth here and you are going to write it because people need to come face-to-face with it. What they do with the truth is beyond my control: I'm not taking responsibility for the human condition. But by God they are going to see it smeared all over the front page of every newspaper in the world. Then if they refuse to face it they are just as evil and just as guilty as the men you're writing about.'

Jake Grafton stood. 'You're going to have to name names. Lancaster is in his office right now playing the tape for Yeltsin. Put that in your story.'

Jack Yocke gnawed on a fingernail as he thought about it. Finally he said, 'You want me to say how you got the information from Tenney?'

'You can do it like an interview, if you want. Don't mention binary poisons. I think that little problem is going to solve itself. Just quote Herb. Don't forget to mention that the interview was recorded and the president got a copy of the tape.'

' "That little problem is going to solve itself." God-damnit, Admiral, shit is shit! If we're going to nail the Commies to the cross we ought to nail our own bastards up there with them.'

'Oh, we will, Jack. We will. But one set of bastards at a time.'

'Who authorized you to release this story? The president?'

'I authorized myself.'

Yocke couldn't think of a reply, which infuriated him since he had known what Grafton's answer would be before he asked the question.

'Wake me up in two hours,' the admiral said, 'and let me read your story. I'm not much of a writer but maybe I can help you with the commas.'

And with that Jake Grafton stretched out on the couch. He turned so his back was to Yocke. In moments, as Jack Yocke stared, he was breathing deeply and regularly. By the time Yocke got his computer plugged in and running, Jake was snoring lightly.

CHAPTER TWENTY-TWO

Boris Yeltsin was a bear of a man, a burly, fleshy Russian with a bulbous, veined nose that one hoped did not indicate the condition of his liver. He shook Jake Grafton's hand and waved toward a chair as he traded Russian with an aide who didn't bother to translate. The interpreter who had led Jake into the room also remained silent.

The sun streamed between the drapes of the tall window on Yeltsin's left. Blinking in the glare, Jake Grafton looked around curiously. It was a good room, a man's room, tastefully decorated and heaped with piles of paper.

Yeltsin kept glancing at Grafton as he spoke. Finally one of the aides said, 'President Yeltsin wishes to thank the American government for its help in this crisis.'

Jake Grafton nodded pleasantly and glanced at his watch. The first edition of the *Post* carrying Jack Yocke's story was probably hitting the streets of Washington just about now. If the *Post* editors placed the story on the wires it was going to be on CNN and every other television and radio station in the Western world within an hour. Yeltsin's phone should start ringing in very short order.

After Yocke sent the story to the *Post* in the wee hours this morning via modem, his editor, Mike Gatler, called back and questioned him for ten minutes. When Yocke was about to lose his temper, he passed the telephone to Jake Grafton, who told Gatler, 'Yeah, I read the story. Every word's true.'

'Saddam Hussein has two *dozen* nuclear weapons?'

'At least that.'

Gatler whistled. 'Can this CIA source – what's his name?—'

'Herb Tenney.'

'Yeah. Can Tenney be trusted?'

'I don't know that I trust him, but I think he told the truth on this matter.'

'Can we quote you on that?'

'If you spell my name right.'

'Rear Admiral, right?'

'Yes.'

'And you and Yocke both saw the base where Hussein got the weapons? Weapons sold to him by the Russians?'

'Yes. Name of the place is Petrovsk. Yocke has it in the story. We went there in a helicopter.'

'This is a *big* story,' Gatler said.

'That's what Jack said.'

'Put him back on, please.' Jake held out the telephone.

'This story just scratches the surface,' Gatler complained to Yocke.

'I know that, Mike. I'm getting all I can. I'll send you more as soon as possible.'

'I want you to work with Tommy Townsend on this. Call him at his hotel.'

Yocke decided to call Townsend in the morning. He went to the bathroom, washed his face and hands, and was just stretching out on the floor with a pillow when Gatler called back. 'The State Department refuses to confirm or deny this story.'

'Nothing I can do about that,' Yocke said, waving frantically to Jake Grafton. The admiral sat up on the couch and rubbed his head.

'Yocke, this is the biggest story since the Japs hit Pearl Harbor,' Gatler said. 'Our White House guys can't get any confirmation, State refuses to confirm or deny, the people at the Pentagon refuse to comment, the CIA press people refuse to confirm that they've ever even heard of this Tenney guy. And CIA says that none of their people would ever talk to the press – violation of security regs and all that crap. So we've got your story and a voice on the telephone who claims he's Rear Admiral Jake Grafton. That's all.'

'I heard the Tenney interview, Mike. I was there in person. I saw the tape being made. I saw the rubble of the Serdobsk reactor, I visited the base at Petrovsk. I saw some bodies. I saw some weapons. I talked to Jake Grafton on the record – he's the deputy director of the Defense Intelligence Agency, for Christ's sake! He explicitly agreed to be quoted. I talked to an Israeli Mossad agent who's now dead – she was shot in my presence. I've got all that I can give you. If you haven't got the balls to run the story, then don't run it.'

'Don't get testy with me, Jack. I'm just explaining how far out on the limb we are with this story.'

'I'm sorry, Mike, but it's a good story. Every fucking word is true. I guarantee it. I don't give a shit what anybody else says, General Shmarov sold Saddam Hussein those bombs and blew up the Serdobsk reactor to cover up the fact that the weapons were gone.'

'Shmarov is dead.'

'I know that, Mike.'

'Heart attack.'

'No, he was poisoned by Herb Tenney.'

'*What?*' Gatler roared, '*Poisoned! By a CIA agent? That isn't in this story!*'

'I know that too, Mike. I can't get any confirmation for that from anybody. But Tenney confessed to the killing in my presence. I didn't put that in this story because I don't know that anyone will ever confirm that Shmarov was even murdered, much less that Tenney did it. I'm telling you that the stuff that *is* in that story is confirmed gospel. I've got a mountain of stuff that isn't in there because I haven't yet got it confirmed.'

Gatler thought that over for five seconds, then said, 'I want a copy of the tape of Tenney's confession.'

'Grafton won't release it. The White House might, but I doubt it. It covers a lot of ground, all of it classified up the wazoo.'

'I want more stories when you get confirmations.'

'I understand. When and if, you'll be the first to hear.'

They said their good-byes and Yocke told Jake, 'He's gonna print it.'

Jake Grafton had grunted from his position on the couch and pulled his jacket around him. He was asleep again in minutes.

This afternoon Jake idly wondered what Boris Yeltsin would do when he heard the story was out. Oh well, he was a politician, experienced in converting lemons into lemonade.

He settled back into the chair and crossed his legs. This afternoon President Clinton was supposed to call to talk to Yeltsin about the mess in Iraq. Last night Yeltsin invited Jake to come here to answer any questions his staff might have.

Now the telephone rang. One of the aides picked it up, said something, then Yeltsin took the other line. Jake looked at his watch. He wondered if the airplanes coming in from Germany would be on time.

But this wasn't President Clinton's call. The interpreter hung up his phone and Yeltsin fell into his chair as he listened intently on his own instrument. Occasionally his eyes swung to Grafton. This went on for several minutes with Yeltsin grunting occasionally. Finally he replaced the telephone on its hook and swiveled his chair to face Grafton. He wiggled his finger at the interpreter and spoke.

The interpreter said, 'A news story has appeared in the *Washington Post*. You are quoted. Did you release a story to the newspaper?'

Jake nodded. 'I did.'

Yeltsin listened to the answer and swiveled his chair nervously. He toyed with a pencil, then stared at it, finally replaced it. He said something to the interpreter.

'The president wishes to know why you released the story.'

'As we discussed last night, it is of critical importance that those weapons be recovered or rendered harmless. We cannot go after those weapons without a public explanation of our actions. So the truth must be told. The truth is that a small group of individuals here in Russia sold weapons to get money to overthrow the elected government. They murdered hundreds of thousands of people to cover up their crime. *This* is the story. The sooner the world knows it, the better — for Russia, for the United States, for the people of the Middle East.'

'*You* released this story?'

'Yes.' Of course he had discussed it with General Hayden Land, but both men had agreed it would be best if Jake took the responsibility. If the story came from Jake it was deniable in Washington, and that might well be the first reaction of panicky politicians with a genetic aversion to telling the public about disasters. In the ordinary course of things weeks might pass before they screwed up the courage to talk publicly about this one. Yet Hayden Land and Jake Grafton knew they didn't have weeks to clean up this mess: at best, they had hours.

'What is going on, Admiral?' In Washington, Yeltsin meant.

'Sir, we discussed this matter last night. Nothing has changed. US Air Force planes are flying in from Germany to take me and the other foreign military observers to Arabia. From there we will go to Iraq to recover the weapons. You agreed that Marshal Mikhailov and General Yakolev would accompany our group on behalf of the Russian Republic.'

'I don't want *them* talking to reporters.'

'I understand. I promise that they won't.'

'I should have been consulted before you talked to the press.'

Jake acknowledged this. He apologized, though not very convincingly.

359

Yeltsin didn't look too put out – the story Yocke wrote couldn't have been more favorable to him even if he had written it himself. Complete innocence was a rare commodity, one to be savored. Being the unwounded target of a cutthroat power play that misfired was even nicer.

'I have a suggestion,' Jake added. 'In an hour or so you, Mr President, are going to be besieged by reporters wanting your comments. The reporter who wrote this morning's story for the *Washington Post*, Jack Yocke, is downstairs. Why not get him up here, give him an interview, and get your side of this on record before the spin doctors in Washington and Baghdad get into the act? Mr Yocke is knowledgeable about this matter and sympathetic to your government.'

The mention of Baghdad did the trick. Saddam Hussein would be on camera as soon as he heard about the *Post* story. Hussein had just two options, as far as Jake could see: deny he had nuclear weapons or admit it and claim that the government of Russia sold them to him. That government, of course, was Boris Yeltsin. Which option Hussein picked would depend, Jake suspected, on the amount of time he still needed to get the nuclear weapons operational. The nearer he was to being ready to push the button the more likely he was to admit that he had them. But this was speculation, and just now Jake was trying to cover all the possibilities.

In minutes Jack Yocke was being ushered into the president's office. He glanced at Rear Admiral Jake Grafton seated at an oblique angle from Yeltsin's desk, then turned his attention to the Russian president.

Yocke knew exactly what his editor, Mike Gatler, wanted – a gold-plated confirmation of the first story – and he went after it without making any detours. Point by point he led Yeltsin through the story and scribbled his answers on a small steno pad.

Yes, it was true that Shmarov had used the KGB to collect money from Saddam Hussein. He sold things that belonged to the nation that he had no right to sell. That was a crime. Such a thing would be a crime in any nation on earth.

Yes, Shmarov allowed the removal of planeloads of weapons from the base at Petrovsk the day before the Serdobsk reactor was destroyed. Yes, Shmarov ordered Colonel Gagarin of the KGB to destroy the Serdobsk fast breeder reactor. And yes, Gagarin committed the crime. Yeltsin was not yet prepared to say what Shmarov did with the money he collected for the weapons – the government was investigating. The new fact to lead off this story – Yeltsin had ordered Marshal Mikhailov, commander of the Russian armed forces, and General Yakolev, commander of the Russian army, to accompany Rear Admiral Jake Grafton and a group of officers from Germany, Britain, France and Italy on a trip to Iraq to recover the stolen weapons.

'Stolen?' Yocke asked, looking up at Yeltsin.

'Stolen,' the interpreter repeated after a burst from Yeltsin. 'The government of Russia has never sold and will never sell or give away nuclear weapons. We have given our solemn promise on that point to numerous governments throughout the world. We have signed treaties.'

Jack Yocke then asked the next logical question: what would Russia do to get the stolen weapons back if Saddam Hussein wasn't gentleman enough to return them? The answer: 'We are cooperating with the United States and the governments of other nations to secure the return of the stolen weapons.'

That should have been the end of it, but Yocke was Yocke and couldn't resist asking one more. After a glance at Grafton, whose face showed no emotion whatever, he said, 'General Shmarov allegedly died of a heart attack the night before last. Was it a heart attack?'

'I don't know,' Boris Yeltsin said. 'An autopsy is being performed.'

Yocke opened his mouth, glanced again at Grafton, then

thanked President Yeltsin for the interview. He was ushered from the room. Jake Grafton remained seated.

Out in the waiting area Yocke grabbed his computer from the chair where he had placed it and opened it on his lap. In seconds he was tapping away while the US marine captain, McElroy, watched over his shoulder.

When Yocke finished and looked up, McElroy and the four enlisted marines with him were no longer in the room. But there was a secretary behind the desk and she had a telephone in front of her. 'May I make a collect telephone call?' he asked.

She merely grinned nervously at him.

'Use the phone?' He reached for it and raised his eyebrows.

She nodded. Yocke snagged the instrument and when he heard a voice addressing him in Russian, asked for the international operator.

The C-141 was somewhere over the Black Sea when Jack Yocke tired of looking out the window at the four F-15 escorts, their KC-135 tanker and the electronic warfare E-3 Sentry that formed this aerial armada. Jake Grafton obviously intended to make it to Arabia regardless of who had other ideas.

As they were boarding the airplane in Moscow, Yocke had asked, 'You don't really expect the Russian air force to try to shoot us down, do you?'

'With the story out, probably not. But we have Mikhailov and Yakolev. Who knows how that will play? It's like trying to figure prison politics.'

Yocke had watched with growing wonder as the F-15s occasionally slipped in behind the tanker for fuel, then slid away afterward. The planes seemed to hang motionless in the sky, a perspective Yocke found unique and fascinating. The noise of their engines was masked by the background noise inside the C-141, so the show outside was a silent, effortless ballet.

He had already tried to interview Lieutenant Colonel Jocko West and the three bird colonels from Germany, Italy and France. None of them wanted to talk, on or off the record. They did spell their names for him, for future reference. Then they shooed him off. As he turned to go back to his seat, West told him with a grin, 'Reporters are like solicitors and doctors – the less you see of them the more tranquil your life.'

Marshal Mikhailov and General Yakolev were in the back of the compartment surrounded by four armed marines. Captain McElroy was seated nearby; he had merely moved his head from side to side about half a millimeter when Yocke looked his way.

Up front Jake Grafton was in conference with Toad Tarkington and Captain Tom Collins. Yocke stood in the aisle and stretched. Even after that hassle with the story last night and just two hours sleep, he wasn't a bit tired. How often is it that you get to interview the president of a big nation and write a story that will make every front page on the planet, then jump on a plane and jet off to do another? Ah, he could get used to this.

Better enjoy it while it lasts, he told himself, because when it's over it'll be really over. He would be back scribbling crime stories and the city council news that was fit to print all too soon.

Yocke passed by Grafton and his colleagues and went forward to the cockpit. Rita Moravia was in the left seat. She turned and flashed him a grin.

'She's not really a pilot, you know,' Jack told the air force major standing behind Rita. 'She was Miss July of 1991.'

'Careful, friend,' the major rumbled. 'This is the new modern American military. Comments with any sexist content whatsoever have been outlawed.

'Sorry.'

'You want to remain politically correct and ideologically pure, don't you? No more male and female pronouns. Everything is *it*. During the transition period you may say *hit* and *sit* instead of *it*, but no *shit*. One slip and the sexual gestapo will be on your case.'

'After they gets finished with you,' the copilot told him gravely, 'you'll have to Spiro Agnew.'

'Actually,' Rita Moravia said, patting her hair to ensure it was just so, 'I was Miz July.'

'Where are we?' Yocke asked when the three stooges had calmed down. All he could see out the window was sea and sky.

'Thirty-three thousand feet up,' the copilot told him, and laughed shamelessly at his own wit.

The reporter groaned. Look out, Saddam! The Americans are coming again. Yocke left the flight deck and went back to the cabin.

Jake Grafton was seated beside Tarkington. Collins was back in his own seat reading something, so Jack sat on the arm of the seat across the aisle from the admiral. 'How's planning for the war?'

Jake Grafton examined Yocke's face. 'Our agreement is still in effect, right?'

'Oh, absolutely.'

'I mention it because last night you flapped your mouth to your editor about General Shmarov's death. That subject was and is off limits.'

'Admiral, Gatler was on the fence over whether or not to run the story. I had to give him a hot off-the-record fact so he would think I had a lot more, that we were scraping the icing off a very big cake. And that tidbit about Shmarov was the only hot fact I could think of just then. I assumed you wanted the story in the paper or you wouldn't have bothered to order it' – Yocke snapped his fingers – 'like a ham and cheese on rye.'

'Then you tried to inch onto that subject with Yeltsin this afternoon with that last question, on the off chance he might spill his guts on the spot.'

'Admiral I—'

Jake cut him off. 'I saw you give me that guilty look,

should I or shouldn't I, just before you put your mouth in motion. Either you play the game my way or you can zip right over to the commercial airport when we land and ride your plastic right on back to Moscow. We are playing with my ball, Jack.'

'Yessir. Your ball, your rules. But for my info, are you ever going to let me loose on the CIA's creative use of binary poisons?'

Grafton shrugged. 'I don't know. Doubtful. That situation will probably solve itself.'

' "Solve itself," ' Yocke repeated sourly, and drew in air for an oration on the hypocrisy of not airing our dirty linen while we launder other people's.

He never got the chance. Jake jerked his thumb aft. 'Those two are a part of our international team.'

'The two Russian prisoners, you mean?' Yocke said, and instantly regretted it. Jake Grafton's gray eyes looked like river ice in winter.

'This may be just a story for you,' Grafton said, almost a whisper, 'but there's a bit more at stake for everybody else.'

'I'm not writing fiction, Admiral. Not intentionally, anyway.'

'I'm not asking you to. But no interviews with them until I say so, if and when.'

'Aye aye, sir.' Yocke tried to keep the sarcasm out of his voice and succeeded fairly well. Tarkington gave him the eye, though.

Grafton went back to studying the photographs that lay in his lap. He used a magnifying glass.

'Aerial photos?' Yocke asked.

'Satellite.'

'May I look?'

Grafton passed him a couple. They looked like shots from just a couple thousand feet above an airfield. He could see the aircraft clearly, the power carts, the revetments, even people and the shadows they cast. 'These are really clear,' he murmured. 'Are the missiles here at this base?'

'I think so. The trouble with satellite surveillance is that you can rarely be absolutely certain of anything. It's true, at times the resolution is so good that you can read license plate numbers, and if people like Saddam think we can see everything all the time, that's just fine with us. But we can't. There are very real technical limitations. The art is in the interpretation of what you *can* see.'

'So are we going to hit this base with an air strike?'

'That would be the easy way,' Jake acknowledged, then selected another photo and bent to examine it. When he finally straightened he added, 'Nobody ever accused us of doing anything the easy way.'

Jack Yocke returned the photos and went back to his seat by the window. He sat staring at the two fighters he could see. They were in loose formation, so loose one was over a mile away.

The sun was setting, firing the tops of the clouds below with pinks and oranges. Beneath that the sea was a deep, deep purple, almost black. He stared downward, between the clouds. That looked like . . . maybe it was land. Were they over Turkey? Or was that ocean down there in the gloom?

He finally reclined his seat and tried to sleep.

Up forward Toad Tarkington muttered to his boss, 'You may trust that jackass, but I don't.'

'To which of our jackasses are you referring?'

'Yocke.'

'Oh, he's got his rough edges,' Jake said, 'but he's an honest man. Rather like you in that regard.' When he saw that Toad was at a loss for a reply, Jake grinned and added, 'You guys are Tweedledum and Tweedledumber. Amy says you're both fun to have around. She's still trying to decide which of you is Tweedledumber.'

'Thanks, CAG.'

'Anytime, Toad.'

CHAPTER TWENTY-THREE

The command bunker at the sprawling military base outside of Riyadh looked like a *Star Wars* movie set. A long rack of television monitors mounted above a huge wall chart of the region displayed everything from the current CNN broadcast to real-time satellite ambient light and infrared views of selected areas inside Iraq, computer presentations of Iraq and UN troop positions, computer presentations of the vehicles moving near Baghdad and Samarra, aircraft aloft over Iraq, Arabia, Kuwait, and the Persian Gulf, ships at sea in the Gulf – everything a commander might want to know was on one of those screens. At computer stations facing the screens were the men and women who punched the keys that made it all work.

Just now all eyes in the room were on the CNN monitor. Jake Grafton and the European colonels stood together in a knot staring upward at the jowly visage of Saddam Hussein, who was busy calling the *Washington Post* and Boris Yeltsin liars. 'Iraq does not possess nuclear weapons. Lies have been told. Yeltsin is desperate, attempting to use Iraq as a scapegoat to prevent political collapse in Russia.'

'What do you think?' Jake asked Jocko West.

'If he has trained Russian technicians, I think he can shoot the missiles on launchers any time. At best, within hours. But he probably only has two or three missiles on their Russian Army launchers. The launchers were just too bulky and heavy to transport. He took as many missiles as he could, probably intending to put them on launchers he already has. And he took warheads, which are small and could be loaded quickly onto his planes. I suspect that he's playing for time in order to load the missiles he stole on old Scud launchers and adapt the warheads for use on his missiles.'

Colonel Rheinhart agreed. 'If he has the people and the proper tools, he can begin placing nuclear warheads on the Scuds in a few days, arm perhaps thirty Scuds in ten days or so. Five or six ready-to-shoot weapons are not enough for a war.'

The Italian and Frenchman nodded at this assessment. Jake Grafton wasn't so sure. A lunatic might start a war even if he had only one bullet.

As Jake Grafton stared at Saddam's image on the monitor, he reviewed what he knew about the Iraqi dictator. Born poor, poor as only an Arab can be, in a squalid village a hundred miles north of Baghdad, he went to live with an uncle in the capital at the age of ten, about 1947. His uncle was the author of a screed entitled *Three Things That God Should Not Have Created: Persians, Jews, and Flies.* This tract became young Saddam's *Mein Kampf.* Within months, according to his official biography, he killed his first man.

When he was twenty, the young thug joined the Iraqi Baath party, where he became a triggerman disposing of the party's enemies, of whom there were many. One of the people he murdered was his brother-in-law. Two years later, in 1959, he bungled an assassination attempt aimed at the current Iraqi dictator, General Abdul Kassem, and was shot by Kassem's guards. Somehow he escaped and fled to Egypt.

In 1963 the Baath party successfully murdered Kassem and took power. Saddam returned to Iraq and ended up in prison nine months later when the Baathists were overthrown by an army junta.

When the Baathists seized power again in 1968, Saddam

was there in the councils of power. In a stunning parallel to the career of Josef Stalin, he took control of the secret police and systematically set out to murder everyone he could not control, thereby becoming the real ruler of Iraq. Before long he took personal control of the nation's foreign policy. The nominal president of the country soldiered on under Saddam's orders until 1979, when he retired, thereby becoming the first ruler of Iraq not to die in office within the memory of living men. Saddam anointed himself dictator and gave himself a new title, The Awesome. Perhaps it loses something in translation.

Yet Saddam never forgot how he got to the top, never lost touch with his roots. New title and all, he still liked to use a pistol to personally execute cabinet officers, generals, and relatives who had the temerity to argue with him or whom he suspected of harboring a nascent seed of disloyalty.

From any possible viewpoint, Jake Grafton thought, Saddam appeared as the master thug, a self-centered man without conscience or remorse capable of any crime. In other words, a perfect dictator.

Oh, he had screwed up badly a time or two – the eight-year war with Iran cost Iraq a hundred thousand lives and $70 billion it didn't have, and the little fracas over Kuwait didn't turn out quite the way Saddam thought it would. But the man wasn't a quitter. After those debacles he had ruthlessly shot, gassed and starved his domestic enemies into oblivion. Iraq was still his: he was hanging tough, arming himself with nuclear weapons. Then he would find who still wanted to play the game and who was willing to kneel at his throne.

Saddam's tragedy was that he ruled such a small corner of the world. If only he could have had a stage the size of Germany or Russia!

A naive person might wonder why the civilized nations of the earth continued to deal with miserable vermin like Saddam, but Jake Grafton didn't. *Realpolitik* kept him alive.

He was part and parcel of the forces in dynamic tension that kept the Middle East from exploding into religious and race war. And Iraq had oil.

Jake wondered if now, finally, the fearful politicians of the 'civilized nations' had had enough. He was still pondering that question when he was called into a room with General Frank Loy, the UN commander. General Loy was talking on the satellite link. He handed the telephonelike handset to Jake.

'Rear Admiral Grafton, sir.'

'Hayden Land. Glad you arrived.'

'I just watched Saddam on the tube.'

'Yeah. They're in a dither here. They're pissed that you gave the story to the *Post* and I had to admit I authorized it. So they're peeved at me. If I weren't black they would have fired me.' He indulged himself in an expletive. 'Anyway, Saddam isn't cooperating. He denied he has nukes, so now the fact that there is no independent confirmation has them in a sweat.'

'So no air strike?'

'No air strike,' Land said wearily.

'Saddam has put his forces on alert,' Jake said. 'It'll take four or five days to bring them up to full alert, so whatever we're going to do we must do quickly. Every hour that goes by is going to cost us lives.'

'I know that,' Land said.

'The German expert thinks that Saddam could have the stolen missiles ready to launch in hours, if they aren't ready to go now.'

Land didn't respond. In a moment he said, 'These people here are trying to figure out a way to blame this mess on George Bush. He had his chance to stomp this cockroach and didn't, so now they have to dirty their shoes with it.'

'Yessir. Should Yocke do another story?'

'Your staff reporter? No. Not right now. They would lock me out of the White House if that happened. Soooo . . . I want you to plan an assault on that airfield.

370

Figure out what it will take, when you can do it, what it will cost.' Jake knew that when Hayden Land talked cost, he wasn't talking dollars: he was talking lives. 'Then call me back. If you and Loy think an assault is feasible, my idea is for you to take some network camera teams along. If we treated the world to a live broadcast showing the Russian missiles and warheads that Saddam says he doesn't have, these people here will be off the hook. Then you can fly the weapons out.'

'We try to fly the weapons out, General, this is going to be a big operation and damned risky.'

'I know that. But these people inside the Beltway don't have the balls to take any flak from the Sierra Club about nuclear pollution. They'd rather take US casualties than Iraqi casualties. It's not that they're callous, it's just the fact that they got in with a plurality of the votes. We're dealing with a president that sixty percent of the American people didn't want. He knows it, his staff knows it – and they won't risk alienating the support they do have. That's political reality. So plan for an airlift.'

'Don't we have a carrier battle group in the Gulf of Oman? If she ran west through the Strait of Hormuz into the Persian Gulf that would help.'

'We'll send her in. Now let me talk to Loy again.'

Jake passed the handset to General Loy and walked out of the room.

'They're in Samarra.' The air intelligence staff officer said it positively.

Jake Grafton needed to be sold. 'A fifty-fifty chance, sixty-forty, what?'

'No, sir. They're there. We saw the planes come in from Russia and nothing big enough to transport a missile has left. We've got round-the-clock real-time satellite surveillance. They're there.'

'The missiles?'

'The missiles are there, yessir.'

'And the warheads?'

'I don't know,' the staff officer said, and shook his head. 'They're so small . . .'

'Have they been moving Scuds around?'

'No. We would have seen that. They've tried to keep them under cover since the war. We know where some of them are, but certainly not all.'

'Let me see if I have this right: the Russian missiles are in Samarra, but we only know where some of the Scuds are. If the Iraqis are mating nuclear warheads to the Scuds, they must have taken the warheads to the missiles, because they haven't brought the missiles to Samarra.'

'Yessir.'

'Then we're fucked.'

'Yes, sir. That's a very apt description. I couldn't say it any better myself.'

'Find the Scuds.'

'Sir, we've been trying to do that for eighteen months.'

'Have the Iraqis taken warheads to the sites of the Scuds we know about?'

'I don't know, sir. We've been trying—'

'You're not trying hard enough,' Jake Grafton said coldly. 'Track every vehicle leaving the Samarra base and see where it goes. If the vehicle visits the site of a known Scud, you've just found one.' Jake lowered his voice. 'They tell me you people are the very best. Your equipment is the best. Find those warheads. I don't care what you have to do, but find them. Now!'

A modern joint military operation is extraordinarily complex and requires extensive planning. The myriad of details cannot be worked out in hours, not even by competent, experienced professionals. Days, even weeks, go into the planning of a successful joint operation.

Jake Grafton was demanding this one be put together and be ready to launch in eighteen hours, by 20:00 local time tomorrow. He would have gone sooner, even in daylight, if the planning could have been completed, but even he had to admit there was no way. As it was there would be no time for a run-through with the commanders involved, no time to sort things out before the starting gun fired, so there were going to be snafus – people getting in one another's way, people who didn't go at all, busted equipment, too many people at one place, too few at others, things that had to happen but didn't . . . He expected all that. But it could get worse – there could be good guys shooting at good guys. He and the troops would have to live with it. Or die with it. Being Jake Grafton, he didn't think much about the dying part, except to ensure that the medical support would be there, all that could be fitted in.

Fortunately General Loy named a competent professional to plan and command the operation, Major General Daniel Serkin, a whipcord-tough soldier with only one pace – fast.

Jake Grafton stood and watched, walked the floor and listened to the planners, perused op orders, conferred repeatedly with General Serkin. And worried that while the allies fretted over call signs and radio frequencies Saddam would start spraying nuclear warheads at his enemies.

At dawn he called General Land and gave him a preliminary overview. The operation would start with a navy SEAL team delayed parachute drop from thirty thousand feet. Chutes would open under two thousand feet. The team would secure the airport perimeter, wipe out anti-aircraft resistance and machine gun emplacements. A battalion from the 101st Airborne Division (Air Assault) would then arrive in helicopters escorted by electronic warfare aircraft – Wild Weasels – and fighters, with helicopter gunships providing close air support. The idea was to quickly overpower any resistance, make the airfield safe for transports. These would come in with their own aerial escort, which would orbit overhead and prevent Iraqi forces from counterattacking. With all the Russian weapons

373

aboard, the transports would leave and the American and allied troops would pull out under air cover. If everything went according to plan, the raid would be over before the Iraqis could bring overwhelming military power to bear.

Fortunately Saddam Hussein seemed to be expecting an air strike. The radars in the Baghdad and Samarra area were almost constantly on the air and mobile antiaircraft guns were moving into the area. But not troops.

Toad Tarkington suggested a name for this operation, Operation Appointment. Jake told him the name lacked pizzazz, but he too had read John O'Hara so he recommended the name to General Land, who accepted it without comment.

'So it all depends on how deep the Iraqi forces are at the airfield?' Land said finally, when Jake was finished.

'Yessir. Intelligence says we'll be facing a battalion of Republican Guard.'

'Armor?'

'Yessir. We have a choice – try to wipe out the tanks with Apaches prior to the SEAL drop, or drop the SEALs and try to achieve surprise, then bring in the Apaches.'

'Has General Serkin made a decision?'

'Not yet.'

'Found the Scuds?'

'Not yet, sir.'

'What if you don't find them?'

'We'll go anyway.'

'And the antiaircraft defenses?'

'We'll use missiles, chaff, and jamming, then A-6s and A-10s.'

'Call me back later.'

Jake went to find a place to sleep. One office had a couch. He was pulling off his shoes when Toad Tarkington tracked him down. 'Here's a message from Ambassador Lancaster in Moscow, for your eyes only.'

Jake tore open the envelope. Herb Tenney was dead. In his sleep.

Half the pills Jake put in Herb's mouth were aspirin, but some of them were part of the binary cocktail. Perhaps Herb already had the other half in his system. *Damn!* Or someone just poisoned him.

Jake replaced the message in the envelope and passed it back to Toad. 'Herb Tenney died in his sleep.'

Toad snorted. 'His tough luck.'

Jake balled his fist and started to pound his thigh, then opened his hand and ran it through his hair. 'I am really sick of this mess.'

'I know,' Toad said. 'I know.'

'Turn the lights out and close the door. Let me sleep for three hours.'

'Yessir.

'And question General Yakolev. Find out if they shot down that Russian helicopter pilot, Vasily Lutkin.'

'CAG, you aren't responsible for that. Yakolev is. You can't—'

'Just do it, Toad.'

'Aye aye, sir.'

He lay in the darkness trying to relax. Too many details ran through his mind, too many questions were still unanswered.

Saddam Hussein was down to his last trick, but it was a dilly this time. He had tried to take the Iranian oil fields and lost, tried to take Kuwait and found out that a second- or third-rate military power could not win on a modern conventional battlefield. So now he was playing the nuclear card. And it would be a winner unless allied forces arrived in time.

In time.

What was happening in Washington?

When Toad woke Jake up, he had a message. 'The president said Go. You're to call General Land.'

For some reason he didn't quite understand, Jake felt refreshed and relaxed after his nap. He followed Toad to the com center and sat drinking coffee while the technicians placed the call to Washington.

Hayden Land's voice had a note of optimism this morning, actually midnight or after in Washington. 'The White House crowd finally faced up to the fact they have no choice.'

No choice! The words echoed in Jake's mind. It's almost as if the grand smashup is preordained, he thought.

'Where are the Scud missiles?'

'They aren't moving on the roads, sir,' the air intelligence officer told Jake Grafton. 'And we can't find any vehicles leaving the Samarra base that go to any of the Scud sites we know about. None. We've used computers to analyze satellite imagery and side-looking radar to track their vehicles. We've come up dry.'

'Maybe most of the warheads are still at the Samarra base.'

'Reluctantly, I come to that conclusion too, Admiral.'

It is never safe to assume that your opponent is doing what you want him to do. Jake Grafton was well aware of that pitfall, and yet . . . 'Perhaps,' he murmured, 'Saddam is having his trouble adapting the warheads to the missiles.'

'It's possible,' Colonel Rheinhart agreed. 'The Iraqis reduced the payload capability of their missiles several years ago in order to carry more fuel.'

'So where is Saddam?' Jake asked the intelligence staff.

'He rode out the Gulf War in '91 in a camping trailer that moved randomly around Baghdad. We told the press we knew where all the command and control facilities were, which was a serious stretcher. Then we blew up a few of them with smart bombs and he concluded we were telling the truth.'

'And now?'

'Well, we've refined our satellite capability since the Gulf War. We have side-looking radar in the air that tracks moving vehicles so that we can find Scud sites. Now we do have all the command and control facilities spotted and we can follow Saddam for five days at a time. Unfortunately, right now we seem to have lost track of him.

'Could he be at the Samarra base?' Jake asked.

'Sir, he could be anywhere.'

General Loy, Major General Serkin, and Jake Grafton reviewed the final plan together. They set H-Hour for 24:00 this night. Serkin said he didn't think they could go sooner, and with yet another glance at his watch Jake acquiesced.

Then he went to find Toad. 'Did you get anything out of Yakolev?'

'He refused to say a word. When he heard the question he looked at me like I was crazy.'

Jake Grafton sighed. 'I'm jumping tonight with the SEALs,' he said after a bit. 'I want you to bring the nuclear weapons experts in on choppers. Get chopper transport for Jack Yocke and a network camera team and as many other print and television reporters as you can cram in. Have Captain McElroy and the marines bring our two Russian friends and Spiro Dalworth. Bring Colonel Rheinhart, Jocko West and the other international observers. You're in charge of that operation.'

'No, sir. I'm going with you.'

Jake Grafton did a double take. 'Toad, I want you to get the press and the international people there. This is the key to the whole deal.'

'Rita can handle it, CAG. I'm going with you.'

'Maybe I didn't make myself clear, Commander. You—'

'CAG, you can court-martial me if you like. But I'm going with you to watch your back. *You* are the key to this operation and if you get zapped, the rest of us are in big fucking trouble. I'd never forgive myself if that happened and Rita wouldn't forgive me either. Now that's *that*.'

'Have you ever made a delayed parachute drop?'

'I've done as many as you have, sir.'

'Okay, smart-ass. We'll hold hands all the way down.'

Jack Yocke had a request of his own when Toad told him he was going in on a chopper with Rita. 'I'd like to go with you and the admiral.'

'Yeah, I bet you would,' Toad said. 'Forget it, pencil pilot. We'll give you a window seat on the executive helicopter if you promise not to pee your pants.'

'No, I want to jump with you guys. It'll be a great story.'

'You don't seem to understand, Jack. We'll be the first guys in. *This is a twenty-eight-thousand-foot free fall at night into a concentration of enemy troops who are probably on full alert.* There'll be bullets flying around, helicopter gunships blasting tanks, the whole greasy enchilada. Get serious! Your mother wouldn't even let you play with a cap pistol when you were a kid.'

'Let me ask the admiral.'

Grafton listened to Yocke state his case, gave Toad an evil glance, and said, 'Sure you can come. Why not? The more the merrier.'

They started sweating during the suiting up at 20:00, after dinner in the main cafeteria. Camo clothing, insulated one-piece jumpsuit, jump boots, helmet, silenced submachine gun, ammo, knife, radio, canteen, flak vest – 'The bullets will bounce off like you're fucking Superman' – parachute harness, parachutes, oxygen mask, oxygen supply system, gloves, jump goggles, night vision goggles for on the ground . . . almost eighty pounds of equipment. They waddled when they were finally outfitted.

'I don't want a gun,' Yocke said.

'No weapon, no jump,' Jake Grafton told him curtly. 'Your choice. I'm not taking a tourist into a firefight, and that's final.'

So they hung a submachine gun and ammo on Yocke and he kept his mouth shut. As a final indignity, Toad Tarkington smeared his face with black camouflage grease.

It was bizarre. The SEALs looked like extras from an

378

Arnold Schwarzenegger action flick. Zap, boom, pow! No doubt he did too. And they were all grown men!

Yocke began really sweating in the lecture that followed. A chief petty officer explained each piece of gear, explained about the wrist altimeter, how they should check it occasionally but wait for the main chute to deploy automatically – 'It'll work! Honest! It's guaranteed. If it doesn't, you bring it back and we'll give you another' – how they would run out of the back of the C-141 in lines, lay themselves out in the air to keep from tumbling, steer in free fall, steer when the chute opened, how they should land.

And when all the questions had been answered from the three neophytes, the final piece of advice: 'Don't think about it – just do it.'

Jake Grafton had too many things on his mind to worry about the jump. As the C-141 climbed away from the runway, he adjusted his oxygen mask, ensured the oxygen was flowing and let the jumpmaster check his equipment, all the while trying to figure out what Saddam Hussein had done with the weapons. Were they still at the Samarra base, or had The Awesome outsmarted the Americans?

Sitting beside the admiral, Toad Tarkington thought about the upcoming jump as the air inside the plane cooled. The red lights of the plane's interior and the noise gave it the feel and sound of flight deck control, the handler's kingdom in the bottom of a carrier's island. And he had that night-cat-shot rock in the pit of his stomach.

He looked at the blank faces and averted eyes of the SEALs around him and thought about Rita. Would she be all right? Had he made the right decision coming with Grafton? If they shot Rita down she had no parachute, no ejection seat – if that woman died Toad wanted to die with her. This thought had tripped across his synapses when he was weighing his request to accompany Grafton. Nuclear weapons to murder millions – with Jake Grafton alive and thinking, they had a chance to pull off this crazy assault. With him dead it would be just another bloodletting and probably end up too little, too late. Although racked with powerful misgivings, Toad had elected to go with his head and not his heart.

The oxygen, he noted now, had a slightly metallic taste.

Maybe, Toad decided, a little prayer wouldn't hurt. He didn't bother the Lord often, just checked in occasionally to let the man — or woman — upstairs know he was still down here kicking, but now, he thought, might be a good time to put in an earnest supplication from the heart.

Dear God, don't let anything happen to Rita.

Jack Yocke was thinking exclusively about the upcoming free fall. Unlike Grafton and Tarkington, he had never ejected from an airplane, nor had he ever jumped out of one. He knew people whose idea of a perfect Saturday was to leap out of an airplane with six of their buddies and free fall, then float down in sport parachutes, those colorful flying wings. He had never had the slightest desire to join the macho brigade. Maybe those folks had maladjusted hormone levels or were trying to spice up dull, boring existences, but Jack Yocke was perfectly happy with his feet upon the ground. He still got dates when he wanted them and his dick got stiff at the right time, so why spit in the devil's eye?

Part of the reason he was here, he admitted to himself, was Tarkington. The Toad-man had a knack of rubbing him the wrong way. That coolest-of-the-cool, studlier-than-thou attitude, that . . . asshole! So now here he was, getting colder and colder, about to fall over *five fucking miles* through the night sky, then ride a parachute — if that contraption of bedsheets and fishing lines opened — right smack into the middle of a goddamn war with a bunch of raghead Nazis.

What if the chute doesn't open? I mean, really! You gotta lay there in the air like a store dummy for two minutes and

380

forty seconds waiting ... waiting ... waiting ... If you panicked and pulled the manual ripcord too high you might run out of oxygen, or drift away from the landing area and the support of your fellow soldiers. Or you might find yourself hanging up there when the helicopter gunships and troop transports came in with their blades whirling around, flak searching the darkness, cannon fire, machine gun bullets ... No, Jack, don't take a chance on pulling the ripcord too early. Wait for this seventy-nine-cent gizmo from Woolworth's to do the job for you.

He would wait. Under absolutely no circumstances would he panic. He told himself that yet again, trying to believe it. He would close his eyes and wait until the chute opened. It *would* open. He assured himself of that for the fiftieth time. If it didn't, by God, they would scrape him off the asphalt in the middle of the runway, his eyes scrunched shut, his hands and legs outstretched, still waiting.

Now, fifteen minutes after takeoff, Yocke was *ready*. He was properly psyched and ready to leap straight into hell. Then he looked at his watch and saw that they had over an hour to go.

Oh, Jesus!

Rita Moravia sat in almost total darkness with her back against the forward bulkhead of the Blackhawk's passenger compartment. Sharing the compartment with her but quite invisible were the four European colonels 'observing' and the two Russian flag officers.

The Russians also had escorts, Captain Iron Mike McElroy and one of his sergeants. Rita had briefed them carefully.

Right now she wasn't thinking about the other passengers. She was listening to the muffled roar of the engines through her headset and thinking about her husband, Toad.

He would be okay, she assured herself. When she heard he was jumping she thought of the two steel pins in his leg and wondered if he should. When she mentioned his leg he glared at her.

Isn't that just like a man? If the man is concerned he's thoughtful, chivalrous, gallant. If a woman voices her concern she's a nag.

So life isn't fair. Tell it to Yocke and let him put it on the front page.

The navy had been a tough row to hoe. First the Naval Academy, then flight training, the squadrons, test pilot school — Rita had encountered subtle covert and overt discrimination every step of the way. Oh, the senior officers thought it would be fine to have women in the navy as long as the pretty ones wanted to be executive secretaries to those said senior officers, but women shouldn't be on ships! Or in cockpits. Or where men were shooting. Or drinking. Or telling dirty jokes. Heaven forbid!

Jake Grafton didn't think like that. Because he didn't Rita had found herself riding the tip of the arrow, slaughtering doomed men with a 30mm cannon.

Here in the darkness inside this helicopter over the desert, Rita Moravia remembered that moment. She remembered the feel of her airplane, the look of the clouds, the look of the Iraqi plane on the parking mat as she dove at it, the Gs tugging at her as she maneuvered, the lighted reticle in the sight glass, the vibration as the cannon vomited out its shells, the smoke billowing skyward as she pulled up and banked away . . . Everything was crystal clear, engraved on her memory.

She had killed.

Oh, it had to be done . . . but *she* had done it.

She thought now that she understood those senior officers she had met through the years, understood that look in their eyes. It had been a tired look, a weary look.

Now she forgave them. Yet they were wrong.

Jake Grafton was right.

You can't avoid it or wash it off your hands just because you didn't get a Y chromosome and a penis. Oh no.

Little Toadlet inside of me, this world you will come into isn't just flowers and teddy bears. Male or female, you are going to have to live, endure, survive, do the best you can. You must be strong, little one. Somehow, some way, you must find the strength to do what you believe to be right. And the strength to live with it afterward.

CHAPTER TWENTY-FOUR

The cruisers were on the western side of the task force, arranged in a broad semicircle over five miles of ocean. The Tomahawk missiles popped out on cones of flame, rising and accelerating, then nosing over and descending to just a hundred feet above the sea as their turbo-fan engines took over. Missile followed missile, a total of fifteen in all. Their targets were five radar sites between Samarra and the southern border of Iraq, with each radar being the target of three missiles.

The last missile had just disappeared into the darkness when the carrier to the east of the cruisers turned into the wind and the first tow of her aircraft rode the catapults into the night sky, one off the waist, one off the bow. The launch took seven minutes. The planes were still climbing away from the carrier when more Tomahawk missiles rippled from the cruiser's launchers.

Meanwhile a half-dozen AH-64 Apaches were approaching their targets, two more Iraqi radar sites, at just forty feet above the desert sand. Apaches from the 101st Airborne Division had made a similar attack against radar sites only a few miles from these on the opening night of the Gulf War in 1991. The Iraqis had worked for two years to build these replacement sites, which now met the same fate as their predecessors. They were turned into twisted junk by a blizzard of Hellfire missiles, 2.75-inch rockets, and 30mm cannon shells.

Wild Weasel antimissile aircraft were already orbiting over Baghdad. Under their wings were the radar-killing beam-rider missiles that would take out Iraqi fire-control radars when they began transmitting. Since the Gulf War allied aircraft had routinely patrolled the skies over Iraq and they were there again tonight, waiting.

The two C-141s carrying navy SEALs crossed the border at thirty thousand feet on a direct course for the Iraqi air base at Samarra. Someone had suggested a feint toward Baghdad, but Jake Grafton vetoed that. The most valuable target in Iraq was at Samarra. Feints were merely a waste of fuel and precious time.

The Iraqi command center duty officer in Baghdad noticed on his radar presentations the flight of aircraft crossing the Kuwaiti border and another flight coming in from Arabia, all converging on Samarra. This was unusual, the deviation from the standard allied patrolling tactics that he had been briefed to look for. He was about to pick up his telephone when the first of the navy Tomahawk cruise missiles struck its target and one of his radars went blank. Then a second, and a third. Frantically he jiggled the hook on the telephone. The operator came on the line. Alas, Iraq's fiber-optic, state-of-the-art military communications system was heavily damaged during the Gulf War and was still under repair. So the duty officer had to use the civilian telephone system.

'The air base at Samarra, quickly.'

What he would have said to the people at Samarra we will never know, for at that moment a Tomahawk missile penetrated the reinforced concrete wall of this command and control center and six-thousandths of a second after the initial impact its thousand-pound warhead detonated. The people inside the structure never felt a thing – they merely ceased to exist.

The battle had begun.

Flights of A-10 Warthogs and A-6 Intruders raced into the area around Baghdad and Samarra and began attacking antiaircraft missile sites. They were protected by electronic warfare jamming planes and a curtain of chaff that a flight of B-52s was dumping from thirty-six thousand feet.

The SEALs in the C-141s were up and in line. Silent, tense, they watched the red jump light high in the rear of the compartment, above the open ramp that led into cold, black nothingness. Jake Grafton, Toad Tarkington and Jack Yocke were in the middle of the line against the starboard side of the aircraft.

Jack Yocke had switched his mind off. He was running now on adrenaline and instinct.

It was like being back on the high school basketball team waiting for a tipoff, all hot and sweaty, ready to go whichever way the ball bounced.

Once his eyes caught a glimpse of the blackness yawning beyond the lead men, but he ignored it. Then the jump light turned yellow. The man behind him crowded him forward, so he took a step, nudging up toward Toad's back.

He was chanting into the oxygen mask: 'Come on, baby, let's do it! Let's go, go, go, go,' so when the light turned green his muscles surged and he was charging right behind Toad and shouting 'Go, go, go,' and the ramp wasn't there anymore and he was falling, falling, falling into the infinite eternal darkness.

Jake lay spread-eagle in the sky and waited for his eyes to adjust to the near-total darkness. It would have been great if they could have worn the night-vision goggles, but those bulky headsets would have been torn off by the wind blast. In seconds he was up to terminal velocity, 120 miles per hour.

He was still getting oxygen. Fine. So how many seconds had it been?

He scanned, trying to pick up the men who were falling with him. He saw a few shapes in the darkness, but that was all. He concentrated on staring into the blackness below. Nothing was visible, of course, since there was a thin cloud layer at twenty thousand feet. After they were through that the lights of Samarra should be visible underneath, perhaps the air base lights if they were still on, and to the south, the lights of Baghdad.

So he lay there in the sky feeling the cold wind tear at him, maintaining his balance. That was important, and extremely difficult to do in the darkness without a visual reference. All you could do was pray you didn't tumble, and if that happened of course you would know it. Even though the wind was cold, he wasn't freezing. His jumpsuit and clothes seemed to be enough. And as he fell the air would become warmer.

What was down there? Were the Iraqis on full alert, or would the surprise be enough?

Toad Tarkington had a problem. His goggles had somehow come off in the scramble out and now he was squinting against the wind. There was nothing to see, so he scrunched his eyes tightly closed and began counting. 'One, one thousand, two, one thousand, three . . .'

He was falling at the rate of two miles a minute, a mile every thirty seconds. At the end of a minute he should be through the cloud layer. Then he would open his eyes.

This fall was a whole hell of a lot different than the last time he jumped, that time in Nevada when he and Rita had nearly bought the farm.

Actually this wasn't bad. He could feel the cold but he wasn't freezing. And nobody was shooting.

They were going to be shooting on the ground. Toad was certain of that. The most dangerous part of this whole jump was the last few hundred feet, when any Iraqi draftee who could lift a rifle would have a free shot.

The thing to do was to get the weapon out when the parachute deployed and be ready. He rehearsed the moves that he would make, how he would get the weapon free and cycle the bolt. Ahmad the Awful might get his shot at the ol' Horny Toad, but it wouldn't be free.

*

Yocke wasn't counting. He was trying to stabilize himself in the spread-eagle position. He could feel the dizziness of rotation, and try as he might, he couldn't seem to stop it. Damn!

And he had lost track of the time. Well, two minutes and forty seconds was an entire lifetime. He would still be falling like this in the middle of next week if he didn't get stabilized.

He forced himself to spread his arms and hands to full extension. According to the chief who had briefed them, that should stop the tumbling.

But he wasn't spread out. Now he realized that he was almost doubled up at the waist. He was so pumped up he couldn't even tell what position his body was in!

He forced himself to full extension. The rotating feeling slowed. And stopped.

And he was still chanting. 'Go, go, go . . .' He stopped and took a deep, ragged breath.

He stared straight ahead, which must be down. The wind was in his face, trying to pull his arms and legs backward, so straight ahead must be down.

Thirty years of life, and all of it led up to this. School, work, family, women, good moments and bad, and all of it was mere prelude for *this* moment, this free fall into a cold, black eternity.

Jack Yocke began to laugh. He laughed until he choked, then decided he might be getting hysterical, and stopped himself.

How long has it been?

Does it matter?

And the answer came back. *No.*

He fell on toward the waiting earth.

Jake knew he was through the cloud layer when lights suddenly appeared in the velvet blackness below. There was Samarra, and the base almost directly under him. He twisted his head so he could see Baghdad. The navy and air force were doing their job, he noted. In the blackness he saw the wink and twinkle of explosions, here and there jeweled strings of tracers streaking through the darkness at odd angles. No sounds, just muzzle blasts and flashes of warheads and those twinkling strings of tracers.

He tried to steer toward the center of the air base below, that black spot where the runways must intersect.

Now the two-miles-per-minute rate of fall was quite discernible. The lights below were coming up at sickening speed. Even though he had spent years flying tactical aircraft at night, the visual impact of his rate of descent was disconcerting. Would the parachute open?

This question must run through the mind of every free fall parachutist. Jake Grafton had a pragmatic faith in military equipment – through the years he had occasionally witnessed the spectacular, usually fatal, outcome when vital equipment failed.

He pulled his left wrist in and examined the luminous hands of the wrist altimeter. Three thousand feet still to fall!

How many seconds?

The math was too much. He waited, noting the absence of muzzle flashes. Maybe they had achieved surprise!

Toad's eyes were slits, staring at the lights rushing up at him. He reached for and grasped the manual ripcord. And waited.

The runways were plainly visible, and the hangar. There was a plane!

How high was he? Still a couple –

The opening of the chute almost tore his boots off.

Toad took off the oxygen mask and threw it away, then began checking his equipment. He still had it. All right! He got the submachine gun unslung and checked the magazine.

Still no muzzle flashes on the airfield directly below. Please God, let them be asleep!

*

Jack Yocke was chanting again, some mindless sound he repeated over and over as he fell toward the lights on the earth below.

The air was warmer here. In one corner of his mind he took note of that fact, but the flashing, twinkling lights embedded in the velvet, Stygian blackness claimed the rest of his attention. The lights were coming closer, growing larger. He could even hear muffled explosions. They were having a war down there, and he was falling into it at two miles per minute.

He caught himself fumbling for the ripcord. No. No! *No!*

The lights were rushing toward him now, faster and faster and fast – a tremendous jolt jerked his head up and tore at his crotch.

He yelled. Into the oxygen mask.

And he was hanging by the harness, the fierce wind now a zephyr. He tore at the oxygen mask and succeeded in freeing one side of it.

He was drifting. Where? What was that lighted complex there?

The city! God, he was coming down into the city of Samarra, not the airfield, which was over there to the right. Buildings below, streets . . .

He pulled on the left side of the parachute risers and felt himself slowly turn in the air. Now he was going toward a street. Good! He looked up, trying to see the parachute. He could just make out its vague, winglike shape. Where are those cords that you use to steer it? He fumbled, trying now to find them. Oh well, he was coming down into that street –

Something tore at his feet and he tumbled forward all in a heap, the wind knocked out of him.

He rolled over on his back, gasping.

Alive! Thank God!

Something tugged at his shoulders. The chute was on the ground, tugging in the gentle breeze. Clumsily he got to his feet and fumbled in the darkness for the Koch fittings that held the parachute on. He got them released. The chute began to move away.

He let it go as he stood there staring all about him at the buildings, the windows, the empty street lit by the occasional streetlight. No one about. No Iraqis, which was wonderful, but no SEALs either.

In the pregnant gloom of an Arab street his euphoria gave way to fear.

He scuttled to the doorway of a building and stood sheltered there, looking and listening as the sounds of battle echoed off the buildings. The swelling, fading, then swelling sound of jet engines set his teeth on edge. His hands were shaking, he realized, and he was biting his lip.

Which way was the airfield?

He had no idea. It had been on his right as he descended but he had hit the street and tumbled and lost all sense of direction, so now he gazed upward at the three- and four-story buildings, trying to decide in which direction the airfield lay as the fear congealed into a lump of ice in his chest.

He found that he had the submachine gun in his hands. The hard coolness of the plastic and metal should have comforted him somewhat, but if it did he didn't feel the effect.

As he tried to remember what the map had looked like when he studied it several hours ago surrounded by SEALs — in his former life, before he leaped through that extraordinary threshold from the airplane into the void — he drew a total blank. He had absolutely no idea where in the city he was or in which direction the airfield lay.

He stood paralyzed. He was panting and he was desperately afraid, a freezing, numbing fear that left him unable to think, unable to move.

The parachute finally brought him out of it. The white silk had draped itself around a car and fluttered ever so gently in the wind. Anyone looking out a window would see it. Anyone who came along, anyone who —

Jack Yocke stepped from the safety of the doorway and started along the sidewalk. His steps quickened. He ran.

He had gone several blocks and just crossed a fairly wide street at a hell-bent gallop when he heard the truck. The noise of a big engine at full throttle boomed off the buildings and penetrated his fear-soaked brain. He dove into a doorway as a large army truck thundered across the intersection he had just crossed.

Follow it! Yes. It must be going toward the base.

He waited until the engine noise died away, then willed his legs to move.

He was in the middle of the street when a jet streaked overhead just above the housetops – the thunder of its engines arrived all at once and temporarily deafened Yocke. The glass in several windows broke and fell to the sidewalk. The roar faded almost as fast as it came and left a terrifying silence in its wake.

Someone was looking out a window. He caught a glimpse of a face. He kept going. His pace was slower now, more sure. He wiped the sweat from his face with his right hand, then grasped his weapon again. He held it in front of him, ready.

He had walked for five minutes or so when he heard the first rifle shots. Single shots, then the staccato ripping of an automatic weapon. The reports seemed loud.

When Jake Grafton's chute opened, he bounced once in the harness and breathed a tremendous sigh of relief.

He quickly took off the oxygen mask and grabbed for the steering cords on the parachute risers. He was directly over a big hangar. He didn't have a lot of options, so he steered for the dark area behind it. He seemed to be covering ground quickly. Going downwind. There was no help for it.

The breeze carried him well clear of the hangar. He tried to make out the terrain where he would be coming down. Vague shapes – was that a truck? Then his feet struck something and he took a vicious rap on the left shin.

He smacked into something else, then was on the ground with a thump.

Opening his eyes, he found he was in a parking lot. He had bounced off two trucks before he got to the ground. His shin felt like it was on fire.

He rolled over and tried to get up. His leg took his weight but the pain brought tears into his eyes. Holy—!

He pulled the chute down with the risers. Only then did he unfasten his Koch fittings.

Aagh, his shin! He sat down heavily and felt his left leg. It was swelling rapidly and maybe bleeding, but it didn't seem to be broken.

He got the goggles off, the helmet off, then donned the infrared night vision goggles. He found the switch and adjusted the sensitivity. After replacing his helmet, he wiggled out of the parachute harness and the unopened backup chute. Now for the silenced submachine gun. He tilted the goggles up and made sure it was loaded, with the safety on.

Massaging his shin, he sat there trying to recall where the truck parking area was on the field.

Yes, the hangar he wanted was that big one he had floated over, that one over there.

Jake Grafton got to his feet and gingerly hobbled to the gate. It wasn't locked. He stood there scanning with the goggles.

He could see figures moving out beyond the hangars. These blobs of red stayed low, moving swiftly and surely, then stopped to reconnoitre. SEALs! But closer in . . . there! A sentry by a guard shack, looking out into the darkness. Even as he watched, the sentry contorted and collapsed onto the concrete. Jake scanned. The shooter who had drilled the sentry with a silenced weapon from almost a hundred feet away began to creep along the side of the hangar toward the door.

Jake opened the gate and hobbled toward the hangar as fast as he could go.

The shooter by the hangar wall watched him come. When he was five feet away, the man said, 'Jesus, CAG, what happened to your leg?'

Toad Tarkington!

'Banged it up. You okay?'

'Yeah, I think so. Landed on some concrete. But I don't think this hangar is the one we want. Aren't we on the wrong side of the airfield?'

'You're assuming this is the right airfield.'

'Don't tell me.' Toad Tarkington pulled a compass from his shirt. He consulted it. 'This has got to be the right airfield, but the wrong hangar. Ours is over there.' He pointed.

Missiles streaked overhead before they could react. They heard the explosions of the warheads detonating, then the roar of jet engines at full military power.

More jets. One went over with his cannon spitting bursts.

Jake Grafton sat on the ground. He pulled his map and a pencil flash from a leg pocket and studied it while the jets worked over the Iraqi armor beyond the field perimeter. Finally he replaced the map and flash in his pocket. 'Help me up.'

'How bad's your leg?'

'Ain't broke. Come on. Let's go.'

With Toad leading and Jake hobbling along behind, the two of them headed into the darkness of the center of the field toward the distant hangars on the other side.

They had gone no more than a hundred feet when they heard the small-arms fire. It seemed to be coming from the perimeter.

'Well, they know we're here,' Toad muttered.

They came to a drainage ditch and were wading through the mud in the bottom when they heard the first chopper. It swept across the field only a few feet above the ground without a single light showing. Somewhere off to the left it slowed, almost a hover, then kept going toward the airfield perimeter.

*

Jack Yocke heard the background hum of the chopper engines, and he heard several more of the machines coming across the city. These were the Apaches, he assumed, the gunships that were to act as heavy artillery under the direction of the SEALs on the ground.

But he was on the wrong side of the flight. He was supposed to be inside the airfield perimeter, under cover.

Goddamnit!

Nothing in war ever goes the way you planned it. Wasn't that what Jake Grafton told him as they waited to board the plane?

Explosions ahead. Flashes, and after a few seconds, the noise, which swept down the night streets in waves that could almost be felt. And the roar of automatic gunfire. Burst after burst.

A man opened a second-story window and stuck his head out. He saw Yocke and ducked his head back in.

That lump in the pit of Yocke's stomach turned cold. He was sweating profusely now. Unable to do anything else, he kept going, toward the gunfire.

He came to a corner and approached it carefully. The firing was loud now, no more than a block away. Close against the side of a building and sheltered in darkness, he waited until a helicopter swept over and eased his head around. And found himself staring straight into the face of a man just a few feet away.

Yocke swung the weapon and pulled the trigger. Nothing. *Mother of God! The safety! He tried to find it.*

There was no time. The Iraqi came for him in a rush.

Yocke swung the gun barrel, still trying to find the safety, and literally pushed the man away with the barrel. But he kept coming.

Galvanized, Yocke pushed him again, this time using his left hand.

He felt the bite of the knife on his arm. It stung.

The knife gleamed in the man's right hand as he crouched, then flung himself at the reporter.

Yocke was at least six inches taller than the Iraqi and twenty pounds heavier and his terror gave him tremendous strength, which probably saved his life. Somehow he got hold of the Iraqi's right wrist and began to twist. As the two men fell to the ground the knife came loose.

Yocke got it.

And rammed it into the Iraqi's body. Twice, three times, jabbing with all his strength.

The Iraqi groaned once, almost a scream, then the strength drained from him.

Yocke stabbed him three or four more times, then rolled away.

He lay beside the dead man, trying to get his breath.

Sticky. His hands were sticky and wet.

His arm was burning.

Horrified, he looked at the blood. On his hands, his arm, his clothes, the gear he wore. On the Iraqi. Smeared on the sidewalk.

Jack Yocke managed to get to his feet and stood swaying as the sounds of battle came echoing down the empty street. Amazingly, he discovered he still had the knife in his hand. He opened his fingers. The knife made a hollow sound when it bounced on the sidewalk.

Sobbing, Yocke examined the submachine gun still slung around his shoulders and found the safety. He flicked it off.

The Apache helicopters were pouring fire into an area by the main gate, about two hundred yards away, as Jake Grafton and Toad Tarkington lay in the darkness on the edge of the concrete parking mat and studied the hangar looming ahead of them. Lights mounted above the center of the main door and by a sentry box at the left corner were still illuminated.

What the lights revealed were bodies. Jake counted. Eight. Even as he watched, one of the men lying near the hangar moved, and drew immediate fire from out of the darkness on Jake's right. With the goggles on, Jake could see the prone figure who had just fired.

'The SEALs are here,' Toad whispered. 'Isn't this Saddam's safety-deposit box, the Treasure Chest?'

'I think so.'

'There's a personnel door over behind that sentry box. We might be able to get in there.'

'Let's check in first. Keep an eye peeled.'

Jake extracted his radio and fumbled with the switches. Then he held it to his ear and keyed the mike. 'Snake One, this is the Doctor.' Snake One was the commanding officer of the SEALs team, Commander Lester Slick. Slick was a hell of a name for a naval officer but if anyone snickered they did it well away from Lester, who had the body of a professional wrestler and the scarred face of a man who liked to fight and had done far too much of it.

'Snake One, aye. Say your posit.'

'By the target hangar, west side.'

'Wait one.'

They waited in the darkness, listening to the battle. Jake removed his night vision goggles and let his eyes adjust.

The radio squawked. 'Snake One, this is Snake Four. There's four of us out here in the middle of a whole god-damn raghead platoon.'

'Fight your way in, Snake Four. You're behind schedule.'

That was Lester Slick. If you wanted sympathy, write home to mama.

'Roger.'

Jake looked at his watch. In six minutes the first of the Blackhawks was scheduled to arrive.

'Okay, gang, this is Snake One. Let's start moving in on the Treasure Chest.'

Jake and Toad rose from the ground and scuttled toward the hangar. As they came into the light he saw five other men, SEALs, coming at a trot. 'Let's get inside,' Jake told Toad, and went for the personnel door by the sentry box.

Jake opened the door and stepped into a foyer, a dead

space to keep out blowing sand. Toad was right behind him. They paused and listened, then Toad opened the inner door several inches while Jake peeked through the opening. He stepped back and motioned for Toad to close the door.

'Over a dozen men. Some armed,' Jake whispered.

'The nukes?'

'A lot of them.'

'Whoo boy!'

'There's a door in the east side, by the aircraft door,' Jake said. 'It's open. I'm gonna step out and look around the corner. Open the door for me.' His heart was hammering, he was perspiring freely, and he was breathing hard, as if he had run ten miles, but when Toad opened the door he slipped back outside.

The light over the doorway outside had to go. Jake reached up and broke it with the silencer on the end of the submachine gun. Then he inched his head around the corner of the hangar. Just bodies visible. He ran the length of the building as fast as his sore leg would allow and paused at the next corner by the sentry box, then cautiously inched his head out.

There was a trailer or something, a dozen or so armed Iraqis, some of them looking this way. He jerked his head back.

The fat was in the fire. They must have seen him. A grenade!

He got one from his web belt, pulled the pin, then threw it as hard as he could around the corner. When it blew he leaned out a few inches and let go with the silenced weapon.

Three men were down. The nearest man was picking himself up off the concrete, just twenty feet away. Jake's slugs smacked him and he went over backward, his weapon flying. Jake sprayed another burst at the men by the trailer, then ducked back into shelter.

Bullets splattered into the metal of the hangar just above his head as the ripping of a weapon echoed off the clustered buildings. Jake crouched, looking for the muzzle blasts. There! He squeezed off a burst as he scuttled sideways for the dubious safety of the sentry box.

More bullets spanged in.

Now he took his time, sighting carefully: this was what the Iraqi hadn't done. He squeezed the trigger and held the muzzle down. And saw the Iraqi fall from behind a barrel where he had taken cover.

Quickly he took the empty magazine from his weapon and inserted another. Now back to the corner. Another burst at figures now trying to get behind the trailer.

There was a car there. A car? A limo, it looked like.

Shots from inside the hangar. Toad must have gone in.

Jake heaved another grenade.

After it exploded, he looked again. The car was right beside the trailer, the passenger door open. Two men were hosing lead in this direction. The car was also facing this way.

Jake got down on his belly and aimed his weapon at the front tires of the car. The two men who were upright now went down, dropping their weapons. Jake gave the tires a whole clip.

New magazine inserted.

Even though its front tires were flat, the limo started to move. Grafton pumped a burst into the engine compartment and watched as a cloud of steam came out. The limo stopped.

The gunfire on the western side of the base was building into a sustained racket. Grafton looked around. A SEAL was running toward him, his weapon at the ready.

The SEAL flopped down behind Jake. 'Go into the hangar and help out,' Jake said. 'One of our guys is in there. Be careful where you shoot.'

Without a word the other man got up and went into the hangar.

Jake lay where he was, watching the limo and the trailer by the hangar wall. No one moved.

A helicopter swept over. Then another. Running without lights. Rockets rippled from a third machine and streaked away to the west. Now Jake heard the roar of a 30mm cannon. This machine was barely moving, pouring fire at several tanks just outside the perimeter fence. The wash from the rotors of this machine fanned Jake.

Two figures rose from a low place out on the airfield and came slowly this way, bent at the waist. They stopped and crouched occasionally. They approached the car.

'Don't shoot him,' Jake shouted during a momentary lull in the gunship barrage going on just behind him. 'Take him into the hangar.'

With that he got up and opened the hangar door.

Inside the foyer he wiped the perspiration from his eyes, got a good grip on the submachine gun, then jerked open the interior door and dived through.

He slid right into the body of an Iraqi soldier. His throat had been cut. More bodies lay near the eastern door, the one that led to where the trailer was parked. Jake inched forward and looked carefully around. A group of Iraqis was standing near the west wall of the hangar with their hands up. Three missiles on trailers sat against the north wall, and here and there, several compact, cylindrical devices – warheads. Piles of wooden crates sat in one corner. A Scud on its launcher sat against the west wall.

'Toad?' Jake made it loud, because the noise from outside was reverberating inside the large metal building.

'Over here, CAG.'

'Everything under control?'

'Seems to be.'

'Are you behind something?'

'Yes, sir.'

'Stay there. I'm gonna take a look out this east door.'

Jake walked across the hangar warily. He didn't take time to count the warheads, but there were a lot of them.

Approaching the door he stepped to one side. The door was ajar. He eased it open and inched his head around the jamb for a look. This was, of course, an excellent way to get his brains blown out, but right now didn't seem to be the time to play it safe.

Three bodies were lying near the door. Four more were visible to the right, toward the south. And fifty feet away the limo still sat, the two SEALs kneeling behind it. Jake stepped out and walked toward them.

'There were about a dozen men here when I first saw them. Did you guys see where the others went?'

'They went hoofing it toward the north. There's a network of trenches over there, I think. You'll find their bodies about fifty yards up that way.'

As helicopters crossed above and the whuff of Hellfire missiles and rockets being launched washed over them, one of the SEALs seized the front door of the car and jerked it open. The driver sat with his hands on the steering wheel, offering no resistance. 'This guy's been watching too many American cop movies. Okay, Ahmad, outta there.'

The rear door on Jake's side of the car opened. He stood ready, the submachine gun leveled, his finger on the trigger. First a leg came out, a leg clad in uniform trousers. Then an arm and head, then the man was standing there. He was bareheaded, wore a long-sleeved uniform shirt without a tie or jacket, and had a thin brush mustache on his upper lip.

Jake gestured with his gun. 'Raise 'em.'

The man obeyed.

'Okay, Saddam,' Jake said, stepping aside and jerking his left thumb at the door, 'let's join the others at the party.'

Jake stopped outside the door and got out his radio. He selected the proper channel and checked in. 'The weapons are here. The dance is on.'

He waited for an acknowledgment, then turned down the volume of the radio to save the battery. He kept it in his hand though.

Right now the SEALs were establishing a perimeter around this building and locating the remainder of the Iraqi Republican Guard troops. The Apaches were working over the Republican Guard camp and the nearby barracks. Yet this was makeshift, a temporary expedient until the helicopters with the 101st Airborne Air Assault troops and their heavy weapons arrived. Outside the base fighter-bombers would attack the Republican Guard without mercy and hopefully prevent Iraqi troops from amassing sufficient combat power to retake the base or hinder the American buildup. As usual in modern war, timing, mobility, and firepower were the key.

Commander Lester Slick came striding in. His radio was also squawking in his hand. 'Admiral, we have four dead that I know of and about twenty men unaccounted for. One of them is the reporter.'

Jake merely nodded.

'We've scouted out most of the base and neutralized some of the opposition, but the bulk of my men are setting up lights for helo landing zones. The choppers should be here in about a minute, sir.'

'Runways intact?'

'Appear to be, sir.'

'So how are we doing?'

'We're right on schedule. Less resistance than we anticipated from the Republican guard, which is a blessing.'

'Let's stay on schedule. When you can, send me a couple more men to guard these prisoners. And if you come across the reporter, send him in here.'

'Aye aye, sir.'

The buildings of the town ended abruptly. Beyond was a sandy area, then the fence that encircled the airfield. And the fence had a hole in it, a fairly big hole that was just visible in the muted light from the town. The edge of the wire was curled and one post was awry. Beyond the hole was nothing, just darkness.

Jack Yocke lay against the side of a building facing the fence. From where he lay he could see the body of a man lying facedown, half-buried in the sand. Yocke could see the entire length of the body, which lay about twenty feet away. The US style helmet was quite plain, the parachute pack on the back, the weapon, the desert camouflage trousers, the desert boots.

From the angle of the head against the shoulders, it was obvious that the man's neck was broken. And probably half the other bones in his body.

Yocke shifted his gaze. He watched the muzzle blasts of the helicopters making runs on the Iraqi troops outside the base and the streaks the Hellfire missiles made.

To the east pulsing fingers of antiaircraft fire was rising into the night sky. The strings of tracers seemed to be probing randomly, without purpose. Even as he watched he saw the flashes of bombs exploding on the horizon, where the guns must be. The guns fell silent.

He picked up a handful of sand and idly let it run through his fingers. Then he studied the hole in the fence some more.

Well, there it was – a way into the air base. All he had to do was run for it.

It was too good to be true, really. And that was why he was lying here looking.

He concentrated on the problem, tried to think objectively about the hole in the fence. Why was it there? Perhaps the Iraqis were just sloppy. Well, that made sense. The streets and buildings he had come through were certainly Third World ratty.

He looked left. No one in sight.

Right. The same.

But . . . it didn't feel right. Something was wrong.

His contemplation of the problem was interrupted by a chopper that came from over the city behind him and swept across the fence, merely a black, fast-moving shape, then laid into a right turn. He was watching as the streak

403

came in from the right and intersected the chopper. Then it exploded. A white flash registered on his brain, then a red-yellow fireball, then the wreckage was angling downward. It hit the ground and fire splashed forward in the direction the machine had been traveling.

Even from this distance, Yocke could faintly feel the heat against his cheeks.

The fire burned fiercely for several minutes, then subsided. Finally it winked out, leaving the darkness beyond the fence even blacker than before.

Yocke looked right and left again, then began to crawl. Across the street onto the sand, toward the dead American sailor. Murphy. That was the name on his clothes.

After one more look around, Yocke got to his feet. Hunched over to present the smallest silhouette possible, he made for the fence.

He was twenty feet from the hole in the wire when he saw the helmet. He took two more steps before he saw that the helmet still had a head on it. And there on the wire, a piece of cloth. No, an arm, with a hand attached.

Jack Yocke froze.

Now he saw the hole in the ground under the tear in the fence.

Mines!

He was standing in a minefield.

He looked wildly around, trying to see the triggers. All he could make out in the gloom was sand and trash.

Off to the right – there, something moving. Only Yocke's eyes moved. A soldier, coming this way. An Iraqi!

In front of him was the hole that led into the beckoning darkness. More pieces of the American sailor who must have tripped the mine. Fifteen feet. No more. Tracks.

Tracks! He could see where the doomed man had stepped.

Yocke moved. One step. Two. Three.

A bullet sang over his head. And another.

He ran. Straight through the hole in the wire and on for

fifty or sixty feet as bullets cut the air near him and one tugged at the equipment on his back.

Finally he threw himself down and spun around facing back the way he had come. The land was so flat that through the fence he could still see the Iraqi who had been shooting at him. The helmeted man was bent over, working with the action of his rifle. A bolt action rifle!

Jack Yocke's weapon was in his hands. He sighted it carefully, as carefully as he could as he struggled to control his breathing. Now he pulled the trigger. He held the trigger down as the weapon vibrated in his hands.

The last shell flew out and he wrestled the empty magazine out of the gun and slammed in a new one.

Now he saw that the Iraqi was down. Lying on the sidewalk, barely visible in the half-light.

Yocke sighted carefully at the prone figure. Again he pulled the trigger and held it down. He fired the whole magazine, then lay still in the darkness listening to his heart thudding. Only then did it come to him that the man he had just killed had probably been even more scared than he was. A bolt-action rifle – missing bang, bang, bang . . . at that range! Probably a recent draftee, maybe militia.

Yocke began sobbing again.

CHAPTER TWENTY-FIVE

Rita was wearing the headset and listening to the radio traffic and conversation between the two pilots as they approached the Samarra air base through the southern corridor. Two sanitary corridors had been hacked through the Iraqi defenses by the allied jets and attack helicopters, which had pulverized every antiaircraft weapon and fire-control radar that they could locate.

Still, there was no way that the gunships could kill every Iraqi with a rifle, so Rita and the people in the chopper with her were wearing flak vests and sitting on extra ones. They were also trying to make themselves very small.

You hunch up, move self-consciously into the fetal position, and you wait. You wait for that random bullet to find your flesh.

Those bullets were out there zinging through the darkness. Occasionally one struck the helicopter. Several times Rita thought she could feel the delicate thump and once the pilot commented. Fortunately the helicopter was flying perfectly with all its equipment functioning as it should.

Still you draw your legs up and tuck your hands under the flak vest and wait for random death. The seconds tick by. You become aware of the beating of your heart. Stimulated by adrenaline, your mind wanders uncontrollably.

Violent death happens to other people — it won't happen to me. No bullet will rip my flesh or open arteries or smash bone or tear through that delicate mass of neurons and brain cells that makes me me. No.

She was focused inward, waiting, when she heard the pilot gag and felt the chopper pitch abruptly sideways. The copilot cursed.

'Let go of the stick, Bill! Goddamn, *let go of the fucking stick!*'

Standing in the door, Rita reached over the pilot slumped in the right seat. He had a death grip on the stick. The bucking chopper threw her off balance.

'Unstrap him,' the copilot urged Rita over the ICS. 'Get him out of the seat. Bill, leggo the fucking stick!'

She released the shoulder Koch fittings of the pilot's harness and leaned forward for the lap fittings. The cyclic stick and his hand were right there. The copilot was wrestling the cyclic with both hands. The chopper was bucking. Rita grabbed.

'Get him outta the seat,' the copilot demanded.

She released one lap fitting and fumbled for the other. The dying man was jerking the cyclic stick and the machine was obeying. Rita lost her footing. She regained it and hung herself over the back of the seat.

There. He was no longer attached to the seat.

'Get him *out!*'

Rita grabbed his shoulders and pulled. Oh God, he was heavy.

She braced herself and gave a mighty heave.

The pilot came half out of the seat but he still kept his death grip on the cyclic stick.

His helmet, with the wires. She tore it off his head.

She grabbed him again, two handfuls of harness, braced her right leg against the back of the seat and pulled with all her strength.

He came out of the seat and Rita kept pulling and the two of them tumbled backward into the passenger compartment, the wounded pilot on top.

She fumbled for her flashlight. The beam showed blood. He was shot in the face. His eyes were unfocused, blood flowing.

'He took a bullet in the face,' she told the copilot.

'Five minutes. We'll be on the ground in five minutes. Keep him alive.'

How do you keep a man alive who has been shot an inch under the right eye?

Then she realized that the convulsions had stopped. He was limp. Rita Moravia found a wrist and felt for his pulse. Still a flicker.

Since there was nothing else to do, she cradled him in her arms and hugged him.

How long Jack Yocke lay in the sandy dirt he didn't know. The noise of the helicopters and the explosions and concussions that reached him through the earth finally subsided, so he levered himself from the ground and began walking. He walked until the exhaustion hit him, then he sat down in the sand beside a runway. He was sitting there unable to summon the energy to move when he heard the crunch of a boot in the sand.

Yocke grabbed his weapon and ran his fingers over the action, trying to brush off the sand.

'Hey, shipmate! What're you doing out here?'

'Uh . . .' Relief flooded Yocke and he tried to collect his thoughts. He gestured toward the fence, back there somewhere behind him. 'His chute didn't open. Murphy. His name was Murphy.'

The man came over for a look.

'You're one of the SEALs, right?'

'No, but I jumped with them.'

'Better get over to the hangar. We're setting up a perimeter along the fence.'

'There's mines on the other side.'

'You came down in town?'

'Uh-huh.'

'How bad are you hurt? You got a lot of blood on you.'

'Most of it isn't mine.'

'Medic over by the hangar. Move along now, buddy.'

'Where?'

The sailor pointed.

'Thanks.'

Yocke placed his weapon in the crook of his arm and began walking. He had gone about ten paces when the man behind him called, 'Better move it on out, shipmate, because the main wave of Blackhawks are overdue. They're going to land right here. Fact is, I can hear 'em now.'

In spite of his exhaustion and all the gear he was still wearing, Jack Yocke dutifully broke into a trot. When he too heard the swelling whine of the oncoming engines his gait became a run.

Yocke paused by the door of the hangar and watched four Blackhawks settle in and disgorge more troops. The men came pouring out just before the wheels hit the runway, then the choppers were gone in a blast of rotor wash and noise. Choppers with underslung artillery pieces were next. When the slings were released, these machines also kissed the earth and more men came out running, then they were gone.

The choppers brought machine guns, ammo, artillery, antitank weapons, com gear, and men, many men. By the time the fourth wave came in, the artillery pieces from the first wave were banging off rounds toward the east.

Above him three huge choppers materialized in the darkness – Sky Cranes, with pallets under their bellies.

Jack Yocke turned his back and went through the hangar door.

The first things he saw inside were the missiles. The long, white pointed cylinders still wore red stars on their flanks. He stood for several seconds staring before he saw the warheads – yes, those things were warheads – sitting on wooden forklift flats. He began to count.

Thirty-two of them. And missiles sporting red stars.

And against the far wall, a missile on another truck, but

this one was different – it had Arabic script on the side near the nose and sported a black, white and red flag. A Scud!

In front of the Scud launcher stood a row of Iraqis with their hands up. Several SEALs and US soldiers guarded them.

He was still standing there inspecting the warheads, taking it all in, when a group of people came trotting through the door with Captain Collins in the lead. Yocke recognized the British soldier, Jocko West, who was carrying a box of something. Another of the men was Rheinhart. West and Rheinhart immediately opened and began unpacking the box they had slung between them. Jack stayed behind Collins and watched as the muffled noise of war thudded through the hangar.

'The hot stuff is still in these warheads,' Collins said to Colonel Galvano, who was busy with a radiation counter.

'There is much background radiation, *Comandante*.'

'I'll bet these idiots didn't even hose down these weapons when they brought them here,' Jocko West muttered, then added, 'Let's open the hangar doors and start loading these things.'

Yocke wandered over to look at the prisoners. Most of them were Iraqis, but several were Russians. They didn't look happy. One of the Russians was trying to talk to an American soldier in English. 'I go, *da*? With you? You take us?'

'Keep your hands where I can see them, Boris.'

'Seen Admiral Grafton, soldier?' Yocke asked.

'He's in one of those offices behind the missiles,' the soldier said.

Yocke thanked him and walked in the indicated direction. One of the office doors was open. Yocke stepped in.

'Didn't fit. They're too big,' Spiro Dalworth was telling Jake Grafton. Three Russians sat in chairs. 'They cannot be made to fit without completely altering the structure of the missile.' More Russian. 'Hussein shot two of our men. Shot with a pistol, one bullet each. In the head. He told us we would make the warheads fit.'

'Are these all the warheads and missiles? Have the Iraqis taken any of the warheads anywhere else?' Jake asked this question and Dalworth spewed it out in Russian.

'*Nyet.*'

'All the weapons are here.'

Toad moved over beside Yocke. 'You look like one of Dracula's afternoon snacks,' Toad whispered. 'If all that blood is yours you must be a couple quarts low.'

Jack Yocke just shook his head. 'What's happening?'

'It was screwed up from the beginning,' Toad muttered. 'The warheads are out of bigger, heavier Soviet missiles. Saddam wanted them installed in the Scuds but they wouldn't fit. World-class problem solver that he is, he wouldn't take no for an answer.'

'So he shot two Russians?'

'To motivate the others. Terrific leadership technique, huh?'

'How about the missiles they have sitting out there? Why didn't he roll them out and tell the world to kiss its ass good-bye.'

Toad leaned closer to Yocke's ear. 'Those missiles don't have any guidance systems. Oh, the warheads are there, the fuel and all the rest of it. But without guidance systems . . .'

And Jack Yocke nodded. Russia, the land where nothing works, where shortages are endemic. It was sort of funny, really. Saddam, The Awesome, makes a sharp deal and the Russians give him the shaft.

'Can I print this?'

'That's up to the admiral.'

'This whole . . . thing, a goddamn fuck-up?'

'Sometimes the best-laid plans . . .'

A half-million Russians dead, another half-million or million or two million doomed, Americans dying outside, Iraqis . . . all because some Russian politicians desperately needed money and Saddam Hussein wants to be the Arab Stalin!

411

And he himself had just killed two men. So he could go on breathing and write the big stories . . . about how fucked up the world is!

Yocke walked over to a corner and plopped down. Suddenly he had a raging thirst. He got out his canteen and took a long drink, then another. He was nursing the water and listening to the translators when the first television crew arrived. The camera man was dragging the end of a cable, which went out the door. Another man set up some lights.

'Can we film in here?' the reporter asked Grafton.

'Have right at it,' the admiral said, and got out of his chair. 'Interview these Russians.' Jake gestured at Toad. The two of them left the room together.

There was a massive steel beam that formed an angle with one of the upright supports on the wall. Staring at it and listening to the CNN reporter's breathless delivery into the camera, Jack Yocke got an idea. He removed the magazine from his weapon. Then he wedged the silencer and barrel of the piece into the junction of the beam and angular support. Now he pulled with all his might. He paused, braced his feet, then put his weight into it. The barrel bent. With sweat popping on his forehead he made a supreme effort. The bend got bigger. When the barrel had bent about thirty degrees the stock shattered. Yocke removed the remains of the submachine gun from the joint, inspected it, then tossed it on the floor.

Everyone was watching the television reporter interview the Russian technicians.

Jack Yocke wandered out of the room with his hands in his pockets, lost in thought.

The air base was secure. For the moment. Approximately a hundred casualties, about thirty of them fatal. The 101st Airborne assault commander wanted to be gone in three hours, at least an hour before he estimated that the Iraqis could put together an armored assault. Although he had real-time communications via satellite with headquarters in Arabia and thought he had the air power available to stop any conceivable Iraqi military effort, he didn't want to take any more chances or casualties than he had to.

Jake Grafton listened to the report and nodded. He had no questions. The little knot of officers stood in one corner of the hangar watching technicians load the warheads onto pallets with forklifts. Through the open doors came the whine of helicopter engines at idle and the pulsating thud of turning rotors. This noise almost drowned out the distant bark of artillery, which was shelling known remnants of Iraqi forces to prevent their concentration. Almost drowned it out, but not quite.

Someone handed Jake Grafton a paper cup full of coffee. Beside him someone else lit a cigarette.

'Can you spare the rest of that pack of cigarettes?'

'Sure, Admiral.'

'And the lighter.'

The staff officer handed it over. 'I didn't know you smoked, sir.'

'I don't.'

As he walked across the hangar Jake saw Jack Yocke standing with his hands in his pockets. He looked tired and pensive, the flesh of his face tightly drawn across the bones. 'You okay?' Jake asked.

'Yes, sir.'

'Come with me,' Jake said and walked on.

'I've seen enough,' Yocke told the admiral's back. Jake Grafton acted like he hadn't heard. Yocke quickened his pace to catch up. 'I've had enough.'

The admiral didn't even look at him. 'Who hasn't?' he muttered.

The marine guard outside the door of the room where General Yakolev and Marshal Mikhailov were being held saluted Jake as he approached. Rita Moravia was standing beside him, and she also saluted.

'Are you injured?' Jake Grafton asked. She had blood on the front of her flight suit.

'No, sir. We arrived fifteen minutes ago. Our pilot was killed by small-arms fire.'

'Is the machine airworthy?'

'I think so, sir. We took a couple of other hits, but nothing vital. They're refueling now from a bladder that one of the Sky Cranes brought in. We'll be ready to leave in another fifteen minutes or so.'

'Fine. Have the Russians had anything to say?'

'No, sir. Lieutenant Dalworth is inside with them now, just in case.'

Jake nodded and opened the door. Jack Yocke followed him into the room. Dalworth stood up. 'Thank you, Lieutenant. Let me have a few minutes alone with these gentlemen.'

'Yessir.'

When the door closed behind Dalworth, Jake sat down at the table across from Yakolev and passed him the pack of cigarettes and the lighter. Yocke took a chair in a corner.

'A last cigarette, Admiral?' Nicolai Yakolev muttered. He took one and offered the pack to Mikhailov, who also stuck one in his mouth.

'Perhaps. We'll get to that.'

'At least these aren't Russian cigarettes.'

Yakolev glanced at Yocke, who was getting out his notebook. Mikhailov concentrated on savoring his cigarette and ignored Jake. He looked exhausted, shrunken, the lines around his eyes and mouth now deeply cut slashes. He looked old. The marshal didn't speak English, Jake remembered.

'Who is he?' Yakolev inclined his head an eighth of an inch at Yocke.'

'A reporter.'

'A *reporter*?'

'That's right. His speciality is news that isn't fit to print.'

Yakolev closed his eyes. He took an experimental drag on the cigarette, sucked the smoke deep into his lungs, then exhaled through his nose.

'So explain to me, General,' Jake said, 'how the hell you got yourself into this fucking mess.'

'You want the history of Russia in the twentieth century? For an American newspaper? Will this be deep background or a Sunday thinkpiece?'

'Just curious.'

'Another philosopher,' Yakolev said heavily.' I give you some good advice, Admiral. While you wear that uniform you cannot afford to be a philosopher, to ponder the nuances of good and evil. You do the best for your country that you can and live or die with the results. That's what the uniform means.'

'Blowing up a reactor? Poisoning hundreds of thousands of your own countrymen? You did *that* for your country?'

Yakolev smoked the first cigarette in silence, then lit another off the butt of the first one and puffed several times to ensure it was lit. Under his heavy eyebrows his eyes scanned Jake Grafton's face carefully.

'Russia is disintegrating,' the Russian general said finally. 'Very soon it will be like Somalia, without government, without law, without civilization, without food for its people. We are not talking about a return to the Dark Ages, Admiral, but a return to the Stone Age. Roving bands of armed thugs, mass starvation, epidemics, a complete breakdown of the social order – to survive, future Russians will become vicious, starving rats fighting on the dung heap.'

Yakolev glanced at Mikhailov, then continued. 'Already it has begun in the countryside, in the republics, in little towns in Russia that your news media does not cover, on the farms where there is no one to see the babies and old people starve, no one to watch or care as people die of pneumonia and tuberculosis. No agriculture, no food, no fuel, no transportation, no medical care, no electricity, no one to protect those who cannot protect themselves, violence leading to ethnic warfare, feuds building toward genocide – it is here *now!*

'In Moscow the ministries are corrupt from top to bottom. A small number of bureaucrats trade in dollars and live well while the rest of Russia – the rest of the Soviet Union – sinks deeper and deeper into the morass of starvation. *This* is what the future looks like when this grand scheme you call civilization collapses.'

He shifted his weight in his chair. Mikhailov said something, to which Yakolev gave a short reply. Then he turned his attention back to Jake. 'You Americans, with your television eyes. You look at Yeltsin and expect him to create miracles with his mouth! Those political swine – hot air is all they are good for.'

Yakolev leaned forward and reached for another cigarette. 'That is why.'

In the silence that followed, the sounds of a helicopter going overhead penetrated the room, followed by distant explosions.

'Do you have any regrets?' Jake Grafton asked when it became obvious Yakolev felt his explanation was sufficient.

'Regrets?' Yakolev said the word bitterly. 'Oh, yes!' His head bobbed. 'I wish the God the Communists swore did not exist had given this stupid sack of shit sitting beside me some balls. If he had had some balls we would have shot Yeltsin. We would have thrown the selfish swine out of the Congress of People's Deputies. We would have gone through the ministries and shot every corrupt bastard that we could lay hands on. We would have hunted down the thugs terrorizing the countryside and slaughtered them like rabbits. Then we would have made the farmers grow food and the trains run and people would have had food to eat. Regrets? To watch your country die while the politicians argue and the cowards wring their hands? Yes, Admiral, I have regrets.'

'Why didn't you shoot him first?'

'That is what I should have done.' Yakolev leaned back in his chair and rubbed his face. 'Ahh, I am old and tired. I have lived too long. I have seen too much. I am ready to die.'

'The world is going to hell, so you played God.'

'You Americans have a phrase that seems a perfect reply to sanctimonious comments like that: fuck you.'

'You won't get off that easy,' Jake Grafton said. His voice had an edge to it. 'Russia is in the mess it's in because of people like you, because czars and dictators and administrators used pens to authorize murder. "It had to be done." "*I* had to do it." "*I am responsible and I know the way things have to be, so they have to die!*"

'You Commie messiahs think your people are pigs. For them you have the profoundest contempt. They are too ignorant, too stupid, too blind to see what's good for them, so they must be taken care of by wise men like you. You feed, clothe, and house them, keep them warm in the winter, and slaughter them when necessary. All for their own good. It's just too goddamn bad they don't understand how wonderful it is that learned, wise, responsible men like you are willing to get their hands dirty running the hog farm.'

Jake Grafton leaned forward in his chair. '*What if you're wrong?*'

'We weren't wrong.'

'Don't give me that *shit!*' Grafton roared. 'Lenin was wrong, Stalin was wrong, you're wrong! I'm sick to death of you self-anointed messiahs willing to murder half the people on earth to save the other half, the half you're in. You make me want to vomit!'

Yakolev said nothing, merely reached for another cigarette.

'We have another one out there' – Jake pointed toward the hangar bay – 'ready to slaughter everyone alive who doesn't agree with him. Now I tell you this – it's time for all of us little people to take a page from the book of you prophets of doom and damnation.' He stared at Yakolev.

The Russian sneered. 'So you brought two Russian villains to Iraq to parade in front of your cameras. The folks at home can see the dirty devils on CNN, prisoners of the victorious, virtuous Americans.'

'No. I brought you here to help me solve a problem. I need your help.'

'Help?' Yakolev laughed, a dry, vicious bark.

'As one soldier to another.'

The laughter died. Nicolai Yakolev's face twisted again. 'You tell me I have no honor, then you appeal to it.' He spit on the table, in Jake's direction. 'I am not a coward! I am not afraid of death. I do not fear a bullet.'

'I know that,' Jake said gently.

'I have two sons and a daughter. They have children.'

'A trial . . .'

'When?'

'You'll know when the time comes.'

Yakolev glanced again at Jack Yocke, then shrugged. 'I'll think about it. For you personally I would do nothing.'

Jake Grafton rose from the chair and started for the door. 'Come on, Jack.'

Out in the hangar bay Yocke wanted to know, 'What was that all about?'

'About doing the right thing, for a change.'

'Like what?'

'You'll figure it out.'

The room had a table in it about eight feet long. And chairs. At one end of the table sat Saddam Hussein, who glowered at Jake Grafton and Jack Yocke when they came in. He roared something in Arabic. The translator said to Jake, 'He wants to know if you are in charge, sir.'

'I'm one of the officers in charge, yes,' Jake said as he motioned to the two soldiers on guard duty to leave the room.

Hussein ignored Yocke, who leaned against the wall opposite the translator, and directed his remarks at Jake.

'The United States makes war upon Iraq,' the translator said. 'You meddle in affairs that are none of your business.'

Hussein's hands were bound with a single plastic tie in front of him, so he waved them, now stopped and shook his doubled-up fists: 'How long, how long, until you nonbelievers stop raping our daughters? How long until you stop defiling the sacred places? How long until you leave the children of God to worship as the Prophet taught us?'

Toad came over to Jake and handed him a pistol, a 9mm automatic. 'We took this off him.'

Saddam thundered on: 'You violate the sovereignty of this nation, of this people. You shoot down Iraqi airplanes over Iraq, you send inspectors to hunt through our offices, you—'

Jake Grafton fired the pistol into the ceiling. The deafening report stopped the flow of words.

The spent casing slapped against the wall and fell to the floor with a tinny, metallic sound.

'I have a question,' Jake said softly to the translator. 'Ask him how many Iraqis he has killed with this pistol.'

The translator did so.

Hussein sat in silence, saying nothing.

'How many Iranians?'

Silence.

'How many Kuwaitis?

'How many Kurds?

'How many Shiites?

Unbroken silence.

'If you don't know or can't remember how many men you have personally murdered, perhaps you can tell me how many have died at your orders?'

Saddam Hussein's eyes were mere slits.

'When you are dead will they hold a great funeral, or will they drag your corpse through the streets and burn it on a dung heap?'

When he heard the translation Saddam Hussein opened

his mouth to speak, then apparently decided not to. He looked at the translator, at Jack Yocke, then let his gaze return to Jake Grafton.

The automatic was heavy. Jake Grafton stared at it, examined the safety, the hammer, the maker's name stamped into the metal. Then slowly he removed his own pistol, a .357 Magnum Smith & Wesson revolver, and hefted it thoughtfully.

He laid the revolver about a foot from his right hand, then gave the automatic a gentle shove with his left. It slid down the table and came to rest about a foot or so in front of the Iraqi dictator, the barrel pointing out to one side.

'Let's settle this right there,' Jake said. 'You have killed many men – one more certainly won't matter on Allah's scales. And an unbeliever to boot. Go ahead! You grab for yours and I'll grab for mine and we'll kill each other.'

As the translator rattled this off Jake studied the Iraqi's face. It had gone white. Beads of sweat were coalescing into little rivulets that ran down beside Hussein's nose and dripped off his mustache. Stains were rapidly spreading across his shirt from under each armpit.

'You've seen cowboy movies, haven't you? Let's shoot it out, you simple, filthy son of a bitch.'

Hussein sat frozen. He didn't even glance at the automatic within his grasp.

'*Pick it up,*' Jake Grafton roared.

Hussein sat silently while Jake regained his composure. He took several deep breaths, then said, 'This is your last chance to go out like a man. The next time you will get the same chance you gave your minister of health, the same chance you give the people you send your thugs to kill, the same chance you were going to give the people those bombs out there were meant for, which is none at all. *This* is your *only* chance!'

Seconds passed. A tic developed in Hussein's left eyelid. As the twitching became worse, he raised his hands and rubbed his eye. Finally he lowered his hands back to his lap.

Jake reached for the revolver. As he grasped it the Iraqi started visibly. The admiral rose from his chair, and holding the revolver in his right hand, retrieved the automatic. He stuck it into his belt.

After one last look at the dictator, Jake Grafton turned and left the room.

Jack Yocke had stood throughout this exchange. Now he pulled a chair away from the table and dropped into it. He got out his notebook and mechanical pencil and very carefully wrote the date on a clean sheet of paper. Beside it he wrote the dictator's name.

He looked at Hussein, who was staring at the open door. An armed American soldier stood there gazing back at him.

Jack Yocke cleared his throat and caught the attention of the interpreter, who had also pulled up a chair. 'I was wondering, Mr President,' Yocke said, 'if you'd care to grant me an interview for the *Washington Post*.'

Fifteen minutes later Jake Grafton came back through that door, followed by the two Russian generals. Captain Iron Mike McElroy was behind them, cradling a submachine gun in his arms. Then came a television reporter and cameraman and two technicians with lights and cables in coils over their shoulders.

Jack Yocke got out of his chair and leaned against a wall. Toad Tarkington eased in beside him, but he said nothing. Then Jack realized that Toad was holding a pistol in his hand, down beside his leg, hidden from sight.

Spiro Dalworth was also there. As the television reporter gave orders to his cameraman and the technicians discussed where to put the lights, Yocke heard Jake say to Dalworth, 'Ask General Yakolev if Lieutenant Vasily Lutkin is still alive.'

'Lutkin?'

'Lutkin, the helicopter pilot. Ask him.'

Dalworth stepped over to where the general sat and asked the question in a low voice. Yakolev glanced at Jake, then shook his head from side to side. Mikhailov, Yocke noted, sat staring at the top of the table in front of him.

The television types opened a discussion of lighting and camera angles. Later, when he tried to recall exactly what had happened, Jack Yocke was never sure of the sequence. He remembered that someone else from a television crew came in carrying a floodlight and several people began looking for plugs. Another cameraman came in and his helper began unrolling cable.

The television reporter was talking to Admiral Grafton about the possibility of moving the news conference out into the hangar bay so they could use one of the missiles for a backdrop when Toad went over to where General Yakolev sat. Yocke caught that out of the corner of his eye, but he didn't pay much attention.

Toad must have laid the pistol on the table in front of Yakolev, because he was standing there opening a pocket-knife – probably to cut the plastic ties around the Russian's wrists – when Yakolev elbowed him hard and he fell away, off balance.

'No!' Yocke yelled, almost as the first shot hammered his eardrums. Mikhailov's head went sideways – a bullet right above the ear. Then Yakolev was shooting at Saddam Hussein.

Boom, boom, boom – the pistol's trip-hammer reports were painfully magnified in the confines of the room.

The Iraqi dictator came half out of his chair on the first shot into Mikhailov, so he took the next three standing up, at a distance of about ten feet. A burst of silenced sub-machine gun fire followed the pistol shots almost instantly. Yakolev went face forward onto the table as Saddam Hussein fell back into his chair and the chair and the body went over backward with a crash. The whole sequence didn't take more than three or four seconds.

'Shit, I think they're all dead.' Tarkington's voice. He stood and slowly looked around.

Jake Grafton got up from the floor and examined the Russians. Yocke tried to recall when Jake went down and couldn't.

'Yakolev is dead,' Jake said. 'Mikhailov is still breathing. One right above the left ear. I don't think he's gonna make it, but . . . Dalworth, go get a medic.'

Yocke pushed by the horrified Iraqi interpreter, who stood frozen with his hands half-raised. Toad was bending over the body of the dictator, which was lying on its side. Toad rolled him over. Saddam had three holes in his chest, one in the left shoulder, one dead center, and the other a little lower down. His eyes were fixed on the ceiling. Toad released a wrist and announced, 'No pulse.'

Saddam Hussein was as dead as Petty Officer Murphy . . . and that Iraqi Jack Yocke had knifed in Samarra, the soldier with the rifle he had mowed down. Dead.

Toad Tarkington stood looking down at Saddam's face as he folded his pocketknife and dropped it into a pocket. He held the pistol Yakolev had used with his left hand wrapped around the action, so the barrel and butt were both visible. That looks like Saddam's pistol, Yocke thought, but he couldn't be sure.

Toad glanced up and met the reporter's gaze.

Jack Yocke took a last look at the Iraqi dictator, then walked for the door. McElroy was replacing the magazine in his weapon. He didn't bother to look at Yocke as he went by.

Out in the hangar bay the reporter ran into another television crew, this one still shooting footage of soldiers loading nuclear warheads onto pallets and the pallets into helicopters.

'Were those shots we heard in there? What happened?' The reporter shoved a microphone at him.

'Saddam Hussein is dead,' Jack Yocke said slowly. 'A Russian general killed him.'

'*Holy . . . !* C'mon, Harry, grab the lights. Ladies and gentlemen, we are broadcasting live from the Iraqi base at Samarra and we have just learned that Saddam Hussein is *dead!* Stay with us while—'

Yocke walked on through the hangar and went outside. One of the Sky Cranes was lifting off with a Russian missile slung beneath.

The rotors created a terrific wind that almost lifted Yocke's helmet off. He watched the machine transition into forward flight and disappear into the darkness.

CHAPTER TWENTY-SIX

Jake Grafton was asleep when he heard the knocking on the door. 'Just a minute.' He pulled on his trousers and opened it.

Yocke walked in lugging his computer. 'I've written a story and I need to phone it into the paper. You'll have to read it on the computer.'

He turned on the desk lamp and set up the machine.

Jake seated himself in front of the screen and put on his reading glasses. 'You push the buttons.'

'Okay.'

As Jake finished each page, he nodded and Yocke brought up the next one. The story was an eyewitness account of the air assault on Samarra, the recovery of the nuclear weapons, and the death of Saddam Hussein. Yocke got down to cases on the third page.

Just before the news conference was to begin, General Yakolev seized a pistol from an American officer and shot Marshal Mikhailov and Saddam Hussein before he himself was shot by a guard. Hussein was shot three times and died instantly. Mikhailov suffered a severe head wound and died approximately an hour later. Yakolev was dead at the scene.

Jake got out of the chair and switched on more lights.

'I thought you weren't going to write fiction,' he said to the reporter.

'There isn't a word in there that isn't true.'

'Well . . .'

'Look, you're doing the best you can with your weapons, I'm using mine.'

'You know, Jack,' Jake Grafton said softly, 'that's the nicest thing you've ever said about me, but I don't know that it's true. Arranging that little shoot-out was the dirtiest thing I ever did.'

'You were going to shoot Saddam yourself, weren't you?'

Jake Grafton ran his fingers through his hair. 'Well, not at first. After that talk with Yakolev I thought he'd do it, and I felt dirty. *I* wanted Saddam dead! But if I killed him the political implications would be unpredictable, and perhaps profound. Then in that room listening to him spout bullshit, I thought what the hell, maybe we'll kill each other.'

'He wouldn't play, so you let Yakolev shoot him.'

'Something like that.'

'I'm not ever going to print this.'

'I know, Jack.'

'But did someone in Washington want Saddam dead?'

'If they did they never said it to me.' Jake met Yocke's eyes. 'I learned a long time ago in the military that you can have all the authority you are willing to use, but God help you if you screw up.'

'Did you know Yakolev was going to shoot Mikhailov?'

'No. I'm sorry he did. That was his decision.'

'So what are you going to do now?'

'Hell, what is there to do? I'm going to live with it.'

'Do you feel guilty?'

Jake Grafton made a gesture of irritation.

'You did what had to be done.'

Jake Grafton rubbed his face. 'I thought so then, and I thought so when I sent Lieutenant Lutkin on to Moscow in a chopper that I suspected was going to be shot down, when I stuffed those damn poison pills into Herb Tenney's mouth . . . but!' He gestured helplessly. 'When all the

426

preachers have shouted themselves out, the bottom line is that people shouldn't kill people who aren't trying to kill them.' His gaze shifted to Yocke's face. 'The easiest lie ever told is that old nugget you tell yourself, *I'm doing what has to be done.*'

'You're not feeling sorry for Saddam Hussein and Yakolev and Herb Tenney, are you? They were *guilty.*'

Jake Grafton laid a hand on Yocke's arm. 'I'm feeling sorry for myself, Jack. They got what they deserved all right, but what do I deserve? I'm not God. I don't want his job.'

'This is the real world, Admiral, not some class in metaphysics. Herb Tenney murdered people with poison and died of it himself. An absolute despot and two wanta-bes are dead – they did it to each other. *You* didn't pull the trigger.'

'That's sophistry, Jack. You should have been a lawyer.'

Jack Yocke exploded. 'Goddamnit, Admiral! I've had it with all these people who tut-tut over the state of the world and won't *do* anything. Mass murder, starvation, tyranny – it's damn near two thousand years since Christ and . . .' He gestured helplessly. 'Guilt seems to be the in drug of the nineties. Okay, I'll drink my share. I'm *glad* Saddam's dead . . . and those two Russian gangsters in uniform. Looking back, I wish I had pulled the trigger.'

Yocke swallowed hard. 'I killed a man last night with a knife. Honest, there was no other way. I had to do it. It was him or me. Then I panicked and gunned a soldier or militiaman who was banging at me with a bolt-action rifle. I wish I hadn't shot him. I shouldn't have shot him.' he wiped the perspiration from his face. 'I knew at the time that he was no threat, but you know . . . I *wanted* to kill him. Do you understand?'

Jake Grafton nodded.

'I've been thinking about those two men all day,' Yocke continued. 'Thinking about guilt, about what I should have done, what . . .' He took a deep breath and exhaled audibly.

427

Now he looked at his hands. '. . . what I wish I had done. But it's over. And *I* have to live with it.'

Jake Grafton cleared his throat. 'I can live with it too.' His voice became softer. 'Maybe that's why it worked out the way it did.'

Jack Yocke bobbed his head.

'How's your arm?'

'Fifteen stitches, but the cut wasn't deep.'

Grafton stood. 'Call your story in. I'm going back to bed.'

'Toad says you always try to do the right thing. I think he's right.'

'I hope he is,' Jake said. He extended his hand. Yocke took it and squeezed.

Yocke closed the door behind him and walked down the hallway of the makeshift BOQ. He called his story in as it was written, not changing a word.

Then he stood looking out the window at the desert. The sun was overhead and heat mirages distorted the horizon.

After his return to the United States from Saudi Arabia, Jack Yocke threw himself at the word processor. His articles on the upheaval in the former Soviet states were well received and widely reprinted. He called the Graftons and invited them out on two occasions, but the first evening he had to cancel and the second time the admiral got tied up at work.

Yocke understood. Jake was the new director of the Defense Intelligence Agency and was busy trying to stay on top of rapidly changing events in the former Soviet states and the Middle East.

As Jake Grafton had predicted, the CIA problem took care of itself. As September turned into October Jack found the obituary of Harvey Schenler buried on a back page. Although the story didn't say so, by Yocke's count Schenler was the fourth high-ranking CIA officer to die since mid-

August. According to the press release, all died of natural causes. In their sleep.

Jack called Admiral Grafton at the office, and got him.

'Congratulations on the new job.'

'Thank you, Jack. How are things going for you?'

'Oh, just sitting here reading the obituaries. Seems that a deputy director of the CIA died in his sleep last night. Guy named Schenler. Heart failure.'

'Well, all things considered, it's not a bad way to go,' Jake Grafton told him.

'Fourth CIA bigwig in the last six weeks. Must be something in the water over at Langley.'

'It was their choice. Protects their families and the institution.'

'How is the Toad-man?'

'Doing fine.'

'Think I'll ever get to write anything about Schenler and his pals?'

'I doubt it,' Jake said promptly. 'Certainly not anytime soon.' He paused, then continued with a hint of concern in his voice: 'You aren't running out of stuff to write about, are you?'

'We're managing to keep the paper full – turmoil in the Middle East, a revolution in Iraq, Yeltsin still riding the tiger and trying not to get eaten. Same old song, different verse. How's Callie and Amy?'

'Doing fine, Jack. Doing fine. I'll tell them you asked.'

'Well, I'll let you go, Admiral. But the reason I called – I just wanted to say thanks.'

'For what?'

'For taking me along, for keeping me alive, for making me a part of the team. Thanks.'

'Take care, Jack.'

In October Jack was notified by the Russian embassy that his request for an in-depth interview with Boris Yeltsin had been granted.

When he checked into the Metropolitan Hotel in

Moscow there was some difficulty about the bill from his previous visit – they had held his room for a week after his hurried departure to the US embassy. He had a tense conference with the manager. After a call back to Washington, he agreed to pay the disputed amount.

Once again the barman greeted him by name. The oil painting of the nobleman outside the Kremlin walls hadn't been cleaned. Jack Yocke sat staring up at it and thinking of Shirley Ross, or Judith Farrell, as Toad and Jake had called her.

After his interview with Yeltsin, he took a taxi to the entrance to Gorky Park, then walked east. The statues of Stalin and his henchman now lay in the early winter snow surrounded by naked trees. The branches swayed in the bitter wind.

Jack found where a bullet had scarred the last bronze standing upright. He fingered the mark as he took in the scene one last time, then buried his hands in his pockets and walked back to the waiting taxi.

In November Yocke was invited to speak on the problems facing Russia at a symposium at Georgetown University. He was seated on the stage near the podium nervously fingering his notes and waiting for the lights to dim when he saw them come in: Rita Moravia, Toad Tarkington, Amy and Callie and Jake Grafton. They found seats along the left side of the auditorium.

Rita looked pregnant, Yocke noted with surprise.

Amy Carol waved, so he waved back. Jake and Toad returned his grin. Both the women smiled at him.

A warm glow settled over Jack Yocke. It's good to have real friends, he told himself, and he was very fortunate – he had five. Perhaps they would like to go out for coffee and ice cream later this evening when the lecture was over. He would ask.

Jake Grafton put the bottle containing the tablets of binary poison into a desk drawer at his office and forgot about them. Through the winter and the rains of spring, through meetings, briefings and staff conferences, through turmoil and upheaval in Iraq and Russia, through coups in South America, through wars in the Balkans and another round of mass starvation in the horn of Africa, the pills stayed in the drawer.

He found them one evening in late May as he rooted in the drawer for a fresh pen. He fingered the bottle, then pried off the cap and dumped the white tablets on the desk in front of him. As he looked at the pills, the whole experience came flooding back.

Toxic waste. That's what these pills were. If he dumped them down the toilet the man-made chemical compounds would go through the sewage treatment plant into the Potomac. Too dangerous to just toss them into the garbage for burial in a landfill. Can't throw them into the ocean. If he burned them . . . but Lord knows what that might do to the active ingredients. And the resultant fumes might be poisonous.

These things were like plutonium pellets, their components deadly in the most minute quantities, difficult to dispose of safely.

That evening on the way home he bought a new battery for the car and asked if he could bring in the old battery in the morning for recycling. Sure.

After he had the new battery installed, he opened one of the plastic cell caps on the old one and dropped the tablets into the acid. Then he quickly screwed the cap back on.

When he looked up he found Callie was standing there in the garage with her arms folded across her chest, watching him. 'What was that stuff you put in there?'

'Ahh . . .'

She stood looking at him with raised eyebrows.

What the hell! 'Binary poison. This was what all the hassle was about last summer.' He told her about Herb Tenney.

'Do you think putting that stuff in there is safe?'

'Should be. They'll drain this battery into a huge vat of acid and that will dilute the poison. Whatever they do to the acid should destroy the compound, I think.'

'It's a risk then.'

'Life's a risky business,' he told her as he wiped his hands on a rag.

'Jake, what really happened in Iraq?'

'That was ten months ago, Callie. Does it matter?'

She shrugged. 'I suppose not, but on some level it does. Last fall when we went out for ice cream with Jack Yocke after that lecture, he and I talked. I read his story in the *Post*.'

'And?'

'Well, I never understood exactly what happened. Why did Saddam get killed? The Russian generals?'

'Yocke talked to you about that?' The words came out sharply, and Jake regretted it.

Callie didn't seem to notice. 'No,' she said slowly, recalling that conversation. 'He said his story covered it. That was the problem. The story just explained what happened, not why. I kept the clipping. I was looking at it again last week. You usually never talk about things like that – which I can understand, although at times it seems hard, unfair even. There's a whole side of you I don't know about.'

'Why did you wait until now to bring this up?'

'I wasn't going to,' Callie said. 'Then you brought that poison home. So I'm asking. If you don't want to tell me, I understand.'

Jake Grafton stared at his wife. After a moment he said, 'Yocke's story is true. He reported what he saw.'

'But not everything he saw.'

'No, not everything.' Jake ran his fingers through his hair. 'We were in the hangar at Samarra. Toad put the gun he was holding on the table in front of Yakolev and bent over to cut the plastic tie that held his hands. Yakolev grabbed the gun and killed Mikhailov and Hussein.'

'Toad wouldn't make a mistake like that. You set it up?'

My wife knows me very well, Jake reflected. Too well. 'Yes,' he said softly.

'And the marine captain killed Yakolev?'

'Yes.'

'Shot him in the back?'

'Yes.'

Callie thought about it. 'Why?'

'I thought the world would be a lot better place if Saddam Hussein wasn't in it. My responsibility. But if I shot him he would be a martyr. So I had a talk with Yakolev. We both knew that if he went back to Russia he would be shot. He said he was a soldier, he didn't fear a bullet. I told him I knew that and wanted his help.'

'And what was his reply?'

'He just looked me in the eye and said he would think about it. So I set it up. When Yakolev saw the pistol placed on the table within his reach, he knew what it was I wanted. And he knew how it would end. He made his choice. Mikhailov didn't know what was going on but perhaps he would have wanted it to end the way it did. Maybe. He was old and tired and wanted to die . . . that was my impression, anyway.'

She stepped toward him and touched his cheek. 'Why didn't you tell me about this sooner? You shouldn't have carried this by yourself.'

'Yakolev and Mikhailov were soldiers. They screwed up big-time. I think they realized that toward the end.'

'And Hussein?'

'Saddam Hussein was a thug who clawed his way to the top of the neighborhood dung heap, like Al Capone, Joe Stalin, Adolf Hitler, Attila the Hun and a hundred others. I have no regrets.'

'General Land? The president? What did they think afterward?'

'They liked Jack Yocke's version. After they put down the newspaper they probably said, Next problem.'

He flipped off the garage light as he followed her out the door into the late spring evening.

'How many times,' she asked, 'can you take on the Herb Tenneys and Saddam Husseins of the world and come out alive?'

He looked at her with raised eyebrows. 'Gimme a break, Callie. I lead a very sedentary life. I'm a bureaucrat, for heaven's sake. You know me!'

'I know you better, Jacob.'

He examined her face, pushed a stray lock back from her forehead. 'I'll fight the good fight as long as I have any fight left in me.'

She smiled, then brushed her lips across his cheek as she took his hand. 'Come eat your dinner,' she said as she led him toward the house. 'You can't fight on an empty stomach.'

The Intruders £6.99
STEPHEN COONTS
0 75284 908 5

The Red Horseman £6.99
STEPHEN COONTS
0 75284 907 7

Under Siege £6.99
STEPHEN COONTS
0 75284 861 5

Final Flight £6.99
STEPHEN COONTS
0 75284 266 8

The Minotaur £6.99
STEPHEN COONTS
0 75284 860 7

Fortunes of War £6.99
STEPHEN COONTS
0 75282 641 7

Cuba £5.99
STEPHEN COONTS
0 75283 418 5

Hong Kong £5.99
STEPHEN COONTS
0 75284 400 8

☐ Combat £7.99
STEPHEN COONTS
0 75284 478 4

☐ America £5.99
STEPHEN COONTS
0 75284 792 9

☐ Saucer £6.99
STEPHEN COONTS
0 75284 895 X

☐ Liberty £6.99
STEPHEN COONTS
0 75284 263 3

☐ Deep Black £6.99
STEPHEN COONTS AND
  JIM DEFELICE
0 75285 901 3

☐ Deep Black: Biowar £6.99
STEPHEN COONTS AND
  JIM DEFELICE
0 75286 538 2

All Orion/Phoenix titles are available at your local bookshop or from the following address:

Mail Order Department
Littlehampton Book Services
FREEPOST BR535
Worthing, West Sussex, BN13 3BR
telephone 01903 828503, *facsimile* 01903 828802
e-mail MailOrders@lbsltd.co.uk
(Please ensure that you include full postal address details)

Payment can be made either by credit/debit card (Visa, Mastercard, Access and Switch accepted) or by sending a £ Sterling cheque or postal order made payable to *Littlehampton Book Services*.
DO NOT SEND CASH OR CURRENCY.

Please add the following to cover postage and packing

UK and BFPO:
£1.50 for the first book, and 50p for each additional book to a maximum of £3.50

Overseas and Eire:
£2.50 for the first book plus £1.00 for the second book and 50p for each additional book ordered

---

BLOCK CAPITALS PLEASE

name of cardholder _____

address of cardholder _____

_____

_____

postcode _____

delivery address
(if different from cardholder)

_____

_____

_____

postcode _____

☐ I enclose my remittance for £_____

☐ please debit my Mastercard/Visa/Access/Switch (delete as appropriate)

card number ☐☐☐☐ ☐☐☐☐ ☐☐☐☐ ☐☐☐☐

expiry date ☐☐☐☐   Switch issue no. ☐☐

signature _____

prices and availability are subject to change without notice